HE SAVED HER FROM CERTAIN DEATH....

The worst part was feeling the noose around her neck, grating harshly against the tenderness of her throat, itching and bruising.

"Hang her," a furious voice called out, and the chant was quickly picked up by those who wanted a show.

"Hold your peace!" the local magistrate cried out. He was silent as the crowd toned down again, and in that silence Ondine asked miserably, "What are they waiting for now?"

"Marriage offers. 'Tis custom. If a lad will step up and marry ye, girl, ye'll be set free."

Ondine stared about her at the crowd. There was not a man in sight who would not gag her if he touched her. And yet her heart had quickened, for in these seconds she knew how deeply she cherished life.

"Stop!" a voice in the crowd roared. It was deep and sure, accustomed to authority and brooking no opposition. The man it belonged to stepped forward. He was obviously of the aristocracy, but his face was . . . hard. Something about his eyes was chilling. "Release her so I may marry her."

"What?" the magistrate shrieked, his fleshy cheeks puffing out. "But, my lord! The girl is nothing but a thief. A pretty piece, I'll warrant, but—"

"Sir, the law reads that she goes free if a man takes her for his bride. I am a man. Now get that rope off her neck."

Raves for Shannon Drake

"[A writer of] engrossing, sexy historical romance!"
—*Publishers Weekly*

"Shannon Drake knows how to tell a story that captures the imagination."
—*Romantic Times*

"A writer of incredible talent!"
—*Affaire de Coeur*

ONDINE

Shannon Drake

Zebra Books
Kensington Publishing Corp.

http://www.zebrabooks.com

*To Tony and Vivienne French
of Cobham, Surrey
with many thanks*

PROLOGUE

Fate, and ships that pass in the night.

The Palace of Westchester
June 1678
The Reign of Charles II

A shimmering sun cast furious rays of heat and light upon men and horses alike. There was no fog, no hint of rain, nothing to cool the dead heat of the afternoon. As Warwick Chatham sat upon his restless horse he silently cursed the heat. He was not fond of pageantry or games, but this joust had been ordered by the king, and being honest with himself, Warwick had to admit that he was exceedingly grateful for the chance to do battle against Lord Hardgrave, viscount of Bedford Place. Hostilities had been rising between the two of them since they had been children. Both families had proclaimed for the old king, Charles I, but the Chathams had fought against Cromwell while the Hardgraves had allowed their loyalties to sway with the winds of fate. Then, of course, there had always been this dispute over border lands.

"Easy, Dragon, easy," Warwick murmured to his mount, a massive chestnut stallion, bred for strength and speed from champion lines of the fleetest Arabians. Dragon was far more accustomed to the action of actual battle than to the niceties of the lists. So was Warwick. On his northern border lands he had grown up waging war against marauding Scots to secure his inheritance, fighting battles of life and death, not participating in pretty shows.

Warwick glanced to the stands. In the center box sat the king and his queen, Catherine. For all that Charles was a flagrant lecher, he was a gentleman, ever kind to the queen he so dishonored. At the moment Charles's dark head was bent toward Catherine; he was giving her his full attention and holding up the joust for her to speak.

Row upon row of benches were filled. The closer seats to the jousts held the nobility in perfect rank and file, and beyond them were the lesser lords and ladies. The commoners did not have seats; yet they were out for this holiday with their "Merry Monarch." They loved Charles, and they loved the pageantry. Banners were flying high in support for a favorite knight, and screams and cheers were rising high in abundance. Looking at the stands, Warwick smiled with faint amusement; the ladies—and the men— seemed to form one colorful rainbow. Silks and satins and velvets—and, even in the terrible heat, furs!—were in abundance. There was a holiday spirit and a holiday mood. After the jousts, there would be feasting; many of the poor would find their bellies filled this night.

Ah, but let's have with it! Warwick thought. Dragon, lathered with sweat, began to prance in small anxious steps.

"Steady, steady," Warwick murmured, but he was as anxious as the horse. Dragon was dressed in all his trappings. His blanket bore the gleaming blue-and-gold insignia of the ancient lords of Chatham; his insignia was the "forest" beast, a mythical creature created as a cross between a lion and a dragon. Warwick's shield bore the same crest, and he was garbed in the same colors as the horse. His hose, beneath the steel of his armor, was a gold weave. His shirt and breeches were royal blue. And it was so damned hot that sweat was running miserably beneath his clothing. He thought with some humor that both he and Lord Hardgrave would rust if they did not move soon.

It was then that Charles raised a royal hand, and the trumpets came to life. The master of the joust rose to read out the dispute between the Earl of North Lambria and the Viscount of Bedford Place. They were commanded to come before the king.

Warwick had difficulty keeping Dragon down to a dignified pace as they observed etiquette in slowly approaching the Royal Box. Warwick and Hardgrave dismounted and knelt before Charles, muttering out, "For God and our sovereign, Charles!"

They were asked if they agreed that the joust would settle the dispute; they were warned that the joust was not to the death. Warwick glanced up to see Charles's dark mischievous eyes upon him.

He grimaced and shrugged, then snapped his visor into place.

There would be only one more piece of pageantry before the joust began. Warwick mounted Dragon and pranced his way down the stands until he came to a certain lady. She was very blond and very lovely—delicate and pale as she sat in the lists. He smiled at her encouragingly. She stood, and his heart went out to her. She drew her scarf from about her hair and throat and stretched it out to him. Warwick nodded to her, smiled again, and gave Dragon free rein to race back to his position. The crowd roared loud with approval, for it was right and beautiful for a knight to wear his lady's colors.

Jake—Warwick's squire when the occasion warranted, his valet and coachman when it did not—came running to him with his shielded lance. "God is your right, my lord!" Jake called encouragingly.

"Let's hope God does not require a large quota of blood for a pretty play," Warwick returned. They grimaced and then parted.

Before the king's box the master of the joust stood at the ready, banner bearing the Stuart crest raised high. There was a flash of color as the banner fell.

Dragon bolted, flying into the fray like a trained and ready warrior. Warwick felt the great strength of the animal beneath him, and that strength gave him a sense of flight. His lance was held straight and still as he raced along the lists. Beneath the horse the earth churned. The world—the cheering spectators, the colors, the vibrancy—was blurred. Cries on the air melded with the soaring wind as Hardgrave and Warwick came closer and closer.

Warwick saw only his foe. One more second . . .

The sound of his lance striking Hardgrave's shield seemed deafening. Warwick's arm, from the wrist to the shoulder, stung as if a thousand bees were on it. He was wrenched and tottering, but experience, strength of will, and the power of his thighs kept him horsed. His eyes were blurred with pain and the salt of his sweat, and it was not until he had run out the distance that he heard the roar of the crowd and knew that he had unhorsed Hardgrave.

Warwick pulled Dragon about, and the great charger reared and spun. Warwick dropped his broken lance, and Jake rushed up to hand him his sword. He raced along the length of the lists once more until he reached Hardgrave, who was now standing, his sword raised high in his hand. Warwick dismounted with a leap, a few feet from his enemy.

Warwick could see by his foe's curiously blue, yet nearly color-less, eyes that Hardgrave was furious. That fury might well be his undoing, Warwick realized quickly. Hardgrave lunged for him immediately, and Warwick ducked the blow. Their swords met in a tremendous clash. Both sought a weakness that neither could find.

Their swords met again, and they came face-to-face as they struggled to untangle. "One day I will kill you, Chatham," Hard-grave promised savagely.

"Will you?" Warwick queried. "I've seen little to fear yet!"

They broke. Hardgrave attacked too quickly, and Warwick found his advantage. Ducking the blow, he brought his sword upward against Hardgrave's and sent it flying far out into the dirt. When Hardgrave tried to chase it, Warwick caught his enemy's ankle with his foot. Hardgrave went sprawling to the ground, and War-wick quickly seized that additional advantage by bringing his sword point to his foe's throat.

He saw Hardgrave's eyes, filled with venom. But the king was standing, calling bravo, and complimenting them both.

Warwick pulled his sword from its threatening point at Hard-grave's throat.

Hardgrave stood. Both men were tense as they clasped hands, then approached the king, kneeling down before him. "Well done, well done!" Charles claimed. "Lord Chatham, the disputed land is yours. Lord Hardgrave, you have promised to abide by the decision. I'll see you both at the banquet."

Warwick bowed. When he rose, he whistled for Dragon. He mounted his horse, turned, and allowed the stallion to race across the field.

He should have sought his tent to assess his wounds; instead, by whim, he rode until he reached the forest trails. The forest offered coolness and a certain peace.

He came to a brook where he paused. Sliding from his saddle, he tore his visor and helmet from his head and drank thirstily from the water. When he'd had his fill, he sighed and sank back on his haunches, tearing away his heavy armor. Stripped of it at last, he just sat, grateful for the cool feel of the earth and grass.

Nightingales were beginning to sing, the breeze was soft, and the trees rustled gently. Here was peace—so rare, even in moments. Here was bliss. He lay back, welcoming the forest. The sunlight played over his closed eyes and then faded. Dusk was coming, a time of twilight shadows that eased his mind. No worry, just peace. And in that peace he dozed.

Something interrupted his oblivion. He started and sat up, puzzled. There'd been a rustling across the brook. He frowned, narrowing his eyes against the coming darkness that cast everything into shadow. Was he dreaming?

Then he heard the woman's voice, hushed by the heat of her fury. "No! No! Never—murderer!"

A man's voice followed, low and threatening and filled with taunting laughter. "Ah, but you will, my heiress. Your father is dead now. My father will be your guardian—legally, in complete charge of the estates and of you. My father, who shields you now, yet can produce proof that you conspired with your father!"

"Forgeries, lies!" she choked out.

"But brought before a court of law, quite damning! You've two choices. One is my . . . protection. The other is a headsman's ax."

"You go to hell! I despise you!"

There was a silence then. Warwick, stunned, shook himself and stood, striding out into the water to cross the brook. He would demand to know what was going on. But before he could cross the stream, the woman screamed out a furious oath.

A second later there was a thunderous crash of brush and trees. Something flew out of the trees like a cannon shot.

It was the woman.

He could not see her face, only her form, a silhouette against the twilight. She saw him and started, standing as still as he. She was young, he thought quickly. The twilight touched her hair as it spilled about her in wild and beautiful disarray. It was shadowed with the night, yet it shimmered a rich burnished chestnut, or perhaps gold. There was little else that he could see, except that she was slim and tall and that her breasts were high and firm and heaving with her fury and exertion. He reached out a hand to her as she stood there on the bank, but she gasped out a startled sound and ran, diving into the water.

"Wait, dammit, wench—I'll help you!" he roared out, racing toward the point where she had disappeared. But she had vanished beneath the surface of the cool brook. Warwick dove after her, again and again. Frustrated and incredulous, he kept trying until he was panting and exhausted. The poor fool girl! It appeared that she had cast her life into the water.

Warwick came to the opposite shore and searched, but could find no one. At last, puzzled, he swam back to the opposite shore, collected his armor, and whistled for Dragon.

As he rode back he could not forget the girl. Or had it been a dream? When he neared the tents once again, Jake came running out to him. Warwick was about to tell Jake what he had seen, but Jake was brimming with news himself.

"Ah, my lord! You missed it. There was an attempt on the king's life! What excitement!"

"Excitement?" Warwick queried darkly, frowning.

"His Majesty was not harmed! It was all settled quite quickly. I barely saw a bit of it myself. Seems an old lord who sat in the Parliament against His Majesty's father was determined to end the life of the son. But he was suspect ere it could happen and slain himself. His Majesty seemed only sad at the death; he insisted that the feasting for the people go on."

Warwick could not dismiss the thought of an attack upon Charles's life so easily. Charles Stuart was a decent man, wise and keenly intelligent despite his humor and his open marital indiscretions. He was a good friend.

"What were you about to say, my lord?" Jake asked.

"What? Oh, nothing, nothing really." The incident in the forest now seemed hazy, definitely an illusion. "Nothing but a dream. I saw a mermaid, perhaps."

Jake stared at him with a worried frown. "Were ye hit in the head, milord?"

"No, no, Jake—never mind." He was anxious to assure himself that Charles was all right. And, of course, Genevieve would be worried if he didn't hurry to meet her.

"Come on, Jake. I've a few wounds to tend to before I see my sovereign—and my lady wife."

Warwick limped slightly as he later entered the solar that adjoined the bedchamber assigned to him by Reemes, King Charles's master steward at Westchester Palace. As he at last reached the carved chair before the fire, he grimaced, then sighed with ease as he sat, taking the weight off his twisted ankle.

If Hardgrave only knew how he sat now! Sore buttocks, wrenched shoulders—and the ankle. He had barely managed to limp unescorted to the solar!

But the day was at last at an end. Genevieve had tired quickly at the banquet and had returned before him. He had gladly stayed behind at Charles's command, for he had seen that Charles was truly well. But he was sad, for Charles had no love of bloodshed.

Warwick tensed suddenly. Beyond the crackle of the fire, he had heard a rustle of sound. He made no move, but muscles that had sought relaxation tensed. When the furtive rustling sounded again, he spun about. His arms moving out with the speed of a shot, his long fingers became a shackle around the wrist of his secretive visitor.

"Warwick!" a feminine voice protested indignantly, and he was staring into the very beautiful but very petulant face of Lady Anne Fenton. He released her wrist instantly with a frown of annoyance, settling back into his chair.

"Anne," he muttered dryly, "whatever are you doing here? Have you given up your quest for the king?"

Anne pouted prettily, batting jet-black lashes at him as she knelt by his booted feet. She leaned against the chair—not without a practiced and alluring expertise—so that her rounded cream bosom met the pressure of the wood. She looked very appealing indeed. "Warwick!" she reproached him, and then her voice became soft, sensually husky. "You know you have always been my first love!"

"Really?" he queried her with a broad grin. "What about your husband, milady?"

Anne laughed; her sense of humor and honesty were traits as compelling as the simplicity of her beauty.

"What about him? He has no desire to come to court."

"Nor would I, were my wife the latest whim of the king."

"Warwick!" Lady Anne snapped, this time with a *tsk* of irritation. She stood, aware that he was no longer appreciating the fine view she had afforded him of her assets. "I don't remember you worrying so about Geoffrey the last time we met!"

Warwick opened one eye and scanned her angry features. He sighed. "Anne, I am married now. To Genevieve."

"Genevieve!" Anne exclaimed heatedly, stalking behind his chair like a caged tiger. "Gentle Genevieve! Sweet Genevieve! Innocent, wonderful Genevieve. Warwick, I warned you not to marry her." Anne laughed, and a bitter twist made her words sound like the shrills of a harpy. "Do you know they say that she trembled, knowing that she was to marry you! The man who was the rage of the court—so handsome, but so rough and battle hard. A demon on women! The great magnificent beast, so exciting— and so distant! Many would have died for your touch, but not Genevieve! You fool! Your wife fears you, just as she fears your specters—the ghost of your grandmother and more ancient haunts! If a beast of a husband is not enough, he adds a family curse—"

"Anne!" Both eyes snapped open. His voice was quiet, but it carried the dangerous edge of a razor. He was suddenly on his feet, stalking her in a way that both thrilled her and made her wish uncertainly that she might take back her taunts. He began to speak again in that soft tone that was also threatening. She backed toward the solar door. "On many things I agree with you, Lady Anne. My wife is a gentle creature, and, yes, she has been called upon to face a legend-riddled past! But she meets no beast in her bed at night, I assure you. Where gentle is, gentle comes. When you have craved a beast, my lecherous lady, you have received one. But that is in the past, Lady Anne. Genevieve is two months with child, and beast that you call me, I would not hurt that gentle lady I call wife upon the forfeit of my own life."

"You don't love her!" Anne cried out. "You married her only to fulfill a promise! You—"

"Anne, I pray you! Ply your charms upon Charles this evening, for I am sorely vexed. No matter what your feeling for Genevieve, she is my wife, and she carries my heir. Anne, leave me be."

She paused at the doorway, then tossed her beautiful mane of

black hair over her shoulder. "Carries your heir, does she, Warwick? I doubt she expects to survive its birth!"

A step brought him to her. His fingers bit into her shoulders,
and he shook her so that her head lolled; but though her teeth
rattled, she did not care. She was in his arms, if only for a moment.

"Anne, by God! I dislike the thought of force against your . . .
fair sex, but twist your knife no further!"

"Warwick!" she cried out, leaning against his chest, a sob
catching in her throat. "I love you, I need you! And I can make
you happy, where she cannot!"

"Anne!" he exclaimed, more softly now, for though he knew
she could easily sway to one lover from another, he felt that she
did care for him. "Anne . . . I have taken a wife. A gentle wife.
And I will not bring pain to her soul, for I do love her gentle
heart."

Anne jerked from him with a scowl darkening her features.
"You will come back to me, Warwick Chatham! I swear it! By
Christmastide next, you will seek the passion of my arms!"

She spun about and left him. Warwick sighed, feeling again all
the little strains and bruises in his body. He started to limp back
to his chair, then paused, staring at the door to the bedchamber.

Genevieve stood there.

She appeared almost ethereal in the fire's gentle glow, her hair
so pale a gold it neared white, her lovely flesh so light as to be
translucent. Her eyes, fine powder blue, were wide and stared at
him. Her delicate fingers held tight to the door.

"You heard?" he asked her, regretful that she had witnessed
such a scene.

Genevieve nodded, but then she smiled. "I . . . had a nightmare,
Warwick, and I hoped . . ." Her sentence faded as she walked to
him. She slipped her slender arms around his neck, and her eyes
held gratitude as they sought his. "Thank you so much, my dear
lord!"

Her lashes lowered and she rested her cheek against his chest,
feeling the hard, sure pounding of his heart. She knew his virility;
she knew his strength. Yet no man could have dealt more gently
with his wife.

"I . . . I fear that I have disappointed you greatly," she whis-

pered, ''and yet in this court, you cling faithfully to me. What . . .
pride it gives me, Warwick.''

Warwick lifted his hand to smooth her pale shimmering hair;
then he lifted her into his arms and returned to the chair, holding
her in his lap. ''You do not disappoint me, love,'' he told her,
cradling her close.

Genevieve, with her head bowed, smiled sadly. She knew that
he lied, but did not accuse him of doing so. For all his great
tenderness, she could not accustom herself to his strength in their
bedchamber. She feigned sleep many nights to avoid her duty,
though she had found that she loved him dearly. She knew that
he was aware that she pretended sleep, yet he would sigh and stare
into the night and allow her that pretense. One day, she promised
herself nightly, she would make it all up to him. She knew—as
the ladies who sought his favors did not—that he was far more
the gentleman than the beast. She had come to him in fear. He
had seen her fear, cast aside his own needs, and cajoled her from
it. Sometimes she was still frightened; he was so strong, she was
so . . . so very weak! He exercised such patience. She had always
planned on entering the convent where she had been schooled.
Her father, on his deathbed, had asked Warwick to marry and care
for her, and for his deep friendship and loyalty, Warwick had done
just that.

A log crackled in the fire, and she jumped.

''Genevieve!'' he admonished her softly.

''I'm sorry!'' she cried.

''Nay, nay! Just be easy, my love, be easy,'' he crooned to her.
Again she settled in his arms, content with his strength about her.
If only it was all like this!

They sat in silence for many moments, feeling the warmth of
the fire surround them. Warwick's thoughts were remorseful—
and painful. One of Anne's vicious taunts was true. He should not
have married Genevieve, even though he had vowed to do so. By
nature she was timid, such a gentle, ethereal beauty. Too gentle
for a beast, he told himself wryly. And too gentle to combat the
rumors.

''Genevieve?'' he said softly.

''My lord?''

''What Anne said isn't true, you know. There are several legends about the family, but my grandmother's death was an accident. We're really not beasts—no more so than the rest of England! All the stories about the family come from the days of the Conqueror.''

"Except the one about your grandmother," Genevieve murmured.

"My grandmother fell through a staircase, Genevieve. There was nothing 'cursed' about it. Rotten wood brought about her death.''

"I know," Genevieve whispered. "But—but, Warwick, the dream that awakened me—I saw her! Warwick, I saw her!''

Suddenly she tensed in his lap, sobs catching in her throat, her fragile hands pounding against his chest. "Warwick, she came to me! She was green and rotting with the mold from the grave, and she told me that I would join her, that I would come—''

"Stop it, Genevieve! You saw who? My grandmother? No, my love, you did not see her. Genevieve, I will let nothing harm you!''

She heard the passion in his voice, and she thrilled to it, just as she felt the terror leave her trembling limbs as he warmed her with his all-encompassing strength.

"Oh, Warwick! I will try not to be such a coward.''

"You are not a coward.''

"Then I am weak—I have no strength.''

"You have the strength of my love.''

"Warwick . . .'' He was so good to her! She lifted her eyes to his, and they dampened with the tears of her love. She huddled to him, and she determined that she would love him as a wife should. She forced herself to push her fears to the background, remembering that they had come to Westchester to settle a dispute. "Oh, Warwick, I do love you so, and I was so very proud of you today. You were magnificent. No man is a nobler knight!''

He laughed. "If I am so to your eyes, it is all that I ask. And now, my sweet, my beloved wife who carries a beloved child, you must be off back to your bed! I crave but a glass of port, then will come and sleep beside you.''

She smiled at him, finding her courage in him.

"I will wait for you, my lord husband," she told him.

He touched her cheek gently with his knuckle. "You needn't do so, sweet. I know that you wish to rest—''

"Nay, Warwick, I wish to wait for you.''

He smiled at her tenderly, then set her on her feet. "I do love you, Genevieve. And I have never been disappointed in you."

She knew this was another lie, but it was wonderfully stated, as wonderful as the virile, handsome man who was her husband. She would be brave! She would not give into phantom terrors in the night!

"I await your leisure," she promised. With a little flush, she hurried into the bedchamber.

Warwick limped around the solar, then poured himself a glass of strong port from a decanter on the sideboard. Anne, he reflected, had taunted him far more than he cared to admit, about Genevieve and their child and the supposed "curse," and about himself.

Tension held his body in a firm grip as memory heated his blood to a painful boil. How he longed to hold a woman like Anne; one strong and ripe and primed for passion, willing to welcome his desire! He stood still and swallowed fiercely, desperately trying to swallow down that blaze of longing.

He tossed back his head and finished the port. His wife was good and gentle—in truth, he would not betray her. Yet, in truth, it was sometimes most painful to restrain all his passion and need.

Curiously his thoughts turned to the woman in the forest again. Had she been real? Or had he been dreaming?

A man had been threatening her, and she had been fighting back. Then she had taken to the water and disappeared. Real—or imaginary? Though he hadn't really seen her, he could remember that she was beautiful. Passionate and glorious. Thoughts of her made him hungry now, eager to hold such a sprite of fire and fury in his arms.

Genevieve, he reminded himself, was his life. He owed her his life and his loyalty—and his dreams. Warwick sighed and sat again to cast off his boots. They made a thud as they hit the stone floor.

And then he heard another thud.

Curiously he turned, stunned to see that the door between the solar and the bedroom had been closed. He frowned; Genevieve had never, even as a new bride, sought to close a door against him. And tonight she had not been afraid of him at all. She had invited him in.

"Warwick! She comes! Oh, she comes!"

He sprang into action at the scream of anguished fear and beseechment, throwing himself at the door. It was bolted.

"Genevieve!" he thundered, but there was no answer.

He threw his shoulder against the door, again and again, ignoring the burning pain that tore through him with the effort.

"Genevieve!"

The door gave, its hinges broken. He staggered into the room. But Genevieve was not there. The curtained, canopied bed was empty. A breeze stirred from the balcony, sending the pale gauze drapes drifting about like whispering ghosts.

A scream sounded from below.

Dread filled him; his legs seemed leaden as he forced himself to the balcony. The scream came again, and his eyes were riveted downward.

"Genevieve!"

Genevieve was set in the king's own chapel as prayers were offered up for her soul. Warwick barely left her side until the day came to lead the black-shrouded hearse back to North Lambria, where she could be interred in the family crypt.

And on that day he sat in the bedchamber they had shared and brooded deeply on the folly of taking such a tender maid to be his wife. It was at that time that he noted a draft where there should not have been one. Pensively he studied the tapestries that hung on the walls flanking the fire and mantel.

Then suddenly he pulled aside a tapestry, discovering that it concealed a break in the wall. When pressure was applied, the wall slipped silently back, creating a small passageway.

He followed the passageway, almost tripping down a flight of dank, dark, and treacherously curved stairs.

He returned to the chamber for a torch, then followed the stairs. They lead to an old, long-deserted dungeon. Amidst the rats and ancient slime Warwick found something peculiar—a monk's cowl and a Greek theatrical mask.

He stared at them in a dark and furious silence, bundled them into his arms, and returned to his chamber.

* * *

Everyone in the king's court knew that the Earl of North Lambria was disconsolate. He withdrew to his estates, isolating himself.

Charles, who sorely missed his friend's visits, at last journeyed out to North Lambria. He was greeted as befitted the king, Warwick was polite; he offered his finest hospitality, and he tried to laugh at the king's renowned witticisms. But the coldness in his heart could not be warmed.

Charles, a wise and shrewd man despite his reputation for levity, came quickly to a somber point.

"You did the girl no ill, my friend. You were a better husband than most by far, including myself, God and the queen forgive me! You must continue your life. Marry again—"

"Nay," Warwick stated. "I'll not take another to her death!"

The king snorted. "You know as well as I, Warwick, that no curse from heaven hounds the family! Ghosts do not exist, nor kill—"

Warwick at last flared into a passionate fury, pounding his fist hard against the table so that the plates and goblets before them rattled. "Her death was no suicide, Charles! I do not believe in ghosts, but I do believe that she was murdered."

"Murdered?"

"Aye, My Grace. She was murdered." Warwick hurried to his sideboard and produced the cloak and mask. The king was stunned.

Charles lowered his eyes. "By whom?"

"I don't know," Warwick muttered in dismay, sinking back into his chair and rubbing his temple. "Charles, I do know that she was killed. Unless I discover why, I cannot take another wife."

"God in Heaven!" Charles exclaimed. "This must be madness. Who do you suspect? Justin, Clinton? I cannot believe—"

Warwick laughed bitterly. "I pray not!"

"Then—"

"There is Lord Hardgrave," Warwick said bitterly.

"Oh, come!" Charles muttered impatiently. "You two have your differences, but for such an accusation—"

"I am sorry, perhaps it was unjustified. But who, dammit, who? Mathilda loved her dearly, as did Justin. Even Clinton thought her entirely too good for me! Charles, it leaves me cold. I must discover the truth, else spend my life in the company of paramours.''

Charles sighed. ''Warwick, I tell you, this is a plague of your imagination. Genevieve was . . . I'm sorry, Warwick, but I believe that she was suicidal. You found an old mask and a cloak. Many wear masks at court to hide their true identities when planning a tryst with a lover! You must get over this. You are coming back to court with me.''

At the king's insistence, Warwick returned to court. Not only did Charles miss his friend, but there was the business of a kingdom to run.

And as the lady Anne had prophesied, he spent the Christmastide next in her arms, where she worshipped an ardor grown silent, roughly passionate, strangely distant.

She took to calling him the ''beast'' again, for he went to many women. He claimed their desires; yet gave none his heart. He was a heated lover, but a cold man, harder than ever before.

A year passed. Time healed the rawest pain, but Warwick's suspicions did not die, and his determination never wavered.

''You need to marry again, my friend,'' Charles advised once more.

Marry . . .

Nay, he needed to bait a murderer first. But he did not feel like arguing with Charles.

''Aye, Your Grace,'' he would say, smiling. ''I need a wife.'' But to take a wife, he firmly believed, would be to risk that lady's life. He was certain that someone was determined he should leave no heirs.

Lady Anne's elderly husband, Geoffrey, succumbed to a fever and died. In bed Anne turned impetuously to Warwick.

''We could marry now, my dearest!''

Warwick rolled from her side, planting his feet upon the ground as he ran his fingers through his hair.

''I will never marry again,'' he told her.

The lady Anne chuckled huskily, rising upon her knees to rake her nails sensuously along his back. ''I shall change your mind!''

Nay, she could not change his mind, but she could ignite his senses. He turned, taking her into his arms, fiercely easing the tempest in his body. But when dawn came, he left her.

Genevieve haunted him always. Dear God! But he owed her justice! There had to be a way to flush out the killer!

In April of 1679 Warwick walked with Charles along Market Street. The king sought trinkets for his wife, and Warwick, in a rare light mood, sought to purchase an ivory fan for the lady Anne.

He and the king stopped in a tavern for ale. Charles, a king easily accessible to his people, readily sat in the common house. He made the serving wench gasp with pleasure when he discreetly pinched her rump, and he rewarded the innkeeper with a fat gold coin.

The king's guards stayed far behind them as they laughed merrily and ambled into the streets again.

Suddenly a flurry of darkness descended upon them, and a sword was raised against the king. Warwick sobered quickly, drawing his own sword. The skirmish was swiftly ended with the man, a hearty if filthy and toothless soul, panting at Warwick's feet and begging for a quick death.

"Slay me, my lord! I beg you! 'Twill be Tyburn Tree—"

" 'Twill not be Tyburn Tree for a traitor against the king's own person!" A guard, rushing upon the scene, declared, "Ye'll know the agony of being drawn and quartered, scum, or perhaps the fires of death will rise to the sky!"

The beggar was dragged away. Charles, his dark and handsome eyes upon his friend, sighed wearily. "Would that I could do something to save such wretches. The man was surely mad."

"Then surely he should be mercifully hanged!"

"Hanged? Nay, man, hundreds hang for far lesser crimes. They rot for debt, they die for stealing bread."

"You are the king—"

"I rule by Parliament," Charles said huskily. "I do not ever forget that my father's head was severed from his body; I rule by the law. I am fond of my neck and the crown upon it."

A week later Warwick traveled the streets again in his coach, homeward bound for North Lambria. The coach came to a halt, and he leaned from it to speak with Jake, serving then as his coachman. "Why do we stop?" he queried.

"A death procession, my lord," Jake replied. "A lot of three poor wretches, bound for the Tyburn Tree."

Warwick gazed out the window. Crowds gathered about a cart as it moved down the street. He saw a youth, an old man—and a woman.

The woman turned suddenly. She was filthy, tattered, but something about her compelled his further scrutiny. Her hair, tangled with filthy straw, still caught the sun's reflection. It was long, waving, and curling down her back, a rich auburn when the sun caught its highlights. She was young . . . surely less than two decades of life had passed her by. She held her chin high. Her face was smudged and filthy, but her eyes burned with a haunting defiance. She was thin and pathetic.

Yet it was not with lust or love that he looked upon her. Warwick Chatham's eyes narrowed, and he tried to imagine her scrubbed and scoured. Her life would be forfeit in a matter of minutes.

And wasn't any extra moment of life precious?

"Jake!" he said suddenly. "I've heard tell that a man or woman can be saved from the gallows if taken in marriage before the rope is pulled. Is that true, Jake?"

"Aye," Jake muttered. "So reads the law."

"Jake," Warwick commanded tensely, "follow the procession."

PART I

Ondine

A water nymph by legend;
one who gained a soul through
marriage to a mortal.

Tyburn Tree
May 1679

Chapter 1

The worst part was feeling the noose around her neck, grating harshly against the tenderness of her throat, itching and bruising until she longed to scream and wrench herself free.

But she had promised herself that she would not scream, that she would not create any more of a show for the spectators than they were already going to see. She reminded herself that she was no martyr. It would be best to die as a common thief, rather than to have her head severed from her neck on a charge of treason. She could at least assure herself that she had fought a valiant battle against the odds. She'd lost, and now that it appeared her last hope was gone, she was determined not to falter—or further entertain a rabble that found amusement in death.

"How are ye doing, girl?"

As the cart jolted along, Ondine turned to the old man beside her who had voiced the question. His dark sunken eyes were full of sadness, and she longed to reach out and comfort him, but she could not, for her wrists were shackled together.

"I think that I would be doing fine, Joseph, had they but waited to tie the noose . . ."

Her voice faded away as she noted a pair of scruffy children following alongside the cart. Children! Mother of God! What kind of a woman urged her offspring to ogle suffering and death? But then, since they had first been dragged from Newgate an hour ago, she had been appalled by the throngs of people who had crowded the streets for a glimpse of the hanging. And the people had followed them from Newgate to St. Sepulchre, when she and Joseph and a terrified youth known as Little Pat had been given nosegays. The crowd was still with them now as they traveled down Holborn, High Holborn, St. Giles High Street . . .

"We're coming to the corner of Endell and Broad Street," Joseph warned Ondine.

Again she glanced at his dearly beloved face, wrinkled and etched from a life of poverty. "I'll not drink myself to a stupor to amuse this rabble," she told him with softly spoken dignity.

Joseph smiled wanly at the girl, seized with a heartache that had nothing to do with his own impending death. He was old, he had seen enough of this life and was ready for the next. But the girl! She was young, and before Newgate gaol had robbed her bones of flesh, her cheeks of color, and her hair of luster, she had been very beautiful. Even now, with filth dusting her translucent features and her clothing reduced to tattered rags, there was something fine about her. Perhaps it was in the way she stood, straight and proud, her chin high, her blue eyes shimmering with dignity and defiance.

His heartache was for her, for her youth. She had the vitality and exuberance of a spring morning, a natural exhilaration for life. Her true nature, beneath an outer layer of determination and fierce cunning, was sweet and sensitive; even in the bowels of hellish Newgate she had looked to her fellow man, sharing a crust of molded bread with anyone who appeared in greater need. She had cried out furiously against their jailors. She had planned an escape for herself and Joseph that had almost succeeded. And if she hadn't paused to care about Little Pat, she would have escaped.

Joseph sighed. This girl, this Ondine, was surely not the common lass she had claimed to be when she had joined their group of poor and homeless in the forest. She moved with too great a grace, spoke with too melodious a tone. She had dressed in rags, but her manner had been that of a lady born and bred, even if she had fought against injustice with the rugged verve and vigor of a fishwife! She had defended them all, and they had accepted her with no questions. She was a mystery they had never attempted to solve.

And it seemed that the mystery would die today. Joseph was suddenly furious. They were going to die for trying to live. Maddie, Old Tom, and crippled Simkins last week, and today the three of them. They had committed no crime but to struggle to eat. Joseph did not care for himself, but that they were to take this girl with all her spirit and snuff out her life—that was a crime.

"Drink the ale that they give you, girl," Joseph advised. He swallowed suddenly and painfully as he struggled to speak the truth kindly. "Sometimes the rope . . . sometimes 'tis not quick. Don't mind these gawkers. The ale can make it easier. Let it."

Their procession—the two of them and Little Pat in the cart, the friar who waddled beside it, two guards, the black-cowled executioner, and the magistrate—came to a sudden halt. They had reached the Bowl, and as was the custom, the innkeeper came out, and they were offered ale.

Ondine hesitated before stretching her wrists to the limit of her shackles to accept the cup offered her.

I am not afraid, she tried to tell herself. I am not afraid. God knows that I was guilty of no sin against Him. Every step that I have taken, I have taken with care; I could have changed nothing. And now I must find serenity and not be afraid.

But she was afraid, and still unwilling to accept her fate. God! How she had longed to clear her father's name of the injustice offered him in death. She had dreamed of returning home to avenge that death and prove the devious treachery behind it. But she'd never had the chance. Along with the beggars in the forest to which she had run—the kind people who had become her friends— she was to die. She accepted the ale and prayed that it would give her courage so that she could scorn those who so unjustly took her life and made a mockery of her death.

Ondine drank deeply and discovered that the bitter ale only added to her misery. With each swallow the noose about her neck chafed her throat, and the liquid running through her offered no warmth, no courage to sustain her.

The spectacle at the Bowl came to an end, and the cart began to move once more. Ondine tried to close her mind to the shouts about her, to the hoots and catcalls of the men who told the executioner she would be more sport alive. They were nearing Tyburn Tree now, the three-legged structure where their ropes would be tied. Then the horses would be whipped to frenzy, and she, Joseph, and Little Pat would dangle by their necks until dead.

Let it be fast, God, Ondine prayed silently. She felt a dizziness sweep through her so that she thought she would falter and fall as she saw the open galleries that flanked the gallows, galleries where spectators paid two shillings apiece for a bird's-eye view of the execution.

The galleries were filled.

Ondine closed her eyes. She could feel the sun on her face, and a soft damp breeze that promised rain swirled lightly about her cheeks. She opened her eyes. She would never see the sun again.

Ridiculous things came to her mind. She would never know what it was like to be clean again, to feel her hair, freshly washed, fall softly about her shoulders. She would never run across a meadow, pluck a wildflower from a clump of dew-damp earth . . .

"Hold fast to God, girl!" Joseph said softly. "For His is a better world, and He knows the goodness in you and will be there to embrace you."

Die—no! She couldn't be about to die! She would fight until the end. She would kick and scream and bite—and gain nothing, she told herself bitterly. There was no escape now. She would not give the crowd its money's worth!

She tried to nod and found that she could not; movement was tightening her noose.

They were beneath the gallows. The fat friar was muttering unintelligible benedictions, and the executioner was demanding to know if they had any last words.

Little Pat started to scream, begging for his life, crying out his fear. Ondine bit hard into her lip. The lad couldn't have been more than fourteen, and he had been condemned to die for cutting down a tree that happened to grow in an earl's forest. Not unlike her own "crime."

And the spectators were enjoying every minute. Ondine stepped forward in the cart. She did, indeed, have a number of last words.

"What is the matter with you?" she demanded, her voice ringing out loud and strong and clear. A murmur rippled through the crowd, and then a hush followed. "Can you truly enjoy this boy's plight? If so, I pray that you find one day that you are in dire need of the two shillings you paid for your seats, and that you find you are tempted to fish a stream that belongs to some gentry, just to feed your empty bellies. Suffer with this boy! Else you could well find that his suffering could be your own—"

"Hang her!" a furious voice cried out, and the chant was quickly picked up by those who wanted a show, not a sermon that could touch their hearts with guilt.

"Hold your peace!" cried out Sir Wilton, the local magistrate.

He was silent as the crowd toned down once again, and in that silence Ondine looked miserably to Joseph. "What are they waiting for now?" she begged him, suddenly anxious to have done with it.

"Marriage offers."

"Marriage offers!"

Joseph shrugged. " 'Tis custom, girl. Just like the travesty of this procession, just like the cup of ale. If a lad will step up and marry ye, girl, ye'll be set free."

Ondine stared about her at the crowd. There was not a man in sight who would not gag her if he touched her. They were lecherous and filthy, the lot of them. And yet her heart had quickened, for in these seconds she knew how deeply she cherished life. She thought she would face anything just to live.

"I'd love like heaven to take on the girl!" cried out a potbellied balding merchant. "But me wife 'ould have us both beaten to death before nightfall!"

A roar of laughter rose like the wind. Filthy scum! Ondine thought. Perhaps she *would* rather die than be touched by the likes of him. Her eyes narrowed sharply. Marry, yes! The words would mean nothing to her except escape! The leering buzzards! If one would only offer for her, she could live—and then teach him what rot he was before disappearing!

And then she thought of her own appearance—and her smell! Dear God, but what two weeks in Newgate could do to one! She knew her hair was tousled and wild, streaked with bits of hay and dirt. Her cheeks were pinched and filthy, and her ragged gown hung about her like a muddied sack. No one would ask for her.

"Well, then," began the magistrate, "I've no maid for the old man or boy, and no lad for the girl. The hanging will commence—"

"Wait up there, guv'nor!"

Ondine was startled to see a sprightly little man jump close to the three-legged structure called Tyburn Tree, that instrument of misery and death. Tears sprang to her eyes. He was an ugly fellow—short, sallow, with a beak for a nose—but his dark eyes were bright and warm, and there was a whisper of command to his voice. He was not one of the lascivious gawkers. He was decked out as a coachman. His breeches and jacket were a dignified black, his shirt white. His appearance was that of a well-kept servant, yet he spoke as one accustomed to voicing his own mind.

"I'll wait up for a moment, I'll warrant. What is it, then? Do you wish to wed the girl?" The magistrate guffawed loudly. " 'Tis the only way a jackanapes with such a face could hope to win a wench of youth or beauty—be that beauty filthy and grimed!"

"I'd have a word with the girl," the ugly little man said. He came close to Ondine and spoke softly, not willing to entertain the crowd with his business.

"Be ye a murderess, girl?"

Ondine shook her head, aware that she barely kept the tears that hovered in her eyes from spilling down her cheeks. She'd been accused of murder—but not here, and not now. And she was guilty of nothing.

"Yer crime?"

"Poaching."

The ugly little jackanapes with the warm eyes and beak nose nodded, smiling at her not unkindly.

"Would ye be willing to wed to escape the hangman's noose?"

The executioner began to laugh loud and laboriously, the sound muffled by his black face mask. Apparently he had been close enough to hear the words of the swarthy little man.

"Ha! 'Tis like as not the maid would choose death o'er marriage to the likes of you, gnome!"

The little man flashed a look of scorn to the executioner that silenced the hooded man immediately.

The thought of refusal had never entered Ondine's mind. She had been wondering furiously at the terrible seconds between life and death, imagining one moment the feel of the sunshine and the breeze, and the next moment . . . the rope snapping tight. She might have died instantly, entering what great chasm she did not know. Or perhaps she might have strangled slowly, knowing horrible agony as the sunshine paled to webbed shades of gray.

And this little man, this ugly little gnome of a man, had come to save her. She began to feel guilty, knowing that he was a good man and not a cruel one, and that despite his kindness, she would have to leave him, too. If he was serious, if she managed to live!

"Sir," she said loudly for the benefit of the crowd, for she could, at the very least, commend his kindness to those who mocked him. "I would gladly wed a beast of the forest, a dragon or a toad, so dear to me is life. I should be forever grateful to call you husband, for you are none of those, but a man of greater mercy than any who calls himself gentleman here."

The jackanapes smiled at her reply, then chuckled softly. "'Tis no toad you'll be receiving, but some might say as that ye have joined up with a beast of the forest—or a dragon, mayhaps. 'Tis not me ye'll be marryin', girl."

"Here! Here!" the magistrate protested. "The law does not hold for you to take the girl away for another! You wed her here and now, as is the law, or she swings—"

"*Stop!*" was suddenly roared in interruption. "If you must bluster out the law, I charge you to uphold it!"

The voice, coming from the rear of the crowd, was deep and sure, accustomed to authority and brooking no opposition. Ondine frowned, trying to stare through the crowd and discover the speaker.

Then the crowd began to mumble softly and give way to the man. Ondine emitted a little gasp when she saw him, for he was not one of the common crowd.

He was a tall man and appeared to be more so because he was lean, and his clothing—tailored tight-fitting breeches, elegant ruffled white shirt and frock coat—clung to the handsomely proportioned muscles with a negligent flare. He was obviously of the aristocracy, but though he had condescended to the ruffled shirt, there was nothing else frilled about him. His hair was a tawny color, not at all curled, but clubbed severely at his nape. He wore no beard or mustache, and though his features were handsome— his cheekbones high, his nose long and straight, his eyes large and wide set beneath arched chestnut brows—he had a look about him that was unnerving. His face was . . . hard. But something about his eyes was chilling. Ondine thought, surprised that she could think this at such a time. They were bright, sharp, alert, and thickly fringed with lashes, but like his features, they were hard.

And, apparently, they made as much an impression on the magistrate as they did upon her, for he stepped away from the cart as the man stepped forward. It was not just that the man was obviously of the nobility, it was the threat he offered as a man. His appearance was arresting and promised an uncompromising danger, should he be crossed.

Ondine saw a glimpse of warmth about him as he nodded briefly to the little jackanapes, a single brow raising as if the two exchanged a thought, the thought being that the magistrate was a man contemptible, beneath dung. A slight smile seemed to tug at his lips, but it vanished quickly so that she thought she might well have imagined it.

"I am the man who wishes to wed her—here, and according to the law. I wish to speak to the girl myself," he said, and without awaiting a reply, he turned to Ondine. She noted that he blinked briefly, offended by her scent, but then he proceeded to speak.

"What was your crime, girl?"

She hesitated only briefly. "I killed a deer."

His brow knit into an incredulous frown. "You're about to hang for killing a deer?"

"Aye, my lord, and it should not surprise you," she heard herself say bitterly. "The deer belonged to a certain Lord Lovett— or at least it lived upon his property. 'Tis your kind that has sent me here." Her own kind, she reminded herself dryly. But she had been with Joseph and his fellows through the long nights at Newgate and aligned herself with them.

He lifted a brow, and she quickly wondered why she had chosen to offend him, and then she wondered why not. That the ugly little serving man might marry her, she had found possible. But not this man, not a member of the landed gentry. Hope had become a twisted torture, a macabre jest. And since he was certainly not about to marry her, he was nothing more than curious. And since she was about to die, she might as well quell his curiosity with a truth that was offensive.

But he did not retort to her insolence. She felt his eyes raking over her from head to toe, and despite herself, she felt a flush rake through her.

"Your speech is excellent."

Ondine felt like laughing. She had met many a lord and lady in her day who could not say a line of the King's English. And then she sobered quickly. If she was about to die, her true identity would go to the grave with her. And if she was possibly to live, then she must be very careful. If she lived, so would her dreams of justice and vengeance. She closed her eyes briefly. She wouldn't live. This was all a merciless joke. But it suddenly seemed senseless to insult him further, so she offered up a quickly fabricated lie.

"My father was a poet. I traveled to many courts with him."

He nodded at her, still watching her. Then, to Ondine's amazement, he turned irritably to the magistrate.

"Release her so that I may marry her."

"What?" the magistrate shrieked, his fleshy cheeks puffing out. "But, my lord! The girl is nothing but a thief. A pretty piece, I'll warrant, but—"

"Sir, if I am not mistaken, the law reads that she goes free if a man takes her as bride. I promise you, I am a man. I wish to marry her. Now get that rope off her neck and take her from the cart."

Too stunned to speak, Ondine stared at the tall stranger. He couldn't be serious. It was a grisly joke, meant to torture her to the very end.

"Do not be so cruel as to taunt me further!" she begged.

He emitted an impatient oath and sprang to the cart himself, slipping the rope from her neck, then lifting her with startling strength that almost sent her sprawling as he set her upon the ground. "Friar!" he snapped impatiently. "Are you a man of God, or aren't you? Certainly you can stumble through a brief wedding ceremony."

"My lord—" the magistrate began again.

The stranger's temper snapped and harsh authority clipped his tone. "Get to the paperwork, sir."

"But, my lord! To whom—"

"My given name, sir, is Warwick Chatham. May we proceed? I am not a man without influence. I would not like to have it brought to the king's attention that his magistrates are slow witted—"

No more needed to be said. An excited murmur rose from the crowd, and the magistrate almost fell over himself in his haste to be efficient. The fat friar began to mumble out some broken words, and Ondine discovered that her shackles were gone and her hand was being held by the firm grip of the stranger.

It was the ale, she told herself. It had cast her into some strange dream that was an illusion meant to ease her death. But it wasn't a dream—she could no longer feel the rough chafing of the noose about her neck.

She gasped as she felt his fingers bite cruelly into her arm, then her eyes widened to meet his hard hazel ones. "Speak your vows!" he told her curtly. "Unless you choose to hang—"

She spoke. She faltered and stumbled, but followed the friar's orders. The friar kept mumbling until the stranger interrupted him.

"Is the ceremony complete?"

"Well, aye, my lord. You are legally wed—"

"Good." He stuffed a coin into the friar's hand. A scroll was set before them, and he signed his name, Warwick Chatham, with a flourish. Then his eyes, still hard and sharp, seemed to sear her with impatience. "Your name!" he hissed. "Or your mark if you are incapable of writing—"

The indignity of his suggestion made her move, but even so, she shook so badly that she did not sign with her usual clear script; the quill wavered and her name was barely legible. Just as well, she thought as her mind began to function again. It might have been recognized.

The friar puffed and blew on the ink to dry it. The document was rolled and tied, then snatched from the friar by Warwick as he emitted an irritable oath. He did not thank the friar for his services again. He turned to leave the Tyburn Tree, pulling Ondine along behind him. She jerked back, tears filling her eyes as she

saw the two remaining ropes thrown over the beams. "Joseph!"
she called out.

He smiled at her. "Go, girl! Long life and a fruitful union. Our
blessed Jesus does provide miracles!"

A whipcrack sounded, and the horses whinnied and bolted.
Ondine screamed as she heard the thud of weight snapping upon
the ropes.

"Don't look!" the stranger commanded. For the first time there
was a rough sympathy in his tone, and despite her stench, he
whirled Ondine comfortingly into his arms as he dragged her away.

She could not see, for her tears for Joseph and the boy filled
her eyes. A moment later she was released and set to lean against
something hard and cold. She blinked and discovered that it was
a carriage with an elaborate coat of arms engraved upon the door.
The little jackanapes who had first approached her stood waiting
for them. "Is it done, then, milord?"

"It is," Warwick Chatham replied.

"What do we do with 'er now, then, sir?"

"Hmmm—"

Warwick's eyes swept over her, and she felt a flush spreading
throughout her body at his cool assessment. She felt somehow as
if he had ravaged her. A slight smile played upon his lips as he
cocked his head toward his coachman and lifted a well-arched
brow.

"She is a bit of a mess, isn't she, Jake?"

Despite everything, anger coursed through her. The arrogance
of the man! Did he think that people emerged from Newgate
smelling like roses? He deserved a night in the pit himself; hours
of dank darkness to quell his pride, and infested water to sap his
well-honed strength. Yet she was glad that she longed to slap him
for his amusement. It would not be so hard to desert the man who
had saved her life if she could resent him so furiously. She was
surprised that he didn't wrinkle his aristocratic nose at her. He
laughed instead, apparently aware that his perusal had left her
extremely indignant, her temper rising despite the circumstances.

"Milord Whomever-it-is-that-you-may-be!" she snapped. "I
do not intend ingratitude for my life. But I am not an animal
to be discussed as if I lacked the wit to comprehend my own
language."

His brow remained high, and he inclined his head slightly toward her, as if both surprised by her words and faintly amused.

"No, madam, you are not an animal. But you are in a truly slovenly form, and something must be done about it."

Ondine lowered her lashes. She was more than slovenly; she was odious. And her temper was fading as quickly as it had come, because when she closed her eyes, she could see Joseph swinging from the rope. She had just barely escaped death.

"I am offensive," she said quietly. "I am sorry."

"You needn't be. A bride from the gallows can hardly be expected to appear her best. And filth is a problem that can be remedied. What do you say, Jake?"

Jake scratched his bewhiskered chin. "I say we head home by way of Swallow's Ford. To seek some—niceties!"

"As in a bath!" Warwick Chatham laughed. "Fine idea. Shall we?"

The carriage door swung open, and she felt the stranger's arms upon her again, thrusting her up and into the carriage—an elegant carriage with velvet seats and silk linings.

"Are you comfortable?" he asked her. He watched her, his foot upon the mounting block.

"Comfortable? Ah . . . quite." She should have swung with poor Joseph, yet she had married instead. Married!

She had married a man with a knight's shoulders and hard hazel eyes, a man decked in the finest garb available. A rugged man, a frightening man, "a forest beast." The little man, Jake, had grinned at the description. She trembled despite herself. She would escape him, surely, she swore inwardly to ease her fear. He was still watching her, waiting. For what? She cleared her throat to speak, politely now. Perhaps he had just hoped to save her.

"Sir, I offer my apologies for my temper, and my most heartfelt gratitude! Yet you needn't feel responsible for me. If you'd just leave me, I do have friends in London—"

"That's quite impossible," he told her.

"But surely—"

"Madam, I could swear I just heard you promise to love, honor, and obey till death us do part."

"It was—real?" she demanded in a stilted whisper.

"It was."

"Why?" she challenged him quickly.

"I needed a wife," he told her bluntly. Then he closed the carriage door, calling to Jake, "On to Swallow's Ford!"

And the carriage jolted into action.

Chapter 2

Ondine understood quickly why they had chosen to come to Swallow's Ford. It was a small place, and the proprietress of the local tavern and inn was a lovely buxom matron, thrilled with Ondine—and apparently quite fond of Warwick Chatham. She was more than willing to keep secret the circumstances of his new bride's appearance.

It was Jake who brought her to Meg, by the rear door. Yet Ondine was glad, for she observed the layout of the barn, determining her chances of later finding a mount and fleeing for freedom. Her head still swam. She was so grateful for her life, yet ever so wary of Chatham. What could he want with her? Her teeth chattered with the thought. He appeared so sound and handsome.

He was not just arresting in appearance, she thought, but a peer as well! Jake had called her "Countess," informing her that Warwick Chatham was the earl of North Lambria. This was a very frightening fact, for as a peer, he might well have recognized her surname on their wedding license, were her handwriting not so shaky! But then, perhaps, he would not know of her, for North Lambria was border country, harsh and rugged and beautiful, according to Jake, and, thankfully, far from Ondine's own home.

Meg's place was sparse but clean. The room to which Ondine

was led was a simple one, offering no more than a bed, a washstand, and a screen, but the shutters were opened to the summer's breeze, and the bedding smelled clean and fresh.

"Get behind the screen, my lady, and shed those rags," Meg told her. "Like as not, they should be burned. You've no need to fear an intrusion; I'll see to the tub and water meself. Just stay here till I give you a call." She didn't wait for Ondine's agreement, but bustled out the door.

Ondine did as she had been told, stepping behind the screen and nervously shedding her garments. Oh, but they were rank! She was glad to cast her gown away, and her shift, yet when she stood naked, she shivered again, her thoughts filled with the man who had so suddenly become her husband. He was so fine a figure of a man: tall, broad-shouldered, appearing lean, yet betraying a startling and frightening strength when his fingers wrapped around her arm, when the muscles of his arms constricted to lift her.

Aye, he was an arresting man, his manner as much as his form— the tone of his voice, the assessive tilt of his head. Was it breeding or life that had given him such command, an air that was totally assured, one that would brook no opposition of his will?

She hugged her arms about herself. She couldn't deny that he both frightened and fascinated her. She could easily see how a woman could fall prey to the proud and rugged masculinity of his features, could long for the sound of his voice, the touch and strength of his hands. But would any woman be welcomed by him for more than a brief respite, an interlude of lusty entertainment?

She didn't believe so. Not if ice hovered about his heart the way it did his eyes.

Ondine stiffened, hearing Meg's voice as the door to the chamber opened. "Hurry now, lads; the tub center, and fill it quickly. There's business aplenty downstairs, and if you'd earn your meals, you'd move quick!"

There were "Aye, Megs!" respectfully given, and the sounds of shuffling feet and spilling water. Then there was silence again after the door closed softly.

"My lady, 'tis only me here now. Come while the water's hot and the steam's arising!"

Ondine didn't want to walk before Meg. She felt terribly thin and horribly vulnerable.

"I'd prefer privacy," she murmured. As the wife of Lord Chatham, she reflected dryly, she could surely issue a firm command that would, by right, be instantly obeyed. But she was supposed to be a common waif, unaccustomed to the firm voice of assumption. Nor would she demand things of Meg under any circumstance, as the woman seemed to have a heart the size of the moon.

Meg chuckled softly. "Ah, my girl, come, now! 'Tis only me, Meg, and I raised a household of young ladies, I did. I've a mind to set into that tangled mop of hair upon your head, and come away assured that the vermin are clean of it!"

Ondine hesitated only a second, thinking of how lovely it would be to have someone thoroughly clean her hair.

She sprinted quickly from the screen to the tub, yelping slightly as her tender flesh hit the heat of the water.

"It must be hot!" Meg commiserated cheerfully. "Now, here's a cloth and two squares of the soap. The first will near take the skin from you, I must warn, yet it will leave you clean as a new-washed babe. Now, the second . . . ah, it was a special purchase when my man did travel to Paris! It has a scent of roses that lingers long and sweetly—just what you might crave now, I dare say!"

"Thank you," Ondine murmured. She accepted the soaps, watching Meg's pleasant and homely features as she did so. "You're very kind."

"Kind, oh, no, dear." She sighed softly. "I've a longing for young people, 'tis all. My girls are all wives now, with broods of their own. Oh, and I do love to have the babes . . ."

Meg chatted on. Ondine began to furiously scrub her skin. Meg had been quite right, she discovered quickly. The soap stung at first—she felt as if it peeled away a layer of her flesh. But it felt wonderful.

"Now, if I get me hands into that mop—" Meg poured a bucket of water onto Ondine's head. Even that felt wonderful, but not so good as the movement of Meg's fingers, scrubbing away at her scalp. "Ah, thank the Lord for this fine soap, for without it, we might've had to snip the length of this. And what a glory it is, dear child. As thick and long as a pelt of fur! Now duck!"

She shoved Ondine's head into the water and vigorously worked her fingers through the young girl's scalp once again. Ondine came up sputtering. Meg stepped back, crossing her arms over her chest and surveying her efforts with pleasure. "Ah, but you're a beautiful child! So thin, so—but no matter! You've breasts aplenty, even if your hips and ribs could use a pound or two of flesh!"

Ondine felt a heated flush flame throughout her body, yet she could take no offense at Meg's words; they were spoken so good-naturedly. She smiled, leaning her head back against the tub and relishing the feeling of being clean—and carrying that subtle scent of roses Meg had described. There was only one thing she thought to combat in the matron's words, and that she did a little wistfully, a little wearily.

"I'm not a child."

Yet how she longed to be one again! With her eyes closed and the steam misting around her, she could see the past all too clearly. A time when she had believed in the goodness of men; when treachery and death, poverty and deceit, had found no place in her perception. A smile touched her lips. Her mother had died at her birth, but, oh! She could remember her father so well, especially the day of the sixteenth celebration of her birth.

He had given her a sword—one that was light and easy to handle, emblazoned at the hilt with their family arms. Delighting in it, she had challenged him in the courtyard, lifting her voluminous skirts. He had been vastly pleased with her prowess, yet as they parried she laughed and quizzed him. What did it matter if she could fence!

"Ah, daughter!" he had told her. "None of us knows how the wind may blow. The day may come when I'll not be here, guarding over you like an old buzzard. And you'll be left to fight off a score of suiters by yourself!"

He had teased her, but his voice had carried an edge of sincerity. She had known she might be vastly wealthy; but it had meant nothing to her. There had been no reason for her father to die.

"Well, Meg, how goes this challenge I set before you?"

The voice was deep and pleasant, yet sardonic and amused. Ondine's eyes flew open with horror just in time to hear the soft click of the door as it closed behind Warwick Chatham.

Too stunned to form a verbal protest, Ondine drew her knees to her chest and hugged her arms around them. She could not speak, for her throat was choked with outrage. Perhaps he thought himself her husband, but he was no more than a disconcerting stranger, intruding far too intimately. Her back was to him, and she stiffened. She lowered her head, hoping that the soaked cloak of her hair would give her some covering, some defense against her nakedness.

"Ah, my lord Chatham!" Meg said happily, clapping her hands together in a pleased gesture that purely denoted her acceptance of his presence. After all, Ondine realized bitterly, from Meg's point of view the great lord Chatham was Ondine's husband. He had done her a great honor by making her, a pathetic waif, his wife.

Ondine squeezed her eyes shut tightly. It was the truth. This man had saved her from death.

Yet it was truth, too, that he was a stranger, alarmingly virile, totally masculine. If she had met him but a year ago, she might have been intrigued. She would have had every advantage, and he would have owed her the chivalrous, romantic code of Charles's court. She might have wondered about him, shivered deliciously and speculated from the safety of her own world.

She had not met him a year ago. She was vulnerable, at his mercy. And just as he compelled, he filled her soul with fear. And somehow he managed to play upon every ounce of her pride. She longed to pitch into battle with him and then run, as far away as she could possibly go.

Something fell upon the floor. She heard his footsteps, light for a man so tall and sinewed.

She heard his voice, and it caused her to tremble to the depths of her soul, to feel a force like fire rippling along her spine.

"Let me see what we've got . . ."

His thumb and knuckle curved around her chin, firmly demanding that she raise her chin. She had no option but to do so. Her flesh was alive with the fire that touched her, and her temper fed upon her humiliation.

"Shall I suffice?" she snapped crisply.

A tawny brow arched against his forehead, a crooked grin tugged at his lip, but his eyes were gold blades as he raked over her features. She had both amused him and irritated him. Her flash of temper might be entertaining, but it was hardly proper when Meg stood by as audience.

Warwick did not reply. He tilted her chin to the left and studied her face as he might the wheels of a carriage. Silently, loathfully, she returned his stare, her teeth clenched tightly together.

He tilted her chin in the other direction. Perhaps she should have been gratified that he gave no notice to her locked and contorted body. But she could not be so pleased, for his cold scrutiny left her feeling ever more stripped and naked—to the soul.

With all her heart she longed to reach out and slap him, to rake her nails across his high bronze cheekbones. She sat deathly still, allowing her eyes to denounce his calculated appraisal. She hated the touch of him, with his long callused fingers, the size of him, so near, and the heat that touched her against her will, like a violation.

He released her chin and stepped back, addressing Meg. "I think I've thought of everything, but it's seldom that I purchase women's wear. What is lacking must remain so, I fear."

"Anything will be better than those rags, my lord!" Meg assured him. She hesitated a moment. "Will you dine in the public room? Or shall your meal be brought here?"

"The public room, I think," Warwick said after a moment's thought. He turned back to Ondine, and she couldn't begin to read the emotion in his features.

He bowed to her with formal mockery. "At your leisure, my lady."

Then he strode from the room without a backward glance.

"Oh! I hate him!" Ondine gasped out, unaware of her words, only knowing that she had been appraised like a calf at market and found to be not intriguing, but rather . . . suitable.

"What?" The startled gasp escaped Meg, and Ondine realized what she had said. Oh, God, she didn't hate him. How could she hate a man who had saved her from certain death? She just felt so . . .

She stared at Meg, then shuddered miserably and drew her hands to her face. "I am sorry; I didn't mean it . . ." she blurted out.

Meg was instantly at Ondine's side, bringing a huge white towel to wrap around the girl as she helped her from the bath, clucking softly, all her maternal instincts rising like a blanket of comfort.

"There, there, dear! 'Tis quite natural for a lass to suddenly hate and fear her man when . . . when the first night draws near! But you've nothing to fear, love. It's true, the earl can be a distant man, hard as castle stone, at times." Meg grinned at her. "But he's a fine man, dear, the best of his kind, I think."

Ondine closed her eyes; her knees felt weak. She was glad of Meg's plump arms about her, leading her to sit at the foot of the bed.

"You . . . know him well?" Ondine asked curiously.

"As well as I might. He travels this way frequently." She chuckled. "He's one of the king's favorites, you know. His Grace is always sending for him to deal with one crisis or the next. And one would have thought that one of the heiresses at court would have wed him eventually—he's been known to have his dalliances there—" Meg stopped speaking abruptly, as if she had said much more than she should have. "All men dally," she muttered, then *tsked* and crossed herself. "And as I do honor and revere our good king, Charles, I still must say that women dally overmuch, also! But, ah, dear! Surely Warwick, Earl of Chatham, honors and cherishes you greatly! Else why marry you, honor you so, when he might have claimed the richest, most noble ladies of the land?"

Cherish! Ondine thought, a chill enveloping her and causing her fingers to shake, her limbs to tremble. Had Meg seen nothing? Or was she blinded by the man? He had no real interest in her at all.

She tried to give Meg a reassuring smile and stood, hugging the towel about herself. "Meg, you've never heard any . . . strange gossip about my lord, have you?"

"Strange?"

Ondine blushed to her toes. "I mean, that, perhaps, he has strange tendencies?"

Meg stared at her for a long moment of perplexity, her iron-gray brows fixed in a deep furrow. Then she started to laugh quite pleasantly. "Nay, love, there's nothing 'strange' about him. He's a bit of a reputation as a rogue—nothing more. His sword arm is famous, he's seen many battles, and he is known to speak his mind. And with our fair sex, I suppose, such a man becomes quite a rage with women." She seemed to wander in her own thoughts for a moment, then shrugged. "And he is elusive. Perhaps that is the greater fascination. But for anything that you might hear, trust me in this. I see the gentry come and go; lords and ladies, kings and queens, must travel. I have seldom seen a man more fair or just, ready to battle his peers for negligence to a servant or cruelty to a beast. He keeps his own council. All who serve him do so willingly, aye, ever cheerfully, for though he can be a hard taskmaster, he rewards labor well.'' She stood abruptly and briskly. ''Let's see what he's purchased for you, shall we?''

She began tearing into a wrapped parcel by the door, the thing that had made the thud Ondine had heard when Lord Chatham entered.

''Oh! How lovely!'' Meg cried out delightedly.

Ondine tried to smile as Meg drew out a silken shift, then an underskirt of flowing blue linen. Meg continued to gasp delightedly as she next discovered a bodice and overshirt in rich teal velvet, then a stiff petticoat in ruffled lace.

''There's even a pair of the loveliest shoes,'' Meg muttered. ''Who would have thought his mind would bend to find such fashionable garb?''

''He probably makes purchases for his paramours,'' Ondine said acidly; then she wondered instantly why she should be so bitter, why she should care. Had she not had the various warnings? She would have known that he was not a man of celibacy. There was something about him, beyond the power of his physique, even beyond the draw of his rawly masculine features; even beyond the compelling fascination of his eyes. It was something in his movement, in his occasional humor, in the sensual way his lip could curl while his eyes blazed their golden challenge.

''Come, dear,'' Meg said a little worriedly. ''I'd not keep him waiting overly long when he wishes to dine.''

Let him wait! Ondine longed to cry out. She lowered her eyes quickly, at a loss with herself. She was famished. There was no reason to keep him waiting—not when he meant to offer her a meal!

She hurried over to Meg, dropped her towel, and mumbled out her thank-yous as Meg helped her into the clothing. He had not only done well with style, he had done remarkably well with fit. And no matter how she resented him, she couldn't help but feel glorious in the new clothes. Gloriously alive. She was clean—and alive—by way of his curious bounty.

"Oh, love! You're beautiful—really beautiful!" Meg gasped out happily. Her bright blue eyes were alight with pleasure. "So very lovely. I see now what it was that so beguiled Lord Chatham to snatch you to his heart! All we need is a brush now. We won't pin your hair. You're a bride tonight; we'll just brush it to a gloss. Oh, I did do marvelous work, if I must say so myself!"

Ondine couldn't help but smile at Meg's sheer delight, yet as she sat for Meg as the woman lovingly worked the tangles from her hair, she gnawed her lower lip. She would be no bride tonight. One day she would find a way to repay Lord Warwick Chatham for his generosity—a generosity that had meant her life. Though he touched her temper and pride like a raw, taunting blade, she knew she owed him everything, and she meant to be entirely grateful. Yes, one day . . .

But not tonight. Tonight she would escape him and run into the forest, a place where she had found refuge before. There was no reason she should have any difficulty. Who would think that a humble waif would wish to escape the company of a nobleman, one not only wealthy, but extremely fine in stature and appearance?

Tonight, yes, she could easily be gone, ready to survey her situation once again, ready to battle the treachery that had brought her so low.

But not until after dinner. Were the public room below peopled with all the demons of hell, she would have hurried to it anyway, such was the depth of her hunger.

"Ahhh . . . copper, my dear!" Meg wasn't calling her "my lady" at all anymore; they had somehow become very close, and the words would have been ridiculous between them. To Meg, she was another daughter; a girl to be cherished and reassured.

The feeling was nice. If only she had been simply a starving waif that Jake had found wandering the streets of London. She could have stayed with Meg, worked so very hard that the woman could never have doubted her worth.

But she hadn't been a waif; she had been a criminal at Tyburn Tree. Her only recourse now was escape.

"I wish I had a glass that you might see yourself, but, alas, I haven't one! But surely you will see your own beauty in your husband's eyes, when they fall upon you. Come—you're ready to meet your husband."

But she wasn't ready. Her fingers were shaking and she clasped them together, wondering desperately why she was so afraid of him. She didn't want to meet his eyes again and feel that strange heat that raked the length of her spine when he touched her.

"And there's a fine rare roast today!" Meg said cheerfully. "Summer potatoes, and carrots, swimming in gravy—" Ondine could almost smell the dinner from Meg's words alone.

"Yes, I'm—I'm ready," she murmured.

Meg opened the door and hurried her down a long hallway. They passed a common men's room, where there were at least twenty pallets, and there were private rooms for those who could afford them.

And then there was another stairway. From the top of it Ondine could hear voices, mainly male. Men were laughing, drinking ale, relaxing from a hard day's labor, unwinding from a long and jolting carriage ride. And every once in a while there was softer laughter, a woman's voice.

"You must go down, my dear, if you're to eat!" Meg prodded her.

As if awakened from sleep, Ondine nodded. She started down the stairs, then paused again.

She could see Warwick pacing impatiently. He paused with his back to her, then slowly turned as if a sixth sense had warned him of her presence.

She held still, her heart pounding. He was truly an indomitable figure standing there, so tall. He wore a plumed hat that added to his height and to his air of a buccaneer, as the brim fell low over one brow. She noted again that his appearance of leanness was deceptive. His shoulders were very broad, his back strong before tapering, his legs heavily muscled beneath the taut material of his breeches, so fashionably buckled beneath his knees. He'd shed his coat, and his shirt was very white against the deep bronze of his features. His eyes, in contrast to that white, seemed to blaze with startling color.

He stared at her for the first time. Like a deep and blazing touch of the sun, his eyes raked over her, slowly, openly, offering no apology.

A rakish grin tugged upon one corner of his lip; a gleam of laughter touched his eyes. They were gold and seared into her, and it seemed again that her blood heated and sped thoughtout her, causing her limbs to grow weak.

He lifted a hand to her, the gesture a command. She started to walk down to him. His fingers caught and curled around hers, and still she couldn't draw her eyes from his.

Again he chuckled, a deep, husky sound, and his eyes moved from her face to regard her breasts where the mounds rose smooth above her bodice. He lowered his gaze to her hips, to her toes . . .

"You'll do quite well," he whispered, a breath that touched her throat and the lobe of her ear and made her shiver all over again.

She swallowed, bracing herself mentally against him. "I shall do quite well for what, my lord?" she inquired coolly.

He laughed.

"For my wife, of course. What else?"

Chapter 3

Their table was by the rear wall. He sat across from her, and that fact alone caused her heart to pound more quickly. There would be no escape from this table. Should she rise, he could quickly stand and block her way.

There was food, and she was famished. She would not run now. She grabbed at the bread, and as his hand came down on hers, she raised her eyes, startled, to his.

"No one is going to take it away," he promised her in a voice that was gentle. "You mustn't eat too quickly, or you'll become ill."

His hand lifted from hers and he poured out two goblets of ale. He broke the bread himself, handing her a piece. She was still staring at him. He grinned and leaned against the wall, resting one foot idly upon the bench, his hand dangling nonchalantly over a knee. "I didn't mean that you couldn't eat," he told her, a little amused.

Ondine kept her eyes warily on him while she bit into the bread. He seemed well aware of her nervous perusal of him and quite entertained by it. His smile was almost genuine as white teeth flashed against his candle-shadowed features. He suddenly had the look of a very rakish demon, a man casually aware of his effect upon women—upon her in particular—and totally amused by it.

"Where is Jake?" Ondine inquired between bites of bread.

"He is my servant, not my property. His free time is his own."

Ondine tried to sip her ale with an element of delicacy, but she was too thirsty, and she drained half the goblet.

Somewhat surprised, he filled it for her again.

She sighed with the sudden flooding warmth of the ale. She determined to disconcert him as he did her.

"You do not consider your servants property, sir?"

"No man can be owned. To think so is folly."

"And what of a wife?"

"Ah, well, that's rather different, isn't it?"

"Is it?"

"I dare say," he replied slowly, drawing a finger about the rim of his chalice. His head was bowed now, not quite close to hers. The candle flame seemed to grow larger, and the room became quite hot.

"Yes, I dare say. A wife, you see, swears a vow of loyalty."

"Servants can be loyal."

"Aye, but a servant who fulfills his duty owes no more."

"And a wife?"

"Ah, but a wife should not tire of her . . . duty, should she?"

"Depending on what those duties be," Ondine replied coolly.

"None so difficult, I should think. For what one may call duty, one who has spirit would call pleasure, wouldn't you say?"

Where did this lead? she wondered, a dizziness sweeping through her. She had drained her ale far too quickly. She *was* his wife; they spoke as if he mused on someone else. Her fingers trembled as she made a display of nonchalance, pecking at the bread again. It had lost its delicious flavor; it seemed thick in her throat.

"What is owed to one is owed to the other, is it not?" she said serenely. What did it matter what words they exchanged? She would not stay with him long enough to discover the meaning of his taunting wordplay.

He seemed to tire of his game, sighed, and sat back, reflective as he drank his ale. "I think I should tell you something of the manor. We've another night on the road, yet if we travel hard, we will come to North Lambria by the second eve.'' He broke off. The tavern lad was back with a platter filled high with beef and new spring potatoes. Warwick dismissed him, preferring to mound a pewter plate for Ondine himself, going lightly with the food. He laughed at her expression and reminded her, ''I've no wish to be mean with food, girl. Yet it seems it's been long since you've known regular substance, and I've no mind for a sickly hindrance.''

Sickly hindrance!

He didn't seem at all inclined to eat himself, and again he leaned against the wall, casually resting that elbow on his knee as he spoke. ''Mathilda keeps the house, so you will have no difficulty with its management. If you've questions, come to me. The servants you will meet, and Jake you already know. Clinton is in charge of the grounds, the tenants, and the stables. And there is my brother, Justin. He resides at the manor, so you will see him frequently.''

The roast beef was delicious. It was ecstasy to Ondine's palate, so much so that she gave his words little attention. After all, they did, in truth, mean nothing to her.

She was, in fact, so involved with her food that she did not realize that he was aware of her total lack of interest until he swept the plate suddenly from her, bringing her eyes to his once again.

She gazed into his eyes. All amusement had fallen from them, as had any sensual taunt. She stiffened, sensing the sudden flare of a cold and ruthless anger within him. Her mouth went dry. She thought again that there was no escape, that he could catch her before she could rise from the table.

''Listen!'' he snapped at her. ''You've a role to take on, my gallows' bride, and I'd appreciate a modicum of effort on your part. Rather, dear wife, I demand it.''

A pulse ticked at his throat above the fine white linen of his shirt. Ondine blinked and nodded, wondering at the many faces of the man. The charming, seductive rake, the steel-edged autocrat, and the sensitive gentleman who had set his arms about her to buffer her view of the hanging. Which, then, of these faces, was the man?

Irritably he repeated himself. ''Justin is my brother. Clinton manages the estate. Mathilda is the housekeeper. She is quite proficient, and if you listen and follow her lead, you'll have no difficulty acting out the titled dame. They have long been with

Chatham; it is their home as it is mine. I rule my land, as it is mine, but we live pleasantly there. None is cruelly treated. Do you understand?''

She was quite tempted to pull her plate back and see how he appeared with gravy framing his insolent eyes. Who did he think she was? Surely she had managed a household of far grander scale than his ''manor'' in the barely civilized north.

She opened her eyes with wide and malicious innocence. ''Dear Lord Chatham! I shall certainly do my best to refrain from flying into a 'common' fit and thrashing your servants. Is that what you wish me to comprehend?''

He leaned back again, annoyed. ''Madam, you'll learn to watch your tongue.''

Long seconds passed as their glares locked, and Ondine's eyes were the first to fall. She folded her hands in her lap, discovering that in one thing he was right. She hadn't eaten much, but it seemed all that she could manage. It was imperative now that she be humble and gracious, lest she arouse his suspicions.

''I beg your pardon,'' she told him demurely.

''Why don't I believe that?'' he muttered so softly that she might have imagined the words.

She looked at him, careful to keep the discussion focused upon her future life with him. ''When Jake first came to me upon the cart, he said that some might say that I had wed a 'beast.' Are you a beast, milord Chatham?''

He made a ticking sound of annoyance and downed more ale. ''The beast sits upon my armor, lady, nothing more.''

''Pray tell, what is this beast?''

He gazed at her dryly. ''A dragon creature. Half lion, half myth. They say that once such 'beasts' roamed our forests, protecting Saxons from Normans—and Royalists from Cromwell's wrath. I've yet to see one, myself, except in art and whimsy.''

Ondine smiled at little wistfully then, noting the charm of his grin. She was clean, her stomach was comfortably fed, and the promise of a new freedom loomed before her. She could afford to exchange a few words with the man, moments in which to lull him further to trust.

''When you wear the armor, sir, are you then the beast?''

He cocked his head slightly, arching a brow. "What we are is in how we are beheld, is it not?"

"So it would seem. Are there those who might behold you, then, a beast?"

"How can I judge for others?"

She picked up her goblet, twirling it idly in her hand, and scrutinized him quite openly, narrowing her eyes as if she gave the matter great thought.

"Aye, my lord Chatham, I can see where you might upon occasion appear the beast."

"Do you? But then beasts can be quite tame, can't they? And, my lady, my given name is Warwick. You must use it, at least upon occasion."

He reached across the table suddenly, catching a lock of her hair between his fingers. Her flesh seemed to burn as his fingers brushed over her breast, and her breath caught in her throat with both indignation and a startling sensation. He didn't notice. His interest in her was very keen; yet again, she felt much like a purchase, to be appraised for the value of appearance' sake.

"You really are very beautiful," he mused, as if such a thought should give him great surprise. "For a commoner."

She could not help herself. She wrenched her hair from his grasp and moved as far to the wall as she could.

"Are commoners usually ugly, then, Lord Chatham?"

He sighed, as if weary of her troublesome behavior. "Nay, and I meant no offense. You've merely features very fine—far more so than many of the great and 'noble' beauties of the land." She might have been a diversion, one with whom he had allowed himself to tarry, yet now found tedious.

"Have you quite finished?"

"What—"

"We've made our appearance. Word will spread quickly that you appeared at this table as my bride, a lady of bearing surely fit for mistress of the manor. Your past shall rest between Jake, yourself, and me. We need no longer stay here, and I, for one, am weary. I would think that you, too, would long for the comfort and cleanliness of a bed such as Meg offers here."

A bed! With him in it beside her . . .

The dizziness swamped her in a burst of alarm and searing heat that brought a weak quiver to her limbs. Was he the beast, the rake, or the gentleman? She didn't want to know. It was time to be the charming damsel now, herself; time to make good her elusive goal of freedom—and vengeance.

"Is appearance so important, then?" she murmured, stalling for time.

"Aye, especially so with us, milady."

"Then why did you marry me, a common poacher? Please, don't tell me you needed a wife! Surely you could have secured a dozen wives from better places, had you so chosen!"

"A dozen wives? A man may have but one, milady." He hesitated. "I've grown tired of the pressure to marry, that is all. And I did not care to have a clinging countess about my neck, quizzing my movements. A gallows' bride, madam, best suits my tastes. You are alive. I may be at peace and live my life as I choose. Does that satisfy you?" he inquired coolly.

"It must, if it's what you wish to tell me."

She lowered her eyes, fluttering her lashes carefully. A flash of guilt caused her heart to skip a beat. He *had* saved her life, had given her the pure ecstasy of cleanliness, and had caused her stomach to cease its habitual growl. Perhaps she could get an annulment for the marriage. She fervently hoped so, since there would be nothing she could do for quite some time. And she didn't forget for a moment that she meant to pay him back.

"My lady, may we leave?"

She raised her eyes, allowing her lip to tremble. "Dear Lord Chatham, I implore you, may I have a minute for myself?"

"What?" He crossed his arms over his chest, scowling with a sudden impatience.

A flush that could not have been enacted rose to her cheeks, and she stuttered out her request again. "I'd have a moment. I— I wish to take care with my—"

"You needn't—" he interrupted her abruptly, but she would not allow him to go on. She reached across the table, resting her fingers lightly on the top of his hand, staring at him with all the tender innocence she could muster.

"I implore you!"

He shook off her touch—almost with distaste—and lifted his

hands into the air. "Do whatever pleases you. It makes no difference to me."

Smiling graciously, she lowered her head and stood, willing her knees not to wobble. Hurriedly she swept from the bench, but she did not breathe until she had passed by him.

And then she gulped for air, blindly making her way through the tables for the stairway. There were still voices and laughter in that room; they all blended together as she raced up the stairway, aware only that Warwick's eyes followed her intently all the way.

And, sitting still at that table, he frowned slightly as he watched her retreating back. She quite astounded him, for she was far more than he had imagined possible; slim, erect, shapely, dainty. As hollow as her cheeks were, their texture was as soft and pure as silk. She was truly a stunning beauty. None would doubt his attraction to such a woman; nor would anyone think to question her background.

Still scowling, he poured himself some ale. The only flaw seemed to be her temper. He had expected a great deal more humility and appreciation. She should have listened eagerly to his every word and not only been willing, but grateful to accept the life he was offering her.

Warwick leaned back and drank a long swallow of his ale. Then he grinned slightly. Her apprehension had been so evident, he'd been unable to resist the desire to taunt her.

To be fair, he should have told her bluntly that he had no intention of touching her—ever.

His smile faded. She assumed he would require the "duties" of a wife. He should have informed her that he would never desire such duties just because she was his wife and that, in time, he would see that she was freed from all obligation, yet supplied with an income to live out her natural days as she chose.

His fingers curled around his goblet, and he slammed it against the table with such vehemence that it almost cracked. He couldn't tell her that, not yet. He pushed the goblet away, frowning with weariness. He might as well go up and let her know she need have no fear of him, "beast" that she claimed him to be.

And yet . . .

Strange how the memory of her eyes, deep and hauntingly blue, remained with him. And her scent . . . now one of the richest, sweetest rose. And the velvet touch of her hair between his fingers—fire hair, dark in shadow, yet gleaming with strands that caught the color of the sun.

He smiled slightly. He even liked the pride she wore as a shield about her, though it could irk him sorely. The cast of her chin, the haughty retort in her eyes.

Yes, she might well have been born to rule a manor. And—by God!—he would see that she survived to have her freedom.

Warwick frowned suddenly, his muscles tensing as an inexplicable sensation of danger seized him. He thought of his new bride: the utter disdain in her delicate features when he had surveyed them, cleansed, for the first time; her quick temper; her immeasurable pride. She was not ungrateful for her life, yet it seemed that she had no intention of compromising her newfound freedom.

She hadn't appeared really frightened of him, but she had been wary—and suspicious. She was prone to staring him straight in the eye, instead of batting her lashes with the charming ease of the born coquette.

"Damn!" he swore suddenly, furious with himself as his jaw locked grimly. She'd played him for an idiot and done so very well.

"Beauty" was attempting to escape the "beast."

Still swearing softly beneath his breath, Lord Chatham traversed the stairway, two steps at a time.

Ondine had managed to walk sedately up the front stairs from the public room. Once upon the darkened landing, she ran. Her heart was thudding as she passed the common rooms and the more expensive private rooms . . . the door to the room where she had so recently bathed and exchanged her rags for riches.

At the back stairway she paused for a moment, clutching her hand to her heart as she gasped for a deep breath. The kitchen, she knew, led off the door where she had entered earlier. It was time to remember all that she had learned about evasion; not to bolt, but to wait and listen, carefully . . .

There was no one near the door. She forced herself to ascertain that fact as a surety, then glided silently down the back stairs. The tavern was busy now, for the tables were filled when she fled the public room. All the lads and maids and Meg herself should be busily occupied. And which of them would think that the common bride of a great lord would think to elude him?

The wood of the back door seemed to have swelled with the coolness of the night. Ondine gnawed at her lower lip, fighting a wave of panic as the door refused to give. She tugged upon it with greater effort and almost gasped when it sprang quite suddenly from the force of frantic desperation.

Collecting herself, she sped outside, bringing the door shut behind her, and leaned against it for one moment to collect her breath. She stared out across the dirt and pens of the yard, across the rolling fertile fields to the forest beyond. Her heart seemed to sink within her, for the distance to that forest was great, far greater than she had realized before. On foot, wearing the delicate pumps her strange "husband" had purchased for her, she would take forever reaching the ebony haven of nature's succoring retreat.

Think! Quickly! she warned herself. By God, she hadn't escaped the king's guards and dozens of petty sheriffs to find herself frantic against a single man. It had taken a posse of fifty trained horsemen to capture her party of poor men and thieves in the forest outside London. And if Little Pat hadn't fallen then, she would have eluded even them.

There was no way out of it, she decided quickly, drawing upon learned instinct. She was going to have to steal one of Lord Chatham's carriage horses. Nor could she allow herself to feel guilty for the theft; she hadn't the time. She could only vow to herself once again that she would find revenge against those who had so tricked and used her—and her poor woefully betrayed father! And she would pay the Earl of North Lambria back for his gift of life and substance at a later date.

So determined, Ondine raced across the dirt to the stable, praying that no one would be about. The massive doors were still open to the night, and a single lantern burned near them, high on the wall. Despite the flame, she blinked as she swept around the open doorway, pausing once again with her back to the wood structure as she attempted to see clearly. The stable was as neat as the inn: fresh hay was strewn richly over the ground; harnesses, bits, bridles, and saddles were polished and hung on pegs by the entrance.

Horses pawed the ground from two opposing rows of stalls, separated by low, thin barriers of wood.

The right horse . . .

She had been condemned to die one time too many and was determined now to steal only one of her "husband's" horses, lest she be caught with the beast. She didn't intend to be caught, but having borne the label of "traitor," felt the promised horror of the headsman's ax, and, in truth, the scratch of the rope, she was hesitant despite herself. Another man could claim her a thief, but not the man who had so curiously chosen to marry her.

She reflected briefly that she would almost rather face the law again than the man with the chill gold gaze once she had crossed him. That thought caused her to shiver, but shivering set her into action at last. She gazed to the doorway once again, assured herself that no tavern lad was about, then silently skimmed across the hay, looking for one of the chestnut mounts that had pulled their carriage. She paused at last behind a high rump, certain she had found the right horse. It was a tall creature, like its master. And like its master, it had broad, powerful shoulders, and a sleek and fluid body, well muscled and long in the legs.

"Shhh, my fine lad!" she murmured to the hrose, closing in on its hind quarters lest it should choose to kick. She moved along its flanks to its neck while stroking its glossy coat. The animal snorted; its great dark eyes rolled to survey her. Ondine rubbed its velvet-soft nose. "You're really a love, aren't you?" she murmured, finding no resistance to her touch. "We're going to take a ride, you and I. Do you mind?"

The horse was tethered by a halter to the wall before it, and Ondine slipped the rope quickly and led the horse to the center of the stable. Swearing softly against the volume of her skirts, she slipped the guide rope over the animal's head to secure it on the other side as a rein, then collected her skirts in one hand before leaping upon its back. The animal made no protest and stood still while she awkwardly mounted.

She nudged her heels against his ribs. "Now, my lad," she whispered, "we've a need to leave here quietly and then race like the wind."

The horse pranced obediently toward the door. But just as he did so, a shadow streaked into the opening. Cast against the glow of the single lantern, Ondine could see nothing but the figure of the man, looming tall and stalwart, legs apart, hands on his hips.

"And to where, madam, might you be 'racing like wind'?"

It was a question most cordially voiced, but there was an edge of steel behind it, low and throaty and menacing in the very control with which it was spoken. He stepped forward, and the candlelight fell on his face, the jaw slightly twisted and clamped hard, the lean features taut. His eyes seemed to catch the energy and fire of the candle's glow; they were alive in themselves with a blaze of taunting gold. He smiled as he stepped forward, surveying her, his movements curiously negligent, as if he had truly come to offer no more than his casual interest. His head tilted toward her, the tawny arch of a single brow raised pleasantly, a mockery of concern. Yet beneath the fine white cloth of his shirt she saw a ripple in the sinewed breadth of his shoulders . . . and in his arms, as if they twitched with the desire to lash out. And beneath his tight breeches she saw the powerful knots of muscle in his thighs, so restrained was his stance.

When it would have served her best, Ondine did not take the time to think. Seeing him caused her heart to catch, then race in a flurry of raw panic. She gasped, throwing her heels hard against the horse, praying madly that she could race away. But even as a cry escaped her and she thought to rule the horse, Warwick's arm streaked out and caught the halter rope. The animal reared high, snorting. Ondine fought to stay mounted, but to no avail. She slid from the horse's back to the hay and cried out again, closing her eyes and praying that the massive hooves would not fall upon her.

They did not. She opened her eyes. The horse was standing at his master's side, shivering but still to Warwick's soothing whisper. Ondine scrambled to her feet, trembling like the horse, yet taut and ready to run.

He still blocked the doorway—the beautiful entrance to the cool breeze of the night and freedom.

He stared at her for long moments without moving, long moments in which dread rose in her to a point where she thought she would scream and collapse with it. And then he spoke, quietly, pleasantly.

"Perhaps you would be so good as to return Wick to his stall."
He patted the animal's gleaming neck, eyeing him with affection.
"Good carriage horses are hard to come by, my lady. I'd just as
soon not lose him to the night."

Abruptly his gaze returned to her. Ondine did not think she was
capable of moving forward to reach the horse's halter. Yet caught
by the blaze in Warwick's eyes, she did so, stepping with stiff
and jerking motions, touching the halter with care to avoid any
contact with him. Shaking, trembling, her feet leaden, she walked
the horse back to his stall, fumbling with the lead rope as she
tethered him there. Her breath caught as she realized that Warwick
had followed her and that she had not heard his movement. He
stood behind the horse. Gazing beyond the animal's tail, she could
see only his legs, spread slightly with his feet planted firm upon
the earth.

Her mind seemed to spin and then go numb. Then suddenly it
took flight again. He was to the left of her now, no longer between
her and the doorway. She pretended to take her time with the rope,
and then she bolted, pitching all her speed and strength and youth
into her sudden run. The door, the sweet scent of night, was before
her.

She might have been afloat in the clouds, so desperately did
she hurl herself along. And then it seemed that she was flying, for
there was a moment when there was nothing beneath her, nothing
but the air.

Yet that moment was horribly fleeting, and when it had past,
she was back in the hay, gasping for breath, her mind reeling with
the thud of her head against the hard earth of the stable. She closed
her eyes, fighting the pain and the swamping sensation of dizziness.

Then she felt weight about her, a tight and heated vise. Gasping
out a scream, she opened her eyes, only to find a less than gentle
hand clamped over her mouth and her husband's burning eyes
searing into her own, his thighs straddling her hips.

"What would you, madam, make a beast of me in truth?" he
demanded in a harsh and furious whisper. He moved his hand
from her face quickly, distastefully, assured that she would not
dare to push him further.

In that, he was right. Dazed, she returned his stare, too keenly
aware of the hard cold floor beneath her, the terrible heat of his

thighs around her, and the subtle scent of him, clean like the night, but carrying a hint of raw masculinity that was so threatening, her limbs seemed to grow warm and uselessly weak. What would he do to her now? she wondered despairingly.

He leaned low against her, surveying her again with fury. "Ingrate!" he spat out suddenly, and she gasped again as his fist clenched and muscles bunched beneath his shirt with the thunderous movement of his arm. Instinctively she closed her eyes against the coming blow, but there was none. His hand slammed into the earth at the side of her head, and a second later he was on his feet, staring down at her.

"Get up," he told her coldly, and when she found that she could not move, he impatiently reached down to her, dragging her to her feet, swearing beneath his breath. "So I saved a horse thief as well as a poacher and God alone knows what else! Pray, tell me, my lady," he mocked tightly, a pulse ticking with a fervor in his throat, his fingers like steel as they held her, "what is it I did to you that you are ever so determined to leave me for the life of a starving, filthy renegade once again?"

Ondine could not look into his eyes; she stared at his hand, and its brutal hold about her own, wondering if her bones would snap beneath it. Didn't he know, didn't he care? Or did he intend far worse?

He released her so suddenly that her instinctive pull against him sent her back to the front wall of the barn, where she stood still, her hands braced against it. "By God, what will I do with you?" he muttered, and at last she was ready to strike back.

"It matters little to me, my lord!" she cried with sudden passion. "There is naught that you can do"—she choked on her own words—"little that can compare to Newgate, to running, to starving, to vicious murder by tra—"

She cut herself off suddenly; desperately she fought back tears. At this moment, she needed her pride. It was her only remaining source of strength. She lifted her head and met his curiously narrowed eyes with despair, bringing her voice to a casual disregard.

"Beat me, lash me, hang me—I care not."

He took a step toward her and for a moment she regretted her hasty words, certain he intended to take her up on one—or all—of her suggestions.

His fingers twined around her elbow, but their touch now, though firm, had no painful bite. "If starvation is so appealing to you, my lady," he drawled sarcastically, "I must then apologize for keeping you from it. But you're not leaving, and I pray ask you not to contemplate such a thought again. I'm weary. Let's end this night."

There was no fighting his grip. Still feeling her heart beat so quickly that she feared it would tire and cease, Ondine came along with him. They crossed the yard and reached the rear door. He opened it, and his gaze and the inclination of his head suggested that she precede him. Ondine did so, but when the span of his fingers fell on her waist, propelling her toward the staircase, dread rushed up to flood her features once again, and she couldn't help but turn to him. "My lord . . ."

"Go, my lady."

She closed her eyes, fighting the sensation of faintness. She remembered that upon the gallows she would have willingly married any man, and that men naturally demanded intimacies of their wives. Old men, ugly men, fat men, stinking men . . .

Yet in her heart and mind she had counted, even then, upon escape. She had been saved by marriage. Her husband was neither old nor ugly nor fat, and his scent was a fascinating one, like the night wind . . .

But she had not escaped. And so she wondered with a quiver what it would be, how it would feel to have those hard thighs, naked and demanding, against her own. She bit her lip, promising herself that she would scream, and she began to wonder a little desperately how vehement his passion would be, if he would hurt her, if she could endure intimacy without longing to rake his eyes out, without fighting . . . Would he be cold and brutal, furious at rejection? Where would his lips touch her? Would she be split by his size, bruised by his strength?

"My lady, walk!"

Swallowing, shaking, feeling a tremor as if the earth moved, she walked up the stairs. She could not open their door when they reached it.

He did so. His prod sent her forward into the room, and he bolted the door firmly once he, too, was inside. Ondine floated nervously to the window. Her body seemed to be nothing but hot liquid as she waited, wondering again if she wouldn't shriek out with fear of his next movement.

He sat upon the foot of the bed and doffed his boots, giving her no heed. And when he was done, he rose, stripping the white shirt over his head and casting it upon the footboard of the bed. Ondine felt her heart flutter and seem to sink ever deeper as she watched him. His appearance of leanness, brought on by the casual wear of his fashionable clothing, was totally deceptive. Bands of muscle, defined and well knotted, rimmed his shoulders, back, and chest. His waist was flat and slim, also a band of muscle. His figure was that of a fighter, of a man who had learned to handle heavy weapons. She could not draw her gaze from his chest, slick and powerful in the moonlight, and when he turned to her, he must have seen her dismayed anticipation, for he suddenly, wickedly smiled and approached her. She would have backed away, but there was nowhere to go. He paused before her, and his fingers moved deftly to the ribbons at her bodice, brushing her flesh upon the valley between her breasts.

"You must be quite exhausted," he told her, his words husky and pleasant. Still smiling, he reached for her hem and brought the overskirt high over her head. Ondine could not help a little sound of protest, a gasp that brought her own hands to her breasts, warding him off. He ignored her, moving quickly to strip away the elegant underskirt and bodice, mindless of her wild attempts to resist him, her outraged whimpers when his fingers raked over the rounded curves of her breasts. His touch was barely upon her, yet she felt it so fiercely—his taut power and that essence that was so alarmingly male . . .

Left with only her flimsy shift, she clasped her arms over her chest, ready to plead with him. He'd married her; she had no recourse, and so she was shaking. Yet she prayed that she could at least move him from what seemed to be a cold and ruthless determination and anger.

Soon his hands, his searing touch, would be upon her naked flesh.

"Please . . . I . . ." She felt so naked, even in the garment. So vulnerable. His eyes were upon her with such contempt and scorn, seeming to mock what she might offer him.

He stepped backward, a wry and humorless smile on his lips as he bowed to her. "Madam, your chastity is yours—to savor, or rot with, as you choose. I ask only that you play the countess—a role for which you seem amazingly well suited—with a pretense of effort. Good night."

He turned from her abruptly, strode to the bed, and cast his length wearily upon it, far to the right side.

Stunned, Ondine stared at him. Incredulous words came to her lips unbidden.

"That is . . . all? You expect—nothing else of me?"

"Not a thing, madam. You are the last woman upon whom I would think to force my affections," he replied, his tone one of total disinterest.

She could not believe him, and she stared at him. It was then that he moved again.

"For God's sake, might we get some sleep!"

She took a step forward, and, dazed, she again spoke without thought.

"You wish me to—to sleep in the bed?"

"In the bed, on the floor. You may levitate for all I care. Just give me some peace."

He meant it, yet still barely able to believe the turn of events, she moved hesitantly to the bed and sat upon it. His back was to her. At length she stretched out, but so nervously so that she was ready to spring at his least movement.

He did not move. It seemed he barely breathed.

And so Ondine lay tensely, her eyes open to the night. She could not resist turning to the broad, muscled expanse of back offered to her.

The bed shifted; Ondine froze. Seconds passed, and at last she twisted her head. He was on his side of the bed, his back turned to her. She could not help but reflect that he was indeed a fascinating man, incredibly fine and sinewed and . . . striking, in manner and person.

She shivered and closed her eyes. He was her husband. He had saved her from death . . . he wanted nothing from her.

She would play his wife, play the countess to a perfection that would surely astound him. Aye, she would play the role—and seek out her own revenge from the safety and security of the noble wing of his protection. She smiled. Unwittingly, he might even help her . . .

Chapter 4

Warwick awoke with the sun slashing in through the panes he had forgotten to close the previous night. He cast his arm over his eyes for a moment, groaning. Then, with a start, he remembered the woman at his side.

He turned to her. Ondine's back was to him; and she was curled far from him. Warwick swung his legs off the bed, ran his fingers through his hair, then planted his feet on the floor and strode silently around the bed. She was sleeping soundly. The light didn't appear to bother her in the least.

He meant to move quickly from her; he found that he could not. He studied her in sleep instead. The morning sun caught her hair, so fragrant with its scent of roses. Disheveled and scattered over the white bedding, it gleamed deep and rich, dancing with fire, framing her flawless complexion like a silken fan of intrigue. Her lips were parted slightly as she breathed quietly and peacefully. He noted what a beautiful design they were, the lower lip fuller and hinting of deep and secret sensuality. Her cheeks were a pale rose, high and lovely; her brows high, arched, and enchanting. He shook his head slightly as he viewed her, somewhat bemused. He had noticed something about her when he had seen her in the hangman's cart, but not this exquisite beauty. Long of limbs, she

was still too slender, yet beautifully lithe and curved. Her breasts
rose firm and high against the flimsy material of her shift, as if
they strained against it, full and round and tempting. Their rouge
tips were a dimly veiled taunt. They seemed an invitation, beckoning a man's caress . . .

Warwick suddenly scowled. He had no intention of becoming
enamored of the prickly little thief!

He cast his head toward the open window, decided it was still
quite early, and padded to the door in his stocking feet. Outside,
he hurried to the landing at the rear stairwell and called down to
Meg, ordering that a bath and food be brought.

Lads came with the tub and water, and Meg cheerfully brought
food. Ondine slept through the entire proceedings. Warwick discovered himself pitying her and wondering what in life had brought
her to such despair that she should fight even him.

He turned away from her, shedding his hose and breeches, and
climbed into the tub, wincing at its heat. He could not allow
himself to care for her, admire her, want her.

He leaned back, closing his eyes, wondering if this impulsive
plan of his would draw out the murderer.

He opened his eyes, puzzled by a moaning sound that came
from the bed. It was Ondine, of course. No longer did she sleep
peacefully, her lashes leisurely resting against her cheeks. She
tossed about, tangling herself in the sheets and fighting them ever
further. Her moans began to take on meaning. Whispered tears,
vehement vows.

"Merciful heaven, *you* killed him! Oh, sweet Jesus! No! No!
Never could I forgive you! Treacherous monster! I'd far prefer
death."

Frowning with perplexity, Warwick stood, the water sluicing
from him. He snatched up his towel from the floor, wrapped it
about his waist, and hurried, still dripping, to her side. He sat upon
the bed and caught her shoulders, shaking her, hoping to wake
her gently.

Such was not to be the case. At his touch, she went wild. "No!
No! Murderer! Your hands are stained with blood, the blood of
my own! No! I'll kill you first—"

"Girl!" He shook her more irritably and was startled when her
fist flew out, catching him soundly in the jaw. He released her to

rub that sore part in astonishment, then swept both arms about her, crushing her against his chest. "Girl! Who in God's name do you fight? It is me, your—husband!"

Her head fell back, her eyes open fully at last, huge and luminously blue, like a storm-tossed sea.

"Oh!" she gasped.

He smiled and spoke softly. "You were dreaming."

"Oh! I'm sorry. I . . ." Her voice trailed away as she noted her circumstances. Still dripping bits of water, he was clad only in a towel, and she was now damp from the contact with his bare chest, in the shelter of his arms. Alarm sprang to her eyes before she could hide the emotion, and he couldn't help but chuckle.

"I am sorry if my presence distresses you. As it was, though, my lady, you were the one to bring me from my bath."

Her eyes darted from him to the tub, to his pants strewn beside it. Then her lashes fell again, and Warwick followed her gaze. They realized together that she might have been as bare as he, so transparent did the dampness make her shift. A swift and merciless shaft of heat tore through Warwick; again he felt the blinding need to touch the fullness of her breast, graze the pouting nipple with his thumb, explore the fascinating fullness of her youth and beauty . . .

He rose, abruptly turning from her. He cursed himself for having naught but a towel to cover his flagrant response to her sensual appeal. "Go back to sleep if you wish!" he snapped to her far more harshly than he would have intended. Not caring in the least whether he alarmed her or not in his present discomfort, he turned his back, dropped the towel, and quickly descended into the tub. She remained silent, which continued to irk him, and on top of everything else, he had somehow lost the soap.

"There's food on the tray," he tossed out over his shoulder, less than graciously.

"Thank you," she murmured.

"Not at all," he responded. " 'Tis not a favor, it seems, lady, but the only bribe I might have to keep you at my side."

He heard her rise from the bed and collect very quickly the clothing he had shed for her the night before. She did not approach the food tray, but moved to the window, leaned against the sill, and stared out at the day.

"You needn't worry about my disappearing again," she murmured.

"Oh—and why is that?"

"I have—uh—taken a thorough assessment of my position. And you're quite right. If all you wish is a young female—'suitable,' as you are so apt to say—to play your wife, then I am happy to play that role. What better have I?"

"Umm." His eyes turned to her. The water was growing cold and his teeth were chattering.

He watched her, curious at the straight grace of her back, her slender hands upon her lap as she reflected, her eyes on the window.

"Who did you think I was?" he quizzed her suddenly.

"What?" He so startled her that she turned to him, then flushed and stared down at her hands. "What . . . do you mean?"

"In your sleep, in your dream. You battled someone and battled him fiercely. Who was it?"

"I . . ." Her voice seemed incredibly soft. "What did I say?"

"Lady, I am questioning you."

She shrugged, as if the motion could force his inquiry to slip away. "The hangman, I suppose. Or the keeper at Newgate."

"You accused the hangman or jailor of treachery and murder?"

Her head lifted, and her eyes blazed into his. "And why not? Spend some time in Newgate, dear sir, you or your precious king, then perhaps you might be fit to judge my words!"

The water seemed to steam again as his temper rose in reaction to her words. "Taunt me, my lady, and you but tempt my wrath at your own peril. Lay taunt against the king again, and you will assuredly draw my vengeance. You, madam, do not know the king."

She slid from the sill to present her back to him—and hide the sudden rise of tears to her eyes. She did know the king. His sincere interest in others was a large part of his charm, as well as his pleasant wit and his gallant appreciation of women. But Ondine knew that Charles's years in exile, his bitter decade-long struggle for his crown, had also worn him. The king kept his own counsel; no one knew what truly lurked within his mind. He detested violence, though no man had been a braver fighter. He despised duels, and he abhorred executions.

But that did not mean that traitors had not gone to the headsmen.

He was loath to sign a death warrant, yet he was the king, and he had done so when required.

And to his eyes—as surely as to the eyes of all who had witnessed the event at the joust that day—she was a traitor.

"I hold nothing against the king," she murmured out loud, having learned that her husband's temper was something she did not care to test.

He said nothing else on the matter. An explosive silence seemed to reign between them, then at last he spoke, still tensely.

"Bring me the soap, if it will not too sorely tax you," he drawled sardonically. " 'Tis by your foot, and it was your scream that caused me to lose it."

Ondine stared down at the soap a little blankly, suddenly loath to go too near, especially in his present temper and lack of dress.

"I'm well folded, lady. I can hardly offend your preciously delicate sensibilities."

After enduring that last mockery, she determined never to let him see her distressed. She plucked the soap from the floor and walked to the tub, smiling quite sweetly as she dropped it down to him.

"You're mistaken, sir. Nothing offends my sensitivity; I come from Newgate, lest you forget."

He caught the bar of soap and returned her regal stare, tempted to rise and embrace her and force her bluff to a test. He reminded himself furiously that he wanted his distance from her; it was merely difficult with her standing there, so damned assured with the promise of abstinence he had spoken to her last night! Women . . . nothing would give him greater pleasure at the moment than to leap from the tub, give her a full view of her effect upon him, and sweep her to the welcome softness of the bed.

He contented himself with snatching her wrist and allowing a warning to gleam from his eyes.

"Ondine, did no one ever warn you not to play with beasts?"

She did not tug at her wrist; her eyes remained locked with his. At last her lashes swept down, but they rose again, and a flush touched her cheeks as that chance gaze enveloped more of his muscled form than she had expected.

"I—am hungry," she murmured uneasily.

He released her. "Go eat."

She hurried to the tray across the room. He closed his eyes, wondering at the sudden misery he had cast upon himself. He hadn't felt like this . . . ever. He was fascinated, almost compelled, and so at war within his mind and heart. With a sudden fury he began to scrub a foot, and then an arm.

"Ex-excuse me, my lord Chatham," she murmured suddenly.

"What?"

"Is this . . . is this how we are to live at your home?" Her words were faint and a little shaky.

A long sigh of relief escaped him. "No. You've your own chamber, beyond mine." For several seconds he was silent. "One which you will keep bolted at all times. Do you understand?"

The last was husky, yet underlined with absolute command. A command so tense that it was repeated when she didn't instantly reply.

"Do you understand?"

"Aye!"

"There will not be many rules by which you must abide, yet those I do give you must be followed explicitly. And I'll not listen to any more of your knife thrusts regarding Newgate. I did not put you there, though you proved your own folly last night by attempting to steal my horse."

"You don't understand—"

"Nor do I care to. From this day forward, you have no such past. Your father was a poet, you say. We'll change that subtly. He was an impoverished French nobleman—dear God," he interrupted himself, sighing, then muttered, "nay, they'll expect you to speak French."

She hesitated briefly. "I do speak French."

He did not face her; she sensed the probing cock of his brow.

"My—mother was French. And she was an impoverished noble." She winced a little. Lying was coming to her with such astounding ease! She could only pray she didn't forget her own inventions.

"That better explains your speech," he murmured, then suddenly he spun about, apparently irritated again by something. She looked at the breakfast tray and realized that she had consumed all of the food. Dismay touched her; she couldn't help her temper flaring to his words, but she had no wish to be blatantly rude.

Color filled her face, and she said miserably, "I am sorry, truly I am—"

"What?"

"The food—"

"The food was there to eat," he said impatiently.

"But I've left none—"

"Lady, if I wished it, I would order more."

"Then—"

"I merely wish to go down and see what that rascal Jake is about in the public room. I wish to be out of here. Now."

The word sounded quite like a growl. Ondine was only too glad to leap to her feet. "I'll tell him!" she promised, and the door closed distinctly behind her.

Warwick let out a long, shuddering gasp of relief. Then he rose very irritably, swore at himself, and donned his clothes.

Meg was at the doorway to see them off. Ondine decided wryly that while both the bride and groom were tense and moody, Meg and Jake continued to be both highly amused and delighted.

Right before Ondine was handed into the carriage by her husband, Meg swept warm and tender arms around Ondine. "Don't forget, child, he's made you a countess!"

Ondine tried to smile; her effort fell flat. She wanted to cry out that she was a duchess in her own right, that she should have been able to spit at her arrogant earl of a husband's sharply voiced orders.

She didn't speak. As a duchess she was wanted for complicity in murder—and treason. Better to play the countess until she could prove the duchess innocent.

Once again Ondine rode in the carriage alone. Warwick slammed the door shut and rode up top with Jake.

She had long hours for introspection as they rode that day. It proved painful; she could come up with no brilliant plan, and in time her mind wandered to the past—and the pain. Perhaps her wretched fight for survival in the forest—even her days in New-gate—had been better in a fashion. There had always been others more wretched than she to comfort. Now all she had was her own sorry company.

Near nightfall the carriage stopped. Warwick came back to tell her that she would have a few moments to stretch her legs, and that Meg had packed them some cold fowl, wine, and cheese.

Jostled, rumpled, and weary, Ondine merely nodded to him. She didn't protest his hold when he lifted her from the carriage, but hurried off into the trees by herself. She found a stream where she could wash her face with fresh water, and she felt a little better.

Returning to the carriage, Ondine paused. Both Jake and Warwick were on a spit of roadside grass, a cloth with a hamper on it between them. Jake sat cross-legged and merry-eyed as he bit into meat; Warwick was half reclined on his side, long legs stretched before him, an elbow supporting his weight. He wore a broad-beamed hat in fine Royalist tradition; its plume was red and dashing. In all he cut a striking and rakish figure, but that was not what gave her pause—it was the sound of his laughter, pleasant and easy. His face was ever the more attractive for it. The full sensuality of his lips was visible, the glitter in his eyes an endearing fascination. Like a bold cavalier he lay there, paring an apple with his customary ease of movement.

"Ye never heard that?" Jake was chortling to him. "And, now, how did ye miss it, ye being so close with His Grace?"

"I don't believe you!"

" 'Tis God's own truth! There was Nelly Gwyn, caught by the mob and yelling back to them, 'I'm not the Catholic whore! I'm the *Protestant* whore!' "

"Like as not, if I know Charles, he enjoyed the story as well as anyone might." Warwick chewed a piece of his apple, then waved the paring knife toward Jake. "I've another for you. Nelly once told Charles she could help clean up his kingdom. All he had to do was send all the French back to France, send her back to the stage, and then lock up his codpiece!"

Jake chortled, then sobered suddenly. "What's 'Is Majesty going to say about this sudden marriage of yours?"

Warwick shrugged. "I didn't steal anyone's heiress."

"But perhaps he had something in mind for you."

Warwick shook his head. "Charles would never think to twist my hand so. I've stood by him too many years, as my father did before me. He knows where loyalty lies. I think that Charles will be quite pleased. He has not stopped me since Genevieve . . .''

"Since Genevieve!" Jake muttered as Warwick's voice died away. "And that's the crux of it, right there, milord! I've an affection for that girl, and I don't wish to see her come to harm. Ye should have seen her on the gallows, coming at them like a righteous angel. And, sweet Jesus, if she isn't a greater beauty than even you imagined. She has courage, Warwick, real courage, and determination. She's not . . . meek, and she'll not be easily frightened—''

"She has nothing to be frightened of, Jake. I'll see to that."

"I pray 'tis so. But, sir, apart from any danger to her, I think your marriage whim of yesterday the finest move yet! She's refined, sweet as—"

"Sweet, my . . . rump!" Warwick retorted. "Don't let pretty faces deceive you, Jake." But he paused then. "Nay," he mused.

"Mayhap I haven't seen as many as Your Lordship!" Jake parried. "Now, the lady Anne, I'll warrant she has an angel's face, but a heart like a stone. Pleasure in the flesh perhaps, but she's longed for some time to get her talons into you. For my money, I'm waiting to see her reception to the news."

Warwick shrugged again, his knife slipping over the apple. "I never intended to marry Anne; she has always known it."

"Nay—you've known it. Not—"

"Shh."

Warwick looked up suddenly, staring straight at the trees, his eyes narrowing. He stood with a single fluid movement and strode through the brush, reaching Ondine before she could back away, barely holding his anger in restraint as he pulled her forward.

"How long have you been there?"

"I just came—"

"Liar. Lady, I tell you this once. I will not be spied upon, by you or anyone else."

"You've nothing worth spying upon!" Ondine raged out indignantly, and she flushed, for she did like Jake, very much, and she was heartily embarrassed for him to be witnessing the episode.

Jake jumped to his feet and uneasily balanced his weight from one foot to the other.

He cleared his throat, knowing from his master's eyes that an explosion was in the brewing. "Milord! We shouldn't tarry if you have a mind to reach the crossroads tonight!"

Warwick cast his gaze upon Jake, then upon Ondine once more. He seemed to relax a bit, but then he caught her chin between his thumb and his forefinger. "I don't care to warn you again. I'll not be harped upon by a lying, thieving chit of a girl!"

"Don't harp at me, milord!" she retorted, mindless of his touch upon her. "And I'll not harp at you."

He threw up his hands in disgust and swung on Jake. "She'll need your championship, old fool, if she remains determined to have the last word. And if she can't learn to mind her manners, she will have something of which to be afraid—me!"

He stalked off through the brush for the stream. Jake looked at Ondine and shrugged his shoulders.

" 'E's really not such a bad sort, really, milady."

Ondine laughed dryly, but hadn't the heart to fight Jake. She came to him and sat in the grass where Warwick had been and looked into the food basket.

"You're the one who warned me he was a beast, Jake, I'll not let you change your tune now!"

"Nay—"

"Never mind, Jake. I am here because I 'suit his purpose.' I have now decided that he suits mine." Smiling, she bit into an apple. Jake returned that smile uneasily.

The carriage stopped so late that night that she had long been sleeping; indeed, she did not even wake when it stopped. She was vaguely aware that the door opened, that there was an annoying light all about her.

"We're here," Warwick said.

"Where?" she murmured.

"Another inn. Come on—nay, don't bother, I'll get you," he muttered.

She did wake when his arms came around her. "I—can walk," she told him, her thoughts dazed, stolen from the mists of sleep to confront the alarming strength of him, the golden glitter of his eyes, shadowed and shielded by the brim of his hat.

He shrugged. "This is not like Meg's, but a meaner place. 'Tis probably best this way." He led her in and procured a room.

The bed was clean—at least the room and the linen smelled fresh. Warwick, still holding Ondine, surveyed it sternly beneath the meager glow of the lantern. Then he placed her on the bed.

He snuffed out the lantern and the room became as dark as pitch. She heard him shed his own things in the darkness, and she felt his weight when he climbed into the bed. She heard then the oppressive silence of the night.

Nervously she disrobed to her shift. She thought that sleep would elude her, but it was morning when she opened her eyes again. Warwick was not beside her, nor was his clothing anywhere to be seen. There was a large tray of food awaiting her, filled with fresh meat pies and a large pewter tankard of fresh milk. She dressed quickly and then ate, amazed once again when she consumed everything in sight. She mused that she was perhaps still afraid that there might not be another meal for days.

There was a sharp rap on the door just as she had washed her face and rinsed her teeth in the room's chipped washbasin.

She dried her face quickly and rushed to the door. It was Warwick, resplendent and regal once again in a black cloak and plumed hat. "Are you quite ready?"

"Aye."

He caught her hand and led her down a flight of stairs. The tavern was quiet this early; only one drunk snoozed away the night's entertainment at a corner table.

They walked out into the sunshine. The carriage was before the door, but Warwick led her past it to a charming walkway that fronted a number of shops.

"Where are we going?"

"Shopping," he said briefly.

And though she objected to his charity, she had little choice; he stated that his wife would be well clad.

She spent the day in a new fury, for as the dressmaker worked over her, tailoring chemises, petticoats, gowns, silks, and satins, Warwick stayed near her, observing the situation with a keen eye.

But soon it was over. Some gowns were completed, others would be shipped on to North Lambria.

That night, they slept together, silently. The next day was spent on the road, and again it seemed long. But when the carriage next stopped, Warwick joined her. He sat beside her, too close beside her, his presence filling the small space.

"We're coming upon the manor," he told her. "You'll remember that we met and were wed in London, that your father was a Frenchman. You bring no dowry, so please try to be charming before the servants. They'll need to believe I married you in such fascination that I did not care that you brought nothing to the union. If they bear the brunt of your charming tongue, despite your beauty, they're liable to doubt my sanity."

"I doubt your sanity!" Ondine retorted, stung.

She was rewarded with one of his steel-hard stares of warning.

"Countess, there is one more order I would give you now. I've a neighbor, Lord Hardgrave. Ours has never been the best of relationships; I'll thank you to take care if you meet him. Nay, avoid meeting him, lest I am with you. I do not trust the man."

Ondine glanced his way; his arms were crossed over his chest, his eyes were ahead, intent upon his own reflections.

"I'm hardly likely to meet him."

"Don't ever, ever be alone with him. Do you understand?"

Ondine sighed softly. "Aye."

Warwick pulled the drape from the window. "This is it. The drive to Chatham." Ondine, curious, could not help but lean past him.

Chatham Manor loomed immense and grand down a huge double drive, cut through by a row of manicured gardens. The structure itself seemed to touch the sky. It was stone, beautifully adorned with arched and chiseled windows, towers and buttresses. Sloping fields surrounded it—grass as green as emeralds—with forest to the east, pasture to the west. Mountains rose in purple splendor to the north. It was stunning, as rich and elegant as any a royal palace.

Yet, staring upon it, she suddenly shivered. The setting sun reflected off the windows. Beyond the glow was darkness, and she felt an inexplicable terror of what the shadows might hide.

Ridiculous, she told herself. It was beautiful; it was the home of an earl, an important peer, a palace in truth. It was a perfect place to be, far to the north—a place where she could spend her days in peace, wrestling with her own dilemma, seeking out the answers and the vengeance she so craved.

Her husband's hand was suddenly laced tight with hers, drawing her gaze up sharply. He smiled, a flash of white teeth, a devastating, wicked gleam of burning gold eyes.

"Countess, we're home. And, my love, you will behave the charming bride."

Chapter 5

The "beasts" that heralded Warwick's carriage were cast in massive stone, one on each side of the marble staircase leading up to the doors. Ondine stared at them while Warwick gave Jake instructions regarding the baggage. Jake replied cheerfully, tipped his cap to Ondine, and disappeared around the carriage.

At the top of the dignified staircase double oak doors opened silently. A woman stood there, tall and slim and very erect. She was dressed in shimmering gray, a simple gown with no adornment that was high-necked and as stiff as her posture. Ondine tremored slightly, aware that a "masquerade" was about to begin. And it was to begin with this severe and dour-looking woman.

"My lord Chatham!" The woman stepped upon the marble landing and smiled warmly, somewhat easing Ondine's apprehension. She was severe, yes, in dress and appearance, but when she smiled, she came to life. She must have been near sixty. Her hair was dark as pitch except for one attractive streak of silver that might have been painted in from her temple to her neck. Her features were nearly gaunt, yet her eyes were a bright and luminous green, and when she offered that welcoming smile, she gave an illusion of youth and a hint of the beauty that must have once been hers.

''Mathilda.'' Warwick returned the greeting. His footsteps were quick, causing Ondine to pant as he hurried her up the steps. Ondine felt the squeeze of his fingers, a reminder that he had warned her of the importance of those she would meet.

The housekeeper's eyes fell to Ondine with an expectant curiosity. She seemed familiar with Warwick, but not beyond the bounds of propriety, for she made a small curtsy as he reached her. ''I did not expect you, milord. Nor did I know of guests—''

''Not a guest, Mathilda, my wife, the lady Ondine.''

Surely Mathilda could not have been more surprised had the stone beasts before the steps come to life and rushed the manor. Her jaw fell, her lips pursed, and she stared at Ondine speechlessly before managing to gasp, ''Your wife?''

''Wife, yes,'' Warwick replied, bemused. ''And we've been in the carriage for quite some time now.''

''Oh!'' Mathilda recovered herself quickly and inclined her head in a low bow to Ondine. ''Countess, please, this way . . .''

She led the way into a grand foyer in the French manor, one with marble flooring of a lighter shade than the steps. There appeared to be entrances to the foyer also from the east and the west, but Ondine was not to see them then, for Mathilda was leading the way up a wide and curving stairway to the apartments above. Warwick no longer held her arm; he followed behind her. Mathilda spoke over her shoulder to Ondine, a little too quickly, perhaps, as if she struggled to regain complete composure.

''There's a dining hall beyond the staircase, my lady, and the old counting house. The living apartments are here, as you shall see, and the family takes its meals in the west wing. Justin's apartments are also in this wing. The Earl's are in the east, and the servants are quartered upon the third floor. Of course, any changes you might care to make—''

''Mathilda, it appears that the manor is most graciously run,'' Ondine said pleasantly. A small and welcome thrill of excitement gripped her; it was all marvelous. After a year of running and filth, fate had cast her into a most comfortable situation. Her clothing was beautiful, her surroundings were more so, and Warwick Chatham was anxiously expecting her to play a role. She determined suddenly to do so with complete élan.

She paused on the landing, a long carpeted hallway that appeared to be the family portrait gallery. "It's lovely!" she applauded sweetly, startling Warwick when she gripped his elbow and stretched upon her toes to plant a kiss upon his cheek. "My love, you did not tell me quite how grand . . ."

She lowered her lashes quickly to hide her amusement at his quickly suppressed amazement, then spun elegantly from him to approve the portrait of the handsome middle-aged man, amazingly like Warwick, yet more elegant in style, with a head of white hair to match the king's in curls and abundance. "Your father, my love? Surely it is by Van Dyck?"

"Aye," Warwick said smoothly, striding to her and managing to conceal his surprise at her knowledge of the painter. "As I told you, my lady," he continued with equal ease, "my father stood by Charles the First until the end. Then he hastened into exile and fought by his son. Charles himself commissioned the portrait."

Ondine moved down the hallway lightly. Ladies and lords of the centuries past stared upon her with different expressions, some merry, some melancholy, and many bearing Warwick's golden gaze and arresting features. She paused before the most recent portrait, finding again a resemblance to her husband, yet certain that it was not he. Warwick totally eschewed the fashionable mode of rich curls for men; hair seemed to him a distraction, and he knotted it at his nape. The man in the portrait had a rich array of golden locks, and his eyes were a valley green. He appeared younger, as handsome as Warwick, but more . . . carefree. Lines of character were not yet etched into the face.

Warwick's hands came to her shoulders. "Justin, my love," he reminded her.

"Aye, of course!" She spun to him, laughing, and tapped her fingers gently against his chest. "When shall I meet this young rake of a brother-in-law?"

"I'm sure that Mathilda will see that he is summoned immediately," Warwick replied, his eyes upon her quite wary at the very sweet and tender nature of her act, since he was painfully aware of its mockery.

Mathilda cleared her throat. Warwick gazed at her. "Justin is about, I presume?" he asked with an undertone of annoyance.

"Aye, milord, and he's been the model of endeavor in your absence, I will say, if I may."

"I doubt that!" Warwick responded, taking Ondine's arm firmly to lead her back along the hall. "If there's a fire going in the family hall, we'll await him there. And, Mathilda, see if Irene can hurry dinner, please."

Warwick pulled her past Mathilda, throwing open a set of doors. Ondine found herself prodded through them; she stared down a long length of polished wood floor to a massive fireplace. Brocade chairs and settees surrounded the fireplace, and not far from it loomed a gleaming table, large enough to seat six, surrounded by straight-backed claw-footed chairs, all carved with the insignia of the beast. Rich panneling flanked the walls to the many windows, which spanned both sides of the wing, all with coves and shining wood seats before them. Plain dual candelabra in muted silver were set between each window. The great room was both elegant and comfortable, and Ondine found herself a bit amazed; she had not imagined wealth such as this.

Warwick drew the doors closed upon them. Ondine moved swiftly to the fire, feeling his eyes upon her.

"I had not imagined," he murmured, "that I came across an actress of such caliber."

Ondine sat daintily upon a fine brocade chair. "I told you, my lord. I've traveled to many a court, manor, and castle."

He strode by her, leaning an elbow upon the mantel to survey her. "You amaze even me, my love," he mocked slightly.

She opened her eyes wide, glad of his apparent unease, since he had so chosen to taunt her before the seamstress. "Have I misjudged something, Lord Chatham? I thought that I was to appear the lady sweet and gracious, well bred and . . . adoring?"

"Warn me next time you intend to be 'adoring,' " he murmured acidly, and she chose to focus her attention upon the windows, as his gaze was searing at least, dry and probing at best.

She stood again, hurrying to one of the west windows. "What lies beyond?" she asked him lightly.

"The stables," he replied curtly, and she was further unnerved that he followed her closely as he pointed over her shoulder to the outbuildings. "Far beyond, over the hill, lie the cottages of the tenants and farmers. On Sundays, after services, there's quite a lively market. We've our own chapel—ground floor of the east wing—but the Chathams now attend public mass in the village.

Not to worry, my love, I'm sure you'll play the femme royale quite as competently . . . anywhere.''

She longed to reply to the taunting lash of his words, but the doors opened again and a husky, pleasant laughter filled the room.

"Married! Warwick, you scoundrel! Not to mention a word, but to stun us all. Where is this rare beauty who could so capture your heart?''

Ondine swung around to see the young man in the flesh whom she had surveyed earlier in the portrait.

He was perhaps five or six years younger than his brother, yet with Warwick, it was difficult to judge age. Justin was young, and charmingly so. His eyes danced with amusement; upon seeing her face, he pulled off his plumed hat and gave her a sweeping and elegant bow. Standing once again, he breathed out his introduction almost reverently. "My lady!''

"Ondine, I give you my brother, Justin Chatham,'' Warwick said most dryly, yet he accepted his brother's embrace of greeting with warmth before bringing her farther forward. "Justin, Ondine.''

"Ever so surely a name of magical connotation, a creature of magical beauty!'' Justin proclaimed.

Ondine bobbed an elegant curtsy, enjoying Justin's good humor and outrageous compliments. She had yet to be looked upon by his brother as anything other than a commodity.

"I thank you, Justin Chatham.'' She offered him her hand, and he kissed it slowly, his eyes sparkling as he raised his head.

Warwick snatched her hand back suddenly, caught her shoulders, and drew her to rest against his chest. "Dear brother, 'tis my wife you mawl! Seek your own, if you must dally so!''

The words were spoken lightly. Ondine was somewhat surprised at the camaraderie between them, for it did seem also that Justin sorely wore upon Warwick's patience.

Justin laughed. "Tell me, Warwick, where you found this lady, for alas, I would hunt the same grounds.''

"Why, the streets of London!'' Ondine replied quickly, escaping her husband's grasp to whirl around the table and keep its solid breadth between them. For her life, she did not know what drove her to goad him so, yet it seemed that she had been given a chance to do mischief, and after his treatment of her, the sweet demon would not leave her soul. She smiled sweetly at Justin. " 'Tis quite true! We met upon the streets and then and there chose to marry."

"An elopement?" Justin queried, enjoying himself tremendously. "How romantic."

"Umm," Warwick murmured, striding toward the table. Ondine moved quickly around another side.

"Oh, tremendously so!" Ondine declared, sweet irony dripping from her tongue. "I shall never know quite what . . . hit me that night. Yet your brother was a determined suitor, and I quickly realized I'd not escape him."

Justin stared from Ondine to his brother, then laughed. "Forgive me, sister-in-law, but I must say, well, I will be damned. My brother, you see, has lived his life the rage of beautiful women— though I can't say why; he's quite the cold and distant rake, or has been of late—yet he's eluded all the most determined heiresses of our good land. And the greatest beauties. Are you, then, incredibly rich?"

"Justin!" Warwick snapped.

"Not at all," Ondine said sweetly.

"We must celebrate this event!" Justin proclaimed. He strode across the room and opened a panel beneath a window seat that proved to hold elegant crystal goblets and flasks. "Nothing so bleak as native ale," he muttered. He pulled his choice forth, balancing the goblets. "The vintage of Aquitaine. I think! Rich and fruity wine, red like love's sweet passion!"

"Is passion red, then?" Ondine inquired innocently. Too innocently, perhaps. She had given her attention to Justin and had not noticed Warwick slipping up behind her.

His arms swept around her, his fingers spanning her waist, their tips hovering below her breasts as he pulled her taut to his hot, tense form, dipped his head, and whispered to her throat. "Very red . . . think of it, milady . . ."

"Warwick, cease!" Justin pleaded. "You draw my attention from the wine!"

Warwick did not release Ondine, and she began to repent her flippancy. She could not speed from him again, for his hold was one of steel. And she could not fight the sensation that was pressed into her by his warmth, causing her to tremble, to loathe him . . .

and to feel beguiled all the same. She seemed to become liquid at his touch.

Justin saved her, approaching them both with the goblets balanced precariously in his hands. Warwick reached for two, released her, then offered her one with a quick fire-gold gaze of warning that assured her he would follow her game, step by step.

She turned back to Justin. "Why is it, sir, that you—charming as you are, and more vulnerable as you pretend—have not fallen prey to one of these heiresses yourself?"

Justin chuckled, sipped his wine, then lifted his goblet to Warwick. "I am not the earl, and though charming—I do mind my manners!—it seems that women, alas, do fall prey to his very aloofness. Ah . . . that which cannot be obtained! As it is, little sister, here's to you! The best . . . with the beast!"

Warwick responded with a dry smile. "It runs in all our blood, Brother."

"I suppose," Justin agreed amiably. His gaze grew speculative over Ondine suddenly. "I've a mind our new countess would not be afraid of a beast—or aught else, for that matter."

Ondine felt a sudden chill in the room as the brothers exchanged gazes. It was not anger between them; it was a thought that was passed and shared, and one from which she was excluded totally.

She had little time to think on it. There was a tap upon the doors. Warwick bid "Enter," and Mathilda came in, followed by two maids and a lad, all bearing cutlery and great trays that exuded wonderful scents.

"Dinner, milord, as you requested," Mathilda said simply. With a wave of her hand, the others moved, quickly setting a linen cloth, china plates, and silver knives and forks upon the table.

Warwick inclined his head toward Ondine. "My lady?"

He pulled out a chair and she swept into it. As platters of eel and smoked sturgeon, boiled new potatoes, and garden greens were passed about, Warwick informed her that the girls were Nan and Lottie, the cook's daughters; and the lad was Joseph, who doubled in the stable. The three had pleasant smiles and an eagerness to serve that reminded Ondine of Warwick's previous warning to her about the gentle handling of his people. It amused her somewhat, for she did think of him as cold, indomitable, and forbidding—even at those times when he made her senses burn.

Yet surely he must be a fair and decent master, to create not only respect but happiness.

He was not always glacial steel, she thought, an inexplicable pain seeming to claw about her heart. She had heard him laugh so easily with Jake . . . and even in his taunts to her, his words were often laced with wit and wry humor.

When the meal was served, Mathilda ushered the servants out, then backed through the doors herself, drawing them closed. Ondine tried to pay attention as Justin gave Warwick a quick accounting of household affairs in his absence, then quizzed him in return about the state of things in London. Justin's eyes fell quizzically upon Ondine once again, a hint of delighted interest in them as he asked, "And what does Charles think of your new countess, Warwick? If I know His Grace, he's surely tossing with regret that he did not seduce her first!"

"They have not met . . . yet," Warwick replied, sipping his wine. He, too, stared at Ondine; she tried to smile, but the sound of her heart suddenly seemed to overwhelm her.

"Were she my wife," Justin mused, "I'd take grave care to see that they not meet!"

The conversation then veered again, to matters in North Lambria. Ondine noted that both brothers grew serious as they discussed matters of business, and that Warwick seemed a little hard upon a man who was his brother.

Justin explained the matter to her, with the same use of wit against himself she had seen in his brother. "I was expelled from His Majesty's court—for dueling. My brother decided that it was high time I avoid the company of the likes of Rochester and others, due to their influence upon my, er, weak character. So, I am, alas, a man now under duress to prove my worth."

He didn't seem to mind the rebuke, or the fraternal clamps set upon him. Ondine was certain that she would have sorely resented Warwick, but they were of the same blood; Warwick merely enjoyed the fortune of having been born the elder.

She smiled at Justin. "Do you find your brother a hard taskmaster?"

"The worst," Justin replied cheerfully. "But then . . . he is the family legend. Ah, the fates of life! You see, I was but a child of ten when we so misfortunately waged war with the Dutch. Warwick was fifteen, but we Chathams rise to height quickly. He ran off and joined the Royal Navy beneath the Duke of York, and as luck would have it, he became a naval hero at sixteen. No one can best my brother with a sword, so I find it most comfortable to remain on his good side.''

''Justin,'' Warwick interrupted impatiently, '''twas the present we were discussing. What of the horses?''

''Ah, but the foals are coming beautifully! Clinton was right about the breeding of those Arabians—we've the fleetest mounts upon four legs! They'll do quite well for the races.'' He turned to Ondine. ''Have you been to Newmarket for the races? What sheer joy and excitement.''

''I daresay,'' Warwick murmured, ''had you avoided the races, you might have avoided the duel.''

Justin grimaced. ''Had Charles but arranged a joust for me as he did for you and Hardgrave—'' His voice broke off suddenly, pained, as if he had brought up something extremely unpleasant.

He had for Ondine. Her breath drew in sharply against her will, and her eyes were drawn to her husband's at the head of the table. Him! He had been one of the armor-laden knights on the field that day; on the day her life had gone from fantasy to nightmare. Dear God, it was but just a trick of fate that they had not met before, that he hadn't known her for . . . the fugitive, daughter of a traitor, traitor herself.

She lowered her head quickly, hoping to hide the naked pain that had streaked to her eyes. Yet with her head bowed, she realized that Warwick had not even gazed her way. His attention had been on his brother, his features gone taut and severe.

Justin cleared his throat. ''Dragon fares as well as ever, like as not to tear down his stall when you're away. He'll be eager for exercise.''

''He'll get it,'' Warwick replied, and the moment seemed to have past. ''Tomorrow I'll take him the stretch of the county, and he'll regret that he was not left in peace.''

Justin went on to mention that several farmers were seeking audiences to settle petitions, then apologized to Ondine for boring her with such matters. She replied that she was certainly not bored, since she was new to it all. She felt her husband's pensive eyes upon her, yet when she caught them with her own, she could not tell if he was pleased with her performance before his brother or not. But she realized then the depth of his deception; only Jake knew the truth of their marriage, as Warwick was not willing to share that information even with his brother.

There was a rap upon the door, and at Warwick's command, a man entered. He was dressed in plain brown breeches and the leather jacket of a groom, but he was clean, neat, and young, near to Warwick in age. His hair was so black as to be jet, he was tanned, and his face was leathered with exposure to constant wind and sun.

Warwick rose at his entrance, his lips curled in a smile. "Clinton."

"Warwick," Clinton said, approaching the head of the table to clasp the other man's hand. Ondine watched the exchange curiously; Clinton was obviously in Warwick's employ, yet they met with no formality. Indeed, it was a very odd greeting. She had always seen her husband courteous to those beneath his station, but that station had also been apparent.

"Ondine, Clinton is master of the stables," Warwick informed her. "Clinton, the lady Ondine."

Clinton turned to her. She noted that his eyes were a dark forest green, that there was something very familiar about him, but that she could not determine what. It frightened her somewhat, yet his words and manner soothed her fear, for she became quite certain that he did not know her.

He bowed low before her. "My lady, your servant."

"Shall you have some wine?" Justin asked him, and Ondine again wondered at the familiar relationship between the earl, his brother, and the stable master.

"If I'm not interrupting."

"Nay—I wish to hear more of the horses!" Warwick said and grinned, a flash of youthful excitement sparkling in his eyes, which gave him again the look of the devilish rake. Ondine did not wonder that were he to give a woman such a gaze, she could easily fall prey to that promise of wicked passion and dark excitement, even knowing that it was the devil's own danger.

Even as he replied to Clinton, he suddenly rose. "If you'll excuse me first, I'll see my wife to our apartments."

"But—" Ondine began. Warwick was already behind her chair, pulling it so that she might rise.

"You've had a long day," he reminded her in such a tone that she chose not to argue. Justin and Clinton were on their feet, bowing, bidding her both welcome and good night.

Warwick's fingers were firm about her arm, giving her little chance for response. Minutes later they were traversing the portrait gallery. It seemed dark here now; night had quite completely fallen, and few candles gleamed along the deserted hall. Ondine shivered slightly, hurrying to keep pace with Warwick's sudden determination to be rid of her.

"Milord!" she protested, but by then they had reached a second set of doors, and he threw them open. They entered a room similar to that which they had just left, but differently arrayed. Shelves of books lined the eastern wall; a massive desk and a small, more elegant secretary sat opposite each other to the left. To the right were a spinet and a harp, facing each other upon a woven rug. Candlelight blazed here, as if in ready welcome for them.

"Our private quarters," Warwick stated simply, but he did not stop to allow her a decent surveyance. He continued through a smaller door at the rear of the room. It opened upon a massive and very masculine bedchamber, one with a huge canopied bed set high upon a step, another desk, a dresser, and a washstand. Cloth embossed with small green dragons adorned the walls, and rich draperies cloaked the windows.

But they did not stop in that room. Warwick opened a second door to a room as large as the bedchamber itself. Toward the rear was a white enameled bathtub, quite huge, with a pipe leading through the floor. There was a stand there with a shaving mirror, a dresser with a washbasin, and row upon row of latticed doors that were surely wardrobes.

Even this Ondine was scarce able to see. Warwick pushed open the third door, and there, at last, they stopped.

"Your chamber, madam, and"—his brow rose to her as he released her—"quite private, I do assure you."

Ondine attempted to ignore him, moving more deeply into the room. It was beautiful, and as elegantly feminine as the chamber before had been fascinating. The bed was as large, but delicate gauze hung from the finely carved canopy, and the color of the bedclothes and window draperies was a misty silver blue. The dresser was finely polished cherry wood. The pitcher and bowl upon it were white enameled and covered with blue daisies. There was a dressing table with a framed mirror, and a stool to set before it. In the far rear was a built-in alcove, draped, too, in the silver blue that covered the windows.

"The latrine," Warwick informed her.

"Thank you," she said stiffly.

"You should find your undergarments in the dresser; your gowns, I'm sure, have been hung in the dressing room. The pitcher is always filled, should you desire water in the night. Is there anything you lack?"

"No," Ondine murmured.

"There is no lady's maid at present, though Lottie—"

"I don't require anyone."

"Well, you must," Warwick said impatiently.

"Then Lottie will be fine."

He nodded. "Then if there is nothing else you require this evening—"

"There is!" She flared suddenly, facing the blazing gold sparks in his eyes.

"And what is that, madam?"

"An explanation!"

"For what?" he demanded, arms folded over his chest, his voice deepening, as it was prone to do, with anger.

"This charade!"

"Would you prefer, my lady, that I return you to the gallows?"

Her eyes lowered. He rumbled out an oath of impatience and queried with a sudden passion, "What is it that does not appeal to you? You are fed and clothed, and not by a pittance. The manor is yours, girl. Gardens, leisure, pleasance. And—as seems a matter of grave import to you—you have total privacy. All that is asked of you in return is that you rise to greet the station, which you know you do remarkably well, with a flair—and a vengeance." He strode the few steps to her, gripping her shoulders so suddenly that she could not avoid him, but was forced to tilt her head back and to meet the fire in his eyes that so belied the chill that could rule his manner. "Where is your difficulty with this?"

His mouth was too close to hers, curled with a sensual flash of contempt. She could feel his breath, sweet with the scent of wine, brush against her flesh, and the finely honed pulsing of his muscled form. Heat suffused her with a trembling, and she wanted nothing more than to elude his disturbing presence.

"Nothing!" she cried out, seeking to jerk away from him, yet he held her still and seemed further angered that he did so, his eyes locked so strangely upon her.

A strangled oath escaped him, and he suddenly tore from her, striding quickly to the door. "There is one more thing—Countess," he mocked. "This is the bolt. Use it. Once I have gone through this door, you will bolt it—immediately. And you will open it only upon my command. Am I clear?"

"Aye!"

He threw the door open, then paused, but spoke to her next with the breadth of his back to her. "Your performance, as surely you are aware, was quite incredible. Pray, do not beguile my brother so that he forgets you are mine."

The door slammed shut. Ondine stood still, dazed and confused by the miserable rush of emotions within her.

"The bolt!" The command came from outside. Swearing like a fishwife, Ondine flew to the door. "I'll be most happy to bolt my door!" she muttered and slid the heavy iron bolt into place.

Only then did she hear his footsteps striding away.

She was shaking as she strained to reach the hooks and shed her clothing; shaking still when she dug through the dresser to find one of the wonderfully clean and elegantly laced new nightdresses.

Still she shook when she crawled into the gloriously comfortable bed. God in Heaven, what was it about the man that did this to her?

She lay awake a long while, so puzzled by her husband that she could think of nothing else, nor could she sleep. She tossed about, agonized by the restless heat that remained within her body; she flushed and burned, she remembered his features so clearly, his touch . . .

She must have lain so, furious, bewildered, and shivering miserably, for about an hour.

Then a sound of horse's hooves upon stone below her window brought her curiously out of her bed and to the drapes, which she carefully pulled back to look out upon the courtyard below.

It was Warwick. She did not see his face, but she recognized his stance as he led a huge shining bay from an archway beneath her. He wore his hat with the single red plume, high riding boots, and a flowing black mantle—with the "beast" embroidered in golden thread. She heard him chuckle affectionately at the horse, then swing upon it, lithe and agile. The animal pranced and reared with excess energy, and then the two were racing away, westward, merging with the night.

Where are you going? she longed to shout. Yet she did not. She stamped her foot with a sudden irrational fury, then scampered back to the warmth of her bed, her heart racing.

He was off to see a mistress, no doubt, she determined shrewishly. And wasn't that why he had married her, a gallows' bride, since no high-born noblewoman would have tolerated his desire to leave her side each night for the life of heedless passion he wished to live?

Ondine slammed a fist into her pillow. What did she care, as long as he let her be. But she did care. She fought her fury, and her ridiculous pain, for what seemed to be forever.

For the life of her, she could not get the sensation of heat to leave her body.

"Damn you to a thousand hells, Lord Warwick Chatham!" she whispered vehemently, so tired that she was near to tears.

And then she froze, for there was a light rap upon her door, and she heard his voice.

"Girl—are you well?"

He had returned . . . she hadn't heard him!

"Aye . . . aye!" she sputtered. "I'm . . . fine."

He said nothing else. Ondine released the breath she had not known she held.

And curiously, in moments, she slept.

Chapter 6

Ondine awoke to discover Lottie tapping upon her door, offering Ondine a scented bath, and food in the salon when she should desire it.

Ondine, quite delighted with the thought of the bath, flashed Lottie a smile and hurried for the dressing room, hastily shedding her gown.

She sank her feet into the water, then more carefully her rump, for the water was hot indeed. Sweeping her hair about her head, she leaned back with a contented sigh, luxuriating in the swirling caress of the bath oil. After a moment she opened her eyes curiously, surprised to find Lottie still stationed before her, waiting with a massive length of towel. Catching her mistress's eyes upon her, Lottie flushed again and bowed.

"Lottie, whatever are you doing?" Ondine inquired gently.

"Why, I—" She broke off, dropping her chin. "I don't know, milady. I've never held such a position before."

Ondine chuckled softly, then sobered, for she had no wish to hurt the young girl's feelings. She liked Lottie; her broad face, farm-fresh smile, and cherry-red cheeks.

"Then, Lottie, I shall tell you a secret," Ondine said, giving the girl an encouraging smile. "I'm a bit nervous myself, so we shall bluff our way through it together. If you would, I'd enjoy a cup of tea while I soak. Then, perhaps, you could lay out a gown for me.''

Lottie nodded eagerly. Ondine closed her eyes again as she heard the girl scamper through the master's chamber to the room beyond. Seconds later she was back, a cup of tea in her hands. ''Perhaps you could draw that little stool near, and I could use it for a table,'' Ondine suggested, and again Lottie nodded eagerly.

It was as Lottie brought the small stool that Ondine noted how badly she shook. Curiously she set her cup upon the stool and asked, ''What is it, Lottie? Surely you're not afraid of me?''

''I'm not afraid of you—you seem ever so kind! It's—'' She broke off quickly, alarmed at her own words.

''It's what, Lottie?'' Ondine demanded with a sigh of exasperation.

Lottie looked anxiously to the door of the master's chamber, as if she were afraid someone might be hovering there. She knelt down by the tub and stared wide-eyed and frightened at Ondine. ''I'm afraid *for* you, milady!''

''Afraid for me!'' Ondine repeated, astonished. ''Why ever would you be?'' Ondine felt a furious tremor shake her. Was there, then, something more about the handsome, tyrannical, and secretive rogue who had married her than she had dared to guess? Something of the demon that hinted only in his eyes? Was there an intrigue dark as his brooding perusal?

Once more Lottie's glance skittered to the door; then her timid gaze returned to Ondine. ''Didn't you hear them?''

''Hear what?''

''The wolves—blessed Jesus, did they howl last night!''

Ondine started to laugh, relief flooding muscles she didn't realize had gone so taut. ''Lottie! Wolves are prone to prowl forest land, and to howl with the moon when they do so.''

Lottie shook her head with frustration, saying, ''Lady, I fear for your life! The first countess was sorely afraid—poor delicate thing!—and she did die, sweet lady!''

''Lottie! She was afraid—of her husband?''

''Oh, nay, lady, 'twas never him, though others sometimes thought so! Genevieve had her own maid, a Yorkshire girl, but she did speak with me oft in the kitchen, and she was so afraid!''

Ice suddenly seemed to sluice through Ondine's veins, yet she fought to maintain control. She could not let the girl see how very ignorant she was of her husband's affairs, else she might lose all she was gaining in truth.

"Of what was she afraid?" Ondine tried to ask casually.

"The ghosts."

Lottie spoke so solemnly that it was all Ondine could do to keep from laughing and submerging herself deeply into the water with pure relief.

"Lottie, you must not fear for me, then, for I have no fear at all of ghosts." She smiled brilliantly. "All great castles and manors have ghosts, Lottie. But my father, who was a dear and wise man, taught me that the dead were the safest men that one could meet; the only ones who could not—assuredly not!—harm you in any way."

Lottie did not appear at all soothed or appeased.

"How did the countess die, Lottie? Childbirth? It is a cruel trick of fate, yet does occur—"

"Nay, nay, my lady! They all said that she was unstable—all but the earl, that is—"

"Unstable?"

"Mad! But she was not! Just fragile and—frightened. She had been promised to the Church, but her father pleaded that the earl take her to wife on his deathbed, and"—Lottie quickly crossed herself—"such a request needs must be met. The two were wed—"

"Lottie, how did she die?"

"She heard voices, you see. The ghosts' voices."

Ondine was growing impatient, yet she could see how deathly serious it was to Lottie. "Lottie, what ghosts?"

"Why, of His Lordship's grandmother, of course. Dead—fallen from the old wood staircase to the chapel. And of the old lord's mistress, hastened to her own death. Genevieve died the same, poor, most noble lady! From a tower at court, she fell, and I knew she had heard the voices, calling to her again!"

"Lottie!" The shocked and horrified gasp came from the doorway. Both girls—Ondine and Lottie—found their startled, guilty attention drawn there. Mathilda stood there quite white-faced, one hand to her heart, the other leaning against the doorframe.

"Lottie, you wretched child! How dare you upset the countess with such wicked gossip!"

Lottie, stricken, fell back on her heels beneath the tongue-lashing. Ondine, irritated at being so disturbed in the bathtub no less, attempted to assert her opinion.

"I'm not upset! I questioned the girl, she but—"

Mathilda had reached Lottie by then and was wrenching the girl's arm angrily.

"I meant no harm!" Lottie cried out.

"Horrid child! You should have remained in the kitchen!"

"Nay!" Ondine proclaimed, gripping the rim of the tub on either side, determined to outrule Mathilda. "I don't wish—" she began, but her words were curtly cut by a masculine voice, thundering in upon them with aggravated authority.

"By the rood—what in God's earth goes on here?"

Warwick now stood at the door, decked in riding coat and breeches, tall with hat and boots, dominating the scene. His eyes, searing points of gold, leveled upon Ondine, were alight with accusation, as if she were surely the cause of this uncustomary domestic upheaval.

She met his gaze with a simmering fury. She was but the victim of them all, trapped within a tub of melting bubbles, naked and waterlogged, and sorely bereft of her privacy. She longed to scream, to throw things at them all! It seemed a horrible invasion, especially so with Warwick there, his eyes upon her, before the other women, and they all decently appareled.

"What is the difficulty?" Warwick demanded of them all.

Ondine bent her knees quickly to her body, alarmed at the crimson color staining her flesh from a vivid flow of humiliation, yet even as she wrapped her arms around them, she was retorting with the best restraint of manner that she could.

"There is no difficulty here, milord. Mathilda was concerned with Lottie's service; I am not. If you would all just leave—"

"And what is your difficulty?" he asked his housekeeper, coldly interrupting Ondine.

"I—milord—I was concerned with the child's choice of rumor to convey to the countess."

"Oh!" Lottie's head fell to the floor as she buried it in the crook of her arm. Her cry was muffled. "I meant no harm, truly! I—"

"No harm is done!" Ondine snapped out, wishing for nothing more than it all to end, for Mathilda and more especially Warwick to depart so that she might rise from the tub and salvage a sense of dignity. "If I might be left in peace with my maid—"

Warwick apparently hadn't heard a word that she had spoken. He was striding into the dressing room and bending to the distraught Lottie. "Come, girl; 'tis the end of it." He brought her to her feet.

"She should be punished!" Mathilda stated.

"I'll not have it!" Ondine commanded in a sudden fury. They were all standing right over her! "Must this go on while I bathe?"

"Mathilda, Lottie, you are dismissed," Warwick said smoothly. "There shall be no recourse, Mathilda, as the countess has requested."

Mathilda, with the still-trembling Lottie at her heels, began to depart. Ondine realized that she was about to lose her maid while retaining her husband.

"Milord, I need Lottie's services. Lottie, you will stay—"

Lottie paused.

"You will go," Warwick said quietly. Lottie nodded mutely and fled, and Ondine learned quickly the lesson that her husband's orders would always override her own, no matter how softly they were spoken.

With their departure, Warwick closed the door behind them, then came forward, resting a booted foot upon the stool and leaning an elbow upon his knee to stare at her.

"Milord, if you don't mind—"

"I do mind. What was it all about?" He was intense, and far too close. She was losing her protective covering of bubbles and was shivering fiercely.

"What was it all about?" she hissed, tossing her head back. She inadvertently displayed a long smooth column of neck and the rise of her breasts. "It was, milord, over things you might have thought to tell me, since it is some role I am to play for you, and I have not been given any lines! You have not thought to warn me, sir, that you were a widower—and the servants claim some ghosts to have lured your bride to death!"

He did not reply, but straightened slowly and walked across the room to lean against the latticed doors of closet space. She could not fathom at all his expression when his eyes touched hers again; he seemed both distant and too near, aware of her in every aspect, yet disinterested.

"Countess . . ." His use of the title was always sardonic. "Certainly you do not believe such things."

No, she didn't, but she found herself shivering fiercely and longing again to know why this conversation, with Warwick so strangely intent, had to take place now.

"Nay," she spat out. "But it would have been reasonable, Lord Chatham, to have given me an explanation!"

He shrugged, and it seemed that the touch of a rueful grin tugged at the corner of his lip.

"Perhaps I feared that you would quake at the thought of ghosts; of a manor where the halls are prone to echo with the howls of the neighboring wolves."

"My lord," Ondine replied dryly, making as great a mockery with the use of the words as he, "you consider my life to be yours; I doubt that you care about my feelings in the least."

He smiled elusively. "You are wrong, Countess. I am quite interested in your feelings . . . and impressions. And if you do not fear ghosts, my love"—his voice fell low—"then why is it that you sit there shaking like an ash in wind?"

"Because of your horrendous lack of good manners, sir!" Ondine cried furiously. "You claim that I am to be mistress of this house, yet not only do servants spat before me in my bath, but you come along to further disrupt my peace and privacy!"

He tilted his head, his eyes glittering as laughter rumbled from his throat. "But, my lady, I am your husband! If I should not disturb your bath, then, pray tell, who should?"

"I should like to get out," Ondine announced icily.

"Then, please do, Countess," he said gallantly, offering her a full and courtly bow.

She didn't move, nor could she think of a scathing retort, so unnerved was she by his taunting charm and laughter. A flush of pink rose instantly to her breasts and face, and she was furious that she could not control it. Instantly he commented upon it.

"You've seen many a horror in your day, lady, as you are so

wont to remind me. Nothing disturbs you—do you recall those words?''

''Get out!'' Ondine railed, shaking suddenly from a frightening savage heat that ripped along her spine.

He did not, but proceeded in long strides toward her again, planting his foot upon the stool, his arm upon his knee, and bending very low to her. ''Never think to order me about, madam. Or out of a chamber that is mine in any way. Where I will have access, I will take it without need of your blessing.'' He spoke pleasantly, but with such an underlying note of arrogant assurance that her temper soared to new heights. She swore out a score of oaths and forgot even herself as she brought her hand flying and spraying from the water with swift vehemence.

He caught her wrist, but not before her palm had caught his cheek. Yet whatever triumphant satisfaction the action had brought her was quickly swept from her soul, for she had not taken time to wonder at his response. And could she not now do more than gasp with sudden and searing panic, for that response was quick. Mouth grim and eyes set, his jaw clamped, he secured her other wrist and pulled her upon her feet with an effortless but ruthless strength. He brought her dripping into his arms as he lifted her from the tub to the floor. Then he lifted her off her feet and locked her arms about his waist, bringing her naked length fully to his. He smiled as her eyes stared up, wide with shock. She knew that her limbs trembled fiercely, that he felt the mounds of her breasts through the fabric of shirt and jacket, that her slim legs were all but entangled with his hard muscled ones, and that surely he felt the rampant thunder of her heart. And he smiled his rake's smile, a flash of white teeth, a bemused glitter of his eyes. ''Lady! It seems I am forever reminding you how little is required of you! Yet it seems you insist upon goading my temper over trifling things, when, alas, you are allowed to escape so very much!''

Then quite suddenly it seemed that his fingers were gently raking into the damp wings of her hair, caressing her nape, arching her throat. She was not prone to seek forgiveness where none was due; and with him she would surely swear in her heart she would never do so.

But she was willing now. Ever so willing, for she was alive with both fear and excitement, and it was the excitement she loathed the most. She felt like liquid silver, and she abhorred him for holding her so negligently, for knowing her flesh and her vulnerability.

"I beg your pardon," she rasped out desperately, but the plea came far too late, for already his head was lowered, his mouth laying claim to hers. She gasped at that contact, and further abetted his intent, parting her lips to his. Theirs was a subtle caress, but firm and yielding, a sweet wine that poured upon her with a potency she hadn't the strength to fight. She felt the searing touch of his tongue stroking into deep crevices of her mouth. Each stroke had a shattering impact upon her trembling body, so much so that she held still, until some good sense showed her the absurdity of it all. With a fervent twist of the head that surely cost her locks of hair, she turned her face from his, gasping out a new spate of oaths that described his behavior and himself in no uncertain terms.

He merely chuckled and slowly allowed her feet to touch the floor, forcing her to slide against him all the while. He did not release her, but kept her pinned to him as he told her, "My love, I but remind you that the rights I claim are simple: your attention when I wish to speak. There are other rights, my lady, that a husband could demand he claim." Smiling grimly, the heat of warning in his dulcet tones, he allowed his fingers to play down the length of her spine, tarry upon its base, then move leisurely over her buttocks.

"Damn you, villain, knave, jackass—" Ondine began.

"You've left out husband and lord," he reminded her, his hand moving again as he held her, the knuckles stroking upward over her hip and waist, and then the length of his fingers closing around her breast in an intimate caress that sent flames racing through her anew. Her eyes were locked with his. Her teeth were clenched, and still they chattered when she lashed out again.

"Tyrant, vandal, blackguard—beast!"

"Ah, and your heart beats like the hare's when that beast is on the hunt, lady! Perhaps that is best; it is well that you learn some recall as to the master of this game."

Abruptly he released her, striding across the room, plucking a towel, and tossing it to her. Ondine caught the towel and hurriedly wrapped it about her, expecting to find his mouth curled in a sardonic grin. It was not; his eyes were very intense, his features masking all emotion.

"Madam," he said harshly, "I'll not disturb you again." He bowed elegantly, sweeping his plumed hat before him, then exited with long, even strides. The door clicked sharply.

Ondine stared after him, alternately shivering with cold fury, and then trembling . . . with what strange searing heat she did not know. At length she swirled about and returned to her own chamber, slamming the door and dressing hurriedly. She thought of her husband and swore silently that she would pay him back one day, in more ways than one.

Then she discovered that she was staring about her room. Genevieve's room? Surely it had to be so.

Poor Genevieve. Ondine realized that she wanted to know more about the girl. And at the same time, she trembled slightly. She didn't want Genevieve's "ghost" in her own life.

Suddenly she felt Genevieve, sweet, gentle Genevieve, in everything around her—in the soft blues and whites of the chamber, in the draperies, in the bedclothes . . . even in the water pitcher.

She turned about, tilted her chin, and left the chamber. Breakfast awaited her in the outer room, and she was quite determined that she would spend the day viewing her new domain.

Warwick had disappeared when she forced herself to walk through the connecting door to his chamber; nor was he about in the music room, as Lottie called it. Breakfast awaited her, and she ate pleasurably alone, then determined to summon Mathilda. The housekeeper came to her, and Ondine gave her a charming smile. "I'd like a tour this morning, and I'm quite sure you know the place completely."

Mathilda's eyes widened, apparently with relief, yet Ondine wondered if the woman wasn't thinking it a very regretful thing that the master had returned with a new wife.

Ondine rose and preceded the housekeeper to the hall doorway, pausing there. "Mathilda, I meant what I said. Lottie is to bear no punishment for the unfortunate episode this morning."

An anguished look appeared upon the woman's features; she began to wring her hands, and her deep eyes carried a hint of tears restrained. "Milady! I beg your pardon! I did not wish you to be upset. 'Tis difficult at best to leave one's home and claim another; I could not bear to see you frightened here!"

"I do not believe in ghosts." She spoke gently, certain that Mathilda had dearly loved the countess Ondine had replaced—in name at least. "I am very sorry about the lady Genevieve," she added softly.

Mathilda nodded her head distractedly, then suddenly seemed to brighten. "Would you like to see her?"

Ondine's heart seemed to leap—was Mathilda mad herself?

"Her portrait, in the gallery, my lady."

"Oh," Ondine breathed, relieved. "I should love to see it."

Mathilda swept by her. They followed the long gallery past numerous portraits of Chathams. Then toward the western wing of the manse Mathilda stopped before a recent portrait of a woman.

Ondine could not help but stare, fascinated and compelled. The woman sat upon a crimson-covered chair, a spaniel in her lap. The artist had captured more than her golden blond beauty and sky-blue eyes. He had found the essence of the woman, a wistful, ethereal look to the eyes, a gentleness about the mouth, caught in a smile both rueful and hesitant—and lovely. She was like soft sunlight, most fragile, and yet so stunning as to capture the heart with a gaze.

"She was—charming, beautiful," Ondine murmured.

"Aye! The earl did love her dearly! Never did I see a man brood so fiercely, so darkly, as when she . . . departed this life."

"I'm sure."

"And she carried his wee babe!" Mathilda added tragically.

Ondine stiffened, but was careful to keep her smile. Perhaps Warwick's behavior did make some sense. He had been horribly in love with his wife, stricken at the loss of his heir—and pressured to marry again, when he had no heart to call another wife. Why not, then, take a gallows' bride, be free to wander callously where he would, and quell all hopes that he might be a delectable catch once more?

"She is lovely," Ondine repeated of Genevieve again to Mathilda. "But now I would see the manor, in its entirety."

"Aye, milady, aye."

A small spiral stairway led off from the gallery to the floor above—the servants' quarters. Mathilda rattled off who slept where, perhaps a little annoyed that Ondine bothered herself with such arrangements. Ondine thanked her quietly, smiling pleasantly.

From the servants' quarters, she discovered that the house was not a U, but a square. The rooms in the top floor connected in a circle, as did the first; the family quarters did not. "There's a passage from Justin's apartments, but not from the master's," Mathilda explained to her. "There used to be many secret passages, hidden stairwells and chambers, you see. Cromwell's men discovered many of them, though, and destroyed them, for the old lord was a Royalist, through and through. 'Tis lucky the manor stands at all—yet Cromwell might have feared a bloody northern revolt if Chatham were destroyed. Even the Scots, with whom the Chathams always feud, would have banded to create havoc. With one Chatham dead upon the field, the lady dead upon the stairway as it was, Cromwell's forces but ordered the passages sealed. The earl's father liked the wing the way it was; privacy, he thought. And it seems my lord Chatham now prefers it, too."

"You've been with the Chathams long?" Ondine queried.

"Aye. I was born here," Mathilda responded. She then led Ondine back to the portrait gallery, and from there they passed through Justin's apartments to the rear wing, where the second floor housed guest chambers. The ground level of that northern wing was an armory, and like the portrait gallery, it was a place where family history was preserved. It was stocked with swords and arms and plates in use by the present generation; it also housed ancient armor, subtly different with each generation and century.

The eastern wing began with the laundry and kitchens, then proceeded to the great hall, an immense place. Once, Mathilda told Ondine proudly, it had been nothing but cold stone wall and a dirt floor. Now it was whitewashed, the ceiling was elaborately molded, tapestries were hung, and rich embroidered carpeting covered a gleaming tiled floor. Mathilda sighed with pleasure as she described the various balls and masques that had taken place in the hall.

Warwick's main office was off the grand hall. The walls here were completely filled with bookcases, and the books, Ondine noted, covered all subjects. Bound volumes of Shakespeare, the French and Italian poets, notes by Pepys, Christopher Wren, Thomas More. There were books on building, on farming, on breeding, on horses, on warfare. An oak desk angled so that sunlight poured in upon it, and there was a settee invitingly placed in a corner—almost a perfect scene. Ondine could well imagine that the master of the manor could sit at work while his beloved lounged nearby, a book in her hand.

And she imagined Warwick at the desk, the fragile, gentle blond in the picture curled in the settee, her wistful smile upon her features; Warwick, looking up, offering his flashing white devilish grin in turn, golden eyes softly amber with tenderness.

"Let's go on, shall we?" she asked Mathilda.

They passed through the grand foyer and through a set of double doors. "The chapel," Mathilda announced.

Ondine had expected something quite small; it was not. It seemed to stretch forever, a hall with Norman arches, a stone floor with a length of red carpet leading to the main altar and to numerous smaller chapels along the sides, each with wondrous sculptures atop their altars.

"It's most . . . unusual," Ondine breathed.

"Memorials," Mathilda informed her. She pointed to the chapel nearest them, where an angel of mercy with gilded wings held a sword against her heart. The sculpture was stunning. "The earl's father."

"He lies in the altar?"

"Nay, he lies in the tombs beneath."

Mathilda walked forward, crossing herself and genuflecting as she paused before the main altar. A beautiful gold cross hung down from the ceiling. Ondine followed suit, then swept around to the left with Mathilda, where they came to an antechamber. It was a square room with an exit to the courtyard at the right, and an exit leaving the manor at the left. At its rear was a long wooden staircase that seemed to lead nowhere. The antechamber was small, the staircase flanked against the wall. At the upper landing there was simply nothing but paneled archways—nowhere to enter the second story, nowhere to go at all except for the narrow landing.

"The cause of our ghost," Mathilda explained with impatience, pointing at the stairway. She seemed eager to exit to the courtyard beyond. "The earl's grandfather was killed upon the battlefield, not far from here. Upon hearing the news, the lady fell against the wood. It caved in, and she joined her lord in death."

"The staircase goes nowhere?"

"The earl plans to destroy it. Once there were cubbyholes above for Chathams in hiding and runaway priests. When our sovereign Charles was on the run, he learned to love many Catholics for their support of him."

Mathilda obviously did not like the antechamber; they quickly left it to enter the courtyard. Ondine discovered where Warwick had ridden from the night before, from the archway far beneath her window.

"That is it, my lady, unless you wish to view the crypt."

"I think not," Ondine said.

"May I serve you further?"

"Nay, not now, thank you, Mathilda. But I think tomorrow that I should like to see about changing some furnishings."

"Change?" Mathilda inquired, appearing surprised and some-what stricken. "You would change Genevieve's bed—" She broke off, lowering her head.

"Genevieve is dead, Mathilda. I cannot take her place, but neither can I bring her back. And I am not her."

Mathilda nodded. "If you'll permit me to return to my duties, then, Countess . . . ?"

"Certainly, Mathilda, and I thank you again. You were very thorough and helped me greatly."

Ondine remained in the courtyard, staring up at the windows about her.

Mathilda lowered her head and started hurrying to one of the eastern archways, an entrance to the kitchen.

But she was muttering, and Ondine was sure she heard the housekeeper's words correctly. "Change! Oh, nay! I think not when the lord Chatham hears of such plans!"

Ah, Mathilda, I am sorry! Ondine thought. The lord Chatham may think himself master of this game, but there are two who must play it, and at times it is my move.

Then she felt a strange tingling at her nape; she was quite sure she was being watched. She looked up, scouring the windows, and saw high above that a drape fell back into place.

The tingle became a warm and swelling sensation that ebbed and flowed throughout her as she identified the window. It was in Warwick's chamber; it was her husband who had stared down upon her.

Chapter 7

Dinner was a surprisingly pleasant affair, certainly not because of any effort on Warwick's part, but because Justin was so good-humored. He told her tales about the first Norman lord to lay claim to the Chatham land. The Norman killed the old Saxon lord and consequently married the Saxon's daughter—a wise political move, one that Henry VII would utilize centuries later upon marrying Elizabeth of York to put a final end to the War of the Roses.

"They say our Chatham ancestor was quite a wild man," Justin told her, lavishly spreading thick roe upon a chunk of bread. "Red-haired and red-tempered, his thirty-pound battle-axe—a relic from his Viking ancestors, no doubt—eternally at his side. From such a man, it seems but natural that our arms carry the legend of the beast."

Ondine took a sip of wine, ignoring her husband's silence to enjoy her brother-in-law. " 'Tis quite an interesting history you Chathams have acquired." The wine tonight was potent, and she felt brash. Heedless of a possible rising of Warwick's wrath, Ondine determined to quiz his brother.

"The legend that intrigues me most, Justin, is that regarding your grandmother, the poor lady who lost her life upon the sealed stairway, the—uh—ghost the servants claim to haunt the manor."

Warwick emitted an impatient oath beneath his breath, and Ondine felt his eyes upon her, hot with brooding annoyance.

Justin didn't seem to notice. "Ah—that is tragic and recent history!" His eyes twinkled as he leaned toward Ondine. "I never knew my grandfather or grandmother—it all occurred before my birth. Warwick was scarce born. It was in the days right before the old king's execution, when the war was coming to an end. The battle came to our very doorsteps, the Round-heads and the Cavaliers! Our grandsire and father cut dashing figures, so we were told! Battling the enemy ... upon their own land! Alas, grandfather fell, and the news was rushed to the house. Father was of age then—and married, naturally, since my elder brother is quite legal!—but Grandmama was nowhere near aged; she was a beauty rare, so they claim, and so her picture shows! She would rush to her lord's side, disbelieving that he could have been slain. The staircase fell in, tragically. But, according to rumor—"

"Justin!" Warwick interrupted impatiently. "Must we further rumor amongst ourselves?"

Justin looked at his brother innocently. "Warwick, I air family linen only before the family! Your bride must be aware of the full story of our haunts, lest she should hear of them elsewhere!"

Warwick did not dispute him, but rose, his teeth set in a grate, and carried his wine to the mantel, as if he did not care to hear a recital of his family's past.

"They say," Justin told Ondine quietly, "that the lord's mistress did murder his wife, casting her from the staircase!"

"His mistress! What was she doing in the house?"

"Well, she lived here, of course. She was the housekeeper."

Ondine gasped. Justin chuckled.

"But you see, the mistress received her just reward, for she, too, stumbled from the stairway and died, her neck broken."

Warwick groaned from the mantel. "Rotting wood—and we are endowed with two crying haunts!" He stalked back to the table, setting his goblet down upon it hard. "Ondine—"

"My brother is quite right," Justin interrupted hastily, worried that he might have truly upset her. "You mustn't let servants' tales upset you, you know. Our parents lived out lovely lives; they've been gone but a few years now, succumbing to lung fever, rather than any curse or ghost upon us."

"I'm not upset, Justin. Merely curious. And you're quite right; I should have learned these things from my husband—or my dear new brother!—rather than the servants!"

Justin appeared a bit surprised by the low hostility in her voice, either that or the fact that Warwick had obviously told her nothing of his land or his family.

Warwick had his hands upon the back of her chair, and he pulled it out abruptly. "Milady, I believe you've heard quite enough for one evening. Bid Justin good night, my love, so that we might retire."

"Retire? 'Tis so early!"

"We're retiring," Warwick informed her, an edge of steel to his voice.

Justin laughed delightedly. "Ah, newlyweds! What can I say, Ondine? The family abounds with hungry beasts!"

Ondine flushed. Justin rose, offering her a deep bow and her husband an encouraging grin. "Remember that second sons tend to be more courteous, should you find my brother's temper too fierce to endure!"

He was gallantly teasing her, of course, yet Ondine felt Warwick's body grow stiff behind her. He did not seem so angry at the words as he was speculative. He set an arm about her, pulling her to him with a groan for Justin. " 'Tis a pity you may not yet return to court!"

Justin chuckled. "Alas, 'tis true. I am doomed to languish here, an unhappy voyeur to the lovers' tension that steams betwixt the two of you. Good night! Leave me to wallow in my wine!"

"Do not wallow too far, Brother. I'd see you in my apartment in, say, an hour. I wish to discuss the building project."

Justin sank back to his seat and raised his goblet to his brother. "An hour, then."

Into the gallery and out of Justin's sight, Ondine pursed her lips, shaking Warwick's touch from her shoulder and stamping somewhat inelegantly ahead of him. She remained silent as he opened the outer door and shut it, then turned on him angrily.

"Why is it, Lord Chatham, that you refuse to alert me to that which it seems imperative to know? Then, when others would do so, you growl like a beast, thus adding fuel to your own legends! You wish me to play your wife, yet you order me about and lock me up at night like a possession, like one of your horses or hounds—''

He watched her silently, slipping from his jacket to toss it upon the spinet bench, then interrupting, ''Madam, you are a possession, purchased upon the gallows. Well kept, I might add.''

Ondine fixed her hands upon her waist, too feverish with temper and wine to take heed of her words.

''You are the one, my lord, who took care to inform me that the gallows were not to be mentioned again.''

He moved over to the large desk, sat upon the chair behind it, and stretched his legs atop it, crossing his booted feet and wearily pressing his fingers to his temple.

''Perhaps, my love,'' he said lightly, ''I should return you to the gallows, since like the horse or hound, you seem prone to bite upon the hand that feeds you.''

''You cannot return me to the gallows, my lord. You chose to take me from there, to marry me. I no longer stand condemned.''

Dear God, Warwick mused, he was acquiring a racking headache. Between this vixen and his brother, he was sorely vexed, irate, and burning with emotion both perplexing and annoying. Damn her! Would she not let him be? Watching her at his table, smiling, laughing—no, flirting, rot her!—with his brother. Acting the grande dame with all finesse and graciousness, far too stunning and feminine in her elegant dress, her hair a soft flow of curling silk and chestnut. It was a blaze of fire and glory about her, and her eyes, so deep a blue as to bewitch the beholder with their gaze . . .

''Perhaps I cannot return you to the gallows,'' he snapped, then found control and continued negligently. ''Perhaps I can return you to the mysterious past that brought you there—to those whom you fight in your dreams!''

''What?'' The gasp came from her in a startled rush, and he frowned, his body tensing. He had really meant nothing by the words; they had just come to him. But at their utterance she turned pale, her eyes vast pools of indigo, and her slender hands, still set upon her hips, tensed with alarm.

And suddenly she appeared both very beautiful and proud and very vulnerable. Despite himself he wanted to assure her that he would do nothing to harm her; that he would never cast her to the pit of demons she so feared.

And yet . . . hadn't he brought her here, hoping that her presence would bring his own demons to the fore?

He longed to go to her, touch her, hold her with all that was chivalrous in him—and all that was not. He was reminded of her naked form that morning, so slim and yet so wondrously curved, the weight of her full young breast in his hand, the sensual beauty in the curve of her hip, the sweet taste of her lips, parting to his with surprise.

Desire shuddered through him, hot and potent. He swung his feet from the desk and turned from her, closing his eyes, clenching his teeth, and lacing his fingers together with all his strength. No! He would not think of her so; he had made her his wife, but— by God!—He would spurn her for the lying, ungrateful horse thief she had proved herself to be.

Slowly, achingly, he began to ease and reminded himself that his behavior was that of the brooding tyrant. And she was many things he admired, courageous and able to carry out his charade with far greater talent than he had ever imagined. Nor did he wish her ill; he craved to give her freedom in the end, a life that might truly have been saved. He had been irked beyond reason to find himself jealous of his own brother. And he had to be as wary and suspicious of Justin as he was of anyone else; Justin stood to gain the most if Warwick gave Chatham no heir.

He turned back to the still ashen beauty who was his wife. "My lady, my apologies," he said wearily. "I did not mean to touch upon a wound; I'd not leave you to any harm, be that harm hunger or one of human threat. It is true—my grandmother died upon a stairway, and you are my second wife. If I do not care for talk of either, it is because I grow vastly impatient with talk of ghosts."

She lowered her head; slowly color returned to her cheeks, and with a rustle of silk and scent of flowers, she impetuously came toward him, kneeling to place elegant fingers tentatively upon his leg, her eyes now deep with a searching compassion.

"My lord, I understand that you loved her dearly. I am so very sorry, sir, that words do come to dig further into your heart. But, milord, if Genevieve was . . . mad, then—"

"Mad!" He shouted the word, riddled with fury again. Mad, nay—tormented, on some mysterious behest.

His hand shot out to the desk, sweeping charts and pens and ink from atop it to the floor; then he rose so hastily that she was cast back upon her heels. He stared down at her, but barely saw her.

"Genevieve was not mad!" he informed her curtly.

Ondine rose with such a dignified elegance and glare of fury that he realized the brutality of his movement. He reached out to touch her, but she gasped and edged back, her eyes upon him as if he were half dragon, half wolf. Emitting a furious oath, he strode across the room and leaned an arm against the window frame to stare into the night. "Ondine," he breathed at last. Then, curiously, he repeated her name again. "Ondine . . ."

Then he lifted his hands, a bit impatiently, a bit helplessly. He didn't look at her. "Go to bed," he told her softly. "Again, you've my apologies."

She was still for a moment. Then he heard the rustle of the skirts once more and found himself turning in time to see her disappear, her chin held high, her movement a study in grace, as if she had, indeed, been born to her role, and not dragged into it upon fate's cast of the die.

The door closed. A shaft of staggering longing, desire like the blade of molten steel, swept through him again. Swearing with a vengeance, he strode to his desk, halfway dislodging the bottom drawer as he ripped it open, intent upon the bottle of whiskey within it.

He didn't bother seeking out a glass, but drank deeply, gasping at its solid trail of fire. He shuddered, then sank into his chair. Damn her to a thousand riots of thieves' hells!

He had to learn to keep his distance from her.

He set the bottle upon his desk, then stared ruefully at the havoc he had created around it. He stood slowly and began to retrieve his papers and quills. Justin would be along soon. And Warwick would be damned if he'd have his brother wondering at his domestic tranquility.

* * *

Alone and furious upon her bed, Ondine suddenly started, hearing the sounds of horse's hooves beneath her window again. She bolted to it and carefully edged open the drape.

It was Warwick, astride the great bay again. Both elegant and masculine in his plumed hat and black mantle, he rode the horse as though one with it.

He rode west once again, and she wondered painfully—jealously!—if he rode to another woman. Nay, she did not trust him, and he infuriated her.

He could drown, for all she cared! She swore silently. But the vow echoed with plaintive discord, and she grew irate with him—and with herself that such a maelstrom of emotions could exist within her.

At length she moved from the window, shed her finery, and donned the nightdress Lottie had left upon the bed. She doused the lamp and curled beneath the covers.

But she didn't sleep. She thought of him, thought of his touch, felt a sweet, aching yearning to know that touch again.

Fool! She reprimanded herself in fury. He was indeed the master, the master of the art of seduction. How often had he played the rake with little thought and little care? She would not fall prey, she would not. And surely she had too much pride, too much fury to do so . . .

And still, the night passed as the one before it. She did not sleep until she heard the quiet closing of the apartment doors that assured her he had returned.

The days that followed brought an uneasy peace. Lottie and she fell into a morning schedule for bathing and dining, and Ondine moved about the estate, learning its domestic management.

Warwick seemed to avoid her.

Ondine met the entire staff of servants; Mathilda arranged that all of them be gathered at the landing to pay their respects to her, and Ondine greeted them cheerfully, drawing, she hoped, their respect.

Old Tim and Young Tim were the gardeners, and she spent many hours choosing flowers for her apartments, for the family dining hall, and for the chapel, which seemed far less a place of gloom when roses were set upon the altar.

There were scores of books to read, and the spinet and the harp to play. She saw Warwick only at dinner, where he was unerringly courteous, perpetually distant. Yet Justin was always charming, and so their trio surely appeared to be a happy and normal one.

Without fail, each night would end the same. Warwick would silently walk to her chamber, she would stiffly wish him a good evening, and he would remind her to bolt her door. Out of five nights, he rode away on three; the two nights that he did not leave, she heard him pace his chamber until she fell asleep.

On her fifth day in the manor she decided to implement her determination to change her immediate surroundings. The servants obeyed her orders without question until Mathilda appeared upon the scene, dragging an irritable Warwick behind her. Mathilda wanted nothing moved. But Warwick's command came in Ondine's favor.

"The lady Ondine is mistress here now, Mathilda. She must arrange things as she desires. It makes no difference to me."

He left them. Ondine ached for Mathilda, yet she could not live with Genevieve's things. Gently she reminded the housekeeper that Genevieve was dead. Mathilda started to cry, and Ondine tried to soothe her, and—ridiculously—they wound up hugging, at peace with each other.

That night, Warwick rode away again.

Restless and angry, Ondine left her bedchamber for the music room. She sat before the harp, idly strumming tunes, and was heartily shocked to feel an unease rippling at her nape. She turned quickly and discovered that Warwick was there, silent and straight, not three feet from her, and still decked in his hat and black mantle.

He smiled sardonically when she saw him. He closed the distance between them, catching in his hand her slender fingers, paralyzed upon a string.

He held her hand between his own, brought her fingers to his cheek, then studied them once again while she remained mute, her heart thudding in sudden alarm. At last he released her, smiling once again.

She did not like the keen interest in his eyes, nor the subtly mocking tone of his voice.

"You do play especially well, milady thief."

"How—how did you get in? I locked the outer door—"

"I have keys to slip every bolt in these apartments, Countess."

"Then—"

He chuckled. "Madam, if I wished to enter a chamber in my domain, I would do so, bolts and keys or no. I was saying that I enjoyed your performance upon the harp, and I've noted, too, your prowess at the spinet."

"You have . . . heard?" she queried with a startled gasp, her heart seeming then to sink while her body flared to heat at his unnerving nearness. His scent was that of the night, fresh cool air, leather, and horses. Even when he touched her lightly, she felt the strength in his fingers.

And she remembered his more intimate touch, even while she feared his suspicions. She felt so defenseless, clad in nothing but one of "Madame's" sheer gowns, and a cloak to match that was of no greater substance.

His grin curled more wickedly into his lips. He offered her a full and courtly bow. "Aye, milady, I've heard you . . . often. And I've come to wonder how you grew so proficient at these instruments while poaching in a London forest."

Ondine lowered her lashes quickly over her eyes and set the harp forward carefully. "I've told you, milord Chatham," she murmured. "My father was a poet. We moved from place to place, and there were always music masters about."

"Ah, yes! I forget. The man was a poet. Perhaps, my love, you would be willing to entertain me with a brief recitation of his work?"

Dear God! Her thoughts went blank. She could not think of two words that rhymed or sounded remotely melodious to the ears. Her fingers knotted in her lap.

"Don't mock me!" she finally cried to him, and her emotion then was real. "His death is too near, and he was too beloved a man for me to bear such memory now!"

Her eyes were a tempest; her hair was a flame that spewed down her back. She thought to escape him, but had he reached out, he would have captured her.

He did not. He offered her only that enigmatic smile, and the gaze that told her clearly he was far more frighteningly aware of her every movement than she had ever guessed.

He moved aside, inclining his head toward her and saying softly, "Sleep well, milady."

Ondine fled past him, reaching her chamber and closing the door quickly to lean against it with a trembling gasp. By habit she slipped the bolt, then wondered why.

She closed her eyes, willing her heart to slow its frantic thunder.

And then she began to wonder if her husband was not a mythical beast, or a manner of demon, he was so able to touch her with the golden flames of his eyes, casting a fire to blaze throughout her.

She raced for her bed, pulled the covers about her, and slowly, slowly, tormented herself to exhaustion and thence to sleep.

Chapter 8

She fell asleep in misery, and restless, she began to dream.

The scene! She saw it—the hall where they walked . . .

Her father, the Duke of Rochester, out of favor with Charles for many years, since he had been against the old king's autocratic policies, though he had fought the execution vigorously.

But they'd been called to court at last. The jousters had been upon the field, the audience assembled. Charles greeted them alone; even his guards stayed far behind, laughing, for it was a lazy day!

There had been only Ondine and her father—and her stepuncle and Raoul. Walking down the hall, they were relaxed, laughing easily, as were the guards, for gaiety lay on the air. It was a great occasion.

Then a sword had flashed. Raoul pretended a fierce grapple with her father, pretending that her father had drawn the sword to slay the king! Oh, well done, well done, for it did appear that the Duke of Rochester had drawn the sword, and that Raoul had slain a heinous assassin! Blood, oh, the blood! Her father had died upon her, his last words a whisper that she must run, for— wounded, bleeding, dying—he realized too late the plot against them both. He who had trusted her uncle! And, oh, God! Her uncle would be her guardian.

The guards, screaming, ran after her.

Raoul caught her, swearing that they would take the estate and prove her complicity! They'd forged letters painstakingly in her handwriting, and they would give them to the king and court to blackmail her if she did not wed him. Raoul! Oh, God!

From somewhere, interspersed with her screams, came the shuddering sound of wood splintering. Ondine fought desperately to rise above the fog of the dream. Hands grabbed at her, and she fought them, too. Then suddenly the room was filled with light; firm arms were about her, and she heard her name whispered soothingly.

"Ondine, Ondine . . ."

Fingers smoothed her hair, wild from her thrashings, from her face. Her eyes opened fully and began to focus, and she gasped, trembling in newfound horror as she discovered her husband holding her, anxiety alive in the golden sparks of his eyes. His chest was bare, all sleek rippling muscle and crisp tawny fur against her, teasing and intimate through the fabric of her gown. His arms were so strong, both secure and frightening. What had she said? She stared at him in wretched dismay, her heart pelting, her limbs quivering.

He shook her slightly. "What was it? Why did you scream? Tell me, I must know!"

She shook her head numbly, noting the rigid set of his jaw, the taut constriction of his body. "No—nothing!"

"Did you hear something, see something—"

She pulled from him, burying her face in her hands, suddenly filled with acute embarrassment. He knew nothing, she realized. She had taken him from sleep by the terror of her dream, and he was gallant enough to search out whatever distress might have plagued her.

"I'm—I'm sorry, milord," she murmured. Her covering was gone; her gown was tangled high above her knees, and the warmth of his thighs seemed to sear her despite the material of his breeches. Nervously she attempted to right her clothing, and more uneasily still, she met his gaze. It remained troubled and suspicious as his muscled frame stayed tense. Ondine brought her knees to her chest, ruefully hugging them there.

"There was nothing," she whispered, trying to smile as the terror receded from her.

"Nothing?" She could not tell if he was relieved or dismayed.

"I believe I was dreaming again."

"Of Newgate?" His brow arched. Candlelight played upon his lean features, sending shadows upon them, and she was not sure if he believed her or not.

"And the hangman's knot," she added on a breath.

He looked about the room and at long last sighed. He stretched, flexing his shoulders, then allowing them to relax as he chuckled. He gave her a crooked smile, devilish and filled with ironic humor. "They will end eventually," he told her.

"They?"

"The dreams," he said softly, and he spoke as one who knew. And watching him, she trembled again and could not help the quiver of her lip, for she had not expected such kindness or understanding from him. He reached out, his fingers touching her lip to still its quiver, and she stared at him, fascinated by the masculine appeal of his eyes. Again he smiled ruefully. "Come here; you're still shaking," he told her.

She must have betrayed some form of alarm, for he laughed. "In the forests, my lady-thief, I do not lay claim to wounded does." With his words he rose and lifted her, taking her place upon the bed, leaning against the pillow to cradle her length comfortingly against his. She dared not move. Her hand rested against his naked chest; her cheek was brushed by its tawny hair. She inhaled his scent and it was subtle and fine, as male as the steel-hewn muscle that forged his frame. Gently he smoothed her hair, trailing his fingers along her back.

"Sleep, my beauty," he teased her gently. "For your 'beast' is standing guard."

She would never sleep, not with him touching her! Not with his heart pounding beneath her ear, the naked feel of his chest like a shield about her.

She did sleep. To the soft caress of his fingers against her nape, to his soothing whisper promising that dreams were fantasy, to his assurance that he would guard her.

* * *

In the morning he was gone. Ondine was in a reckless mood, annoyed with her own weakness, anxious to find some freedom from the manor, from her own haunting dreams, from the ghosts of Chatham.

After she had bathed and eaten, she determined to venture out to the stables. She'd not asked Warwick if she might, nor was she concerned any longer that he might question her riding ability—he'd already caught her at the spinet and the harp, and whether he truly believed her explanations, he hadn't challenged her.

That morning when she left the music room, she was startled to see Jake, seated right outside her door, complacently honing one of his master's dirks.

He stood, apparently as startled by her abrupt appearance as she was at finding him there.

"Good morning, Countess!" He greeted her with a bow.

"Good morning, Jake." She smiled because his warmth was so very real, and yet there was a curious curl to her lips because she was suddenly certain that when her husband was not watching her, Jake was. He came and went swiftly and discreetly, always at a distance so that she didn't notice.

"Do you fare well, milady?" he asked her pleasantly.

"Fine," she answered him, and added with a soft honesty that was pleasant to voice aloud, "far better than in the woods, or in my cell—or with a rope about my neck!"

Jake's eyes glimmered his pleasant humor; he brought a finger to his lip. "Shh, milady!"

She nodded, matching his humor with the sparkle of her own eyes. "By the way, Jake, I've met no ghosts. Am I supposed to do so?"

"Ghosts, milady? Why, I do not believe in them. Do you?"

"No, I don't. But I've an ache for fresh air at the moment. Is the lord Chatham about?"

Jake blinked, as if he quickly weighed her question. "I'm not sure of the earl's whereabouts, milady. Would you have me seek him out?"

"No," Ondine said sweetly. "Excuse me, Jake." She rustled

past him, giving him no clue as to her own destination, yet eager to see if he would follow her.

She left the manor by the west entrance and ambled slowly through the maze of rosebushes before heading toward the stables. She did not see Jake behind her, but she sensed that she was being followed. She pretended not to be aware.

A young lad with a pleasant freckled face cleaned a harness on a stoop before the barn. At Ondine's appearance he leapt to his feet and gave her an awkward bow. "Milady!"

She smiled. "Good day, Tad. I've a mind to ride; perhaps you might suggest a mount for me?"

"I—uh—" He appeared quite uncomfortable and red-faced. "Clinton is yonder; I'll fetch him fer ye, milady—"

Ondine waved aside the offer. "I shall find him myself, thank you, Tad."

She swept into the barn, wondering at the boy's discomfort. But as he had told her, Clinton was inside, currying a huge fine bay. He paused, the brush still upon the animal's rump, as Ondine approached. He inclined his head respectfully, yet she sensed there was a wariness about him as she drew near, and something more, a strange tension. She remembered how he had greeted Warwick upon that first night; the familiarity between them. Clinton was not an ordinary servant, and she sensed that he was a very proud man.

"Good morning, Clinton," Ondine said.

"Good morning, Countess," he said in return, the emotion in his deep forest-green eyes well shielded.

She approached the massive horse, patting the sleek satiny neck. The animal was riddled with strength and sinew, yet as graceful in appearance as any aristocrat.

"He's truly fine," Ondine said admiringly.

Clinton began to brush the horse anew. "Aye, Dragon is as fine a lad as draws breath, milady. Fine and fierce." He cast a glance her way. "He's your husband's favorite, milady. In skirmish, in play, Dragon's his choice. It's well you make his acquaintance."

"Hmmm," Ondine murmured. She rubbed the stallion's soft velvet muzzle and felt warm snorts of breath tease her fingers. "He must be magnificent to ride."

Clinton hesitated. "Magnificent, aye, milady. But spirited. No one rides him but Warwick."

She gazed swiftly at Clinton, wondering if the words were a careful rebuke or a warning. She was the lady of the manor; she could give orders and command, but not where those commands might cross her husband's desires.

But she didn't find herself resenting Clinton, merely finding that again the sense of recognition was strong, as if she knew his eyes from elsewhere, even the fine structure of his face. It was a very strange sense of familiarity, for it seemed as if she knew his eyes from one source, and the handsome structure of features from another.

"Clinton," she murmured hesitantly, frowning; then she said boldly, "why is it that I feel I know you? I look into your eyes and could swear we've met elsewhere." Her voice caught with a little reel of panic. "We have not before, have we?"

He shook his head, laughing a bit abruptly. "Countess, I've heard my eyes are my mother's, and since you see hers quite frequently, 'tis perhaps natural you feel we've met."

"Your mother's?"

He gazed her way, smiling ruefully. "Mathilda, my lady, is my mother."

"Oh." She smiled, unable to suppress a little sigh of relief. He was watching her quite curiously, so she spoke quickly, voicing the rest of her thoughts. "I assume, then, that you were born and brought up on the manor?"

He inclined his head, lashes lowering. "You assume correctly, my lady."

"And you and the earl . . . are, then, very good friends. Raised together?"

He chuckled again. "Aye, milady, you might say that." He watched her, hesitating, then shrugged and fell silent, though she had thought he would speak again.

"You remind me of my . . ." Somehow she suddenly found she could not say the word *husband.* "You remind me of Warwick," she said flatly.

He rounded the brush over the horse's rump silently, then once again he shrugged, paused, and stared at her a bit curiously. "There, again, milady, you are correct. Your husband and I are cousins."

"Cousins!" She could not help her gasp of surprise.

Clinton returned to his task. "I'm surprised that Warwick did not mention the relationship; there has never been a secret to it."

"But—"

"I am the groom, the keeper of the horses, the foreman. I'm also illegitimate. Well, not so myself, since my father did marry my mother before disappearing." He spoke flatly, with more of a sense of humor than resentment. He halted his work again, watching her with a rueful smile. "Surely you've heard the tales of our ghosts, milady?"

"Something of them," Ondine murmured, intrigued.

"Well, milady, there was a mistress accused of helping Lord Chatham's grandmother to crash through the steps to her death. Of course, the accused mistress came to her own death. That lady was my grandmother; Mathilda's mother. We are all, in our way, Chathams."

"Oh!" Ondine whispered, her mind whirling. So Mathilda was Warwick's own aunt—half aunt, out of wedlock! "It's—uh—most unusual," she stuttered, then rattled along with surprise ruling her tongue, "and you find no resentment? Nor your mother? Do you ever—"

Clinton interrupted her with pleasant laughter. "Feel that certain privileges should be mine?" He lifted his arms to embrace the air. "I've all that I need, milady. My mother was abandoned by my father; her half brother—your husband's father—took her in, and in time she was running the house. My uncle was a fine man; we were well treated. And as you suggested earlier, I did grow up with my cousins. I was lectured by their tutors, offered any chance in life I might desire. I've a fondness for Chatham and North Lambria. I've a fondness for my cousin, the earl, who is as fair and just a man as one might wish to claim as kin. I serve him through choice. Does that answer all your questions, milady?"

Ondine kept her eyes upon the horse's large and beautiful head, holding his halter and stroking his cheek as she replied. "I did not mean to quiz you so, Clinton." She smiled at him. "You use your cousins' names when you address them, and you know mine. Would you grant me a like favor?"

He gazed at her, much like Warwick, then smiled slowly. "Ondine."

She returned his grin, then asked, "Clinton, since none may touch this gorgeous beast except his master, could you suggest a mount I might ride?"

His smile faded, and he appeared acutely uncomfortable. He strode to the wall to pluck a small pick from a nail, then clutched Dragon's forefoot and began to clean his hoof, lowering his head as he spoke.

"Have you discussed riding with Warwick?"

"Have I a need to?" Ondine responded sharply.

"Aye, lady, I'm afraid you do." He dropped the horse's hoof and straightened. "I was told that you were not to go out," he said softly. "Perhaps you would care to find Warwick and discuss the matter with him. Then I should be delighted to direct you to the best mount."

She shook her head incredulously, her voice low yet shaking with intensity. "Do you mean, Clinton, that Warwick gave an order that I might not even saddle a horse to ride about the estate? Why?"

Clinton smiled ruefully, and she realized that he was looking past her. "You must ask him yourself, milady," he said quietly.

Ondine turned quickly. Warwick stood in the open doorway, wearing plain fawn breeches and a simple white shirt with wide flowing sleeves, laced low on his chest. His boots were high, hemmed and folded midthigh; he was dressed for work, quite a bit like his cousin. He looked like a buccaneer—wary and careful of stolen gems—as he strode toward them.

"Good morning, milady; Clinton."

" 'Morning, Warwick," Clinton tipped his hat to Warwick. "If you'll excuse me, I believe the lady wishes a word with you in private."

Clinton walked out, whistling. Ondine was instantly reminded that she had been certain Jake had followed her. Now she was positive. Jake had seen her at the stables and had summoned his master.

Warwick smiled and cocked his head politely, lacing his fingers behind his back. "My lady?"

Ondine returned his smile acidly. "I am not permitted to ride, milord?"

Warwick didn't reply. He came to the horse's head and whispered to Dragon affectionately, tweaking his ears, rubbing the velvet nose. The horse nuzzled him in turn.

"Warwick!" Sorely aggravated, she stamped a foot against the dirt.

His quick gaze cautioned her that he did not intend to tolerate her temper; she stood her ground.

"So you ride, too, milady?"

"Don't all horse thieves?" she snapped back.

"No," he replied flatly. "You are not permitted to ride."

She had expected the curt dismissal and a sudden rise of self-pity soared high with her temper. What, in truth, was the nature of the man? Last night he had been seductively gentle; today he was again as cold as winter's ice, cracking whips of rude command by simple inflection.

Her fingers clenched into fists, which she held rigidly at her side. "Why?"

"Because I deem it dangerous."

"Because *you* deem it dangerous? My lord Chatham. I beg to differ! I doubt that your own abilities can be any greater—"

"Than yours?" he flared harshly, turning from the horse. "Lady, my answer is no. And rest assured, I do doubt none of your abilities."

Tears started to sting her eyes; she wanted so desperately to deal with him rationally, but she was never able to do so.

"And am I a prisoner here, then?" she cried in growing fury.

He took a step toward her. "You are whatever you wish to consider yourself, Countess," he said quietly. The smile he gave her was a lopsided jeer, as if he, too, fought for restraint, yet could not resist the temptation to goad her.

"Well, I'll not endure it!" she spat back in her most arrogant tone. She thought of him riding away so many nights, doing exactly what he wished, when he wished, and then having her every movement spied upon. A madness burned inside her, with fury and confusion at all that he had cast into her lap. "I will not endure it!" she repeated. "I am not a possession, not property, not a child to be locked away! I will do as I choose and the devil may take you and your evasions!" She was so fraught that she approached him, ablaze with reckless disregard for the slow narrowing of his eyes. "I will not play your game, milord, and be your prisoner!"

"You will not command me, gutter-bitch—" he began in a low growl, but the thought was not completed.

Her fists, still clenched at her side, rose in a flurry to slam down hard against his while she cursed him. "Vile scoundrel, blackguard—"

The thud of her fists had sent him back a step; now he moved fleetly forward, his mouth grimly compressed. Ondine broke off abruptly, suddenly aware of the silent fury tightening his features. She gasped and turned to flee. There was no chance; he caught her arm, and the impetus was so great that she spun around and fell to her knees. Instantly he was down beside her, his hands upon her shoulders, forcing her to the hay-strewn ground before she could gather breath or wit to escape.

"Milady, it seems we must always tussle in barns!" he growled, leaning over her, the warm pressure of his chest keeping her as still as the power of his hands. "But then, perhaps that is natural. Where else do thieves and poachers and whores frolic but in the hay!"

"Bastard!" she hissed, trembling beneath him, longing to flay him with her nails.

And then she suddenly started to tremble, realizing his power and her own misery. He was so taut about her that she feared she had truly pushed him to his limits of control.

He drew away from her quickly, rolling to his back upon the floor. She remained dead still, terrified that her smallest movement would bring a return of his iron hold.

He cast his arm over his forehead and stared up at the ceiling, speaking with a startling irony.

"I begin to see why men beat their wives!" He came to his side on an elbow, watching her. "Perhaps that is my answer. We've buggy whips aplenty here—"

"You wouldn't!" Ondine gasped, frantic to escape, yet powerless in his presence. She couldn't tell at all from his musing tone if he was serious.

"Nay, I wouldn't," he decided, shaking his head. "Whips are nasty things. They mark up the flesh. The servants would know; the neighbors might talk."

"Neighbors!"

"Aye," he nodded, as if they agreed upon a particular point. "Nay, a whip is no good. And actually, I prefer the contact of the hand . . ." He lifted his left hand, flexed and unflexed his long strong fingers, and studied it thoughtfully. "Aye . . . the hand!"

He stared at her again, gold sparks brilliantly alive within his eyes. And then quite suddenly that hand he had so studied was at the base of her back, pulling her form close to his upon the ground. Instinctively she placed her fingers upon his chest in an effort to ward him off; he didn't appear to notice. His palm made little circles on her spine, then as he smiled quite pleasantly his hand moved lower, firmly caressing the rounded curve of her derriere with an insistence from which she could not escape.

"Ah, yes, milady! The hand . . . when strongly leveled against the flesh of the rump—the bare rump, that is—has long been known as a most satisfactory chastisement!"

She was aware that she stared at him with wide-eyed astonishment, stunned to silence. He was not serious! But yet he might well be, for though his smile was so mockingly pleasant, she could feel the wired tension in almost every muscle of his body.

She lowered her eyes quickly, leaving him to stare at the top of her head, and abruptly she changed her tone of voice to a soft one.

"Milord, I do not mean to rail against you. I am sorry—Nay! I am not sorry that I wish the freedom to ride, only that I attacked you! You must—"

His deep rumble of laughter cut her off. "Oh, milady! You are not in the least sorry that you attacked me! You are only sorry that you haven't the strength to take a buggy whip to me!"

Her eyes flashed back to his with renewed anger, but a warning tap upon her rear and a taunting "Careful, milady!" kept her from the words she meant to voice.

"This is not fair!" she cried in fuming frustration.

"What is not fair?" he demanded. "You have your life, lady. I have a wife. A wife who swore to obey, albeit to save her life. But the vow remains, milady, and it is one that I warn you now—for the last time—that you will honor."

"Perhaps I would honor it with more resolve if you would deign to tell me those things I learn from others! As in Mathilda being your aunt; Clinton your cousin!''

He shrugged, yet it was as if a wary shield fell over his eyes. ''Clinton, Justin, and I bear a resemblance. I am quite surprised you had to be told.''

''Had to be told! Damn you, Warwick! You should have told me, and you know it!'' She pressed more strenuously against his chest, a grunt of effort escaping her. He pulled her closer, shaking his head.

''Nay, lady, you will stay close. Seems that I may only drag assurance from your lips when I have you locked upon the earth of a stable!''

Her teeth clenched, she renewed her struggle. Again he chuckled deeply and swiftly changed his hold, straddling over her and lacing his fingers quickly within hers to bring them uselessly to the side of her head. ''Let's finish this here and now,'' he said sharply as she began to sputter again. ''I do not intend to make you a prisoner. You may not ride alone, because I do not know what danger you might meet in your travels. There are beasts in the forests, madam, boars and wolves and Lord Hardgrave, and I'd not have you come upon any of the three. If you wish to ride, you've only to let me know in the morning, and I shall be happy to accompany you. As to Clinton and Mathilda, it is not something I purposely withheld, but something I seldom ponder, since they are both here by choice, have always been here by choice, and have taken even their positions here by choice. Now, what else have you found here to disturb you?''

She lifted her chin, desperately trying to control her resentment. ''You!''

''Me?'' he queried, hiking a brow. ''My lady, I assure you, I do my best to leave you be! Other than that, I am quite sorry. I am the man who married you, don't you recall. I am not part of the bargain, but the bargain itself. And speaking of such, milady, you do nothing to uphold your end of this arrangement! That is a matter which can always be rectified.''

She tried to ignore the pressure of his thighs about her, the taunt in his eyes and tone. ''You spy on me!'' she accused him. ''You follow me, and watch me—''

''I beg to differ, madam. I am too busy with important matters.''

Ondine laughed bitterly. "Ah, yes! Important affairs! You look to your affairs, then, milord, and Jake is ordered to spy on me! I am locked away at the beginning of the evening, while night after night you ride away in total freedom!"

He grinned, releasing her wrists, balancing his weight on his own haunches as he crossed his arms over his chest. "Madam! Do my absences disturb you, then?"

"Nay—they elate me!" Ondine protested vehemently. She brought her wrists to her chest, rubbing them nervously and praying that he would rise from her.

He shrugged, but his tone hardened as he rose, reaching a hand down to her, which she saw no recourse but to accept. "Milady, I fear you will not find elation much longer. I have received a summons from Charles that I find most convenient. We travel to court in a matter of days."

"What?" It seemed suddenly that the stable spun around her; that mist filled the air. She could not go to court!

"We're going to court!" Warwick repeated, exasperated. "And I've no intent to cause questions there. I shall be beyond your door for all the long hours of every night." He frowned, wondering how her skin had gone from fiery rose to a palor so ashen as to be alarming.

"I have no wish to go to court. Go alone! Indiscretion is quite fashionable this season. You'll be free each and every night to pursue whom you wish. I—"

"You, my lady, are coming with me."

"No! I will not go!" She jerked her wrist from his, backing away from him against the wooden wall. "I am not going!"

He threw up his hands and seemed to growl. "I have had it with this!" Long, angry strides brought him to her; he flattened a hand against the planking beside her head. "Ondine, hear me well. You will accompany me. In the carriage, or tied atop it, I care not. Able to sit—or so ragged and raw of flesh upon the rump that you dare not!"

Chapter 9

Ondine sent Lottie to the dining room with a message that she was indisposed and would not be joining Warwick and Justin for dinner.

She did have a headache, a raging headache. She had no doubt that Warwick meant his words. He would bring her with him, one way or another. She had spent the afternoon pondering escape from the manor; that, too, seemed impossible. She was constantly watched. She couldn't even get on a horse without Warwick appearing.

A rap upon her door startled her and reminded her that if she was "indisposed," she shouldn't be caught nervously pacing the room, fully clothed. She bit her lower lip, took a deep breath, and called out a weak "Yes?"

"Milady, 'tis Mathilda. I've brought tea and broth."

"Oh, thank you, Mathilda. I—I'm not hungry."

"Nay, milady! I will not leave till you've taken something!" Mathilda returned with concern.

Ondine sighed. Mathilda had sounded so fiercely determined— and worried. She felt guilty. She hesitated a second longer, then called out, "A moment . . ."

In another few seconds she had shed her clothing and donned

a nightgown. She quickly ripped apart the bed Lottie had so meticulously straightened. Kicking her clothes aside and nervously composing herself, she came to the door, hoping she looked ill.

"Oh, Lady Chatham! You shouldn't be out of bed in bare feet!" Mathilda chastised her. "You must get back beneath the covers . . ."

"I will, Mathilda. Thank you for the tea."

"I'll not leave until I see you warm and fed, milady," Mathilda fretted, standing staunchly at the door with the tray in her hand.

Ondine lowered her head as another ripple of guilt touched her. Mathilda was really distressed. She had lost one beloved mistress; perhaps it was natural that she grow nervous over the "illness" of the next.

"I shall crawl back into bed right now, Mathilda. And I'm very sorry to have upset you; it's nothing. A slight indisposition of the stomach, that is all. I shall surely be fine in the morning."

Mathilda set the tea tray on the dresser, walked over to the bed, and fluffed the pillow. "You can never be too careful . . ."

She smiled wanly at Ondine. "Come, now, let me take care of you, I implore you, lady."

Ondine crawled back into the bed. Mathilda smoothed the covers over her with a motherly concern. "Now, if you sit so, I can put the tray upon your lap."

Ondine obliged her, touched by her tender care. She found herself watching Mathilda curiously, then saying gently, "My name is Ondine. I do wish you would use it. I—understand that you are a Chatham, too, Mathilda."

Mathilda glanced at her, surprised and smiling. "You didn't know it all along?"

Ondine shook her head, and Mathilda sat beside her on the bed, dropping a cube of sugar into Ondine's tea. She stirred it and handed it to her, smiling again. "You will understand why I am so concerned for your health. The child will be my own blood, you see."

Ondine gasped, scalding her throat on the tea, then choking.

"Oh, dear!" Mathilda leapt to her feet and patted her back.

"The . . . child?" Ondine managed to sputter.

"Oh, dear . . . dear," Mathilda muttered, wringing her hands a little helplessly, then she sighed. "Perhaps you did not wish him to say anything yet? But men are like that, milady! Ever so proud of themselves over an heir. Like strutting peacocks.'' She smiled with a knowing empathy. ''Many women think it unlucky to make announcements early, but you mustn't feel so. And you mustn't be angry with him. He appeared so impatient when your message was brought to the dining table, but then he sighed and started to smile—what a ravishly wicked, pleased smile, but then you do know the earl!—and said it was surely natural, since in the early stages carrying a child did cause a woman discomfort.''

The man was insane! Ondine thought, and barely kept herself from informing Mathilda. Insane—and cruel, to instigate such a falsehood. Mathilda seemed to yearn for the child with a tender and aching excitement.

She lowered her eyes quickly as her heart began to pound. Why the lie? Why was she constantly watched? What in God's name was going on? Was the Earl of North Lambria mad as a rabid hare?

Her temper began to soar. Damn him! He was at it again—throwing these absurd surprises her way without the slightest warning. Master of play, indeed! It would serve him right if she were to tell Mathilda that the earl was either crazy or sadly mistaken; there was no child.

''Milady—Ondine, are you quite all right? Oh, I haven't made you feel worse with my rattling tongue, have I?''

Ondine shook her head and offered her a smile that was truly sickly. ''Nay, Mathilda. I was just taken a bit by my lord's . . . announcement. I—I am not that far along. I had thought we might wish to . . . be absolutely certain.''

''Oh!'' Mathilda chuckled happily, taking her place by Ondine's side once again. ''A woman knows these things, I think!''

''You're pleased?''

''Aye, that I am! A wee babe about the manse again! I beg you, take the greatest care! But then you're so young and healthy. Not at all like—'' Mathilda broke off unhappily.

Ondine stretched out a hand to gently encircle her wrist. ''Genevieve?''

Mathilda's lip trembled. ''Aye, like Genevieve.''

''Oh, Mathilda! You mustn't worry so. I will be fine; truly I will.''

Mathilda nodded. Ondine looked searchingly into her eyes and thought that she must have been very beautiful once.

And then Mathilda flushed, appearing a little embarrassed by her show of emotion. "Well, now, you must eat the broth! For the wee one! And . . ."

"What is it, Mathilda?"

"If you should ever need anything, you must call upon me! Anything, at any hour!"

"Thank you, Mathilda."

"I'm not leaving until you eat the broth."

Ondine obligingly ate the broth and drank the tea. Mathilda moved about the room, collecting Ondine's clothing to hang in the bath closet. Then, seeing that her offering was fully consumed, she smiled with approval and took the tray.

"Rest now!"

"I will, I promise."

Still happily smiling, Mathilda strode to the door with her tray, but Ondine called to her, affecting a bright curiosity before she could exit.

"Mathilda, who was about when milord Chatham made his announcement? Is . . . everyone aware of my—condition?"

"Aye! Justin was there, and a number of the servants. Oh, and Clinton had come in! And, of course, they're both so pleased. Justin and my Clinton, I mean. Justin was himself, laughing and telling his brother he was a rake to waste no moment's time. He said he was green with envy—Justin is quite taken with you, you know."

Ondine kept trying to smile. "Is he? Did he say anything else, or did Warwick?"

"Ah, well . . ." Mathilda suddenly looked uneasy.

"Mathilda! Please?" Ondine wheedled.

"Nothing, really."

"Tell me! I shan't sleep a wink if you don't!"

Mathilda sighed, resting the tray upon her hip. "Well, Justin said that he couldn't wait for the lady Anne to hear the news."

"The lady Anne?"

"His old flame at court . . . Oh! You never met her? I had assumed you met there."

"I didn't meet the lady Anne," Ondine replied evasively, a hot needling of temper pricking at her again.

"Old flames are those that are extinguished, you must remember," Mathilda assured her wisely. "And your husband responded that he was quite anxious for Lady Anne to hear the news, so surely; he wishes her to know how quite settled he is and happily so! And he added that he hoped Lord Hardgrave also learned quickly that there was to be an heir to North Lambria soon!"

Ondine leaned up on her elbows. "Who is this Lord Hardgrave? Warwick mentions him occasionally—and not with pleasure."

"A neighbor, lower in title and stature than Warwick, and hostile for it. Ah . . . admittedly, Warwick, too, is hostile. They met at age three, and even then they were enemies." She stopped speaking, glancing at Ondine with a wary sigh. "There—now I have answered all your questions, even those I probably should not have! You promised to rest."

"Oh, I will," Ondine said, and she forced a sweet and cheerful smile to her lips.

She waited until she heard Mathilda's footsteps pass through the bath, through Warwick's chamber, and the music room. When a soft and distant click assured her that all doors to the apartment were closed and that she was quite alone, she threw the covers off the bed, leapt up, and slammed furiously from her chamber. In Warwick's room she paused, found his brush upon his dresser, and threw it wildly against the wall. "Damn you, knave, what is the game you play?" she whispered vehemently.

She stalked out to the music chamber and sat at his desk, determined to assault him with demands the moment he entered. She sat, barely restraining herself from shredding the chair's brocade with her nails.

And then it occurred to her quite suddenly that she might have at last found her bargaining power. She could tell him that if he forced her to court, she would refute his lie—and inform his household that she was certainly not expecting a child.

Excitement and relief joined with her anger so that she was anxious to see him. She jumped back to her feet and began pacing the room. Again and again, nervous energy drove her back and forth like a caged tiger.

But she began to worry—what if he was a little mad and

considered it all a joke? What if he laughed and told her that he didn't care what she told anyone?

That worry caused her to pause at a window and stare out at the night, fear streaking through her in icy shafts. Should she tell him that she could not go to court because she would be wrested from him, dragged into prison, and tried as a traitor?

No! She could not let it happen. There would be no more such scandal and lie cast upon the family name! They would never prove her a traitor, for she would never let them!

And how was she going to stop them?

She realized bleakly that she could not go with Warwick. He was the king's most loyal servant and friend. She was nothing but a horse thief he had taken from the gallows for whatever absurd reason.

"Oh, damn you, you rogue bastard, a thousand times over!" she hissed, slamming a fist against the wall. Where was he? The hour grew later . . .

In a flurry she gritted her teeth and rushed to the hallway door, wrenching it open.

Jake sat there, apparently having been asleep until her appearance. He was leaning against the wall and quickly lifted the brim of his hat from over his eyes, almost knocking over the chair in his speed to rise and confront her.

"Milady?" he mumbled sheepishly, startled at the sight of her in her nightgown, with bare feet, her hair a web of gleaming, fire-lit disarray, her eyes teal with a passionate wrath. "Can I get you something? May I—"

"Where is he, Jake?"

"My lord Chatham?"

"Aye—your lord Chatham!" Ondine retorted, crossing her arms over her chest. "Jake, don't play games with me! Where is he?"

"He's . . . er, out."

"Out where?"

"I don't know, milady."

"You're a liar, Jake!"

He looked guilty, but also determined. Ondine sighed with frustration, aware that if she held a knife to his throat, he wouldn't betray Warwick.

"All right, Jake. When is he coming back?"

Jake shrugged, scratching his head uncomfortably, then cramming his hat back atop it. He lowered his head.

"You might wish to speak with him in the morning, milady."

"In the morning!"

"He could be . . . late."

She couldn't contain a strangled oath of fury and took a menacing step toward Jake. "What is going on here, Jake? Why is he doing all this to me? You know, don't you?"

"Doing—what?" Jake appeared extremely uncomfortable, but as she had noted before, he was still determined to keep his master's secrets, probably unto death. "Girl!" he said softly. "You have your life! You've clothing, food, and a good home!" He said the words as if he pleaded with her. "Trust him!"

"Trust him!" she wailed, and then she realized that she was venting her temper upon a man who had done her no wrong—who had been as gentle to her when she stood filthy, a rope about her neck, as he was now that she had become "milady."

"Oh, Jake! I am so sorry!" she murmured in atonement. "Truly, I know that you cannot betray him; I did not mean to rail at you. I—" She paused, drawing a deep breath. "I am quite grateful to be alive. I just hope I don't go mad!"

"Oh, lady!" Jake said miserably. "There is naught that I can tell you." He lifted his hand. "Except, trust him. Trust in me, my lady!"

She tried to smile at Jake and failed. On impulse, she clutched his wizened face and kissed his cheek, then hurried back inside.

"Bolt the doors!" he called to her.

She hesitated, then did so.

She turned around and started at the music chamber, then her shoulders slumped with desolation and exhaustion. Her vigil had been a lost labor from the start. A fool's quest. No doubt the proud male was off testing his prowess elsewhere!

Ondine returned to her own chamber, wondering again why it so infuriated her that he should disappear so many nights. And she dared not wonder too closely, for the answers came to her, and they were answers she detested.

Each day she had known him, each time he had touched her, he had fascinated her further. She was haunted by his face, the fine structure of bone, the sensuous curl of his lip, the taunting, brilliant flecks of gold that ruled his amber eyes. She knew the look and feel of his hands—the long fingers, not soft, but carelessly callused, for they were a man's hands. And it was not so much her mind, but her body, haunted by memory of the feel of him, hard as stone, but rippling with heat and life. She didn't know quite what she wanted—because, in truth, his mockery and his wit did rub her sorely!—but there was his gentle side . . . a kindness in him. She had known that side when he had shielded her from a view of the gallows, the painful death of friends.

Ah, yes! she thought miserably. She wanted him, but not as the rogue who callously played the stakes of those cast into the heat of the court. Not that he was interested in being even that passionate rogue with her! She wanted the man who had loved Genevieve. She wanted to see him laughing easily, telling her that she was cherished and beloved, kissing her hand, kissing her lips with longing—and love.

But she was a gallows' bride, a horse thief. A possession.

Angry, frustrated, and hurt in that new and aching way that left the heart and flesh alive with longing, Ondine swore out a last oath and determined to go to sleep. Tomorrow she would blackmail him, since he forced the issue.

Despite her determination, she lay awake a long while. When she did at last sleep, that sleep was fraught with dreams of her cousin, Raoul. She saw his eyes, dark and handsome; his face too gaunt, his lips too narrow and dissatisfied. He had been sullen as a child when she bested him, triumphant when he rose the leader. She had never thought to hate Raoul; he had been a companion, like any other, with virtues and faults. She had never sensed his envy of her, nor his father's simmering jealousy. Surely it was not Raoul who had devised such a plan to strike upon his stepuncle; it had been his father, longing all those years for title and property never to be his.

But it was her cousin she saw in her dreams: holding her hand too long as they journeyed to Charles's court; leaning with amused disdain when she wearily repulsed him. How many times must he be told that they were friends? She could never love him. He had not been angry then . . . merely triumphant. But he had known, as she had not, that he would be the victor; her father the traitor—she totally at his mercy.

Except that she had fled . . .

His face continued to spin before her. Then it slowly took on another look. Dark eyes became Justin Chatham's laughing green. Dark hair took on a hue of gold, and in her sleep Ondine shivered, and she wondered why she should see gallant Justin where she had seen Raoul. Then it was no longer Justin who laughed at her, but Clinton, child of the woman who had been the product of illicit Chatham love.

Chatham. It was her husband then who laughed at her—Warwick, who never doubted his power. Yet his eyes warmed to amber. Suddenly the men were around her, coming toward her, brandishing swords. She knew, as one knew in dreams, that some wanted to save her, that one meant to slay her. Yet she did know which way to run.

She awoke, not screaming, but trembling uneasily. She knew it had been a dream, and she was annoyed that she could not prevent herself from entering these nightmare realms.

"Oh, may they all rot!" she whispered aloud impatiently. She hesitated. "Especially my lord Warwick Chatham!"

She lay silent then, watching the moonbeams playing about her chamber and wondering if she was forced to meet Charles, whether she might find a way to see him alone first and lay her case at his feet, pleading that he give her a chance to prove her innocence. The king was known to be just, to despise violence, especially that violence of death to a woman.

It would be her last recourse. She would do battle against her husband first! Fierce battle, for though she was dearly grateful for her life, he did not now own her!

While her thoughts traveled thus in the darkened room, with only the moonbeams to cast a veiled light, she first heard the whisper.

It was soft, so soft she thought she might have imagined it at first. It carried on the breeze, sexless and plaintive. So very sad.

"Ondine . . ."

She tensed in bed and waited, and it came again.

"Ondine . . . Ondine . . . Ondine. Come to me, for I am cold and lonely. Ondine . . ."

It was not her imagination!

She sprang from the bed, but could see nothing in the darkness. "Who are you? Where are you?" she called out softly.

"Ondine . . ." Only her name came to her faintly, fading wistfully away.

She could see nothing but shapes and shadows in the soft glow of the moon. With shaking fingers she quickly lit a lamp, raising it high. "Please—who are you? Where are you?"

There was no response, except for a rustle of the breeze.

Perplexed, she searched the room studiously, pulling back drapes, searching the latrine, and even opening chests and drawers. She hurried to the window and looked out. There was no one below, nor was there sign of anyone on the slender ledge that ran along the second floor eave.

Frustrated, she sat upon her bed again, then in fury she rose and slammed through to the music room. She rummaged until she found whiskey in Warwick's drawers. Pouring herself a dram, she sat back in his chair, determined that she would confront him— even if she waited all night.

Coming in near dawn, Warwick was quite startled to find her there, a glass in her hand, hair a crest of silken flame about the white lace of her gown, toes resting atop his desk as she stretched in casual rebellion from his chair to his desk.

Her eyes, he noted, were blue fire, and her righteous gaze fell upon him.

Warily he kept his features rigid, bracing himself against the door as he watched her, removing his gauntlets.

"Well," he said quietly, "to what, madam, do I owe the honor of your wakeful presence at this hour of the night?"

She didn't answer right away, but continued to study him with her sea-fire eyes. Irritated to feel himself on the defensive, he strode into the room, casting his gloves upon the desk before her.

She lifted her glass to him. "Milord, I think it is time we had a discussion."

"Oh?" He arched a cautionary brow to her, his eyes narrowing in warning.

"Aye, milord," she replied coolly, contempt pointedly marking her use of the title. Warwick sat upon the edge of his desk, pretending little interest in her words as he drew off a high boot.

"Talk, then, milady."

She took a sip of the whiskey, and he was glad to see it, for in that action he noted her nervousness and sighed inwardly, certain that no matter what her bravado, he would disarm her.

But then her eyes came to his again, blue flames richly edged in darkest lashes that added to their searing intensity and beauty. "I was congratulated this evening upon a child that does not exist. Perhaps it would not trouble you too greatly to explain the lie?"

Warwick reached for the whiskey bottle, returning her stare and swallowing a long draft. He set the bottle down carefully. "What was your response?"

She laughed dryly. "Oh, I did not refute your story, milord." Her lovely lashes tightened about her eyes. "Not yet!"

"Oh—is that a threat, my love?" he queried with a pleasant yet deadly tone.

"Aye, it is," she replied with a contemptuous smile. "You see, milord, you've never explained the game. Therefore, I play at a disadvantage. She straightened, pulling her bare toes from the desk to hide them beneath her on the chair. "It is a cold game, milord. One in which I remain in the dark. I challenge you, I receive but further orders. I am left, then, to create a few of my own rules. And this, then, is one of them. I'll smile sweetly to each lie I hear. I'll cheerfully stand behind your ever absurdity. And in return . . . I stay here. I do not go to court."

He leaned against the desk suddenly, stroking the line of her upturned chin, bitterly returning a twisted smile. "Poaching, thievery, *blackmail!* My, what talents you have amassed at such a tender age, my love!"

"I begin to think you married me for such talents, Warwick Chatham," she returned, unnerved by his touch. He released her and slid smoothly from the desk. He walked behind her to rest his hands upon the top of her head, and cast her into further tumult as he stroked his fingers softly, like a night breeze, through her hair.

"I don't think, milady"—he murmured the last mockingly, bending close to whisper by her ear and tease her throat with the warmth of his breath—"that you will deny anything. The lie is one I so thoroughly wished stressed that I would even be willing to force it into truth."

Ondine closed her eyes, gritting her teeth so as not to shiver or cry out at the ruthless nature of his words. Oh, that there were caring in them! But there was not; only the whipcrack of the master giving orders.

He dropped his hand from her and walked to the mantel.

"Don't ever threaten me, Ondine," he said flatly.

"Don't threaten you!" Her voice rose in fury and she leapt from the chair, despairing and wild from her failure. "Don't threaten you! Milord, there need be no threats! You, sir, should be most grateful that shock alone did not keep me from calling you a liar! By God, you will tell me what goes on here! Not only am I constantly taken off guard by your evasions and deceptions, but I am annoyed at sleep by pranksters!"

"What?" The question was a sharp explosion. He spun to her, his body rigid, his eyes like piercing fires, so intense that she stepped back, her rampantly pounding heart rendering her speechless.

He was instantly across the room to her, his stride so furious that she cried out as his fingers bit into her shoulders. "What?" he insisted, eyes ablaze. "Tell me what you speak of!"

"You're hurting me—" she gasped, her teeth chattering, her head falling back.

His hold eased; he did not release her. "Tell me!"

"Tonight . . . an hour ago, as I lay in bed, someone whispered to me."

"You imagined it?" He asked the question carefully, so intently that she didn't think he doubted her at all.

"Nay! I do not imagine things!"

"What was said?"

"My name."

"And what else?"

"I don't remember—"

"You must!"

"I—I think it was something like, 'I am cold and lonely. Come to me.' "

He released her, turned and strode quickly through his own chamber and the bath to hers. Ondine followed him. As she had done, he searched it thoroughly and looked beyond the window. And as she had done, he at last sat on the foot of the bed and shook his head, pressing his temples between his palms. Then he looked up suddenly, as if remembering that she was there. An elusive shield seemed to form over his eyes.

"You must have imagined it."

"I did not!"

He shrugged and lifted his hands to her. "As you can see, there is nothing."

She laughed dryly. "My lord Chatham, I am all that you say— horse thief, poacher, blackmailer; I survived forests and prisons— but I do not imagine things."

"Be that as it may . . ." He rose and approached her slowly, pausing before her. "Then you must listen again, mustn't you, lady? And if you hear the whisperer again, call me then. Immediately. Do you understand?"

"Oh, aye, sir!" she responded tartly. "Another order, and, yes, orders must be obeyed!"

His fingers closed about her arms, and his face lowered to hers. "Ondine! You must cease to fight me! Trust in me . . . and in the end I will see that you are free and cared for for the duration of your natural life!"

She lowered her head, trembling. Oh, it was true! He was using her for something, and intended only to discard her! She didn't want him touching her, she didn't want him near her, she didn't want to ache and long for what he would never give . . .

She wrenched from his hold, from the vibrant fever of his body against hers, and stood apart from him, trembling.

" 'Twill be hard to warn you, sir, when you are seldom about."

"I will be here," he told her. "And you will leave your chamber door open, as will I. You need only say my name, and I will hear you."

She stood mutely, staring down at the floor. He came to her again, capturing her arm, pulling her to him. When she would have scathingly upbraided him, she fell silent instead, startled by the small slant of a smile, by the gentle amber lights in his eyes. "Ondine . . ." he murmured, pulling her against him. "The name comes from myth and magic. She was, as surely you know, a mermaid. A beautiful seductress of fantasy who enwebbed the heart of a man and, through marriage to him, gained mortal life.

And you have, my beauty, gained life . . . trust me. I will preserve it for you, by my own, if need be, I swear it!''

Stunned and shaken by the heated depth of his emotion, she could do no more than meet his eyes, and cherish the tender smile he gave her. She nodded slowly.

And to her further surprise and fascination, he lifted her into his arms, carrying her fleetly to her bed, where he placed her upon it, pausing still to fan her hair about the pillow with a fascination of his own.

Then he straightened and said hoarsely, ''You are a magical beauty, Ondine.''

His eyes closed; he clenched his teeth and a small groan escaped him. His body stiffened, and when he gazed at her again, he was once more the cold and rugged man who had so coolly ordered her release from the gallows.

''Good night,'' he said brusquely. ''And do not forget that in three days time we head for London.''

''I—I can't go!'' she pleaded in a whisper, a plea that he ignored with an oath of impatience.

''We'll not go through this again! Try to escape and I shall drag you back. Defy me when I seek to leave, and I will haul you, bound and screaming if I must, to the carriage. Have no doubts, madam, that it will be exactly as I say!''

He continued to stare at her. She could find no voice to protest; no magic thought came to her mind. She wanted to lash out at him, but she was still cast beneath his spell.

He turned and walked through the door. He did not close it, and she trembled, painfully aware that nothing but the night breezes lay between them, hating him . . .

Hating herself . . . for loving him.

PART II

The Countess of North Lambria The Game Is Played

Chapter 10

Three days time . . .

Ondine spent those three days in a torment of anxiety and fear. She did not even think of the whisperer—of her name called to her in the night. She was too preoccupied with the desperate search to find a way to avoid King Charles's court.

Warwick was determined; when he was determined, he wasn't to be crossed. There was no help.

She could not escape. Warwick did not leave the manor at nights; he remained in the music chamber while she tossed and turned in her own. It seemed he carefully avoided her during the day, as if he would avoid a headache. During the evening meal, in Justin's presence, he was absolutely charming. Justin liked to tease about the child, and, thought Ondine, surely a lord was supposed to be caring and tender to the lady who carried his child.

On these occasions Ondine gritted her teeth and did not refute the lie.

Mathilda was so solicitous of her that Ondine wished she might crawl into a dark hole each time she saw the housekeeper. How could Warwick be so cruel! Mathilda's hopes were destined to be dashed.

Even Clinton applauded her on the apparent speed with which

she set about to provide Chatham an heir. But at least Clinton tended to be a quiet, straightforward man, and though Ondine knew he would not let her on a horse, she spent a great deal of her time in the stables, stroking the animals, fervently wishing and dreaming that she might find a way to steal one and disappear. As the first day passed she would tell herself that she had time to plan an escape. But as the second day came and went she began to realize that she would never, never have an opportunity to get away. Jake, though quite unobtrusively, followed her constantly. She practically tripped over Mathilda or Lottie anytime she attempted to move. It was hopeless.

Mathilda helped her pack her trunks, with only the best apparel. Charles maintained an elegant court, one filled with artists and poets, women dressed beautifully in designs inspired by the latest fashion dolls from France. She simply must pack her very best— not that Mathilda thought it mattered a whit. With a sniff she informed Ondine, "You've natural youth and the most exquisite beauty! You'll outshine them all! Ah, but it's fascinating. I do love it!"

"You've been?" Ondine wondered.

"Ah, yes! I accompanied . . ."

"Genevieve," Ondine finished for her, and she found herself giving Mathilda a quick hug.

Mathilda wiped a tear from her cheek, then flashed a bright smile. "Ah, but I would love to see you there! To take haughty-tottie Lady Anne down a peg!"

Ondine smiled in return—stiffly. Always she endured the most horrible mixture of emotions! The logical: she couldn't go to court! And the dreadfully illogical: the searing pain of jealousy. It seemed most likely that Lady Anne wouldn't be taken down a peg at all, for she would have her lover in her arms once more.

When Mathilda left her, Ondine threw her pillow viciously across the room. One more night . . . they were due to leave at dawn, and she simply could not go. For her life, she could not go.

And Warwick! Oh, the atrocious nerve of the man, that he should think to drag her—unwilling!—with him to the place of his old immoral haunts. He was welcome to his whore, but not when he shackled her along!

But, no . . . he was not welcome to her! No matter how she hated the feelings, they were there. Ondine cared. She was falling in love with him—loving him almost as passionately as she hated him.

At dinner she was charming, laughing with Justin, quite pleased to flirt with him. Warwick was exceptionally quiet, yet his eyes were always on her, and she knew that he was as wary and tense as she. She tried to disarm him, chatting ridiculously about the gowns she would bring and how dearly she would love to get her hands on the newest fashion dolls. She had barely consumed half the food on her plate before Warwick was standing behind her chair, pulling it from the table.

"Warwick—" Her voice was tinged with annoyance, since she had been quite taken by surprise.

"My love!" he returned smoothly, bending near so that his breath touched her cheek, the underlying danger of his words piercingly clear to her. "We're to leave with the sun, and in such case, I'd have you not lose sleep this night."

Oh, how she longed—just once!—to turn about and soundly box his ears! To destroy his charade. To wound him . . . as he wounded her!

She lowered her head quickly. This was not the time to argue, not if she wished to carry out her plans, her last desperate chance for escape, before it was too late.

She stood quite meekly. Justin was up, kissing her hand, giving her a courtly and courteous bow.

"Sweet sister, this rogue of a brother of mine constantly sweeps you away. Alas, that I could not have seen you first!"

"Umm, alas," Warwick murmured dryly. "Good night, Brother."

Justin laughed. "Good night!"

Beyond a doubt, I am a prisoner! Ondine thought woefully as Warwick led her along the hall. His prisoner . . . and one of my own making. For even as she moved, she shrank from what she had devised. To leave him . . .

Leave the touch like fire upon her. The warmth of his body, close to hers. A mockery, yes. Yet these small crumbs were hers. His hand upon her wrist. His breath, his voice, his eyes. His occasional tenderness, and his passion when he swore to protect her. She closed her eyes tightly as they walked. Fool! He cared nothing for her—she was here to be used.

He opened the door. She started to walk through the music chamber, straight for her own.

"Ondine!"

Her heart faltered, and she paused, turning back. She felt his stare, wary, just as it had been at dinner. He smiled, crossing his arms over his chest, leaning nonchalantly against the spinet.

"Milord?"

"We do leave in the morning."

"Aye, milord."

"My love," he said softly, coming toward her, smiling a warning as he gently stroked her cheek, "I remember your protests were most vehement—so much so that I cannot help but doubt this sudden meekness of yours."

She lowered her eyes and stepped back, keeping her head bowed as she lifted her hands helplessly.

"You have said that I shall go, walking or dragged. I prefer to walk. If you'll pardon me, I am quite tired, and we do leave early."

She turned quickly and fled, not daring to see if he had believed her performance.

In her own chamber she discarded nothing but her shoes and quickly scrambled beneath the covers on her bed. How long would she have to wait? she wondered bleakly. Until she was absolutely certain that he slept?

It was her only hope—to escape their chamber while he slept, to reach the stables when Clinton was absent and steal a horse. And even then she could only pray that Jake did not sleep at the door, since he needn't stand guard when his master was doing so.

Oh, how interminably time passed! She seemed to lie forever, barely breathing, holding the covers closely to her. She could hear Warwick pacing in the music chamber. What was he thinking of? Did he yearn to reach court and the passionate arms of his mistress?

Oh, but it would be best to be away from that arrogant beast! He thrilled her, he infuriated her! He excited her, he frightened her. She wanted all of him and none of him! Be damned with him! She did not want him! She wanted only her freedom, to clear her father and herself.

Finally he went to bed. The candles were doused; only the fires burned. And she had to wait . . .

At least an hour had passed since the last candle had been doused. Oh, surely, God help her, he slept by now . . .

She was about to rise, but instead she went rigid, stunned to realize that he did not sleep at all, that he stood in the doorway, his grim, ever-mocking smile in place against the hard and handsome features of his face.

She swallowed, closed her eyes quickly, and prayed that the shadowed darkness of night had hid her startled glimpse of him.

With her eyes so tightly closed she felt ever more at a disadvantage. She could only wait in the absolute and tense darkness.

More time passed. She tried to breathe easily. He must have decided that she slept, returning to his own chamber to sleep. He must have done so.

She opened her eyes—and let out a startled scream.

He hadn't gone to bed at all; he was standing right above her, hands on his hips, his golden eyes devilish in the glow of the firelight.

He moved like a whip at the sound of her scream, wrenching the covers from her, baring her completely clad figure.

"Dear wife! What is this, then? The latest in bedroom fashion?" He sat beside her, fingering the ruff at her throat. "How remiss of me! I would have sworn I had seen fit to clothe you properly for bed!"

Ondine closed her eyes again, weary, desolate.

"Go to hell!" she said with the little emotion remaining in her.

"Sorry, my love, but it is to court that I go, with my cherished bride on my arm." He stood, caught her arm, and wrenched her to her feet, despite her startled—and guttural—oath of protest. Then she was facing him in defensive fury, aware that her plans were dashed, wondering what new torture this meant.

"What now!" she cried out. "You've found me. I cannot leave—"

"Conniving witch!" he interrupted harshly. "You intended to speed past me? I told you, love, I wake at the slightest sound."

"I made no sound!"

"Ah, but the devious wheels of your mind churned all evening!"

"So! I am caught! Leave me be!"

"Nay, how could I, Countess? Leave you—to sleep in such discomfort?" he cried in a facsimile of gravest concern. "Turn about!"

She didn't have a chance to obey the command; his fingers closed around her shoulders, performing the act for her. Then those same fingers began to unhook her gown.

"Stop! I'm caught! I only wish to salvage what sleep I—"

"You're not sleeping so well prepared to leave, my love. Hold still—or I'll rip it from you."

There was no venom in his words, just truth. Trembling, she stood still as he finished with the hooks; then she wrenched away from him, choking out her words.

"You needn't bother. I'll disrobe myself."

He lifted a hand with casual agreement, but gave no ground. "Then do so, my love."

She stared at him.

"Now," he said.

Labeling him every vile thing that she could, she turned once more, still shaking, and stepped from her gown. He remained behind her, and she could not turn to him.

"Do go on, Countess," he drawled.

She repeated the names she had already called him, having run out of fresh derogatory titles. She still shook so badly that her fingers could not find the ties to her corset.

He stepped forward. Her flesh burned where his fingers touched. Her form had never been more rigid.

Seconds later her corset fell, along with the lace frills of her underskirt. Swearing ever more vehemently, she bent to cast away her hose, then plunge back into her bed, burying herself in the covers.

"Now, will you please go away!" she cried out miserably.

He did not. He sat upon the bed once again, and she stiffened at the touch of his hand upon her back.

"Ondine, why are you so set against a trip to court?"

His voice was strangely gentle and puzzled. She held her breath, listening to the thunder of her heart. She did not open her eyes; she had no wish to see his when they were amber, warmed by concern, curious . . . caring. They could too quickly grow cold and severe.

"I do not like courts," she said stiffly.

"If you told me—"

"I've told you all I intend to!"

She heard his soft sigh, as if he wished he might penetrate her wall of reserve. But then he stood up from the bed, and when he spoke again, his voice was once more sharp with command.

"I'm sorry, then, that the journey distresses you. But it will take place."

She knew that he left her, not by sound, but by the sudden chill that invaded her. She dug her fingers into the sheets to keep from crying out in her desperation, tears of self-pity and fear.

But she didn't cry. She would never let him hear her cry. And then, once again, she began to plot and plan. Once it became morning . . .

It was such a wonderful plan that she slept at last, smiling.

In the morning Lottie came to her. Ondine washed and dressed and instructed Lottie on her hair. She couldn't have been better prepared for a journey.

But as servants ran about with the trunks to be brought to the carriage, with both Mathilda and Warwick in the music chamber, she suddenly gasped out a terrible cry of pain and doubled over.

She was quite good! Ondine decided elatedly. Her act was so convincing that Warwick ran straight to her, clutching her shoulders, supporting her. She could easily have been on the stage!

"My lady—?"

"Oh, my lady!" Mathilda gasped worriedly, rushing to her, too. "Is it the child?"

"Oohh!" Ondine groaned out. "Surely not! Ohh, if I could just lie down again, the pain . . ."

She barely noticed that Warwick released her. Mathilda—dear Mathilda!—set her arms about her mistress and started walking her through to her own chamber.

"We'll get these constricting things off of you at once! You'll lie down and stay down. We won't take a single chance with that precious wee babe!"

"But Warwick—"

"The earl shall have to go on by himself. Now you lie down and I'll find a loose and flowing nightdress—Oh, dear, I fear the best of them are packed!"

Barely able to contain a smile of triumph, Ondine sank back to her bed weakly, casting an elbow over her eyes to await Mathilda's tender administrations.

But the next touch she felt was anything but tender. Hard arms swept around her, lifting her. She opened her eyes wide in alarm, only to meet her husband's fierce ones, narrow and glittering.

"There's nothing my lady needs so much as fresh air," Warwick announced, "and the sooner the better."

"But, Warwick—" Mathilda began.

"My lady is as healthy as a brood mare, Mathilda—just nervous, nothing more! I promise you, the air will do her wonders."

With Ondine in his arms he strode from their chambers at such a furious pace that Mathilda could not keep up to make her protests heard.

Ondine dropped all pretense, glaring at him furiously, pitting her arms against his chest rather uselessly. No struggle would free her. "You—bastard!" she grated out.

"Nell Gwyn never put on such a performance, my love, and she was the rage of the theater before becoming the rage of the king."

"I can walk!"

"I know you can!"

He continued down the staircase and outside to the carriage, where both Justin and Clinton waited to see them off, too startled to hide their surprise.

"A fit of the vapors," Warwick explained briefly.

She did not get to say good-bye to either of them and found herself rather gracelessly deposited into the plush carriage, with the door immediately slammed upon her. She heard the men vaguely. Farewells were shouted out, yet it was all done in a matter of seconds, and before she had a chance to reach for the door handle, the carriage was moving quickly down the drive.

Once again, Warwick opted to ride up top with Jake. Ondine gasped out one sob of frustration, then cast her head against the velvet seat and closed her eyes, so very weary that none of it seemed to matter.

She rode that way for hours, jolting, jostling, numb. But then somewhere along the road and within herself, she began to struggle for reason. There was still hope. As long as one breathed, there was still hope to be found.

She tried to remember her previous rationalization. She really hadn't seen anyone that long-ago day, except the king and a few of his guards. They had just arrived, invited to the joust and banquet.

A page had brought the king to them. The king had been accompanied by two guards.

Charles! She had to see him . . . alone. If she bowed before him bravely as Warwick's wife—and begged him with all the desperation in her eyes—he might gainsay his tongue. Oh, aye! The king was an intuitive man, sensitive to his subjects. It was one of the reasons that he was so loved, as a king and as a man. And he loved women. He had proclaimed himself enchanted with her again and again that day. He was a cavalier—the greatest of cavaliers! Surely if she could but just get to be alone with him, plead her case, he would at the very least give her a chance.

Her heart pounded swiftly. No! It would never work.

But it had to work!

The carriage did not stop until darkness had fallen. When the door opened and Warwick reached for her, she saw that it was night and that they had come to a tavern.

She stared at him loathfully, wrenching her hand from his when he would help her alight. He shrugged and let her be, yet her legs were so cramped from the ride that she stumbled, and his arms embraced her anyway. She did not fight him further, but stiffened against his hold.

Jake followed them into the tavern, arranging for rooms while Warwick found a table where they might order food. Jake returned to them, assuring Warwick that their accommodations would be the best in the house.

They were served roasted fowl and steamed vegetables and ale. Warwick and Jake comfortably fell into a discussion about the road ahead. Ondine picked at her food and swallowed a large quantity of ale. It warmed her, and also exhausted her. She did not realize that she was falling asleep at the table until Warwick touched her, his fingers curling around hers. She gazed up at him, eyes wide, and found that his were warm and curious. But he did not question her.

"Come. I'll see you to bed."

"No . . ."

"Ye're about to fall into yer trencher, lady," Jake said, rising. Warwick had her arm. She allowed him to lead her up the rickety stairs, away from the noise of the tavern.

She realized with some alarm that they were sharing a room. But the ale and lack of sleep had taken their toll—she couldn't really care. Nor could she protest when he turned her about, helping her with her hooks. In her shift she walked away from him and crawled into the one bed. Moments later she knew that he was beside her. Miraculously, though, she slept, slept with his arm around her, and when another dream disturbed her, she was aware of a whispered tenderness.

"Easy, love, sleep, easy. Dear God, what is it that you fear? I am here . . ."

But in the morning he was gone.

And he left Jake to tend to her the next night, when they came to Meg's tavern, so very near to London.

Chapter 11

Warwick was not so far away.

He sat in a dark corner of the tavern, watching Jake—watching his wife—and brooding deeply. He watched her laughter, and he watched her grace, and he swore against himself a thousand times over.

Ah, she was driving him mad!

What manner of fool was he? The inner query brought a pulse ticking hard against the sinewed line of his throat. She was his wife, dammit. If he had any sense, he'd stalk into her room, ignore that wary fear and anger in her eyes, and remind her that she had promised to love, honor, and obey his every command.

His teeth clenched, taut with rising tension. She was just that, his wife—married from the gallows as a pawn, a pawn he had sworn to protect—to whom he had promised freedom. He couldn't think of her as his *wife*. He had to remember Genevieve—young, innocent, slain. Nay, he could not allow himself to *love* his wife! He could only guard her—carefully now!—for Hardgrave was at court, as was the lady Anne. He meant to trap the killer there, for he would not believe the murderer could be his own brother—or Clinton. Surely it *was* Hardgrave.

His attention was drawn to her again. The melody of her laughter filled his senses, and he sighed.

He would not go up until she was asleep. He dared not hold her again, for he wanted her, and deep inside he knew that a storm brewed between them, threatening to sweep them into its tempest and passion.

Ondine was nervous when morning came. Warwick was not with her as she dressed meticulously, praying she would find the king merciful!

She came downstairs to find Warwick in the common room, and she faltered when she saw him, for she was certain he would still have avoided her company. Odd that she should find him so manly in the work clothes he wore so oft about Chatham; stranger still that no matter what his mode and dress, the unexpected sight of him could send her heart reeling, her temper soaring, her pulses racing. Today he was splendid in a lace shirt and velvet coat and breeches in deep blue. His hair was free, dark and thick and wavy. She realized that not even for a royal appearance would he wear a wig. But it didn't matter; he could cater to fashion, he could spurn it. Tall and dark with his ever-changing hazel eyes, he was the height of masculine beauty and rugged appeal. And surely no man had ever worn a rich plumed hat with such flair.

He doffed that hat as she came before him, bowing deeply. He seemed as highly strung as she this morning, fire dancing in his gaze, his manner most strange.

"Milady! How kind that you remain with us!"

"Kind? I'd no choice."

"Yet most common lasses would be most enthralled at the thought of a stay at court."

"Most, perhaps."

"Ah, but then I've never thought that you might be grouped with anything common, my love."

Ondine glared at him uneasily, yet he pushed the point no further. He remained most pleasant as they ate, edging her nerves still further. His arm was about her as he paid Meg. He placed her graciously into the carriage, then bowed to take his leave, apparently preferring Jake's company once again. He smiled when Ondine scowled.

"Milady wife! Where is your complaint this morning?"

"I've none, my lord. Yet I think there's no need to practice your charm, since it is something you doff on and off as a cloak."

He cast her a dry grin. "Practice? And what would this practice be for, Countess?"

"That is your concern, Warwick, isn't it?"

The rising sun seemed to falter in the sky a bit. His smile remained, yet it became cold.

"Aye, Countess, that it is. Excuse me, then. Our next stop will be Hampton Court."

And so it was. It seemed that no time passed before they were upon the Thames, brilliantly blue today beneath a rare cloudless sky. The massive gates of Hampton greeted them. There were guards in livery, scores of people everywhere, lords and ladies in high plummage, pages, clerks, the clergy, scullery maids, stable boys, gardeners, and merchants. The workers seemed to hurry; the nobility to amble. Ondine pulled the curtains back to stare about her, fascinated. The carriage brought them through the main gates, bringing them ever closer to the palace itself in warm red earth-colored tones. Ondine gazed at the giant clock in the courtyard, and only then did she think again that she might be weighing her life not in days, but in hours and minutes.

The carriage came to a halt. Seconds later the door swung open, and her husband's eyes were glittering upon her as he decorously reached for her hand, assisting her from the carriage. She barely glanced his way, wondering in all this milling of people just where the king might be.

Moments later they were entering a grand hall with an even grander stairway, and a man, apparently the head steward of the place, was greeting Warwick, promising that his accommodations were of the finest, seen to by the king himself.

Their apartments were up the grand stairway, down a long hall. The steward proudly opened double doors, displaying a grand den with books and closets, a multitude of richly upholstered chairs and settees, and gleaming round tables set before the windows, where they caught the magic light of the sun.

"The bedchamber," the steward told them, leading them forward, "is beyond."

Another set of double doors was pushed open. It was a beautifully appointed bedchamber, with a huge four-poster bed, heavy and intricately carved. The inner drapes were of gauze and brocade.

A window looked over the gardens and the Thames far beyond. Here, too, were chairs and dressers, and there was another small round table, set as if it might offer an intimate breakfast place for sleepy lovers just come from a tousled bed.

Servants were following with their luggage. The steward showed Ondine where the bellpull was and assured her she could summon a lady's maid within seconds, should she require anything. He was ever so polite and correct, yet he studied her in such a way that she knew she would quickly be the subject of gossip raging throughout the entire compound. And she didn't really care. It seemed that a buzzing had started in her ears, and she knew that that buzzing was fear. Any moment now she would see the king.

Curiously Warwick moved about the rooms, tapping on the walls. He exchanged glances with the steward, who assured him the rooms had been "thoroughly explored."

Ondine tried to question him, but he interrupted her. "His Majesty plays tennis. We'll take the barge to meet him at the courts."

Fine, she thought! For she must get this confrontation over with! Inwardly she trembled, went numb, and trembled all over again. She hurried as they left the palace, traversed the gardens, and made their way for the barge.

"You are eager to do hommage to your king," Warwick observed at last. "Why might that be, I wonder?"

She practiced a sweet smile on him. "Why, because I've heard he's wondrously fair, milord. A gentleman to the core and, by nature, fond of my gentle sex."

She felt his fingers tighten convulsively around her arm; they loosened, and he returned her smile.

"He is as dark as a Spaniard, milady."

"Aye, so I've heard. Fair in beauty, then."

He did not respond, but pointed before them. "A barge, milady. You'll see for yourself in a matter of minutes."

Seconds later they were aboard the small craft that sailed for the sheer convenience of transporting guests to the tennis courts. Warwick brought Ondine to sit, but she could not. She preferred to stand portside and feel the wind. He stood by her, and she knew that again he watched her.

And then the structure—large and covered—loomed ahead of them. The barge docked; the plank was set. Warwick led her along it. Even as they entered the courts, liveried servants presented them with chalices of wine. It was not crowded, but still there were many onlookers. Ladies sat about on chaise longues, watching the play. Regally clad gentlemen urged on the players. The sound of the ball sailing over the net, whacking against the court, was constant.

Ondine did not mean to stop and stare, certainly not in her present state of agitation, and yet she did. She had never seen a tennis court, though she had heard that the king was a great aficionado of the sport.

Her husband's arm came about her shoulder, and for the briefest of moments she allowed herself a sense of security and ease.

She should have told him! Oh, surely, he might well have protected her, held her . . .

No man could protect an accused traitor.

"Queen Catherine," Warwick whispered, pointing to a lounge.

The woman Ondine saw was far from her first youth, yet lovely in the sweetness of her face. She smiled and clapped and chatted with the ladies who surrounded her. "And there, the cutups, Buckingham, Lord Burkhurst; there, that's Sedley."

"The cutups?" Ondine murmured.

"Idle rogues, my love. Tales of debauchery that come from this court come from them, not His Grace, whom they do but amuse. He is not so much a lecher," Warwick mused, "but a true lover. His wife, his mistresses, they are his friends as well. The king also keeps grave council, the likes of Pepys, Wren, and others. Those, my love, are rogues of whom you must beware."

"More so than you, milord?" she asked innocently.

"Infinitely."

"Over there—who is that?" Ondine asked curiously. Far from the queen's lounge across the court was another lounge. The woman within it had lovely features, deep dark hair, and a tiny but glorious physique. The man Warwick had pointed out as being the Duke of Buckingham was saying something to her. She laughed, stretching as luxuriously as a cat.

"Louise, Duchess of Portsmouth."

Ondine gasped. "The king's mistress! With his wife here present, too!"

Warwick chuckled softly. "The lovely creature down there facing the net is Nelly Gwyn."

But it wasn't Nelly Gwyn who caught Ondine's eye; it was a very different voluptuous brunette.

She chatted with Louise, laughed, watched the play. She was stunning to look at, tall, graceful, with full red pouting lips, emitting a lazy ooze of sensuality that was unmistakable. She sipped wine, she dangled grapes from her fingers, and she seemed to brood and laugh again, as if too easily bored.

"Who is that?"

"Lady Anne," Warwick said. "Come; the queen has seen us."

Ondine stiffened. So that was the lady Anne! Wrath rose high within her, then she nearly laughed. What did it matter?—she was about to see the king.

Warwick led Ondine along quickly to the queen's lounge, sweeping a deep bow. "Your Highness."

Ondine curtsied at his side, instantly aware that his affection for the smiling creature before them with the still sad eyes was most sincere.

"Warwick!" The queen still carried the slightest accent of her native Portugal. "What a pleasure, milord!" He stepped forward to kiss her hand, and the ladies with her backed politely away. Catherine disdained protocol and leaned forward to kiss his cheek, but then her bright eyes were looking beyond him to Ondine. "Ah, Countess! Do step forward!" She took Ondine's hand and studied her with open pleasure.

"Oh, but, Warwick, where did you find her? She's lovely! Heads will turn, but they already have! All watch what a lovely couple you make—ah!" Catherine cried suddenly, clapping her hands together. "Game point—to my most noble husband!"

Ondine spun in startled surprise. She had not realized a player to be the king, yet now, too suddenly, she saw that the victor was indeed none other than Charles. He was shaking hands with his opponent, accepting a great sheet or towel from a servant with a friendly thanks, and turning toward them.

He did not see her right away; his great dark eyes were on Warwick. He smiled with pleasure, his trim mustache spreading across his face with the widening of his smile. Ondine felt numb again, staring at him, seeing him anew. He was a tall man, as tall as Warwick, very dark and intriguing. He was a Stuart king, yet as with royalty, he carried the blood of many houses; that of Scottish and French royalty, and the Italian lineage of the Medicis dukes of Tuscany. Perhaps it was from this that he derived his looks, for he was dark and fascinating.

"Warwick!"

The king clapped her husband on the shoulder; Warwick greeted the king with the same enthusiasm.

"And rumor tells me you've brought a bride!"

"Aye, Your Grace. The lady Ondine, my wife."

And then the moment was there. He stared straight at her. Numb, dazed, praying with all her heart, she sank into a curtsy, all the while keeping her eyes mutely locked with the king's deep-set stare. Ah, did he stare! So very long, yet it all seemed too slow, out of a mist. Silently she pleaded; nightmare visions spun like mercury through her head. He would speak, he would summon a guard, he would point a finger and rage out a single damning word: "Traitor!"

He did not say it; the word echoed only in her mind. He recognized her—oh, she could swear, though he moved not and gave nothing away, that he recognized her.

"Lady Ondine," he said smoothly. He reached for her hand, bringing her to her feet. "We offer you our most heartfelt welcome to Hampton Court."

She couldn't speak; she smiled, and her eyes remained tied to his. She feared that the nervous relief welling within her would bring darkness cascading down, sending her to the floor in a dead swoon.

"Married without his king's permission!" Charles laughed.

"But now that I've seen the bride, I can offer only my blessing and my envy. Catherine! Is she not incredible!"

"And chaste, perhaps," Catherine murmured, drawing no offense from the king, merely laughter.

Warwick slipped an arm around Ondine's shoulder, pulling her to him and extricating her hands from the king's. "Chaste, I do swear, my most gracious queen."

"Possessive, Chatham!" Charles admonished. "But, friend, I think you've trouble ahead. Buckingham is near to drooling on my floor over here as he covets your bride. Ah, but he dare not pursue her, while in my presence, and he fears your prowess, Warwick, so perhaps we are all safe. But what—are we? I fear a cat prowls near, ready to shred the bride! Quick—a royal escape!"

Whimsically Charles had her hand once again. In an aside he laughingly informed Catherine he must show Ondine the fields and gardens outside the court, "And save her from the swains we have in abundance here!"

"We'll gladly see the gardens," Warwick said, yet this time, he could not retrieve Ondine from the king.

Charles placed a hand upon his chest and murmured mischievously, "You've matters to settle here, before they can get out of hand, friend. The cat I speak of prowls ever closer!"

Warwick's mistake was in turning, for the king did not lie. Anne, a smile on her face, venom lacing her eyes, was almost upon them. "Lord Chatham!" she cried.

Without cutting her and creating a scene, Warwick had no recourse but to pause, as etiquette dictated. Charles chose that moment to wink and escape with another wink to his wife and Ondine in tow. They were quickly followed by two of the king's guards, but as they broke from the structure of the tennis courts and started upon a tiled garden path, Charles abruptly turned.

"Oh, good fellows! Do leave me in peace for this once. Do you really believe the beautiful lady Chatham to be a threat?"

"Your Grace!" In unison the guards bowed; in unison, they disappeared. Charles led her along the path, deeper and deeper into seclusion, to a place where strange plants grew in profusion. He knelt by one and plucked the fruit from it. He drew a knife from his pouch and slit the fruit, offering a piece to Ondine. "Pineapple. First grown here in England by my own gardener. It's an intriguing fruit. Taste it."

She accepted the fruit, but could not eat it. She stared into his eyes, still numb. "Your Majesty, did you mean that?"

"Of course! I would not lie about such a matter as a pineapple."

"No, no." Ondine shook her head vehemently. "I meant—" She paused, wincing. "Oh, Your Grace! Never would I harm your person! Yet I remain still implicated in treason—"

He waved a hand in the air, smiling, and in that smile she saw all the beautiful things that had made him a beloved man to those closest to him.

"I never did believe your father meant to slay me, my dear Duchess of Rochester."

She let out a long breath. She felt terribly shaky, as if any moment she would fall to the ground. Yes, he had recognized her. She had known it the moment their eyes had met.

"Oh, God!" she whispered, and he touched her cheek with a gentle fascination, then moved quickly away, tossing the remains of the pineapple to the ground.

"Where have you been, Ondine? Where did that deadly rogue of a friend of mine find you?"

"On the gallows."

"Gallows?" Charles turned to her curiously.

"I was caught poaching deer."

"And you were to hang?"

"It's not uncommon, I understand."

Suddenly Charles started to laugh. "And Warwick happened by, to claim you in marriage and rescue the fair damsel in distress. It's wonderful! Ah, what a story! Yet a secret one, I do presume."

"Aye, milord, though I do not know the workings of my husband's mind."

Charles mused upon those words for a moment, then shrugged. "As he does not know yours?"

"I—yes."

"Then you are well met, I believe," Charles said. He started walking down the path again. Anxiously Ondine followed him.

"Your Grace, what am I to do?"

Again he paused, watching her so intently that in the end she flushed. "There were witnesses that day. Two guards; one page. One of the guards has disappeared—possibly he was threatened into leaving? I don't know . . ." he murmured at last. "I searched high and low for the man. I cannot find him, but perhaps he fears to speak the truth. Then there are those papers—forgeries, probably, but good enough to fool a court. If you found those and destroyed them, your uncle and cousin would have no case against you. Still, you would have to trap them to clear your father . . . Ah, Ondine! Legally your uncle is your guardian—in charge of your estates! And legally I cannot pardon you; not unless they withdraw the accusation."

"But you said—"

"I said that I, personally, do not believe you capable of such treason, milady. I suggest that when you deem the time appropriate, you search out the weaknesses in your family yourself. Perhaps you must return to your holdings and play your game for a while. Pretend that you would cast yourself on their mercy. Now, here, you are safe to think—and plan. You are Warwick Chatham's bride. All knew that the old Duke of Rochester had a daughter, but none knew her name. Stay here with your husband, abide awhile in safety. All things will come with time. Ah, Ondine! I am, madam, a popular monarch. Yet I wandered Europe a pauper for endless years; I fought for my crown, I begged aid, I learned to trust good men, and yet the greatest lesson of all that I learned was care. I am here now—the son of a wonderful man, yet a weak king who died by the headsman's ax—not because of battle or debate, but because in the end the people invited me back. They say that I came here affable—charming, if you will—but wary. And they say now that I am a good king, accessible to his people, possibly sly, but indubitably introspective. My charm, they say, can but hide the workings of the mind. Perhaps that is all true. I have grown older, wiser. I have learned that to wait and watch and keep one's own council can bring all things to pass in time. Do you understand?"

Confused, Ondine shook her head. "You said I must act—"

"Nay, I said that in time you must act." Charles leaned against a giant oak, his dark eyes touched by a glitter of humor, his sensual

ace most appealing with its grin. "I've no doubt my lord of
Chatham eyes you, little one, like a hawk. With such a prize, well
might I do the same. Bend to his will, for it is a powerful one,
and if you do not bend, you might well break. Let patience be
your virtue. With a ragged and laden heart he chases a ghost; in
time his own quest will be satisfied. Then you can give measure
to your own."

"You suggest I leave him, then?"

"Nay—I suggest you merely travel alone when you return to
your birthright. For I can tell you this. He married you—"

"For that quest of his you speak of only," Ondine murmured.

Charles laughed. "I think not. I know him well, my girl. As
well as one man can know another. I saw those lion's eyes of his
as I dragged you away. They sparkled with outrage and envy,
possession and frustration. He is shocked that I—notorious as I
might well be—would take a fancy to his wife."

"I—"

The king chuckled again. "You need have no fear of me, my
dear. I offer you no bargains or deals; I ask nothing of you. If
you were not his wife, still I would ask nothing of you. History
will forget that I strove for the arts and excellence in England,
that I fought to make her strong, however I saw fit. History will,
however, men being what they are, remember my liaisons. Yet
no accurate historian shall ever be able to say that I dallied with
any lady not equally willing to dally. Still"—he grimaced, and
smiled once again—"it is wondrously fun to have my friend—
Lord Chatham, known for his stature, his courage, his damned
masculine appeal—jealous of me!"

Ondine lowered her head. She didn't think that Warwick was
particularly jealous, any more than he would be of Dragon, Chatham Manor itself, or any other possession. She did not wish,
though, to argue with the king.

"Come—we must get back. I enjoy a good jest to cast that
husband of yours into confusion, yet I'd not have him truly suspect
I'd accost his wife for a dalliance. But we'll talk again. Tonight.
We'll banquet for dinner, and dance to the minstrels, shall we?"

"Aye, Your Grace! Oh, Your Majesty—"

"Yes?"

"I—bless you, sire!"

He smiled slowly, lowering his lashes. "Don't look at me s
fervently, lady, with those tears upon your eyes. I might easil
imagine myself younger, a less loyal friend . . . Come!"

He took her hand, and they hurried back along the path.

Chapter 12

"Who is this—this common slut!" Anne demanded.

A scene had been brewing, a distasteful scene. For that reason Warwick had allowed Anne to lead him from the tennis courts to the garden, where they could be alone. Now he folded his arms over his chest and returned her glare bemusedly. "Watch your tongue, Anne. She is no common slut, but my wife."

Anne stamped a foot in fury.

"Nay! She cannot be. We were all but betrothed! You swore you'd not marry again! You play some game—yet I will discover it!"

He sighed, wearying quickly, then wondering why. Anne had lost none of her beauty, none of her spirit, and certainly none of the blatant, forthright determination that had once appealed to him.

He was about to answer, but paused, holding his jaw taut, fighting the feelings, the simple answer that swarmed from his heart to his mind.

Nay . . . Anne had lost nothing. It was just that the rich darkness of her hair could not compare with tresses that could rustle through his fingers like fire and sunlight, flame and gold. Her eyes were not like the sea, infinitely deep. Her voluptuous breasts could not compare with the smooth cream of mystery and allure of his wife's; her stance, her grace, her temper, her laughter, her . . .

The bloody little witch! Ah, but she was driving him insane! He could not care! Yet he seemed he could find no fascination for another.

"We were never even remotely betrothed, Anne. And I assure you, Ondine is legally my wife."

Anne sucked in a great gasp of air. "You married her—and would not marry me!"

"Anne! I never pretended that I would marry you! We enjoyed one another with equal desire, and there it ended!"

She raised a hand to slap him. He wasn't about to accept her blow and caught it quickly. "Anne! Cease this nonsense."

Anne didn't wrench her hand away; she used its position to angle closely against his chest, pulling his fingers to the cleavage of her gown and crying, "Feel my heart, Warwick! It flutters and thunders! With desire, Warwick, with desire!"

He chuckled softly; she was a wonderful dramatist.

"Anne, we both know you fulfill your desires whenever and with whomever you so choose."

Her eyes snapped with annoyance. "Warwick!" she cried, and she chuckled softly. "We have been through this before, Warwick. And I will lie with you again . . ."

He had to smile at her sultry determination, yet it was at that moment that the king—and Ondine—suddenly came upon them.

He glanced sharply at his wife. There was nothing of reluctance about her now; no fear, no nervousness. She was breathless and laughing and her eyes were sparkling with a beauty to rival any perfect set of sapphires. Something seemed to strike him, like lightning, a rage of steel tearing into his gut, creating a jagged pain—wonder and envy. Never had she smiled for him so. Never had she stared upon him so radiantly.

Never had he been more painfully aware that, yes, there was a passion within her, deep and sensual, wild and sweet. Seeing her then, he felt it to the core. But it was a thing she kept from him; kept behind her reserve. She fought him, laughing and whispering to the king.

"Men think from their codpieces!" Anne hissed.

Ondine was no longer laughing joyously at the king's witticisms.

She was staring at Warwick and Anne, and he realized that still his hand was entwined with hers upon her breast.

But he would not apologize. He did not wrench his hand away like a flushing lad. He met his wife's eyes defiantly, then moved very slowly.

"Anne, I think you've not yet met my wife, Ondine. Ondine, the lady Anne."

Neither of them acknowledged the introduction. Charles cast Warwick a bemused expression, then broke the discomfort of the meeting by saying, "To a barge, shall we? A banquet, quite fit for a king, is the evening's plan. Let's to it, shall we?"

He turned, leading Anne. Warwick caught Ondine's hand when she would have eluded him. He felt the strength within her and held her tight. He was so riled that he quizzed her in a harsh whisper, "What's this, milady? You fought and spit and clawed like a cat when I would bring you here, yet again you are the cat—a kitten who purrs and teases for the king."

"I find him charming!" Ondine replied evenly.

"Ah, so you would be one of his collection of whores!"

She turned to him, her eyes wide, her voice so sweet it stung.

"His whore? Should I be so? Perhaps! He grants titles and wealth—and is ever so handsome and alluring, gentle and kind!"

The king and Anne were far ahead. Warwick stopped. Smiling, he laced his fingers through Ondine's hair and wrenched it slightly, bringing her throat to an arch, her glittering eyes to battle with his.

"You sweet, chaste, and charming gutter-bitch! You will remember that you are my wife."

"Marital vows?" she retorted. "I shall learn from you, dear husband, how they must be kept!"

He tugged more tightly on her hair, bringing tears to her eyes. "Laugh and tease as you will, my love, but I warn you only once: Watch your step!"

"The king is your dear friend!" she reminded him sweetly.

"My friend, yes," Warwick said softly, a deathly hush that chilled her blood. "But a man. And few men, even when held in check by friendship, can resist a blatant tart's invitation!"

"Something with which you are well acquainted, my lord?"

He held still for several seconds, staring at her. "Aye," he said at last. "But do I resist much temptation, my love. There are ways to tame you, still, my love."

"Bitch, tart—my love! Do make up your mind which of these I am, Lord Chatham!"

"Warwick! Ondine! We sail!" The king's call was a command. Warwick stared at her a moment longer, then once again they walked, his long strides making her breathless to keep up, and she controlled her nearly irresistible urge to tear at him with tooth and nail.

That day, they were surrounded by people. The court was so exciting! She had no chance to be with Warwick alone again. She met a number of lords and ladies about the court, and she was taken beneath the queen's wing. Catherine seemed to enjoy her company.

It seemed but a blur before the banquet began. There was wonderful succulent food that she was full able to enjoy, since the king, all seriousness for that time, spoke to Warwick of his complaints with his Parliament, of his plans to build and broaden, about the Dutch, about the French. And Catherine—his wife on such occasions was always at his side—spoke to Ondine about fashion and fabric, poetry and art. Jugglers performed, minstrels played, handlers brought in a pair of bears to dance. It was a magical evening.

It ended earlier for Ondine than for Warwick; Charles was not through with his friend. There were problems with the Scots to be solved, and Charles meant to discuss them that evening.

Warwick pensively returned her to the door of their apartments, stiffly telling her with no further recriminations that Jake would be there, and departed for further dealings with the king.

Let it only be the king, she prayed despite herself, and not Anne!

She thought she would never sleep with all the joy, the excitement—and the anger—yet she did. Relief and gratitude for her magic meeting with the king was like a potent drug. She tossed and turned and fumed about her husband, but not for long. Just like warm, gentle fingers encompassing her, the night claimed her and she rested, far to her own side of the bed.

But it did not matter. She discovered in the morning that War-wick had slept out on one of the settees. He still slept when she cracked the door in the morning. He was surely uncomfortable, she thought, since his long form did not fit the furniture, his legs stretching over the edge.

He must be exhausted to still sleep so! And then knives cut at her heart. Had he stayed up all night with the king, or with his mistress?

She closed the door to the bedroom and dressed quickly, fuming all the while. She tiptoed to the outer door, but then slammed it hard behind her, smiling with satisfaction as she heard his startled oaths behind her.

Warwick awoke in a foul temper, feeling drugged with weari-ness—Charles had kept him so late. Had he been able to catch her, he thought, he would have surely thrashed her!

"Witch!" he muttered aloud in a plaintive growl as he ran his fingers through his hair, pressing his temples hard to clear them. He groaned. God rot this entire mess! He'd wanted to tempt and trap a killer, to watch Hardgrave and Anne, to observe and discover.

And instead he spent his every moment in heated tempest over his gallows' bride, the bait of his trap! His mind was completely involved with the intrigue of her. She had been terrified to come here, loathe to see the king, yet now she laughed and walked with him as if he were an old friend, a long-lost lover . . .

And it was she that he watched, lost in the intrigue of her eyes, her form . . .

"Lust!" he swore furiously aloud. "And anger. Dammit! She owes me obedience!"

"And love and honor!"

Startled, Warwick turned bloodshot eyes to the doorway to find the king. Warwick groaned; the king laughed. "What is this, Warwick! You would waste the morning! Come! This is the time to swim the Thames. Where is your lady? Up and about already? I do congratulate you on your marriage, friend. Come, now— you're by far the younger man! A swim awakens the senses and the blood." Charles had a number of his beloved spaniels with him; they all yapped and barked and ran about, causing Warwick's mild headache to become splitting. The king most surely realized the torture he brought!

Warwick felt like throwing a boot at him. The king's eyes danced with amusement. Slowly Warwick smiled. He felt a sudden faith that the king would never betray him. Oh, he might with Anne, and a few others, yes; they'd both known some women who had known many men. But he couldn't believe at that moment—or in any sober moment—that the king would ever touch a woman who was his wife.

"Swim, aye, Your Majesty!" Warwick said with high exaggeration. Charles laughed; then, like the friends they were, they departed for the exercise.

Ondine met Nell Gwyn that day and enjoyed her good-natured and down-to-earth wit. She spent the majority of the afternoon, though, with Catherine, surprised by the queen's open admissions. "Never feel anger against Charles for me!" she stated softly. "Parliament wished him to divorce me for my barrenness, and he would not! Ah, and I am no saint! I'm glad to see one paramour squirm—Lady Anne! Oh, you are beautiful—and she is enraged!"

Ondine didn't think that Anne was outraged. She watched Ondine with a feline stare—and a secretive smile of knowledge.

And why not? Ondine had barely seen her husband. Most probably, Anne had seen a great deal of him.

Ondine did not see him until dinner. And it was quite strange then to sit beside him. One minute he offered her his greatest, if feigned, courtesy, and the next he stared at her with an elusive amber fire about his eyes, gravely pondering her.

Then at one point during the meal he stiffened, his eyes focusing across the room. "Hardgrave!" He swore softly.

Ondine, curious, followed his gaze to the newly arrived viscount. Hardgrave was as fashionable as the rest of the company. He wore a plumed hat much like Warwick's, red stockings, cream breeches, and a burnt-orange surcoat. He appeared far stockier than her husband and was a formidable man—broad-shouldered and muscular. He was short, which made him appear broader, and he carried with him none of Warwick's natural grace.

Hardgrave came to offer his homage to his king, and then he and Warwick exchanged courtesies, for the benefit of the company, that thinly veiled their hostility. Warwick did not introduce Ondine. The viscount stared at her, she offered a weak smile, and he left.

"Take the greatest care near him!" Warwick whispered quite

sharply to her, and she found that his eyes were upon her more fiercely than she had ever seen them. She nodded, too laden with the timbre of his voice to taunt him in return.

The meal ended as the king clapped his hands and cheerfully said that with the charm and nobility of the company present, they must all dance into the night.

Food was cleared, and the tables were taken away. In the galleries the musicians began to play. Ondine immediately found herself claimed by the king, and with the pulse and beat of the music in her ears, the king the most charming of escorts, she suddenly found her heart light, youth and laughter bubbling within her.

They paused at last to sate their thirsts with rum punch from a crystal bowl set upon the table, and it was there that Ondine at last met Lord Hardgrave formally.

"Hardgrave!" the king said, sipping his punch. "Ah, what a piece of neglect! You did not meet the new lady of Chatham. Ondine, Lyle Hardgrave, Viscount—"

"The lady knows my lands, Your Grace," Hardgrave said, and his pale blue eyes upon her were both flattering and cold. "As she surely knows of me. Your husband and I, my lady, are bitter enemies."

"Not in my court," Charles said sharply.

Ondine hadn't known much about the man. She was curious about him, yet presumed that men whose lands adjoined might well find friction. Were they not natural friends, it might be quite easy to become natural enemies.

"Never in your court," Hardgrave acknowledged.

She sensed something then, and she knew not how, or why, but she warmed. Looking up, she saw her husband, far across the room. She had known by that warmth that he was watching her.

He was in the company of a lovely young lady that she had not met.

Ondine gave Hardgrave a sweet smile. "It is a pleasure to meet you, Lord Hardgrave."

He clicked his heels and bent to kiss her hand. Perhaps Charles decided the act dangerous; perhaps he had just grown bored. He swept Ondine back to the dance with a sudden flourish and he whirled and twirled so quickly and with such grace and energy that she laughed until she could not stop, and at last begged for mercy, saying that she must escape out the open doorway for a breath of air. The king, waylaid then by his wife, could not follow her.

She was breathless with the dance, breathless with laughter, when she came outside to lean against the stone of the balcony and gasp in air, and cool her flesh and blood. She closed her eyes tightly for a moment. Oh, it was good! Life was good—so very, very sweet!

"I've certainly never heard of her!"

Ondine tensed suddenly, aware that she was not alone outside. Beyond a trellis strung with roses two women sat upon a bench, fanning themselves furiously from the dance—and gossiping.

She clenched her jaw together to brace herself; one of the two was Lady Anne. The voice that had already come her way— imperiously—carried the touch of a French accent, and narrowing her eyes to focus between the slits of the trellis, Ondine realized that the second woman was the king's mistress Louise. And it didn't take long for Ondine to realize that she was the object of their gossip.

"Hmmph!" Lady Anne snorted, in a manner less than delicate, yet she had no audience excepting Louise—and unbeknownst to her, Ondine.

"I tell you she is no 'lady'! And he swore he'd never wed again—not after that fiasco with Genevieve. Ah, what a fool he is! He loves me, adores me! Yet fears to do me ill by marriage. Fool man! Yet still, I shall be content with just his love—until this wretched little bitch of his has played out her role!"

"Wretched little bitch?" Louise inquired sweetly, yet Ondine sensed a hidden malice in the tone. "She's quite beautiful."

"Quite common! That's it! I dare say she's a commoner—"

Louise chuckled, low and throaty, and the tone was definitely malicious. "Not so common! The king is infatuated, as you've seen."

"Oh, men, they all flock to anything new! You wait and see, *ma petite,* they'll all tire soon enough!"

"Perhaps. Perhaps not. Perhaps the lord of Chatham is madly, passionately in love with her."

"His passion, I assure you, Louise, is for me."

"And the king's is for me, *mais oui?* Yet . . . he shares it with others, as well you know. But as Barbara Castlemaine once said of the king, he is exceptionally well endowed for the art of lovemaking." Louise's words were very smug.

"And, as you reminded me, I have known them both! Chatham excels even the king in the absolute wonder of masculine endowments!"

Then they both started to titter with laughter, friends, enemies— competitors.

Ondine felt her face flame with fury and humiliation. All her fascination with the evening came to a crashing halt. Warwick! Damn him to a thousand burning hells! Rake, scoundrel, bastard! He'd dragged her here to be subjected to his mistress, her crass remarks . . . her self-satisfied possessiveness. Oh! She wanted to race back into the ballroom and rip great handfuls of his rich hair out of his autocratic head.

"Ah, you'll miss him, won't you Anne, eh?" Louise inquired then sweetly, still laughing softly. "After all . . . he does have his bride in attendance."

"Trust me, Louise, she'll not stand in my way." Anne's voice lowered to near a whisper. "A bride may, after all, disappear. She is no Genevieve, but one never knows. I may well cause her to run screaming from this place! And," she added maliciously, "it seems the bride has also caught the king's attention beyond all limits. Perhaps she'll be occupied much of the time that she is about."

Ondine could suddenly bear no more. She spun about and stormed back into the ballroom, more aflame with color than she had been from the dance.

She swirled straight into Lord Hardgrave. Hardgrave—her dear husband's enemy! She gave him a beautiful smile, quickly apologizing for her clumsiness.

His broad hands touched her shoulders; his strange pale blue eyes were upon hers, alit with sudden pleasure.

"Ah, Lady Chatham! How long has that name sounded dung to my ears—yet now it tinkles like the melody of a stream. My dear, please do see fit to stumble against me at any time, for it is with the greatest pleasure that I aright you!"

"Thank you, milord, your words are most charmingly stated."

"Ah, lady, you're too fine for the Beast of Chatham! Would

that I had but seen you first, alas!'' His hands lingered too long upon her shoulders; his eyes too long upon the rise of her breasts. She wanted to shrink from him; she did not. ''Still, the day might come that I may yet slay that beast, and then . . .''

He lowered his head; his face was very close to hers. She longed to escape him, yet knew not how.

''Ah, there you are, my dear!''

The king! Blessed good King Charles! How had she ever feared him? Here he was, chivalrously saving her from this man.

''May I?'' Charles asked Hardgrave with a bland smile. ''The lady promised me this dance.''

''In all things, Charles, I would serve you,'' Hardgrave said.

''I dare say,'' Charles murmured, but then he swept Ondine into his arms, and soon they were on the floor, moving to the strains of music that cascaded down upon them from the minstrels in the gallery.

''You laugh, my lady? Is my dancing so very bad, then?''

''Nay!'' Ondine said joyously. ''I laugh with wonder, and appreciation, Your Grace!''

''Ah! I did save you from unwanted attentions!''

''Aye, that you did!''

''Mind like a whip—uncanny intuition, how clever, how charming am I!'' Charles chuckled.

And Ondine, so excellently swirled about his lead, cast back her head and laughed delightedly at his very wry self-evaluation.

And it was then that she saw her husband again. He stood by the wall, watching her with eyes of flame and fury. Stiff and tall and rigid, like a stallion locked in a pen, he watched her. Angry? Oh, more than that . . . yet how dare he! Endowments—his endowments were the subject of general discussion, and he stared at her!

But even as she returned his gaze with her head high and cool contempt in her eyes, he was forced to turn, as a female hand touched upon his chest.

Anne's hand.

And as he turned he smiled, and then chuckled, deep and low, and even that sound, across a crowded room, made Ondine quiver inside. Idiot! she charged herself. She could not care, could not be such a fool as to love such a man. Anne's words, humiliating, shameful, infuriating—painful!—were true. She played a role for him; he would discard her . . .

She felt ill suddenly. Warwick and Anne were now locked close in a tête-à-tête; Anne's hands seemed to be all over her lover. And Warwick was sweeping another chalice of the rum-laced punch from the silver tray, offering Anne a sip, offering her the crooked sensual curl of a grin. Buckingham was with them; they all laughed and drank and it was the most riotous, intimate grouping.

"Sire," she said to Charles, "may I retire for the evening?"

"Leave him to the claws of Lady Anne?" Charles whispered.

"I shall hope that they scratch one another's eyes out," Ondine replied honestly. "Sire, my head suddenly aches."

Most courteously he escorted her to her chambers. Ondine noted that Jake followed them—ready to stand guard over her at the door! Charles kissed her hand elegantly before leaving her.

He walked away. "Good night!" she called to Jake, slamming the door after the king had departed.

Ondine went on into the suite. She stared about the outer room; at the settee where Warwick had slept. She walked over to it and kicked it in a fury, then swept into the bedchamber, slamming the door behind her. She began to mutter as she went through her chest, absently finding a white silk nightdress, with the finest Bruges lace about the neck and sleeves. She nearly tore her dress to shreds in her haste to remove it, then tossed it to a pile in the corner of the room. Oh, damn him!

Decked out in the white silk, she thought to go to bed, to forget the night. The world looked well for her! She had escaped the gallows, and now had the king's own blessing to seek a way to right her wrongs. How could she let this tempest brew within her?

Yet it was true . . . while one lived one felt the furies and glories of life, knew its pains and its elations. Hope, laughter, the coolness of silk against the flesh, the searing blade of jealousy, humiliation . . . and the hurt that she could not shield away.

"Warwick Chatham, damn you!" she cried aloud, but softly. And then she began to pace the floor; she could not help herself. She muttered and raved, thinking that she would tire, that the feelings would at last fade with an onslaught of exhaustion so she could find the solace of sleep.

* * *

Ah, the wretched gutter-bitch!

Warwick stared into Anne's eyes; he smiled bemusedly at her words, yet heard them not. Buckingham pressed another drink into his hand, and he accepted it blindly.

He talked, joked, laughed.

Inside he raged with emotion, haunted, jealous—ragged with the pain he could not quell. She had left on the king's arm, and he could not bear it. All he could think of was her.

He had to have her. Nay, he could not . . .

Another drink, aye! To her sea-witch eyes, her siren's breasts, her walk, her sway, her legs . . .

Stay away, stay away, stay away . . .

He could not. It was late. He had lingered, he had laughed, he had flirted, he had danced and drunk, and none of it did any good.

Quite suddenly he broke from the company. Striding, he left the ballroom grimly, and with his jaw hard, his fists knotted, he headed for his chamber. God rot it, but he could not endure another night like a spaniel on a cushion!

Chapter 13

Ondine was still engaged in pacing her chamber, cursing with every epitaph she had learned from the thieves in the forest, when the wooden door banged open so heavily and with such a ferocious slam that she froze, her blood seeming to chill and cease its flow, her muscles constricted like ice.

Warwick stood there, a great sleak silhouette.

And then he moved. Quietly, elegantly, with all the grace that belonged to the tenor of Charles's court, he stepped into the room. He removed his great plumed hat, and with it in his hand he swept her a bow so deep that its mockery was doubled in its masterful execution.

The act complete, he tossed the hat upon the love seat. And then he reached for the door, closing it slowly so that it moved upon its old hinges, screeching in a way that sent spasms of terror along her spine, even as her mind registered the dangerous taunt in his manner.

When the door was closed, he leaned against it, arms behind his back as he surveyed her. The candlelight flickered. Corners in the room were dark and mysterious; the glow of the flames played tricks. Warwick still had not spoken; he just stared at her, and though his lip curled into the devil's own taunting smile, no sign of warmth touched his eyes. And in that dancing candlelight they were not at all the hazel she knew them to be; they were gold like a flashing coin, or perhaps yellow like a streak of sun. They blazed like fire; perhaps like those of a wolf—a wolf that hunted at night, stalking and cornering its prey. A handsome wolf, stark and powerful with the night—deadly.

Fear plunged into her heart, and then rising anger. How dare he look at her so! How dare he—after his performance in the ballroom, dancing, smiling, laughing with that woman! Dear Lady Anne, who touched him so possessively with everyone looking, knowing that their relationship was indeed intimate. The gall of the man, lord or no! To come here and invade her privacy after his obvious interest in that slut!

Oh, how could he . . . and still she couldn't help the feelings that invaded her, body and soul . . . and heart. Dear God, but he was a striking man! No plume, no lace, no elegance of the cavalier costume, could detract from all that was so very masculine about him. She hated him then, that he could laugh so easily with Anne, that Anne could talk so covetously of him. Yet even hating him, she could still feel a thunder shake her, a storm rage within her. Cold blood sizzled, streaked through her to a mystical core. What was it, she wondered desperately, that touched such a distant and primal level of her being? When she saw him, her heart quaked and her limbs trembled and a secret excitement grazed hot and molten within her . . . even now, when he stared at her so, now when she needed most to despise him, now when the very air warned of tension.

"So—you are in here," he said at last.

He knew that liquor burned in his system; that he was alive with jealousy. He'd never felt like this, never been the victim of such a passion, or such a . . .

Love.

Behind his back his fingers tensed. The wine he had imbibed, silver chalice after silver chalice, had not eased the tempest in him, the brooding, aching, yearning tempest. It was true; he had fallen in love with her. He, of all men, had fallen in love. With the scraggly wretch he had saved from the gallows. Though she was not a wretch at all, as time had proved, but a vibrant woman, clever, mysterious—beautiful. So very beautiful in the candlelight.

Decked in nothing but white silk that lay against her: silk that fell to her feet in graceful lines; silk that could not hide the peaks of her breasts; silk that made him long to reach out. And her hair, floating over her shoulders, down her back. Gold and red, sunlight and sunset, a sea of fire. And her eyes, as blue as the sea, seafire, haunting a man, so deeply that he could not live without her.

Love . . . aye, he was in love with her. Bewitched, as if she were a mermaid, a goddess from the sea. Nay, he could not love her! His soul cried in torment. Yet neither could he shake that fever of fury and lust and . . . love . . . that had brought him here. By God's blood, he would see those cool blue eyes sparkle for him as they had for Charles, he would hear her whispered words, he would be the one to lead the dance . . .

"And where would I be, my lord?" she queried, determined to speak as coolly, yet unable to keep the bitter heat from her voice, or her eyes from glittering, exposing the ire that simmered inside her like bubbling peat.

He arched a dark brow to her. His satanic smile remained in place, and he strode across the room to the fire, turning the logs with the iron poker. "I'd thought, from your behavior, dear wife, that you might be elsewhere. Plying further charms upon the king." He set the poker down and turned to stare at her once more, still smiling in that pleasant, dangerous manner. He leaned an elbow upon the stone mantel and continued. "Like the other very beautiful but rather mercenary whores about court, I thought you might be waiting in line for your turn with the royal bed."

She gasped at the viciousness of his softly spoken accusation, then her temper snapped, and blindly she reached for the nearest thing to throw. Unfortunately, it was nothing more lethal than a neatly embroidered pillow.

But that missile hit him squarely between the eyes, and to her amazement he staggered in his attempt to catch it. She snapped at him furiously, "You're drunk! You've spent the evening whoring with your mistress, Lady Anne, and swilling wines with your grandly titled friends, and then you've the nerve to burst into my chamber with vile recriminations—*out!* Get out of here! Go back to your precious and delightful Anne and leave me in peace!"

He threw the pillow to the floor and hooked his thumbs into his waistband as he took a step toward her. His face appeared hard and dark, his jaw twisted, yet still that crooked grin remained in place while the blaze burned deeper in the golden hearts of his eyes. "Drunk, my lady—my pious, dignified, *virginal* wife? Ah, perhaps, 'tis true! The sight of one's legally wed lady—ever so chaste and pure in her husband's presence—pouring herself over the body of the king like scented oil—"

"Pouring! How—" Ondine cut in, only to be interrupted in return, his voice rising.

"Aye! Pouring, leaning against His Grace, laughing, smiling, with those delectable cherry-red lips, and nearly placing the fruit of those voluptuous white breasts into His Majesty's hands."

"Oh! You are a liar! A drunken sod of a liar! You know nothing better than the sordid tactics of your tavern-slut of a mistress and so you expect the same from others! Well, go back to her, my great lord of Chatham! Go back—"

"And leave you to the pursuit of a royal affair?"

"You're insane!"

"Mayhaps," he said softly. "Ah, yes, mayhaps! Mad with curiosity about the little thieving guttersnipe I married. The ingrate who chooses to make a fool of me—with a man not only my king, but whom I have called the best of friends. Ondine . . ."

He left the fire and came to her. His fingers bit into her shoulders, naked beneath the slim barrier of silk. She did not flinch; she stared up into his eyes. Hers were alive with the heat of candle glow, alive and tempest-tossed with rage. "Get your hands off me!" she enunciated crisply.

"Why, milady, should I do so? Should the husband be denied that which is so freely given elsewhere? What is it that you seek? Nell looks to the king for money and a title; Louise gains in jewels and lands. Or are their depths to the workings of your fair mind that not even I have begun to see? Barbara Villiers claimed the king magnificently endowed for the art of love—is it nothing more than the passion that you quest?" His words slurred huskily; his hand moved from her shoulder, and his thumb grazed her cheek.

"Bastard!" she hissed. Her elegant fingers twined into a knot, and she slammed them against his chest with all her strength. His words were so soft, so lulling, so touched with a huskiness that seeped into the soul, that she was fool enough to feel the hypnotism again—the damnable longing, the wonder . . .

"Oh! I do despise you!" She did not strike his chest again—he hadn't seemed to notice. She slapped him squarely against the jaw, twisted from his hold, and raced to the door, opening it. "Out, my dear lord husband! You are drunk and insulting! Leave me be!"

His strides were long and sure when he approached her. His fingers wound around her wrist, and she cried out a startled little sound as she found herself whirling back into the room. But Warwick didn't leave it; he closed the door once more. The hinges did not squeal or groan; the wood shuddered with the force of the slam.

"What do you think you're doing!" Ondine choked out.

"I wish a discussion with my wife," he said quite softly, but the timbre of the statement was such that she trembled suddenly. Drunk he might be, but not so much that his mind did not remain sharp as a whip, and his demanding nature had not altered in the least.

"I've nothing to say to a wine-sodden whoremonger!" she snapped back defensively. Then the line of his lip became so grim she was forced to remember that its power upon her nerves was nothing compared to his steel strength against her far more meager frame.

"I believe, my love, that you're the whore we're discussing."

"Get out!" she raged, and when she whirled blindly this time, she found the beautiful blue Dutch water ewer. She didn't notice how heavy it was; the fire of her anger gave her strength. She sent it hurtling straight for his obnoxious—and too handsome—head.

His reflexes, it seemed, had not deserted him, for he ducked and avoided the brunt of the blow. The ewer crashed against the door, spraying him with cool fresh water. He paused, startled, then emitted something of a growl as he leapt toward her with the pounce of a wolf, honing in at last upon its prey.

"No!" she shrieked, leaping to avoid him. And avoid him she did, but not completely. She was almost wrenched back to him, but there was a harsh rending sound. Warwick realized it was not his wife he held, but a panel of her gown. Ondine realized she had eluded her husband, but lost half her gown in the process. Dazed and desperate, she rolled over the bed, placing that barrier between them as she sought to drag the skirt of her gown to her breast while parrying his next move.

He sat upon the bed, leaning toward her, and his eyes seemed like narrow slits of fire as he spoke.

"I'll know now what your whispers were to the king!"

"You'll not! You have no right—"

"I've every right!"

"I've nothing whatsoever to say to you! Not when—" She cut herself off, terrified that she would give herself away. She'd never confide in him—never! Never tell him that his gallows' bride stood an accused traitor. And she'd never—please God!—fall more deeply in love with a man who slept wherever he liked and flaunted his affairs! He'd told her what she was to him: a commoner, a thief, a poacher, he had saved from the gallows. Nothing more.

She started to laugh. "Charles," she told him imperiously, "is the king. What I say to him, milord Chatham, is not your business!"

"Ah! So you allow his pawing. You encourage it?"

She wasn't wary enough. He rolled suddenly and with startling agility was on his feet before her, and his tone once more was soft. "Do you smile, my love, just to charm him as a friend? Or do you smile because you welcome his hand upon you as a woman?" He smiled, as if they chatted casually, yet she backed away, arms locked around herself as she sought to maintain what was left of her clothing. Don't taunt him; desist, and he will leave you! Yet she could not obey that logic. Something within her was in a rare impetuous rage that demanded she fight.

"The king is charming and courteous in all things!" she cried.

"And I am not?"

"You are an arrogant, demanding boor!"

"A *what?*"

She was backed against the wall; there was nowhere to go when his arms reached for her, when his fingers locked once more around her shoulders.

For a moment she panicked; then she raised her head, her eyes flashing a blaze of fury. "Dear sir, pray do not touch me. I fear the filth of your hands, for I know that they have wandered far and wide, and upon many an odious creature!"

"What?" Quite abruptly he began to laugh, and she was disarmed. Yet her ease was false, for she was suddenly gasping, swept cleanly off her feet and tossed upon the bed that had so recently been her barrier against him. Stunned, she fought to regain a hold on the remaining material of her gown, tangled beneath her. Yet she could not move, for before she could catch her breath, he was upon her, a haphazard knee cast over her legs and pinning them. His fingers were like steel as they wound around her upper arm.

"I beg your pardon?" he asked pleasantly enough. "You think that *my* hands have roamed too far?"

Her mind was reeling, and there was no release. Each breath she took was of him, his scent, clean and unique, something that spoke of his very masculinity. And she felt the iron-hard tension of his body against hers.

Suddenly he lifted his hand from her shoulder and placed it before their eyes, stretching the long brown tapered fingers. And then his eyes were on her, searing into her. "Is a state of guilt or innocence all that you might hold against my hand, Countess?"

And then, once more, he was watching that hand, that object of discussion. Watching it, because it lay upon her breast, bared by the loss of her gown. Her own gaze fell upon it, upon the fingers, so dark against her flesh, so light in their still caress. His fingers were splayed, her nipple lay between them, and though the touch could have been no lighter, the barest movement, the slightest rotation, was a sensation that ripped into her like a shooting streak of fire, heating the entire length of her. And for moments she lay spellbound, incapable of breathing, hearing only the rampant pounding of her heart, like a rush of the ocean.

Something in her cried out. Something warned her that she would not find him a beast at all. And something warned her that the consummation of her wedding vows would make her secret love for him languish in greater despair.

"Aye!" she cried out, so suddenly that he was taken unaware. "Aye—and I've watched where that hand has lingered all evening! So take it back to where it has been!" Her own words renewed her anger, and she flailed against the hand that dared to touch her. She kicked in a sudden fury against the leg that held her, and attempted to arise.

"Witch!" he raged out in return, but she had pelted herself into such a fury that she found herself the aggressor. She leaned against him, fingers clutched into fists that she pounded against his chest. "How dare you! By all the saints, how dare you!" Surely she sounded like a fishwife or a shrew; she had no thought to care. "You bring me to a place where your mistress speaks freely of your fascinating endowments, hangs on you like an accoutrement, and laughs in my face! Then you dare to—"

She broke off, horribly aware that she was atop him and that she had now lost more than one panel of her once beautiful gown, the silk having caught beneath him. Her legs were bare, her hips were bare, and only one shoulder carried a sign of having been clad. She was all but naked, and astraddle over him.

And she was no longer pelting him because he held her wrists. And his eyes, demon eyes, fire eyes, were upon her with amusement—and with something more, a night glitter, a primal glitter, that somehow echoed the pounding of her heart, the fury of rage and tension that sped throughout her.

"No!" she gasped again, jerking her wrists to elude him. She struggled to rise, but then shrieked with panic when she realized that he had only released her wrists to encircle her waist and send her plummeting down to the mattress once again, his prisoner. She sought to injure him no longer, but tossed madly and futilely against his weight and power.

"Let me—up!"

"Oh, nay! Nay! We've got to talk about this, my love! Am I to understand that you are so vastly annoyed because Anne saw fit to speak about my—endowments?"

"Let me go! I could care less about your—endowments!"

"Ah, because you prefer the king's?"

"Nay! Just let—"

His head lowered, and though she tossed her own, his mouth found hers. His torso covered and held the nakedness of her chest; his fingers moved to her cheeks, stroking her chin as he kissed her. His mouth encompassed hers. His tongue flicked against her teeth with a persistence and strength that sapped her own. Warmth flooded her, and a feeling that was sweeter, more potent than any wine she had ever tasted. Ah, beyond that . . . it felt as if she had stumbled upon a great unknown, a dark uncharted voyage into a strange paradise where she might stumble, and yet could not, for he was her guide. He filled her mouth, tasted and plundered there, and she forgot that she must protest against him. She lay still, aware only of the taste of him, the texture of his tongue as it raked against the crevices of her mouth, leaving the most delicious feeling there, drowning her with sweetness and with force.

He drew away from her, and still she could not move, not thinking to fight him. No humor remained in his eyes, just the darker thing, haunted and tense. His knuckles played over her cheek, swept like air over her throat, then between the valley of her breasts. Once more his dark head bent, and his mouth closed over her breast, the tongue that had been so potent in its play upon her mouth now delivering a sensation so sweet that she cried out. Her body strained with shock, with pleasure. Just the tip of his tongue, stroking again and again, over the tip of her breast, with all the warmth of his mouth around it. And then the force was harder, a suctioning, a caress, drawing rivulets of flame from her, until she did not know where the sensation came from, it had invaded her so. Nor did she understand the soft sounds that came from her, the compulsion that drew her fingers to his hair, to lock there, to find fascination in the thick brown locks.

His teeth held her nipple, gently grazed it, released it, but she was not free of his touch, for his palm moved over her, his eyes burning her with a fire of sensation. His hand, his fingers, traveled over her, her waist, her hip, her belly, her thigh. His voice, too, was encompassing, husky, deep, male, a play upon all the things awakened inside her.

"Ah, Countess, never have I quite realized what bounty I did take from that hangman's noose. What beauty . . ." His lips touched upon her belly, and his whisper was so warm against her flesh. "Be there a comparison of endowments, I would well call yours the finest ever fashioned . . ."

Once again his kiss fell. His fingers strayed in her hair, and she floated in that drugged state that told her this was worth dying for; this was the stuff of ballads, of history's great passions, of—

Comparisons!

Oh, God! That he should think to compare her to that viperous Anne and to a host of others.

"Oh!" she screamed aloud in fury, wrenching his hair in her

grasp, shoving her knee against his endowments. Quite startled, he grunted in pain—and she was free.

"You! You, my lord Warwick Chatham, are nothing but a giant rotting codpiece! You made a promise to me! You—".

"I am what?" he demanded, and his tone seemed laced now with fury as he threw his legs over the bed and rose to face her. "I made a promise to you! Well, what is it, then, my love? Homage to the king, but not to the lord of your own manor?"

"Oh, stop this prattle about the king! You are—oh!"

He was on his feet, not touching her, but grasping the tattered remainder of her gown, and then she wore nothing. She could not escape the determined glitter of his eyes. No anger now could save her, and so she sought belatedly to plead his good graces. "Warwick! Nay, your temper—"

"Is sorely vexed. Just as my—endowments are injured by your less than gentle touch! Yet we'll ease them of such stress, shall we not?"

"Warwick—"

She backed herself once again to the wall, and that was where he pinned her, her hands held in his own. She expected fury and found it in the first onslaught of his kiss, one that conquered and bruised . . . but did not, could not, remain brutal. Even in searing panic and desperation she felt again the call to her senses, to all her aching, yearning excitement and desire. To her love. Again the nectar claimed her, the honeyed feeling, so alive and vibrant. It made her tremble, made her hunger . . .

Her fingers slowly, slowly curled around his. She did not know when it began, but her lips sought his touch as surely as he gave it. Again it seemed as if the pulse of the tide beat within her, as if only the rush of the sea ruled her heart and mind. Her head fell back as he raised her in his arms, her arms entwined around his neck, and there were no words between them, only the golden determination in his eyes and the drugged daze in her own as he returned her to the bed. She thought he would come to her arms; he did not. He shed his boots and his velvet coat, then paused and knelt at the side of the bed.

And then he took her foot into his hand.

He held it first, as if it were a fine porcelain figure. Then he stroked the arch, and the heat of his kiss glazed her toes, an exotic feeling, one that teased, one that burned.

That elusive, maddening touch continued—the stroke of his fingers, nails, the caress of his kiss, the spear of his tongue— taunting, evoking along the length of her. She did not think that she breathed the air; she just lay there, spellbound and sated with each new experience of his touch. The movement of his fingers, his kiss, slowly finding erotic places—the back of her knee, along her inner thigh, the down juncture where her limbs met . . .

A gasp, a whisper, escaped her. A soft cry that she must, must escape his intimate caress, one that blinded her, elated her, made her feel as if her entire body ran rampant with a hot honeyed elixir. She tried so hard to twist from him, yet succeeded only in curling to him, abetting him with the swift and sudden discovery of desperate passion. She knew not where she was, or even who; she did not know herself at all, not this creature who cried out, who writhed and twisted, moaning inarticulate things. She did not know the woman who grasped at his hair, bringing his kiss at last to her lips, bestowing delicious pleasure with her tongue, which nipped and sought and sank, deeper and deeper into the wonder . . .

Suddenly she was bereft. Cold and bereft. He was gone. Dazed, she opened her eyes to the glowing candlelight. He was not gone. His eyes were on her, fire in that light. His features, shadowed, dark and tense. She closed her eyes, trembling as reality came to her. She loved him . . . and she wanted him, she wanted . . . this.

She felt his fingers first, the tips, just streaking along her thigh. Instinct brought her to tense against that pressure; he did not note that last defense of something she held moral. He but leaned down to capture her lips, and the pressure of his knee came between hers, the wonder of his strength enwrapped her. His touch, his warmth, returned her to that mystical plain where she could seek nothing but satiation to all the liquid, burning hunger that rioted throughout her being . . .

She could not have desired any man more, yet neither could she prevent the jagged shriek of agony that escaped her lips when he moved into her at last, a knife that split and tore. She heard him emit a startled oath, and pain helped fuel the anger that speared her, even with his touch. Tears stung her eyes—he had truly thought her so hastily involved with the king, or elsewhere, prior to their marriage. She choked on her tears and could say nothing against him; she pressed her palms desperately against his chest, but she could not move him. And even as the pain blazed and then slowly faded, she heard him again, not in oaths or in question, but in tender phrases, gentle, husky words, words that eased, that lulled . . .

That seduced again . . . seduced with the movement of his hands, his kiss, his stroke upon her breasts, seduced so thoroughly that the ragged moment of agony was quickly but a distant memory.

She would not think till later that he was but the most expert of lovers. That he but knew the trade very well . . .

Now he was a part of her, filling her with bursting wonder, as if he entered every pore of her body. He urged her with whispers, with his fingers cupped about her buttocks, caressing her breasts, lifting her once again. It was a dance, a thing of beauty . . . his shoulders, slick and gleaming golden in the candlelight, his eyes a fire of wanting her . . . He was beautiful, taut, sinewed, a work of art, a man . . .

This was the wonder, the sense of mercury and excitement, that which she had yearned for long before she knew—this sizzling heat that seared the body, made her blaze and soar, ache and yearn . . . explode—with a cry from her lips, a groan from his. Shattering, volatile . . . Oh, sweet Lord! It was crystal magic, enwrapping her, caressing and emcompassing her with the seed of his body. She had something of him . . . Oh, she had never, never suspected that such pleasure could be on this earth!

It took moments, long moments, for Ondine to drift down from that pinnacle of sensation. Yet when she did, she could not look at him. She could not face the wanton display of passion that had seized not him, but herself. She could not believe that she— certainly no fool!—had fallen into his arms . . . arms that had so recently held another and would most probably do so again.

Without a word she buried her face into the pillow.

And it seemed now, too, that Warwick had nothing more to say. She felt him shift; through webs of her hair she saw him rise, still splendid in taut muscular nakedness, and extinguish the candles. She felt him lie down beside her, near, but not touching.

Time ticked by. She lay as tense as stone. How much time? she wondered. She dared to shift, still hiding behind the mantle of her hair. Did he sleep?

He did not. His eyes were on the ceiling, far above him. In the darkness she could not read his eyes. She saw only that his features seemed grim; there was a sense of the ease of the wine about him now. His fingers were laced behind his head, and he seemed to stare at that ceiling in deep thought, pensive and severe.

She froze as he moved, determined to feign sleep.

He rose above her and pulled the hair gently from her face. She kept her eyes tightly closed, and whether he believed she slept or not she did not know.

He shifted again. She felt the covers being pulled warmly around her. And she felt his weight as he lay down beside her again.

And though she didn't see him, she was certain that he had regained his original pose; that he was staring at the ceiling again, and that his eyes would be troubled with secrets and mystery; that his jaw would be hard, pensive . . .

Why?

She ached; she yearned to know. She longed to reach to him, yet she could not. She didn't dare give more of a love than she could receive in turn.

She had her own grave problems to solve, she reminded herself sharply. She forced herself to call to mind the horrid things he had said to her—that she was nothing but a commoner, saved for his use. In time she must escape him—prove herself loyal, regain her birthright. He had taken much of her this night, but he had learned nothing of the king's promise, nor would he.

None of these things could help her; none of them could hold her thoughts, her mind, or her heart. She was changed; he had changed her. She could never forget that her virginity had been shed upon this bed, with violence and tenderness, fury and laughter and—longing.

And she simply couldn't stop thinking of Anne, thinking of her with a furious loathing. If the lady dared speak of Warwick's endowments again, Ondine was quite certain she would tear her to shreds.

The lady Anne, it seemed, had the greater claim.

I am his wife! Ondine thought with anguish.

His gallows' bride . . .

Taken by him at last, and never, never to be the same again.

Chapter 14

Sunlight was pouring into the room when she awoke, streams that danced from the panes upon her. Memory of the night past came upon her in a warm rush, and still dazed with sleep, she smiled, smug and pleased with that memory. Warwick! Ah, memory of his face, his touch, was all that came to her with that first light. Had he been beside her, she might well have sighed with the complacent pleasure of a kitten and cast herself awestruck against him.

But he was not beside her, and as she opened her eyes more fully, she saw him at last.

He stood by the window, completely dressed down to buckled shoes and plumed hat. His foot rested upon the rung of a chair, his thumbs locked into breeches, and he stared darkly and pensively out upon the brightness of the day.

Her heart first soared with the sight of him, then seemed to shatter like the surf against rocks as the grimness of his taut features worked into her mind.

She drew her covers up; she was uneasy, though she knew not why. Her smile slowly faded just as he turned to her.

"Warwick—"

He doffed his hat and bowed low, without mockery this morning, yet with something far worse: the greatest reserve, the most chilling distance.

"My lady, I do apologize for my most atrocious manners of last eve. I fear I drank too deeply, and too well, and matters here are tense at best. Do forgive me."

She stared at him blankly, unbelievingly. Then she raised her own shield of ice to combat the fever of pain, and twisted with her covering so that her back was to him.

"Just do get out of here, please."

He did not move; he hesitated. Then he came to her back, and she shivered as she felt the line his finger drew there.

"I didn't know, er . . . I did not suspect . . ."

She swung around, staring at him. "Know what?"

He grated out some impatient sound, a barely articulate oath. "For God's sake, girl, I married you off the gallows!"

"And . . . ?" she demanded warily, her temper instinctively growing as she sought his meaning.

"I did not expect to find a maid, untouched, but a woman of certain experience."

"What? *Oh!*" She forgot that he was completely clad, that her covers were her only defense, and sat to throw her pillow hard against him. He caught it with a mere tightening of his mouth.

"My God, you'd come from Newgate—"

"Newgate! Ah, yes, my lord of Chatham! I came from Newgate! How dare you assume that all those wretches dragged to that horrid place are whores, since they be debtors or beggars—"

"Or liars, cutthroats, and thieves? Forgive what was stolen, Countess, by a drunken boor; had I known you were among the great virtuous masses of Newgate, I'd never have erred. And then, Countess, there was the matter of the king, you see. You swayed and laughed and teased with him like a mistress well versed in the arts."

Retrieving her covers, Ondine lowered her head. "Get out!"

He bowed low to her once again, and she hated him for it and for the vibrant sarcasm in his words.

"As I said, my manners were atrocious. I shall endeavor, madam, to improve them in the future."

He turned then and strode to the door, but paused there. "I've business with the king this day and the next, yet now that I am

here, I've no wish to stay longer than I must. Be prepared to leave,
for I intend to cut short our stay as much as possible."

He opened the door and closed it behind himself. Ondine stared
after him, still incredulous. Tears burned her eyes, and she dug
her fingers into the sheets, fighting them. She would never, never
understand him. Never in a thousand years . . .

She turned about, burying her head into the pillow as a sob tore
from her. How could she have been so foolish as to forget? Forget
that his reputation was a rage about court, that it seemed that one
woman was but the same as another to him.

She pushed her face from the pillow at last. "Bastard! Bastard!"
she hissed, miserably clenching her eyes together. She had allowed
herself to care . . .

She rose, shivering as she rushed naked to the pitcher and bowl.
She splashed water brutally against her face.

The king had suggested she leave him, and leave him she surely
would. Newgate whore, indeed! She was a duchess in her own
right, and, by God, she would prove it and he would eat the dust
that flew from her heels.

She paused then, shivering once again. No. He had saved her
life in a devil's bargain she still did not understand. She was in
his debt. She would pay that debt, for it was owed. But when it
was paid in full, she would depart as swiftly as the wind.

Warwick spent the day in the king's chambers, listening as
advisors warned Charles about the fear of Papists, still riding high
in England. The king's face was set, for it was his brother, James,
heir to the crown, whom they attacked.

Charles despised intolerance; he had a leaning toward Catholi-
cism himself—yet a penchant for his throne that kept him ever
wary and prudent. As his maternal grandfather—the great Henry
IV—had once claimed, "Paris for a Mass!" Charles would remain
Protestant king to remain a king.

"Leave off with this endless debate!" Charles said wearily.
"We've graver matters at stake!"

And so the business of the kingdom turned to finance, another
endless debate, for Charles was nearly always in need of funding.
Warwick lost touch with the voices around him. He sat at

apparent attention; he was nothing but a marble presence. Hi
thoughts—remorse, shame, hunger, and longing—consumed him
and he feared he would never escape the tangle of emotion. Sh
haunted him more now that the scent and sight and sound an
touch of her were real in his memory, so very real that he coul
see all of her, know the detail, the beauty . . .

He had all but attacked her. His wife. The wretched ragamuffi
he had plucked from the streets—the woman he had sworn t
protect, but never love. Protect! Dear God, from what? Had h
gone insane? What had he expected to prove here? Hardgrave wa
in attendance, as well as the lady Anne. Yet how could Ann
whisper to Ondine in the halls of Chatham Manor? How coul
Hardgrave?

Hardgrave was so near, a neighbor. There were hidden chamber
and false doors within Chatham.

But the hounds would not accept a stranger in the hall, no
could Warwick imagine Hardgrave, with his bulk, scamperin
through the halls to whisper to his wife!

His head was pounding. He had wronged Ondine; wronged he
gravely. She had been as chaste as the snow, yet would be n
more when he released her from this travesty into which he ha
summoned her.

Could he release her? He did not think that he could . . .

God rot it all! But he had never felt this passion so deep,
ruled all thought, dulling the mind and tricking the actions! Th
envy, this jealousy . . . this absolute sense of possession. It was
painful thing. It tore at the gut and the heart and the soul, and h
wished fervently that he'd never seen her face, never felt her spe
entrap him.

Think, man, it was time to watch and judge. Anne was as jealou
as a spiteful little cat, pleading, cajoling, threatening. Hardgrav
and Warwick were keeping their distance, like great wary bear
Hardgrave watched Ondine with hunger lacing his eyes, but wh
man did not? It had all been worthless. All that he had manage
was a time of agony, seeing his wife the center of endless desire-
his own! Taking her . . .

But he could not do so again. He was no rapist, no seducer
innocents. Nor did he dare love her, though love her he did. Sh
didn't know his bargain, but it had been sealed in his heart. Sh

had been bait for a killer, and for that she was due his greatest debt, her life and her freedom.

Two more nights of misery.

No, there was endless misery. For at Chatham she would still be near.

But she would have her own chamber. He could not go to her again; it would not be fair.

Two more days. Days of watching her laugh and smile and charm everyone around her. Days of feeling the coldness of her gaze when it fell upon him. Days of watching Anne eye her in constant and dangerous speculation, while Hardgrave stared after her with lust and cunning in his eyes.

On a sudden thought Warwick made the announcement, the next day, of his coming heir at court. Charles and Catherine were thrilled.

Anne narrowed her cat's eyes furiously.

Hardgrave appeared to plot all the more.

Ondine stared at him, as if her eyes were glittering steel swords and she would gladly use them to disembowel him.

But nothing happened, except that his temper grew shorter as he tried to sleep upon the settee, tried not to think that just beyond the door she breathed and slept, that beneath her nightdress she was warm and supple and curved for a man's pleasure, that she was a woman of grace and passion that raged deeper than even he had imagined . . .

On the third day they left before the sun had risen. Warwick was atop the carriage with Jake; Ondine was alone inside of it.

They reached Chatham, and Warwick found his life ever more miserable. He could not leave her at night, for it was here that she had claimed the whisperer came to her, calling her.

And she was so cool, so aloof and polite, cordial, moving about with the rustle of her skirts, the scent of her perfume, her chin held high, her eyes sweet enigmas. She spoke as if they were acquaintances, and she kept her distance most serenely. She laughed and smiled and chatted—with Justin and Clinton. Mathilda came to adore her more and more.

Warwick grew more moody, more reserved, stiff and straight and cold as ice . . . ice that housed a fire. He could not break the

spell, change the beguilement. Again, he felt something in hir
simmer, and it was dangerous, so dangerous . . .

From Justin, Ondine learned that Anne could be a jealous beauty
though she collected lovers herself as another woman might add
gowns to her wardrobe. She had assumed—after Genevieve'
death and the demise of her husband—that she would marry War
wick, though Justin stated with laughter that Warwick, had he no
been so strange with brooding sorrow and anger after his firs
wife's death, would not have married Anne anyway.

They'd been back at Chatham a week. She walked with Justi
toward the stables as they spoke. Ondine had no permission t
ride, yet she enjoyed seeing the horses where they stood in th
fields, or in their stalls. Jake, she knew, would not be far behin
her, but not close enough to hear her words, and so she easil
plagued Justin with questions that he didn't seem to min
answering.

"You didn't know my brother long before your marriage, di
you?" Justin asked her, his bright eyes alive with laughter.

"No," she admitted, but told him no more. With a winnin
smile she placed a hand upon his arm. "So you see, dear Brothe
I need all your help to understand my lord of Chatham."

That much was true; she longed to understand the man,
discover what role she played, and then leave!

"Ah, fair Sister, touch me not!" Justin implored, smiling h
flattery. "My brother's bride sets a tempest in my own soul, an
I am not made of stone."

"I believe that he is," Ondine muttered, the words slippin
from her without thought.

"Ah-ha!" Justin declared, laughing. "So—this court excursio
brought disharmony betwixt you, because of Anne, no doubt."

She had no desire to explain the details of the estrangement
her marriage that Justin so obviously sensed and viewed wi
amusement. She moved forward to pluck a wildflower from th
heath, then turned back to her handsome brother-in-law.

"Tell me more about Anne."

Justin laughed, taking her hand and swinging it at his side s
that they could continue their walk.

"Anne is a cunning vixen, nothing more, nothing less. She has partnered the king, among others, and from that alone, I can assure you, my brother never thought of her as anything other than amusement alone. The 'beasts' of Chatham are just that at times, my lady—proud and possessive. Beasts play where they will, but when they choose a mate, they do so with the gravest care, and might well be prone to kill for that mate's honor and virtue. Can you foresee such a life with the lady Anne?"

Ondine did not reply. Warwick had, after all, taken her from the gallows, and he had, so it seemed, assumed her to be of the loosest morality.

She grinned sweetly at Justin, enjoying the lightness and laughter in his eyes, the tender flattery of his tongue, when all she received elsewhere was the most distant, forced courtesy.

"Tell me, Justin, do you know so much of beasts since you are of their number yourself?"

"Me? A beast? Nay, lady, never! The second child receives not the title, nor the land—but neither must he go through life with the label either!" Justin laughed.

Ondine laughed along with him, yet suddenly she was uneasy. Justin could hold the same intrigue in his visage as Warwick at times, the same ultimate charm, the same flirtation with danger. Did he ever resent his brother for the accident of birth, that Warwick held the title and the income?

It seemed that a cloud came just then, precisely, to cover the sun, to riddle her with chills of doubt. Ah, it was the madness of this place! It was her husband—oh, the devil should indeed take for a beast!—forcing her to a tempest only to dash her upon the coldness of a barren shore! There was no rhyme or reason to it, yet like him, she watched all with a jaundiced eye and found that mistrust came like a wall between any friendship, any closeness.

"Ah! Speak of the 'beast,' fair sister! There he is yonder, where we walk, with Clinton and Dragon!"

Justin caught her hand and hurried her along. She was flushed when she reached the stable yard, and being so, she felt that Warwick's golden gaze touched upon her suspiciously, and she could not forget that his temper could be sparked to a high blaze with jealousy.

Clinton, observing them all from a casual stance, greeted them cordially. Warwick said nothing, but he had little time, for Justin moved in to touch Dragon's warm muzzle, demanding of his brother, "Have you seen the colt in the field, then, Brother? I do warrant that the son shall rival the father soon!"

Warwick laughed at his brother, seeming to forget Ondine for the moment. "What? You say, for the colt is yours, Justin! I'll wager easily and well that it will take many a year for even his offspring to rival Dragon in strength and speed!"

"Nay! One more year, and we'll see to that wager!"

"Aye!" Warwick declared.

"You're about to ride?" Justin said. "Wait but a moment, and your wife and I might accompany you."

The laughter faded from Warwick's face; again he stared at Ondine in that harsh way she had as yet to fathom. Yet she cared little now; her heart pulsed with the excitement of riding. Surely he could not deny her when he rode himself!

"Ondine may not ride. I've an appointment with a Flemish wool merchant and haven't the time to wait for her to change clothing. Nor should she be so reckless with her health and our— child."

"I beg you, milord!" she said very softly. "I swear, I can ride well in what I wear! My health is excellent. The exercise would do me and"—she paused, challenging him with her eyes—"the child a world of good."

She heard his *tsk* of anger and knew with a fleeting pleasure that she had annoyed and embarrassed him, behaving like an abused spouse before his brother and cousin.

"Come, then!" he said irritably.

"It will take no time to saddle a suitable mount," Clinton said pleasantly, and Ondine gazed at him quickly with wide grateful eyes, further annoying Warwick, yet she did not care in the least.

"I'll tend to my own mount," Justin told his brother, "and there will be no wait at all!"

Ondine did not gaze at Warwick; she sped behind Clinton, finding a bridle even as he selected the saddle for a small chestnut mare. She thanked Clinton warmly for his support, yet thought fleetingly that Clinton, too, had that manner about him! Indomitable; arrogant for all that he was, pleasant when he chose, kind when he chose. But he, too, was a Chatham, not the younger in birth, but of improper birth. Chathams! All possessive, too proud. And around them lurked a shroud of mystery. She should fear, but she didn't know what it was she should fear, only that whispers plagued the manor, and Warwick kept his secrets to himself.

"Come, my lady, now or never!" Warwick called out harshly.

Clinton boosted her onto the mare; she was aware that his hands were powerful, like her husband's.

Justin paused for a word with Clinton; Ondine started off with Warwick. They were but paces from the stable before he turned to her, eyeing her most callously.

"What now, my lady? The king's rapture was not enough? Would you string along my own flesh and blood?"

She was already on the horse; there was no further need for even her customary nominal courtesy.

"The devil take you, Warwick," she said with a condescending smile and a lift of her chin; then she nudged her heels against the mare and felt that she flew—beyond him, beyond his hurting reach.

"Ondine!" The roar of his voice followed her, yet could not touch her. She laughed with delight, laughed with the wind and the freshness of the air and the marvelous feel of the muscular horseflesh beneath her. The mare was sound and small and swift. She raced! But Ondine had forgotten that Dragon was indeed a fierce steed, a stallion as powerful as his master. He was soon beside her.

"Cease this reckless speed!" Warwick blazed out as they came neck and neck. "You know not the terrain! By all heaven I swear you'll never sit upon a mount again . . ."

The threat brought her fleeting glimpse of freedom to a staggering halt. She pulled in on the reins, but not before she discovered what he meant of the terrain. The mare's hoof caught upon a root. The horse stumbled, and Ondine was left to leap quickly away from the falling horse, lest she be crushed.

She landed in a thicket, with Warwick quickly at her side, his hands too intimately upon her as he swore vociferously and checked for broken bones.

"Leave off!" Ondine pleaded. "I am fine!"

"Leave off! Fool! Vixen, you'll not listen, even when it's your life and limb I look to!"

She lowered her head as he dragged her to her feet, loathe that he should know how his touch, even in anger, too vividly reminded her of a different time.

"Ah, marital bliss!"

Both of them started violently at the sound of a female voice. Warwick moved from Ondine, frowning as he turned. They had both been too involved with one another to notice anything else, not even the approaching thud of hooves.

And Ondine could have sworn she was as startled as he at the mounted appearance of Lady Anne.

"Anne," Warwick stated irritably, his hands upon his hips, a frown creasing the line of his brow. "What—"

A second horse moved around the lady Anne's, carrying Lyle Hardgrave.

"Hardgrave," Warwick said quietly, yet the name sounded from his lips like a curse.

"Chatham," Hardgrave returned. He doffed his hat to Ondine. "My lady . . ."

And those words sounded like a caress.

"The viscount so kindly invited me to his estates," Anne said sweetly, "and so here I come upon the two of you! *Tsk! Tsk!* Warwick, I can't imagine that you've not taught your bride to sit a horse properly! Poor lady! Ah, and with child, at that! I shall pray all is well. Oh, my dear girl, you've grass all about you! Such a fall! Or is the grass from your sleeping quarters? Warwick, surely you do not keep her in the barn?"

"Nay, lady, he does not!" Ondine spoke out, carefully modulating her voice to sound cheerful before Warwick could answer in anger. "Do you ask because that is where he might have kept his . . . sluts before? Have no fear, I am well housed. And I ride quite well." She smiled as sweetly as a contented kitten, slipped her hands about Warwick's rigid arm, and moved closer to him with an adoring gaze. "We just discovered that we must touch one another at the strangest moments . . . anywhere, at anytime . . ."

Warwick's arm then locked around her shoulder; he pulled her closer and idly moved his fingers over her shoulder, apparently moved from wrath to amusement, and more than willing to take his cue from her. "Hardgrave, what are you and your guest doing on my land?"

"I beg to differ," Hardgrave responded to Warwick, but his

eyes did not leave Ondine. "This is my land you've stumbled upon."

"Ah, perhaps we have," Warwick said lightly, giving his attention to Ondine, as if she were such a rich distraction that his mind could fathom nothing less. "Ah, love, see!" he accused her as tenderly as a lover. "You've led me far astray."

Anne made an impatient sound from her saddle. "Ride with us a while, Lord Chatham."

"What? Oh?" Warwick tore his eyes from Ondine, lazy eyes that fell over Anne with little interest. "I'm afraid we cannot. I've an appointment."

His chilly gaze then turned to Hardgrave. "We'll take care not to stumble upon your land again, Viscount!"

He turned about swiftly, hands encircling Ondine's waist so that he could set her upon the mare once again. Then he moved to procure Dragon, who had wandered several feet away to feast upon a thicket of high grass.

Anne moved her horse closer to Ondine's. She smiled quite pleasantly.

"Lady Ondine. Lady! I've a mind that you are no more than a common and talented . . . whore! And I will prove it, my lady. Mark my words—I will discover you!"

Ondine smiled in return. "Do your best, Anne."

Over Anne's head she saw Hardgrave staring at her, leering in such a way that her blood ran cold. It seemed that he would consume her with greedy eyes, and despite herself she blanched, even as he bowed from the saddle, spurred his horse, and rode away with the lady Anne following at his heels.

Warwick, mounted upon Dragon once again, came to her side grimly, gripping the mare's bridle.

"Damn you and breakneck paces!" he swore. "I warn you, and my words make no difference! You caused this, girl, and I warn you the two of them will stop at nothing; they are not to be trusted!"

"Trusted! It appears to me that you long and well 'trusted' the lady Anne, with all your heart, mind, soul—and body!"

"Jealous, my love?"

"Nay! Revolted!"

"I am ever so sorry to offend you. Yet something like this

cannot happen again. Perhaps you should be restrained to the house!''

''Were you not such a horrid beast of a jailor, it would not have occurred.''

''Horrid beast! Watch it, Lady! Should you request one, you will get one!''

Justin came dashing up just then, warning them that they crossed the border of their lands.

''I know!'' Warwick spat out. ''And I believe that my lady is now aware of her boundaries, too!''

Justin gazed at Ondine; she shook her head. Warwick rode ahead, and Ondine and Justin followed behind in silence.

Chapter 15

Ondine spoke no more at the stables, except to thank Clinton for helping her from the mare. She turned her back before Warwick and Justin had dismounted from their horses, and hurried back to the house. She didn't have to turn around to know that her husband was close on her heels, but he made no attempt to stop her.

Mathilda was in the entryway, there to warn Warwick that Monsieur Deauvin from Bruges awaited him in his office. She paused in her second sentence to stare at Ondine's state of disrepair. "Oh, milady! What happened?"

"Nothing, really nothing at all, thank you," Ondine replied, striding past her for the staircase. She knew that Warwick stayed below; she heard him ask refreshments be sent to his study for himself and his guest. But seconds later she heard the tread of footsteps behind her. Without turning she knew that Jake had taken his place as watchdog once again.

She slammed into the music room, felt no apology as she rifled through Warwick's desk to procure a bottle of port, then smiled bitterly as she threw the door back open, confronting Jake with the bottle.

"Would you like a drink, Jake? Seems a pity you must suffer constant boredom due to my presence."

"I'm—uh—seldom bored, milady," he mumbled quickly.

"Oh, but you are!" Ondine protested. "You, Jake, are a pleasant man with wit as well as loyalty, and I do think it an eternal shame that you have chained yourself for life to that beastial viper, the Earl of North Lambria!"

Jake grinned at her, apparently unoffended—and equally unaffected by her speech. "You've straws or grass or something in your hair, milady. Shall I send for your maid?"

"No!"

Ondine smiled sweetly and closed the door again. Muttering, she passed through Warwick's bedroom and the elaborate bath into her own chamber, carelessly shedding her gown and donning a new one, then stroking her hair endlessly before the mirror until the grass and twigs were all removed and it again shone like fire.

Dear God! That she could understand anything at all in this household! First, there was a subservient housekeeper who was an illegitimate relative; then there was Clinton, whose illegitimacy didn't seem to bother him in the least; and finally there was Justin—an easygoing rake, fond of his brother, fond of tormenting him too! Then, too, there was a whisperer who crawled the halls—and disappeared into thin air—in addition to a lascivious neighbor with whom Warwick had already done battle. And of course she couldn't forget lady Anne, an ex-mistress, wasn't she? Ah, but she didn't intend to remain an "ex," and there's the rub of it! Oh, they were all insane, and at the top of the group was Warwick himself, striding in upon her to take her in anger, then dragging her back to ignore and chastise her!

She realized that her hand, with her fingers curled taut around the brush, still trembled with a score of emotions.

"Oh, I do hate you! I hate you, vile beast!" she swore out loud. Then she brushed, and clenched her eyes tightly together, because she knew that not to be the case at all, and she could not bear that she—in truth the Duchess of Rochester, the once proud and independent Ondine!—could have stooped to loving a man who might touch her, yet would never love in return.

"Oh, my lord, I will have my revenge on you yet!" she swore, stamping her foot. She tossed the brush across the room, watching it land on the bed. Then she swirled around. She could not stay in the room.

Jake made no pretense of doing anything other than watching her room when she came sailing out once again.

"The garden, I think, Jake."

"But you brought in flowers for the house this morning—"

A small wry smile curled into his lips at the admission that he had watched her all day. Surely they both knew it! There was nothing to hide. Jake was about unless Warwick himself stood over her.

"Then I shall bring flowers to the chapel!" she announced, and he was left with no other choice than to follow her down the grand stairway once again.

At the foot of the stairs she was hailed once more by Mathilda, who came anxiously racing toward her.

"Milady! A spill from a horse and you are up and about again! You must lie down, you must take care!"

Ondine shook her head in confusion. "Mathilda, I assure you that I am fine."

"But the babe! You should look to yourself!"

"Pardon?"

"Your condition, my lady!"

Condition, my foot! Ondine thought furiously. Oh, God, she was forever forgetting that she was supposed to be with child!

"I'm fine, Mathilda, honestly," she said gently. "I'm just going to the garden."

"I shall bring you goat's milk later."

"Wonderful," Ondine murmured. She forced herself to smile, but could no longer abide the manor and so hurried past Mathilda.

She plucked rich red roses from the gardens in back, helped by Old Tim, who provided her with gloves and a basket. When Old Tim disappeared into a small storage shed, Jake came around from the corner of it, panting a bit.

"I do love roses!" Ondine called to him.

He nodded bleakly.

With her basket filled, Ondine swirled about and hurried around the house to enter the chapel from the front. She saw Jake in hurried pursuit, smiled, and closed the doors behind her. Poor Jake! But then he chose to serve his master!

With the doors closed behind her, Ondine paused, leaning against them to survey the chapel. It was a beautiful place with its wonderful stained glass windows and altar sculptures in marble and glass. The afternoon was waning now, but still sunlight flickered through the stained glass in rainbow hues. There was shadow and a pastel glow, and Ondine thought that here one might truly commune with a more ethereal world.

She pushed away from the door, intending to head straight for the main altar. But she did not; she paused along the way, observing the monuments. The most recent memorialized the old lord and lady, and Ondine found herself musing on what they must have been like to have parented Warwick and Justin.

She studied the monument to the Earl and Countess of Chatham who had come before them, he who had died upon the battlefield in defense of Charles I, and she who had died in his wake, pitching through the wood on the staircase. Cherubic angels prayed that they should rest in peace, and Ondine found herself fervently desiring that they did, then wondering where the lord's mistress might have been interred.

"Certainly not in the family vault!" she mused with a touch of amusement curling her lip.

Farther along she came upon the altar dedicated to the first of the Chathams—the Norman who had earned them the rumor of being "beasts." The simple stone was so worn that little could be read of the inscription.

"Ah, but your legend, sir, lives on, long and well!" Ondine murmured. Then she touched the stone, a little tenderly, for despite all, she was in love with that long-ago lord's descendant.

"Except that he is a beast, and it seems I must soon escape him and his madness, else become prey!" Squaring her shoulders as if she might shed her whimsical words of nonsense from them, she returned to the center aisle to reach the main altar. Then she found herself wondering where Genevieve had been interred. She stopped to turn about, and realized that the altar dedicated to Genevieve stood opposite that of the last Earl and Countess of North Lambria. She gave pause, curious, for she was not easily frightened, yet she suddenly felt a tension and a chill. Walk to the tomb, see it! she commanded herself, and she could not do so. She gave herself a furious shake and continued to the main altar, where she dropped briefly to her knees, then stood to set the flowers in the urns there.

She was thus engaged when she heard what first seemed to be a moan. Hands upon a rose, she stiffened, still and silent.

And then the sound came again, like the wind, a whisper, a moan. She spun about, seeking out the corners of the room. But it had grown darker still, and all that flickered about her was blue and red light, a haze of it at that, a swirl of mystery.

"Who is there!" she called out, keeping her voice low and annoyed. Never show fear, her father had warned her once, for it is a weakness one's enemies might feed upon.

There was no answer. She wondered if the air of the place might have played upon her mind, if all the superstitions did not haunt her good sense, and so she turned to her task again.

But the next sound was a husky whisper of her name, a sound with neither sex nor substance, but so clear that she pricked her finger upon a thorn on a rose and shuddered where she stood.

Now she swung in the greatest anger, ready to find her tormentor, determined to challenge him. Yet when she turned now, she was so startled that only a gasp came from her.

There was no need to search out her tormentor.

Not ten feet away stood ... a creature. It was a mirage, an image surely created by the surreal light, by the pall of darkness and shadow, by the fears that lurked in her mind.

It was a creature, completely cloaked in black, its face a demon's mask cast in a hideous leering grin. And even as she stood, stunned and incredulous and gaping, the demon raised its arms to display hands that boasted talons, long and lethal, curled and poised as if they longed to strike, to come across throat and vein and render death with a single swipe.

Somewhere in her heart she knew no demon stood before her; no beast dragged from the bowels of this place of death. It did not matter; be it man or beast, the creature that faced her intended her harm, and she knew she must escape it.

As in a dream, she could not make a sound. She dashed toward the main aisle, yet the creature blocked her, and she was forced to the far right. There she gave no heed to her surroundings; she ran, not daring to see if she was pursued. She found her voice and called out, grateful for once that Jake lurked nearby. Yet she did not know if he responded to her call, for the creature had taken a different path between the pews and awaited her at the end.

She paused, backing away once again. Dimly she realized where she stood—before the ornate and beautiful monument to the last Chatham to have passed beyond the portals of death.

Genevieve's tomb.

And even as she came to that awareness, she discovered that where her sightless journey had taken her there was no flooring. There was stone beneath her feet as she stared at the cloaked creature, then there was nothing. With a scream she pitched downward, and the sound of her voice was lost in echo.

Her skirts saved her from injury as she fell, yet she felt no bumps or bruises, so desperate was she to discover her whereabouts. She stared upward, at the empty space above. She saw nothing but the eerie blue light, and then heard a scraping, a rasping, and realized that a stone—removed so that she might fall!—was being slid back into place.

And once it was done, not even the eerie blue light would come to guide her.

She rose, reaching above her to stop that stone from falling. "No!" she raged, but the sound of her own voice was horrible, echoing all about her.

She closed her eyes tightly, stunned and trembling and afraid. She tried to tell herself that she did not believe in evil death ghosts, in spirits or the like.

Oh, it was impossible not to feel the chill, the terror! Impossible not to know that she was surrounded by the coffins of those Chathams memorialized above her!

She swallowed fiercely and opened her eyes, then half shut them, seeking something, some pencil streak of light to guide her. And, ah, there was light! Oh, vague, vague hope—a ribbon-thin streak that beckoned her, far along a tunnel.

Yet when she would have moved, she paused instead, bumping into the coffin beside her. She had to blink again, strain desperately to see.

And then the most horrible scream welled within, a scream of unspeakable terror.

The coffin had been opened. Within its silken lining lay a body, and even in the darkness Ondine knew it to be a woman, clad in rich velvet, the hands locked in prayer, hair spilling long about

the pillow . . . face rotting, as time and death would have its way
with even the greatest beauty.

Genevieve . . .

She knew no sense or reason, no courage whatsoever. In that
moment Ondine knew nothing but panic, blind and raw. She edged
by the coffin, dimly saw row upon row of those that stretched
beyond it.

Then she ran for that thin streak of light, that one ray of hope.
She was in some tunnel, some tunnel damp and rank with moss
and the eternal odor of death. A place where shrieks that were not
her own, but those of rats and mice, disturbed the silence in a
mortal terror not unlike her own.

She ignored them when they tread over her feet, when they
scampered along her path, and coughing, gagging, choking, she
likewise ignored the spiderwebs that clung to her face and gown.
Spitting, half sobbing, she clawed at them, even as she ran, learning
to place her hands before her.

At long last she reached the source of the light—another wall,
where but a crack lay open. Still sobbing, she raised her hands
against that stone, pulling and prodding, scratching her flesh and
breaking her nails. It refused to give, and she lay against it, panting
raggedly, then set forth once again, feverishly clawing at the stone.
Then she forced herself to stop, stop with her heart pounding like
a hammer against an anvil. Logic, sense, patience, oh, God, how
desperately did she need those virtues! She breathed deeply,
paused, then once again set to her task, pitting all her weight
against the stone.

It groaned, as if long untouched; as if it balked and fought her.
She rested and panted again and returned once more to the labor,
using all the reserves of her strength. And then . . .

Quite obediently and unexpectedly, the stone slid back, as if
on some ancient hinge. Amazed and panting still, Ondine stepped
past it.

A certain darkness lingered here, too, but from the wall, light
glowed from two candles set in service sconces.

She was in the wine cellar, she realized with disbelief. Some
secret path had taken her from the chapel, past the armory, and
below the kitchens. There was a stairway at the end of the room
that would take her to the larder, she was quite certain.

She stared at her hands; they were bloody and raw. Her clothing was covered in a thick mist of webbing, and she knew she was adorned head to toe likewise. Dear God! Loathesome creatures might well crawl in the tangle of her hair even now.

"Uggh!" she spat aloud, still trembling, still terrified—but also furious and determined.

Oh, but Warwick would explain this time! Feet stamping against the stone, she headed for the stairway. Then she paused. She had no wish to scare the servants. She took another breath, pursed her lips in grim demand, and started more quietly for the stairs. She would evade the servants—and accost her dear lord of Chatham totally unannounced and unprepared.

As it was, Warwick was not unprepared for trouble. He was, at that very second, staring at Jake with horror and disbelief.

"What do you mean—*she disappeared!* Women do not disappear. You say you are positive she entered the chapel?"

"Warwick, I swear it! I thought I heard her call, but the door was bolted. In time, I broke it—but she was not there! Her roses were upon the altar—but she was gone!"

"Damnation!" Warwick swore, tense as he hurried for his office door, his heart thundering, his soul in terror. Dear God, but how—

He did not reach the door; it flew open and an apparition in a mist of gray flew into him, slender hands rocketing against his chest in a whirlwind of fury.

"My dear lord of Chatham, I have had it! Beasts and whispers, mistresses, friends, enemies, whores, and ghosts! No more! You! You vile wretch! You and your talk of rescue and salvation! You're mad! You and your entire household! What in the name of all the blessed saints goes on here!"

Warwick was so stunned by her absolute disarray of appearance—and then so taken aback by her fury—that he actually backed away, receiving each of her blows in shocked silence. His head blurred even with his vision; he could think of nothing at first except that she was found; she stood before him. She lived, oh, yes, lived, in a spinning fury, dirtied and grimed and almost comical, but, oh, so alive and vibrant with her special passion for life!

As if awakened by his very thoughts, he stood his ground, catching her flailing fists. "Give pause, madam, I pray you! What is this? What has happened?"

"What has happened?" She shrieked out the words. "From what moment, my lord? Shall I begin with your charitable—diabolical!—plot to steal a woman—any woman—from the gallows? Oh, you bastard! No more! And I was supposed to grovel on the ground where you walked for eternity because you saved my life, only to offer it up for some more heinous death!"

"Nay, that was not the plan!" he retorted harshly, at which point she took a full fisted and furious swing at him. He ducked, grabbed her once again, and brought the two of them crashing down to the floor together, Ondine panting heavily, Warwick amazed at the strength it took to hold her, and Jake quite confused—anxious over her appearance as well as totally amused by the entire matter.

"I'd like to hang you by your toes, Lord Chatham!" Ondine said, pinned at last between his thighs, his fingers twined over hers. "I'd like to see you on the rack! Gibbeted, disemboweled—"

"Shut up!" Warwick hissed, and she did, for they all three heard the footsteps nearing the door, then a tentative tapping.

"Milord!" Mathilda called. "Is something amiss?"

Warwick gazed briefly at Jake; Jake slipped on through the door and murmured some assurance to Mathilda. Ondine did not know why she remained silent, but she did, watching her husband's tense features, seeing the gravity in his eyes.

At last they heard footsteps moving away. Warwick did not change positions; Ondine pressed against his hands, suddenly aware that she was very close to tears and not about to betray them to this man.

"Dear God!" she whispered. "Will you tell me what goes on here!"

He released her hands and sat back upon his haunches, then stood and reached a hand to her. She took it hesitantly. When she was upon her feet, he did not speak, but touched her hair, removing from it a skein of the spiderwebs.

"Aye," he said then softly. "I will tell you. But first . . . "

He absently clutched his hands behind his back and paced the area before his desk. Then with sudden decision he strode to the door and opened it carefully.

"Jake!"

"Aye, milord!"

The little monkey of a man scampered back to them from the ballroom.

"I can't have her running about looking so."

"No worry; I'll call the lads for hot water at your order, thus avoiding my lady's maid."

"Aye," Warwick murmured. "And we'll give leave with a great deal of laughter, climb the stairs as one—young lovers not to be interrupted, even to dine."

Jake disappeared. Warwick hovered by the door, then motioned to Ondine. She could but stare at him as if he had indeed gone mad.

"What—?"

"Get over here!" he rasped in command.

"You've not answered a question yet, Warwick Chatham! I'll not jump at your orders like a frightened hare—"

She halted in sudden wariness as he swore with great exasperation, left the door, and came for her, sweeping her from her feet—cobwebs and all—before she could do more than utter a gasp of protest.

"Laugh!" he prompted her.

"Laugh!"

"Aye, laugh! Slip your arms around my neck, gaze into my eyes as if they held you captive in a sea of adoration. Hold close—"

"I will not!"

"You will! And you will do so now!"

He strode back to the door, Ondine a carefree burden in his arms, tossing back his dark head and filling the evening with the rich and husky tones of a baritone laughter. She tightened her grip around his neck lest she fall, and she stared into his eyes as he had commanded her. She knew that they were to appear as if naught were amiss should someone see them; she knew that Warwick intended to move fleeting and eager. She knew, too, that she was a consummate actress and more—a woman deeply in love with her husband, though he used her, willing with her heart to play this moment to the hilt.

"Warwick!"

He strode so swiftly! She was able to sound breathless, to giggle, to laugh as his quick tread brought them up the stairway.

They passed Jake, who warned Mathilda to leave the young earl and his countess alone. They passed Justin, coming along the stairway, who laughed in turn at their good humor, calling something to his brother about marital quarrels being worth those moments of bliss when they were resolved.

And then they were within their own quarters, where Warwick quickly set her down and hurried into the bath. With a sigh of relief he saw that it had been filled and steamed invitingly with water.

"Come!" he called to Ondine. "I'll help you, since we dare not call your maid."

Ondine followed him through, anxious—so anxious!—to rid herself of the cobwebbed clothing, yet wary as he stood there, for bending to his whim surely brought new misery to her soul. She had little enough pride left; little of dignity.

"Milord, I can help myself," she told him pointedly.

"Milady, plague me not with such nonsense!" he snapped back impatiently, coming to her in one broad step and swirling her about so that he could set to the hooks and tiny buttons of her gown, and the laces of the corset bodice beneath it. She stood rigid, somewhat desperate, for he conjured things she thought best buried and forgotten, sensations of the flesh that were made in Eden, but brought upon the heart and soul the scalding of an earthly hell.

Her thoughts had no import, nor did she have time to expand upon them, for it was surely with a quick and no nonsense approach that she found herself losing her garments. "Nay!" she cried when he would touch her hose, clenching her teeth, lowering her eyes, and removing them herself—then plunging into what little shelter she could find in the steaming water. When she looked up at last, she was surprised to find him still there, hands crossed over his chest, his expression somewhat bemused.

"Haven't you something to do!" she demanded.

"I thought you demanded an explanation?"

"I do! But—"

Her voice trailed as he knelt down beside her, taking up the sponge and soap. She eyed him most warily; his expression was all innocence.

"Woman," he murmured, casually sudsing the sponge, "be it diabolical or no, I married you. I know you, just as I know the movement of my hand, yet again and again you behave as if you've some secret which must not be divulged. The secrets you hide, milady, are known, and so in such circumstances modesty is false."

"Give me the soap and leave me!" Ondine said, but, oh, it was not to be a sharp command, and even as she spoke, her words faltered. This was not an easy man to order about, and ever did it become harder, when it was her own sense she fought more than he!

He shook his head. "I think not. You need help with your hair."

"I've done it many a time my—"

The last was caught in a gulp, for he had pushed her down beneath the surface, thoroughly wetting her head, and when she emerged, sputtering, his fingers had already worked through her temple, her nape, massaging her scalp with the most hypnotic touch. She curled her fingers into her hands, desperately willing herself to be still, for he would complete his task, and she knew in her heart that if she moved, that if he touched her further, she would not gasp or revile him, but twist with the craving of his touch.

She did not look at him, but stared silently at the water, lashes downcast, form rigid, as he manipulated the long waves of her hair. She thought she heard him sigh. With disappointment? With weariness? She did not know. At last he spoke, and it was stiffly.

"That will suffice, I believe."

She nodded and ducked her head, realizing that to vigorously rinse it would require her arms, and then she would need to release their hug about her breasts. Yet there was no need, for he rinsed her hair with his fingers with the same fine expertise with which he had washed it, leaving her to wonder how many times he had performed just such a task, and for how many women.

He was done. He stood and moved to the closet for a towel, and as he sought it she quickly sought to scrub her flesh. Of course he caught her in the act, but he stood silently and waited. Blindly she stretched her arm far from her to reach for the towel. He gave it to her, but when she stood, he was there, mesmerizing her as he wrapped it about her with the greatest care and tenderness, and if she did not know him, she might have sworn that there was a look of wistfulness about him as he touched her eyes.

But those amber eyes of his were at best enigmatic, and his gaze did not tarry upon her long. He swept her into his arms again, completely wrapping her in the towel. He carried her out to his own great chair in the music room and sat her there, finding the brandy and glasses in his desk drawer and pouring them each a portion. She sipped it eagerly, realizing that she trembled from his nearness, and did so, too, from that chill of the graves beneath the earth.

He did not stay near her, but walked to the fire, sipping his brandy, staring into the blaze.

"Madam," he said at last, "it was not with diabolical designs that I took you from the gallows, though it is true that I thought a woman condemned and facing death to be a finer bait than an innocent with nothing to fear but sheer acts of God."

Ondine felt cold, very, very cold. "So. I am bait. For the creature who forced me to the tombs?"

He swung about, staring at her hard. "What exactly happened?"

She drained her brandy. Recall was difficult. She did not want to remember the graves, she wanted to taste more of life.

"I entered the chapel. Jake was with me, but I closed the doors. I wandered toward the altar. Once there, I heard a moan—"

"And you panicked?"

"Milord, I do not panic," she said coolly. "I ignored the sound and set to my task; again it came. And when I turned, I faced a creature—"

"A creature?" he demanded skeptically.

"Aye!" she snapped indignantly. "A figure, capped and cowled and masked! And taloned!"

"Taloned?"

She heard the doubt in his voice, and gritted her teeth, yet the vision had come so clear to her that she trembled, and he saw that shiver in her ill-clad form.

Quickly he was before her, lifting her in his arms again, bringing her to the fire, before which he knelt.

"You are cold; your hair is wet."

"It will dry quickly."

"Go on. Talons?"

"Gloves, then, with talons attached!" Dear God, but it was difficult to think and speak! Fear left her as the warmth and vigor of his body leapt to hers, yet a new fear began, for she could not forget how she had woken once, the spill of virginity between them, only to hear his apology, since he had assumed her a whore!

She stiffened in his arms, wanting only the truth between them now, loathe that she should love him while he scorned her, a gallows' bride.

"Gloves, aye, with nail protrusions—lethal protrusions, milord." She lifted her head, narrowing her eyes, not knowing that the fire gleamed within them, and all along the dancing length of hair that matched its golden glow. "Someone intended me serious harm; I ran, and found then that I must back away. At Genevieve's tomb I found that the flooring was no more; I fell through."

"To the tombs?" he demanded hoarsely.

"To the tombs. And, my lord, you should be aware that your lady's casket has been opened!"

"Opened?"

"Opened, my lord! O-p-e-n-e-d!"

"I know the spelling!" Warwick flared. He set her down upon the floor; she groped to pull the towel about her, stunned as he left her, long strides taking him back toward the bath.

But he had not gone to the bath; he had traveled through to her chamber and returned quickly with her brush. Her shoulders squared as she felt him come behind her on his knees, take up her hair even as he spoke of the matter at hand, fingers gentle, voice as hard as the grate of the stone.

"I shall see to it immediately. And you will go nowhere unattended."

"She was murdered, then. Genevieve."

"Aye," he agreed simply. The brush paused against her hair. "None believed it; not even the king. But I knew, for she did not fear me, nor despise me, and though frail, she was sound in mind."

Ondine was glad her back was to him, for she tightened with a strange pain, a knife that twisted at the sound of anguish in his tone, at the gentle, tender love he had borne another. Oh, she did not envy that poor lady! She only sought the love.

"And so," she said stiffly, "you married me, hoping that the murderer should strike again?"

"Nay!" he charged her impatiently, and the brush tore once again into her hair, not with cruelty but with impatience. He spun her about, eyes burning, searing deeply into hers with intensity and honor.

"I'd have no maid's blood on my hands! Lady, if I did not think that I could preserve the life I bartered for, I'd not have taken it into my hands! I'd thought to watch, to trap, aye to bait, but never leave to danger!"

"I was near killed this night!"

"Never, never will it come about again, for never again will you be alone!" he told her fiercely and with warning.

"Why didn't you tell me!"

"How could I know that you would fill the role if you feared all whom you met?"

"Then whom do you suspect of the deed?"

"No one—and many." He rose again, running his fingers distractedly through his hair and pacing before her with the great cat's energy she so often saw in him. "I know, I know not," he murmured, "only that murder was the truth. Hardgrave despises me; he well would see my house fallen forever. Anne is a jealous witch, yet murder seems not her style."

"Your brother—your cousin. Are they among those you see as candidates for the deed?"

He winced, staring down curiously at his open palms. "My blood, my flesh. Nay! I cannot see it! But Justin stands to inherit if I leave no issue. And should Justin and I both perish, Charles knows I would have Clinton receive both land and titles, legitimized by the law."

Ondine stared into the flames, frowning. "The whispers came from this house. How could Hardgrave—or Anne—be guilty?"

"Hardgrave's land adjoins mine. He or Anne might well know more of the tunnels and rooms than I suspect."

"Clinton, I assume, was never at court."

"But assassins may be hired; life is easily and shamefully little more than the cost of a golden coin."

Ondine fell silent again and then murmured, "Genevieve was not . . . disturbed by the 'ghosts' until she was with child?"

He stopped his pacing, stood still behind her. "Aye."

"And so," she whispered, "your announcement that I, too, was with child?"

"Aye."

She could not help but shudder. He knelt at her side, grasping her shoulders. "Lady, I swear by my life, by my name, by all honor, I'll see you safe of this! Safe—and freed that your life might be your own! It was an oath I took unto God when we married, and here I swear it once again! You will live; live that the years ahead—once to be sacrificed to the noose!—will be my most eternal payment, along with whatever coin will let you lead the life you desire!"

Coin! Oh, God! He offered her coin . . .

She wrenched from his touch and stood, proud and arrogant as she held the towel about her as though it were a cloak woven of gold.

"Milord, this is, I think, a debt evenly met. My life you did save; your mystery I will seek with all I may to bring to a close. Then, milord Chatham, as you've said, we will be quits of all in this life!"

She strode past him in cool fury ; yet something of her manner must have stung his temper despite the passion of his vows. He caught her about the waist before she could leave, spinning her close into his arms.

"Even, milady? I wonder! For about you there are secrets, too, secrets deep and dark, and I wonder what it is that I abet in holding you close to my heart!"

"Wonder away, milord!" Ondine retorted, eyeing him quite regally, for well was her bargain met, or so she thought. "I am your 'bait'; I will, with all my power, play your role. But then, milord, I say that you have had all of me that you will ever touch!"

She twisted from him and walked again, held held high. He watched her through the hallway of the bath; watched her enter her own chamber.

"Ondine!" The passion and the timbre of his voice swept through her. She felt a rage of fire consume her with that sound, and she turned, wary . . . tense . . . frightened, so frightened, deep within her heart.

For even then he closed the distance between them, strong, determined, alive with a sudden fiery temper aglow in his implacable gaze.

Chapter 16

He was almost upon her. Warily she backed away from him, closer to the fire that burned in her grate, cornered against it.

"Nay—get away from me!" Ondine cried, her temper soaring. "You, sir, are a beast! I'll not be among your lusting number, a pet to be pawed and patted and stroked and kept in a cage! I, sir—"

"You are my wife," he reminded her with humor.

"Not your wife!" she corrected him fiercely. "Rather an associate, milord! An accomplice, an abettor, paid for my cooperation, as it were, with life—and coin, so you assure me. Jealous? Nay. Hope, have none! You, sir, will respect me, you will—ohhhh!"

A long and startling shriek swept away her words, for it was not all the heat of anger she had felt, or even that of his presence. So far had she moved that a spark of the fire caught on her towel, and sensation warned her that her flesh was near to scorching.

"Oh!" She spun, on fire, confused, carrying the towel with her. Warwick moved with the swiftness of an arrow hurtling toward her, wrenching the burning linen from her grasp, casting it to the floor and quenching the flame hurriedly with his boot. Ondine stared first at the floor, concerned lest the flame catch, yet so quickly was it out that her concern became far more for her person, flesh now naked to the night—and her husband's perusal.

"Are you hurt?" he asked her.

"No, not hurt!" she gasped out, racing for her bed, wrenching from it the brocade cover to hurl about herself.

He walked toward her slowly, as ever amused, yet imperious as ever in his bold and open scrutiny. "Scorched, milady? It grieves me to think that the purity of your flesh might have been kissed by the flame."

He came too close, and she rolled across the bed, finding her feet quickly, facing him with the expanse of a safe barrier between them.

"You had let me alone at first!" she reminded him reproachfully. "You swore some oath that I should be freed—and you let me be! What is this, then? You foreswore your manners as poor; you promised that they would improve!"

"Aye, I know," he murmured apologetically. "I did long to live with the belief that I could be withdrawn; a cavalier. A man with a haunted past, vowed to release a beauty. Alas, my love, all that I find myself to be in truth is a man, haunted not by the past, but by the present. My vow was that you should live; my manners I demanded of myself lest I should become involved, but that, I am afraid, I am, and manners cannot bend nor ease the torment!" He clutched the bedpost as he talked, in movement slow and silent, yet it brought him around without haste or measure to where she stood, undecided now to keep her ground—or dash across the bed once again.

"Get away from me!" she warned with a shaking voice, but he gave her no heed, just leaned against the second post and smiled with rueful bemusement as he caught her gaze in the fiery glow of his own.

"I have thought, and thought, my lady, of manners, or rights. I have given all the gravest concern. I have thought on the freedom you so crave, and none of these makes any sense, not when memory intrudes. Night after night, milady, I have paced these halls in torment, paced and strode and walked in the night so far that I might have reached London on foot. I have lain awake in my bed, knowing you were not but a few yards distant. I have dreamt of you, imagined you, reached for you in the night, burned in hell's gravest agony as some torture of the mind brought the recall of your flesh bare to mine, tense and seeking. I've twisted, lady, turned and tossed. I've sworn and raged inside, and prevailed upon all that is decent in a man. I've endured rigor, strain, and sleepless nights—all for the honor of her I call wife. Yet tonight, Ondine, even as truth became known, I pondered once again the ungodly restraint, the tortured hours, the high tempered days. And all that I could surmise upon the confused ending of such thought was, For what?''

He came to her, clutching the spread at her throat where she held it close. His smile ever in place, dark lashes over a prism of amber eyes that glowed warm with seduction.

"My dear lady," he murmured, "I did, quite frankly, think merely, to hell with all this! The future is always some distant thing which must unravel itself."

The future . . . oh, the future! It was that one word that loomed before her, that broke the spell of his rugged allure. "To hell with this!" she shrieked, jerking furiously from his touch, choosing that option to bound across the bed once again. Yet she bound with no barrier upon her, for his hand caught the brocade spread, and before she could pitch from the mattress, she found herself captured beneath the lean hard length of him, staring into mocking eyes that glittered with amusement and the triumph they had known all along.

"Nay!" she cried in maddened panic, for if he touched her further, she would be lost, and he would know that all resistance was a lie. She was free and she thought to strike him; her hand caught his cheek, and he reacted with no anger, but twisted her arms beneath her so that she could not lash out more. All that was left was words, and she used those bitterly, the best she could, trembling violently at the impression of his body against hers. "Go to those who long for this caress! Go back to your voluptuous Anne with the feline eyes! I want nothing of your well-worn touch, I—"

His kiss stopped her, the hungry, encompassing pressure of his mouth against hers, filling her with warmth, the taste of brandy, moistness, enveloping sensation. Ah, that kiss! It burned greater than any fire; it reached inside of her, and all of her was alive to the manly feel of him. His tongue moved deep into her mouth, caressing, seeking, creating what was surely madness, an ache of longing within her womb. That kiss was slow, leisurely, creating pressure but no pain, a force not brutal, but undeniable. His hand played upon her naked breast, fingering that bud he called a rose. Subtly, subtly he stroked her, moving the tip of his thumb over the peak, then splaying his fingers to leave it free as he at last took his mouth from hers to use upon her breast, tasting it, suckling so that the nipple came to graze his teeth. Explosive flashes shuddered throughout her; she gasped in pleasure and pain, wishing to wrench herself from him, wishing to hurry that promise of the flesh, which now filled her like liquid fire.

"Nay!" she charged him brokenly, but they were both aware that the denial meant nothing.

He did not respond at first, but nuzzled his head between the deep valley of her breasts, and there her flesh knew all textures, that of his hair, his cheeks, his lips. Then he tended as carefully to one breast as to the other, and she knew that she was betrayed, betrayed by her body, as never by her word or mind. He rose slightly above her, and she saw a different look in him. Humor gone, his tension and passion were foremost.

"Lady!" he demanded, staring hard in heated challenge. "Can you say that I truly wrong you, that this, this wonder between us, is something that you want not?"

She twisted her head to the side in anguish. He caught her cheeks tenderly between his hands and drew her face back, pressing then with the force of his muscular thighs against her long limbs so that they, too, were forced to give. Though he remained clothed, she felt all the strength and ardor of his body fully against hers. She had no control over the mystery of the sexes, no way to ebb the longing that washed over her, hot and pulsing, with the relentless sway of a tide.

She closed her eyes tightly, whispering her answer.

"What choice have I, milord?"

"Damn!" he exploded harshly. "I speak not of choice, but of desire!"

"You, milord, may do so. The power is yours, and the strength. I've no weapons such as yours—"

"Your weapons, Ondine, have always been your beauty and your wit, your pride and spirit, and all those secrets that lurk in your soul. And, lady, you use them well!"

"What is it, my lord, that you wish from me?" she cried. "Surrender? As I told you, it seems I've little choice!"

He shook his head with impatience, pressing his hips against hers with blunt, evocative insinuation. He trailed his fingers from her cheek to her throat and down to her breasts, where he played idly and spoke softly, tensely, almost with anguish. "Nay, lady, never surrender! Admission, nothing more! Say only that this fair flesh craves the caress of my hand, just as that hand hungers for the touch. Say that your fair form is eager to be water for my thirst, for all that I am is arid without your cascading liquid rhythm. Say that the sweet place of nectar between your thighs longs to be a receptacle for my seed, just as I cannot be whole this night unless I fill you, body and soul, with all myself."

"Oh!"

"Ondine!"

"Take me, then, milord!" she cried, hating him afresh. How could he do this to her—draw forth these words she was loathe to say!

"Nay, my countess, there is no talk of surrender; you shall take me, and I shall come eagerly!"

"What . . ."

He was gone from her, at the side of the bed, divesting clothing with the greatest speed. He returned to her naked, and she was in his arms, too quickly at sea, lost and adrift in his kiss, the fierceness of his ardor, the muffled urgings of his words.

"Ah, surely, lady, never hath God created flesh so fine, so fair, breasts so ripe as to haunt a man, waking and sleeping. Never have hips been so sleek and smooth, never have legs been so long and sensually wicked, their movement a lair that might create internal imprisonment . . ."

And, dearest God, all that he said was true! He'd known beauty, vast and wide, in many guises. Anne's feline tempest, Genevieve's angelic delicacy, and many arts and graces in between. Never had there been a woman to occupy him so, to take his heart, his mind, his soul, to shake him with a passion that could not be slaked! Ah, this water witch! Nymph of cascading glory, strong in spirit, unbreakable. Love me! That is all that I command of you, he might have cried, but though he could live sanely no longer without touching her, the vow of freedom was one he could not break, more binding than ever with the tangle of his heart. And he was Warwick Chatham, earl and lord, a man, a champion who did not falter or fail. For all that he was, he could not fail himself now. But neither could he leave her, her beauty, the symmetry of her sweet movement, endless splendor . . .

He caught her hands and brought them to his chest, reveling in their tentative touch, in the sharp and ragged tremble of her breath. "No shyness, milady, for it is this for which we are made, man and woman, and truly given!"

And with that glad cry he kissed her again, giving free rein to the throbbing thunder of his blood, the pulse of his groan. With his hand he parted her thigh, with knowledge and tenderness he moved thumb and fingers against feminine secrets, stroking, soliciting, bringing the blaze that urged her to match his own. All around him he heard the snap and crackle of the fire, the shriek of the wind, even the howl of the wolves in the forest, and they were all a part of him. He led her to touch him further, burst in glory at the tentative measure of her fingers, and shuddered with a new desire, unlike any he had known. He teased her still, in torment that was divine, for when he had her at last, it would be the greatest bliss. He moved and manipulated her, ever stunned by her beauty, the fine perfection of her back, of her buttocks. He stroked her spine and whispered that he would see that the lick of the fire had harmed her not. As his kisses seared her flesh the rasp of his tongue was a greater flame. Never was there such reward, for her whispers came in turn, pleading that he came to her, and he did, a thrust of mercury and steel, heat and midnight magic.

He was all, and more, that she had craved. He was a tempest, giving to her a sweet, shattering climax. What wondrous God had given man and woman! And when they lay spent, he remained at her side.

Ondine awoke, but did not open her eyes. A coldness about her warned her that Warwick lay with her no more, and she could not still the heavy feeling of fear that this morning would bring with it the mockery of that past occasion.

She lay still, not moving, feeling that sunshine entered the room, that the air was fresh, that everything should be beautiful.

Carefully she raised her lashes slightly, then started, for she was not alone at all, her senses having played her false.

He was there, on the bed, an arm's span away from her, watching her curiously, smiling just slightly with amusement at her obvious pretense of sleep. He was completely clothed, leaning upon an elbow so that he might stretch out his length for easy perusal of her while keeping his booted feet from dirtying the bed.

Ondine shrank further into her covers, her eyes wide but wary, tensed as she awaited his words. His smile deepened with a rueful humor, and his lashes shielded all expression.

"We can never go back now, you know," he told her softly, and for a moment she wished that he had left or been cruel, for the sight of his fine chiseled features in that daylight touched her with emotion from the depths of her heart. She did love him, all of him, the hazel eyes that so oft loomed amber and gold; the twist of his jaw, willful, strong, determined, even arrogant. She loved his pride, she loved his stance, the set of his smile, the arch of his brow. The tender, wistful, rueful smile that marked him now as younger, a man not to be bested, but to be met upon his terms.

"No," she murmured.

He sighed, a soft expulsion of air, as if he might have said more, and withdrew his touch. He rose, tense and brooding once again, great shoulders squared as he strode to her dresser, idly drumming his fingers upon it.

"I have been to the tombs."

Ondine frowned, made aware that more was at stake here than the state of her heart. She did not like his tone, and still within the shelter of her sheets, she twisted to watch him.

"And?"

His back was to her, and she saw the dark knit of his brow in the mirror. He turned to her, his questing gaze that of a stranger, one that seared into her as if he might see truth.

"There was nothing amiss."

"What?"

"There was nothing amiss. Stones were all in place; Genevieve's coffin was tightly sealed. There was no sign of cape or mask or— talons."

She sat up, furious at the insinuation that her mind might have wandered, that her imagination had tricked her.

"I tell you, milord, that a creature, caped and cowled and, aye, taloned, did accost me! What is this now, that you doubt my word! How absurd, Chatham! Would I cast myself into a crypt for amusement, run with spiders and rats and mold and darkness for the fun of it all?"

He leaned back against the dresser, casually crossing a booted foot and shaking his head with a grin. "Nay, lady, I accuse you of nothing of the like. I wished only to see that certainty from you. I should have gone there straight last night; alas, you were my concern. I do not doubt your word; I but asked to see that streak of certainty come from you." He hesitated and appeared dark and strained once again. "There were times . . . there were occasions when I knew that Genevieve did see things with her mind, and not her eyes."

Ondine brought her knees to her chest, hugging them there. She lowered her eyes from his absent gaze, swallowing tightly. The pain and tenderness that brought low his voice when he spoke of Genevieve seemed to clench about her heart, and she longed to cross herself, for in truth, she was so sorry for the woman slain, and yet yearning that she herself might be so gently regarded.

Ondine had his care; that much she believed. Yet something about her felt hollow, and she reflected in misery that he might think of her somewhat as it seemed he did of Anne—healthy sport and amusement, to be enjoyed, perhaps even gallantly so, yet never truly cherished.

And did it matter? she queried herself bleakly. She had no more than this time she had sworn him—payment for her life. The king had given her leave and grace to prove her own quest, and it was something that must be achieved. The freedom Warwick had sworn to her was a gift she must take.

She gazed up, startled, when he moved across the room to her, sitting at her side, taking her chin.

"Ondine, I have seen before such a costume as you described."

"Where?" she demanded breathlessly.

He smiled bitterly and released her, walking to the window from where the day streamed in. "At Westchester. After Genevieve was killed, I tore apart her chamber and found a passage, and at the foot of the passage I found a discarded cloak and mask.''

"Then you knew, for fact, that it was murder! Why didn't you go to the king?''

He shrugged. She saw only the movement of his shoulders. "I did go to the king. He thought that the death had unbalanced my mind, because, you see, he hosted many masques and balls at that time, and thought surely that some clandestine lover, innocent and removed from the deed, had lost the cloak.''

"But it is all real," Ondine murmured, then said, eyes widening, "at Hampton! That was why you tested the structure of the chamber, why the steward spoke so strangely.''

He nodded.

"Well, then," she murmured a little tartly, "we have failed at any attempt to find this creature! Last night, milord, was the time to act. To question all, to discover its whereabouts—''

"Do you think me a fool?" he charged her, turning about. "Whilst I saw to you, Jake sought out the others. No one was seen. Clinton claimed to have been at the stables, Justin swore to have been in his chambers. Mathilda said all the servants appeared to have their tasks, and a rider sent to Hardgrave's castle was told that he and lady Anne were dining together at the time. Who lies? Who speaks the truth? We are back full circle.''

"There must be a motive.''

"What motive would you wish, milady? Hatred, revenge, jealousy, greed—they all might be applied.''

"Your brother loves you!" She instantly rose to Justin's defense, though he had not been pointed out.

"Hmm, and I think, perhaps, Countess, you love my brother far too well.''

"Perhaps I should," she retorted. "He, milord, is never brooding or aloof, nor prone to rages, but rather ceaselessly pleasant.''

"Ah, and there lies your truth!" he exclaimed, smiling now, but with a sharpness to his eyes that warned his humor veiled a darker emotion. Returning to her in a stride, he swiftly wrenched her sheet from her grasp and brought her naked breasts hard to his chest in a passion so sudden she could only gasp.

"Ondine! Wouldst you see blood among brothers?''

"Nay! I speak merely of his temperament—and of yours! And you, milord, stray from the conversation at hand!"

"My temper became, from your lips, the conversation at hand. And, aye, sorely has it been vexed as of late. Such is the nature of a beast, madam. Tease it, taunt it—it growls and paces. Offer kindness, and it comes sweetly to heel."

She stared into his eyes, aware that she melted to his touch, the fever of his arms, the passion growing even now in his eyes, in the hands that stroked the length of her back, her naked flesh, silk to his touch. She tilted her head back, prone to whimsy, careless of anything but the moment when he held her so. He was then hers, completely hers, if only for the fleeting glimpse of time.

"Oh?" she murmured sweetly, fingertips light and seductive as the whisper of her voice. She smoothed them into his nape. "Do you say that you—autocrat and beast!—might purr and be gentle at my whim?"

"Aye, milady, be that whim the sweetest promise!"

Then she shuddered, for the whim was his. His lips touched upon her throat, found her pulse there, and wandered lower to close with fiery moisture over her breast.

" 'Tis day!" she gasped, tugging upon his hair, for little will and strength did his purpose leave her to stand. "The light streams in, servants are about—"

"And I, milady, am, above all, master of that which I would call my own castle!"

"The light!" she choked, too late, for she was down upon the bed, he between her thighs.

"The sun casts even greater beauty over you than does the moon," he told her hoarsely. "It brings velvet beauty to the fire of your hair; a satin finish to your flesh; the red of the rose to your lips; a sheen of emeralds to your eyes . . ."

She lost the meaning of his words. He had barely disrobed before he was in her, fierce and storming, casting her to netherworlds of sensation where she could but ride the waves and reap the splendor, stunned and shaken and trembling with awe and the volatile, primal ardor of the man.

She held to him, glad again of the time, gasping to the stroke of the staff that filled her again and again, and left her drenched with quivering elation . . . and then . . .

She twisted from him, worried. He thought her a petty thief, a common wench; he claimed her flesh as his, as if by right, and loving him, she gave it. Oh, that she had some restraint that dignity might remain with her!

Warwick was quickly on his feet, adjusted in apparel. Her back was to him, and to her further outrage he whacked her smartly against her derriere.

"Rise, milady, the day wastes. Rise!"

"The day wastes! You knave! Scoundrel—"

"Up!"

"Up! You, milord, may get out—"

"I give the orders, milady."

"Orders! I am not your servant! Don't you dare think to touch me again! You play the games, you torment me, and then you dare to come with this sudden command! Milord—leave my chamber!"

Dear God, but she was a fool! He was nothing but a lusting autocrat, and, by God, she'd had it with him!

He laughed deep within his throat, sharp now, impatient. "We return to court."

Gritting her teeth, she dragged her pillow to her breast and fought him shrilly.

"You are mad, Lord of Chatham! We've just returned from court! Your quest is to trap a killer, yet you run—"

He came too quickly, strides long, body rigid, knuckles lifting her chin so that her sparkling eyes caught the hardness in his own.

"I never run, Lady. Do as I say."

He strode from the chamber, heedless of the epithets that followed him.

He closed the door that separated the music room from the sleeping chambers and leaned against it.

No, he did not run. But now he did. For he was blinded; he knew not what he sought. And the fear that rose in him was cold and horrible, for he dared not take the smallest chance in the future. An agony of indecision struck him, for each time he touched her, she drove more deeply into his heart, and he could not use her as he had thought that day upon the gallows. He had not been wrong; some lunacy was sworn against him. Perhaps his enemy feared that he, himself, could not be touched, beaten, or slain.

And, therefore, any woman he called wife was in serious peril of her life, a peril that he now feared beyond imagination.

Jealousy had driven him from court. How and when she had become such a part of him, he knew no other desire, he did not know. God! He had tried with all his strength to stay away from her! Better ask man thirsting unto death to forgo water! He was no saint, no monk, and could not watch her without the wanting of her. Nor was he made of steel, but of flesh and blood, and such a man with both health and vitality that natural appetites must be appeased.

He ground his teeth tightly together, remembering his vow. Aye; he had to release her! But first he had to protect her life, and for that time, by God, she would be his! He could pray that in time he would be filled with her, know the magic that so bound him! Find release from it! His promises he would keep . . .

But for now he would go to court, lay his case once more before Charles, and bring the king due on debts of loyalty so that the finest of the king's guards would be set for her protection. None would dare touch her then!

For a moment he reflected on her, Ondine. His brow slowly lifted and he stormed back into her chamber, catching her half clothed. He twisted his lips in a dry smile and taunted her with both gentle humor and warning.

"Lady, remember, wives promise obedience. I am not mad that I say we return to court, but that matters not—the whim is mine. Then, I think, there is much to you we have not touched upon as yet. The reason you so dreaded to meet our king; the reason, too, you caught his fancy—platonic fancy?—is an intrigue that does fascinate me! So, you see, my love, it seems to me that you should scrape and bow, and bend with ease to my slightest wish—lest I find time to dig and discover that which you are so eager to hide!"

She threw her brush at him in one of her sudden piques. Warwick chuckled and ducked.

"And you accuse me of foul temper, love! If I am a beast, I have surely met my match in a water witch! We leave, my love, in an hour. Hurry."

He laughed still as he closed the door on her. Then he sobered as anguish swept through him. He could not bear the danger into which he had cast her. His lips hardened in a line, and he decided that he could count the days that remained to their marriage. He would ask the king for a divorce immediately and make arrangements for her to be brought to the Colonies. If she were rid of him, she would be safe.

We have 4 FREE BOOKS for you
as your introduction to
KENSINGTON CHOICE!
To get your FREE BOOKS, worth
up to $23.96, mail the card below.

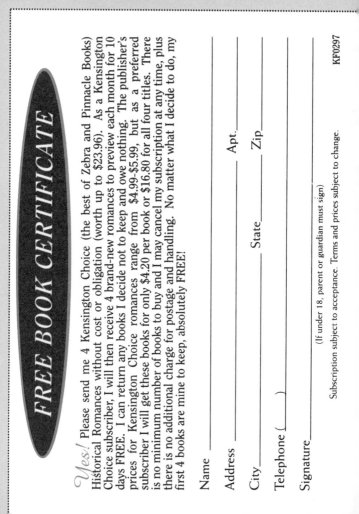

FREE BOOK CERTIFICATE

𝒴𝑒𝑠! Please send me 4 Kensington Choice (the best of Zebra and Pinnacle Books) Historical Romances without cost or obligation (worth up to $23.96). As a Kensington Choice subscriber, I will then receive 4 brand-new romances to preview each month for 10 days FREE. I can return any books I decide not to keep and owe nothing. The publisher's prices for Kensington Choice romances range from $4.99-$5.99, but as a preferred subscriber I will get these books for only $4.20 per book or $16.80 for all four titles. There is no minimum number of books to buy and I may cancel my subscription at any time, plus there is no additional charge for postage and handling. No matter what I decide to do, my first 4 books are mine to keep, absolutely FREE!

Name _____

Address _____ Apt. ____

City _____ State _____ Zip _____

Telephone ( ) _____

Signature _____

(If under 18, parent or guardian must sign)

Subscription subject to acceptance. Terms and prices subject to change.

KF0297

Chapter 17

Warwick most assuredly meant to put his absurd plan into action; he'd barely left her before Mathilda and Lottie arrived breathlessly at her chamber door, prepared to start packing. Mathilda was upset that Warwick should drag Ondine back and forth when a child was expected, but Warwick himself assured Mathilda she would be fine. Mathilda brought her mistress more goat's milk. Ondine hated the stuff, but for Mathilda's sake she drank it with a weak smile.

There was one aspect to the trip that seemed quite nice: Justin was accompanying them. He whispered to Ondine that though he had been in definite disfavor with Charles for dueling, Warwick had spoken to the king, and Justin now had permission to return to court.

Clinton remained behind in charge, and his good-bye embrace to Ondine seemed warm and comforting. She prayed again that neither he nor Justin would be guilty of murder, as she was growing to love them both dearly.

She thought that Warwick might choose to ride above with Jake as was so often his custom; he did not. He seated himself next to her, facing his brother.

The journey went marvelously well, or so Ondine thought, until they had but one night of travel left. They stopped to picnic, and though the lunch was casual and easy, she and Warwick managed to quarrel at its end when Justin mentioned they should stop and rest early—for Ondine's health and the coming Chatham heir. Justin rode with Jake. Ondine and Warwick were alone in the carriage as the afternoon waned.

Yet in the darkness of the carriage she felt his eyes upon her, and a deep tension struck her.

"Warwick—" She said his name, then hesitated, for their relationship was ever strange to her. She knew him intimately; she knew him not at all.

"My love?" It was always there—that bitter twist to his tone when he addressed her so.

She stiffened, staring out into the darkness. "I know what it is now that we set about; I comprehend the reason for your deception. But still I think it cruel. Wouldn't it perhaps be best to tell Mathilda and the others that we were mistaken, there is no child?"

He was silent, and she could not read his mind or expression in the growing darkness.

"Perhaps even now, Countess," he said coolly, "it is not a lie that I perpetuate."

"Trust me, my lord," she replied regally, "it is a lie."

"Is it?" Amusement crept into his voice. "Ondine, you are aware of nature's functions, are you not?" He pulled closer to her, whispering with warm, evocative breath about the things that happened when men came together with women. The sound of his voice—even the words!—sent hot shivers racing through her; she clamped her teeth together in anger, for he seemed unconcerned.

"Leave me be!" she cried, twisting from his touch. "I know what—I know all about—I—"

He laughed, releasing her at her insistence for once. But the sound of his laughter faded into the night, and she felt a touch of cold gravel in his tone when he spoke next.

"You sound quite upset, my love. Does the idea sound so repugnant to you, then? A child of mine?"

A child of his . . .

Nay, it was not repugnant; it was a dream, a fantasy, unreal—a family life, wanted and cherished and . . . normal. She saw years that stretched ahead with laughter and warmth and love. She saw a future together, where he would speak as tenderly of her as he did of his lost Genevieve, where he would laugh and tease and want her forever.

Men! How dare he think to quiz her so, when he thought of nothing but convenience and his own pursuits?

"Of course, Lord Chatham, the thought is repulsive to me! We go our own ways, remember? I'd not be saddled with a child."

He caught her chin quite suddenly, fingers harsh upon her, but still the darkness hid from her all but his anger.

"Lady, this I promise you: No heir of mine will ever leave my presence! It might take you longer to be free, but free you would be—unsaddled. Any child is mine—and Mathilda's, since you show such little concern! And trust me, lady, should she be given the task of raising the heir, she would not note your disappearance!"

"Bastard!" Ondine exploded, continuing heedlessly. "Then—things must cease, ere the lie is truth!"

He released her, leaning back, completely in shadow.

"Nothing ceases."

"You—"

"You are my wife. And there, my lady, the matter ends."

She swore at him with some of the wonderfully apt and colorful phrases she had learned within Newgate, yet to no avail, for soon the carriage jolted to a stop.

Jake opened the carriage door, addressing Warwick by name. "Shall we stop? We've reached the Boar's Head."

"Aye, we'll stop."

Jake called to Justin, who leapt down to the ground. Warwick showed no sign of his temper to Jake or Justin, and Ondine chose to do the same. She did, in fact, think to be utterly charming to her brother-in-law. They teased and laughed all through the meal. Warwick joined in, yet Ondine was certain it was not with his whole heart.

Yet even as she laughed and dined, she found herself praying once again: Dearest Lord, don't let it be Justin! For though he was gallant to her and ever full of flattery and laughter, there was, despite his mischief, a certain care; he knew that she was his brother's—property. In that he took care never to quip too far, never to touch her overly long. Above all there was a certain respect between them, and Ondine believed Warwick might well be ready to die in truth himself, rather than learn that his blood had betrayed him in murder.

It was late when they finished in the dining room, late when they trod the steps to separate rooms.

Ondine feared their conversation that night; she feared his very nearness. But she needn't have. He told her harshly to sleep, and he lay down far from her, partially clothed, and his eyes closed very quickly.

She did not find solace so easily, but stayed awake, torn by misery and emptiness. She wished fervently that she had never spoken in the carriage.

They left the tavern at dawn, Justin riding with Jake, but Ondine still so weary from lack of sleep that she had no thought to carry any further argument with Warwick. Indeed, she tried to rest against the carriage, but it jolted so that he drew her to his lap, and with no protest she sighed and rested.

They had not gone far, though, when the carriage stopped quite suddenly. Warwick, frowning, adjusted to open the door, startled to find Justin in the act of wrenching it from the outside.

"What—"

"We're being followed," Justin said quickly. "I thought you should know."

"Followed?" Warwick queried tensely.

"Lyle Hardgrave and the lady Anne. I saw the stag's head on the coat of arms. They're right behind us."

Ondine, dazed with sleep, still saw the brothers exchange glances, as if they were allies upon the field, recognizing a foe, eager to accept a challenge.

"We'll stay far ahead of that pair, shall we?"

"My thought exactly," Justin replied. He smiled at Ondine, youthful exuberance alive in his gaze, a chuckle in his throat. "Go back to sleep, my beauty—beasts do guard your slumber!"

She returned his smile, casting a questioning gaze at Warwick as the door closed again. He did not return her gaze, but stared pensively out to the great oaks as the carriage jolted forward again.

"Milord?" she murmured. "Do you think—"

"I dare think nothing."

"Can you not clear your own brother from the suspicions in your mind when those two plague your every step?"

"Are you so anxious, then, for Justin's innocence?"

"Aye," she answered honestly.

"You care for him so?"

"Of course!" she cried, reproach lacing her eyes and her tone. "He is your blood, and you love him dearly! And he is young and dashing and seems so loyal to your cause."

Warwick sighed and placed his hand upon her head, urging her back down to rest.

" 'Tis a pity, then, milady, 'twas not Justin to discover you in the hold of the hangman's noose."

She would have answered him; she caught her tongue because he did not speak with anger or mockery, just weariness. His knuckles moved over her cheek lightly. "Sleep, Ondine. The day wears on long and tedious."

The king was in his laboratory when they arrived.

A barge took them down the river, not so far as the tennis courts, but perhaps halfway, where there was a large plain building, recently whitewashed and pleasantly designed with windows. The king's guards stood before the entrance, but they made way for them.

Ondine could not help but smile at the sight of the king. He was clad in a large apron, and he stood behind a table, busy with vials that steamed and smoked, intent as he measured one bubbling liquid against another, his dark eyes alive with interest.

He looked up at their arrival, a broad smile curling his full lip. "I've done it! I believe I've done it!"

Warwick arched a brow, approaching the scene. "Might I ask, Your Grace, done what?"

"Root and herb and sunshine, friend, 'tis the trick. Why, I've 'Bon vivant'!"

" 'Bon Vivant'?"

"Ah, but you're still too young a fellow!" the king said impatiently. "This was taught to me once in my wandering years by an old French chemist—'tis a potion to ease certain strains of age, which we'll not discuss! It's a potion I've at last remembered and perfected, which pleases me so much in fact—Justin Chatham!—that I am glad to see you returned!''

Justin, standing carefully behind Ondine, cleared his throat. The king set down his vials, removed his apron, and stepped forward. He, too, cleared his throat, and Justin came forward, kneeling down to kiss the king's ring.

''Duly contrite, Justin?'' the king queried.

''Duly so, sire!'' Justin replied.

''Then get off your knees—and see that you don't plague me with a knave's behavior in the future. And then get out of my way, so that I might greet Lady Chatham, since I swear she is finer upon my eyes than either of the pair of you!''

Ondine quickly dropped him a curtsy. He drew her to her feet with both hands and kissed her cheeks. ''My dear, you grow more beautiful. I know not why you're here, but I'm glad to see you. Justin, take Ondine for a walk. If you must be about court, be useful. I need a word with Warwick.''

Warwick tensed and started to protest. Ondine felt a sinking misery grip her, for she knew that he feared to have her alone with Justin—for her safety, lest they both be fooled by emotion. Justin frowned, forced to an awareness that his brother did not trust him. But the king stared steadily at Warwick, then turned, saying something that only Warwick heard. Warwick grinned and waved to Justin and Ondine as he followed Charles back behind his laboratory table.

But it was too late, Ondine could tell. Justin now knew that something troubled Warwick deeply.

When Justin took her hand and they left the lab, she knew the king had given Warwick assurance, for guards followed behind them. Justin lowered his voice as they idly wandered trails of oaks.

''What is this, then, that my brother fears my protection is not enough for his wife?''

''Justin, it is not that. He is edgy, nothing more—''

''Nay! Don't take me for a fool!'' Justin cried, and she knew that he had been hurt deeply by his brother's distrust.

''Justin—''

''He suspects me—his brother!—of some foul deed?''

''Nay!'' Ondine protested lightly. ''Surely 'tis a foul mood—''

''Why, then, his mood?''

She managed to laugh at that. "You tell me, Justin! You are the 'beast's' own blood!"

He eased a bit and chuckled with her, but then they both stiffened as the guard that followed them gave way to a woman elegantly dressed in velvet and lace in the deepest sky blue.

Lady Anne.

"Justin Chatham! Why, you lovely boy, so you are here with your brother and his . . . lady."

"Aye, Anne, that I am," Justin replied, bowing to her.

"And lady Chatham! How nice to see you at court again. You are such a fascinating creature. Of such wonderful mystery and intrigue! Oh, I do love a good mystery, don't you, Justin?"

"Oh, most assuredly," Justin replied, but Ondine was certain that he eyed Anne as suspiciously and warily as she did.

For there was, beyond a doubt, something very sinister about Anne today. She was so gloriously . . . smug. And happy. She was so very much like a cat, happy with cornered prey.

"Where's Hardgrave?" Justin asked her.

"Lyle?" she asked, smiling sweetly. "Why, he's about somewhere, I do imagine. A busy man, though, of course."

"Of course. Yet strange, isn't it, that we all travel about the country at the same time?" Justin asked politely.

Anne smiled a vibrant smile, and Ondine felt heat quake through her. Anne was beautiful. A cat that might crawl into beds, she was still stunningly lovely.

"Strange? Maybe," Anne murmured elusively. "And just how are you, child?" she asked Ondine. "Do you survive married life well?"

Her expression was bland. Ondine returned to her with all the sweetness she could muster.

"I adore married life, Anne. And all the wonderful . . . endowments it brings to one!"

"Ah! There they are!"

The king's voice stopped them all. Charles and Warwick appeared on the trail. The king greeted Anne with a frown.

"I heard that you had returned."

"The North was too quiet."

Charles raised a dark brow, but said nothing more to her. He took Ondine's hand and started down the path with her, leaving the others to follow as they chose, but clearly displaying his desire for them to remain a distance behind.

Ondine longed to turn around; longed to discover why Warwick's voice was low, and why Anne laughed so beguilingly.

She did not. In a low voice Charles claimed her attention. "I am deeply distressed. It had been my belief that Warwick was plagued by sorrow and guilt; now I know that murder haunted my hospitality, my court. You were attacked?"

"Frightened near to an early grave," Ondine admitted.

"There will be guards about you always," the king promised. Then he hesitated. "He asked me today that I arrange a divorce. I told him that I am not, of course, the Church." He sighed. "Yet we all know that such things are possible."

She gasped. "He asked you—today—to arrange for a—divorce?"

"Aye." Charles's wonderful dark eyes found hers with empathy and curiosity. "He feels now that his plan to marry you was a careless one. Lady, he does not want you harmed."

He does not want me at all, and certainly not as wife! she thought with such ardent anguish and dismay that she feared she would scream or burst into tears before the king.

"I asked him about his child, and he betrayed by his baffled expression that you are not enceinte. When you leave here this time, he plans to go home but a night to see to all your things, then send you to the Colonies by way of Liverpool."

She lowered her head, still unable to speak.

"I am warning you, my dear, of his plans, for although he is among the best and most valued of my friends, I have yet to betray a woman with your beauty, honesty, passion—and honor. Perhaps you may find you are forced to desert his cause to see to your own."

She found her voice at last, though it was hoarse and broken. "You have not told him—who I am?"

"I do not betray what I consider to be a confidence."

"Thank you. Bless you, sire," she whispered.

"No tears! Tonight we banquet together. And I claim the dances again. The future will come, and when I may help you, know that I will."

She nodded, aware only that they had paused and the others

were behind them. She could not speak at all as they walked to the river to board the barge.

Justin was silent. Only the king, Anne, and Warwick found conversation, and Anne's was exceptionally merry. Ondine caught Anne's eyes frequently upon her, and she was very wary, for it seemed that Anne knew something she did not and was, perhaps, preparing to strike.

Strike? Ondine queried herself uneasily. Was it possible? Could Anne have taunted her in cape and talons at Chatham? Had she, in fact, taunted Genevieve unto death?

This did not seem such a thing. It was more open; blatant, perhaps, as if she held some prize.

Ondine lowered her head, weary of it all, numb. Warwick would have to pursue his own demons. If he intended to send her to the Colonies, she would have to start worrying about her own future. The Colonies! She couldn't leave England! There was still the matter of her own life and the treachery played against it to be solved!

In the courtyard at Hampton they parted ways, Justin seeing Buckingham and determining to speak with him, the king muttering something inaudible, and Anne waving to Hardgrave across the walk, laughing gaily at Ondine, and rushing off to join the viscount.

Ondine had nothing to say to Warwick as they returned to their chambers, nor did it seem to matter; he was so withdrawn. Her head splitting, she decided to lie down for a while and left him in the outer chamber.

Lying down, she slept and, sleeping, dreamt. Her visions came and went like whispy clouds, but none was soft. She saw the jailer in Newgate, rotten-toothed and leering, then that image faded and returned, and the face she saw belonged to the masked creature in the chapel. She fought that masked creature and saw herself on her father's arm, at the king's side at Westchester, saw a sword rise and fall, heard screams and the rage of guards . . .

She saw blood, red blood, staining the stone floor—her father's blood. In her dream she remembered the anguish, the terror, and herself running and running, for if she did not escape, none would believe her pleas . . .

She did not know that she screamed aloud until she was startled awake. Her arms flailed wildly, and the cry she sounded was only stopped by the hand that was fitted tightly over her mouth.

"Sshh! What demon you wrest, lady, I know not, but you're about to raise the palace in arms!"

Warwick's voice was tender; he held her gently to his chest and for long moments she lay there, gasping, fighting to escape all the shadows and lingering ghosts. The strength of his arm was a tower to which she might cling; the steel of muscle beneath fabric was security; the living, vibrant wall of his chest a great harbor.

"Lady, tell me, what battle do you wage?"

She stiffened at the question, pushing furiously from him. He'd asked the king for a divorce that very day, and now he quizzed her. He wanted her to be a commoner, easily cast away. By God, she'd never be more to him! She would never betray the truth of her birth to him, or the mysteries and deceit that plagued her past.

"None who you will ever meet, Chatham!" she snapped. He caught her wrist and forced her eyes to his.

"What new venom is this, lady? You dream, and I soothe you, only to find your claws more deeply drawn."

She jerked at her wrist. He did not release it, but held it taut.

"No new venom," she told him wearily. Perhaps he did care for her safety. "Only that which has always been. Warwick, please! Will you leave me be!"

He released her and stood, staring down upon her. "Aye, milady, for now I'll leave you be! Yet I think there is a graver fear, for Anne and Hardgrave whisper and plot, and I wonder what discovery has been theirs."

She froze, shaken anew. Was that Anne's great pleasure that afternoon? Had she found out that Ondine was the old Duke of Rochester's daughter?

Warwick turned to leave her, bowing deeply at the door. "We leave for dinner shortly, if you would prepare."

She sat long, quaking with fear. Then something settled over her, something that was perhaps a sense of fatality. She stood and was not pleased with the gown she had chosen to wear to dinner. Tearing through her trunk, she sought another and settled upon one with a bodice and looped sleeves in organdy, and an overskirt in deepest mauve. Pearls gleamed elegantly from the hem, and she knew that once she had dressed her hair, she would appear striking in any crowd. If Anne meant to do her harm, Ondine decided she would not hide from the attack.

She exited that inner chamber with her head high to find her husband at the mantel, his elbow against it as he sipped a whiskey. He raised a high arched brow at her appearance and gave her a dashing bow.

"My lady, I grant you this: You are no coward."

"Shall we go?"

"If you've sins in your past, perhaps it might be best to confess them now."

"Warwick Chatham, of all men, you'll never be my confessor."

He shrugged and took her arm, leading her from the room. But at their door he paused and pulled her close.

"Ondine, eternally you forget one thing: You are my wife."

About to be cast out! she thought, feeding the fury that held her tears in check. She could not betray the king's confidence.

"And you eternally forget one thing, great Lord of Chatham. I truly do not give a damn."

"This night you should; the sharks are waiting."

"Sir, then I shall sink or swim."

"Perhaps you might need an arm."

"Never yours!" she cried in fury and watched his eyes narrow darkly, felt the grip of his fingers wind tightly around her arm.

"Then, lady, drown if you will!"

She lowered her eyes, afraid of the fear enveloping her. Why? Oh, why on this night had she battled him so, despised his offers of assistance?

There was no help for it; it was done. Stiffly they walked into the hall, and desperately she worried what Anne might say.

She did not have long to worry or wait. They had barely reached the dining hall, peopled with nobles and ladies, chatting and laughing, when a man's voice, harsh with vengeance, cried out upon them. "There they are now! Chatham—and his lady!"

The last was said with sarcasm. Ondine stiffened. A pathway parted between the crowd, and she saw Lyle Hardgrave, sneering as he approached them.

Warwick stiffened, hard and primed as a blade. A hush fell; the crowd drew back.

Ondine felt herself pulled forward on her husband's arm. She realized that Justin had appeared from the crowd and stood in back of them, ready at his brother's defense.

She doubted if Warwick even knew. His eyes were gold, a blaze upon Hardgrave.

"Aye. 'Tis Chatham and his—lady. Do you say, sir, that it is not so?"

Ondine heard a whisper from the crowd. "Someone should summon the king!"

Hardgrave and Warwick ignored all else but one another. Hardgrave openly leered at Ondine and bowed low with graceless mockery. "Nay, good neighbor! I say no such thing. 'Tis the lady Anne by chance discovered from whence she came."

Anne stepped up from behind Hardgrave's shoulder, in the greatest, most dramatic pretext of agitation.

"Warwick! I am ever so sorry! Let there be no discontent here!"

"Yes!" thundered a voice of authority, and the king stepped in amongst them. "Let there be no discontent here!" He frowned severely at the assembly, whirling to Anne.

"What is this?"

"Your Grace! 'Tis true she is no lady!"

"And why is that?"

"I'd rather not say—"

"Then, madam, may I suggest that you don't?"

Traitor, traitor! She will call me traitor, Ondine wailed within. She didn't know how she stood in those moments, her fear was so great.

"Your Grace!" Hardgrave said. "She came from the gallows! Warwick Chatham married a common poacher, pulled from the hangman's noose!"

"She's a common wench, straight from the streets!" Anne announced.

The king turned about, mildly interested, appearing as if he knew nothing of the matter.

"Is this true?" he inquired with polite interest.

Seconds passed. Ondine did not know whether to be relieved that the real truth was not known, or horrified that Anne had chanced upon this damning information. And, oh, what a perfect moment for Warwick to turn against her! He could cry that she bewitched him, and plead that he be rid of her on account of sorcery . . .

He did not. At that moment he turned to her, his amber gaze a glorious fire. He drew her hand slowly to his lips, bowed over it, and kissed it most reverently. His eyes met hers, lingering, as if he were, indeed, bewitched. And then he returned his gaze to the king, still holding her hand tight.

"Your Grace, it is true. Yet, who could blame me? Across a great expanse I saw her face, the beauty in her eyes, the pride in her fair countenance. Never had I seen a more glorious creature called woman, condemned to such a terrible fate. I came to her and, seeing her, knew that never again would I find such sweet beauty, never would I know such a chance for love, and so, aye, Your Grace, I did marry her, then, on the spot, and, by God, sire, what man would not reach out so for a touch of heaven?"

Charles was still for a moment, slowly smiling, bemused and quite taken with Warwick's witty salvaging of the situation.

Charles laughed and applauded, and the assembly applauded with the king, all taken with the wonderful romance of it. Charles pummeled Warwick upon the back.

"By the rood, Chatham, most wonderously stated, and most certainly, I could not have passed such a great beauty by!" The king bowed whimsically and gracefully to Ondine. "Lovely creature, you are indisputably a countess; I claim you to be among the greatest ladies of all my domain. Now, shall we have dinner?"

The king walked by; the assembly followed him.

Hardgrave and Warwick continued to stare at one another; Anne appeared furious and deflated.

Ondine trembled with a rush of warmth that brought color to her cheeks, and she felt faint. Oh, dearest God, after all, he had defended her, with far more than mere appearance would dictate. She did not want to be grateful, but she was. Breathlessly so. Achingly so. No threat or rage of his could have ever humbled her. The amazing reverence of his kiss upon her hand had done what words and warning might never accomplish. She wanted to thank him; she didn't know how.

"Hardgrave," Warwick said icily, "slander my wife, and you slander me. She might be defenseless to your malice and your sword; I, most assuredly, am not."

He led Ondine after the king. Ondine heard Justin comment cheerfully to Anne as he followed behind them.

"*Tsk, tsk,* Anne. My dear sister might be from the streets, but that's far better than the gutter, from where some females do come!"

Anne snapped out an oath that had definitely been born in the gutter. Justin laughed. Warwick turned to him, and they chuckled together, and each took one of her arms in a most gallant fashion.

She lowered her eyes, deeply in love with both the brothers Chatham.

Dinner came and passed, a feast with many courses. Jugglers performed, a bear danced, and the minstrels played. Ondine danced with the king, with Justin, with the rogue Buckingham . . .

And with her husband.

But Charles never seemed to tire, and even as the hour grew late, he told Warwick that he had a kingdom to rule and needed some counsel, if Warwick thought he might be able to set his personal problems aside for an evening.

Jake materialized to take Ondine to her chamber; she knew that he would remain outside the door.

For a long time she walked the floor, deep in thought. Pride burst in her, for the evening, for the man she loved. Anguish touched her, for already he planned to be rid of her. But—oh, God!—she owed him so . . .

She gnawed upon her nails and walked again with agitation. The hour grew later and later, but she suddenly cast open the door and asked Jake if she might summon a maid and a bath.

Jake seemed surprised and even a little disgruntled, but he called to one of the guards, and minutes later, a sleepy little maid appeared, and then a trail of pages brought a gigantic tub, filling it with steaming water.

Ondine bathed long and luxuriously in wonderfully scented oils. And while she soaked she sipped upon a glass of port for the courage she felt she needed.

When the water cooled, she emerged. She dressed in her sheerest gown, and the little maid brushed her hair to a high gloss, one that rivaled the fire of splendor.

Then the boys returned for the tub, the maid bobbed a curtsy and left, and she was alone. She found a high-backed chair, dragged it to the fire, curled her toes beneath her, sipped more port, and waited.

It was long past midnight when she heard the door twist. A flush rose within her, and an unbearable tingling sensation of warmth and nerves danced inside her.

Warwick strode into the room. She felt his eyes upon her. He walked to a small table and cast his small sword upon it. He saw the port bottle and poured himself a glass, then moved around before her, taking a chair opposite her, and, sitting, watched her over the rim of his glass.

"What are you doing still up?" he asked her.

Courage seemed to fly; he sounded so distant and so cold.

She lowered her eyes and shook her head.

He leaned forward suddenly, fingers tight around his glass, voice harsh.

"What?"

"I—I wanted to thank you."

"For what?"

She paused, hesitant. Surely he knew of what she spoke! But he would not make it easy for her; he awaited her answer.

"Anne wished to make a mockery of me. You did not allow her. There were whispers throughout the night, but no one was appalled, everyone seemed enchanted with your story," Ondine whispered at last.

He leaned back again. She felt his gold gaze so keenly over the rim of his glass.

"You are a Chatham. It is that simple, madam, you owe me no thanks."

She couldn't speak then; she felt foolish and rejected.

"Is there more?" he inquired suddenly.

She uncurled her feet, wanting only to escape. But she didn't have time to rise. He suddenly cast his glass into the flames, creating a hiss and sizzle. He strode to her, hands on the sides of her chair, blocking her in.

"You smell like a garden, madam, as elusive as a dream, as seductive as night jasmine. Your gown leaves nothing to be imagined. Were I not so thoroughly aware of the most ardent hostility of your regard for me, I just might be so intended to imagine an attempt at seduction on your part, a most dumbfounding experience, and certainly shattering to self-control. What was on your mind, Ondine?''

She shook her head suddenly, vehemently. Her hair gleamed and cascaded with that small motion like rivers of molten silk.

"Let me be!" she gasped. Oh! This had taken all her courage, and he mocked her!

"Madam, seduction was your intent. Why?"

"Just let me pass—"

"No. Why?"

She would never break through the barrier of his arms, or that of his harsh determination. She raised her head to his last stern question.

"I told you! I wanted to thank you—"

"Holy Mother of God!" he thundered. "Thank me?"

"I—"

"Lady, come to me for one reason and one reason only. Ever. Come to me because you want me."

"Oh, God!" she breathed, mortified. She couldn't even seduce him properly! What a fool ... "Please!" she rasped out.

He moved. She rose like a bird in flight, but spun back against his chest with another gasp. He caught the fabric of her gown.

"Could you possibly want me, Ondine?" he whispered to her.

And sensation fell all about her—the feel of her own skin, smooth and sensual with oil, the engulfing warmth of the fire, of his body, the feel of his arms around her.

She didn't think. She stared into his eyes. She did not speak, or even nod, but felt compelled by the night, by magic. She stepped back and touched the shoulders of her gown. It fell to the floor, a mystical cloud at her feet.

He did not touch her, but held her eyes as he shed his clothing, hastily, smoothly, letting it lie where it had dropped. When he was naked, when the flames played splendidly in a vast golden glow over his shoulders and chest, he spoke to her at last.

"Come to me."

She did, a step at a time. She fit into his arms and felt the great consuming passion of his kiss, the exciting arrogance of his hands upon her.

Their mouths came apart and met again, came apart and met. She pressed against him and longed to feel him with all her body. She pressed her lips to his shoulder, his chest, his throat, his fingers. She fell to her knees before him and gloried to the hoarse fever of his cry.

They never went into the bed, but made love upon the floor, with no covering but one another, no heat but that of the fire and of their fusing bodies. There was no future for her that night, nor was there a past . . . just the flaming passion of the night.

Chapter 18

Ondine knew that she lay curled on the floor before the fire, a carpet their bed, her husband's chest her pillow, her discarded gown of the night before a covering for her feet.

She was barely awake, drifting in some netherland of soft clouds and ease, when she was jolted to awareness by the heavy sounds of footsteps in the hall outside their door. Then horrendous pounding at that same door penetrated cruelly into her world of pleasant dreams.

Beside her, Warwick stirred abruptly, swearing out a ragged groan. "Damnation!" He rose, reaching quickly for his breeches.

Still dazed, Ondine stared up at him in confusion as he pulled on his pants. " 'Tis the king," he told her, "and yonder door is not bolted; Jake stayed beyond it, and I did not think to come upon you, er, here, and remain here so!" Dear Lord, but she was beautiful! Soft with sleep, touched by daylight, her hair a gold and tawny cloak about shoulders as sleek as satin and pure as ivory. Her eyes were so like the sea from which an enchanting siren might well spring. Ondine, a mythical creature, granted eternal life through marriage to a mortal.

Aye, he'd granted her life. He could not take it, nor could he linger on thoughts of her now, for the door would surely spring forth, since it was unlocked.

He touched her chin, knowing he must repudiate her soon, unable for that moment to be anything but gentle and tender. "My love! The king is here. I was to have met him early, alas! I knew such comfort, I did not awaken. Ondine, the king comes; he'll enter."

"Oh!" she gasped, startled, realizing too late the import of his words. The door flew open as with an impatience of its own. Charles strode within, his retinue pausing behind him at the doorway.

Barefoot, barechested, but decently decked in pants, Warwick by instinct hunched to the floor, holding his wife to him in the gauze folds of her white gown.

Charles paused instantly at the sight. Not in apology, for Chatham had been late, and the purpose for such an outer chamber in a suite was so that a friend or advisor might have a place to greet company. Nay, he paused, touched, lowering his head with a smile, for it was such a lovely scene, the handsome knight shielding his lady—a great beast protecting his delicate wife.

He bowed low. "Lady Chatham, my apologies. Warwick!"

"Sire!"

"You're late! The lords of Sudbury and Wane await, and they mean to plague me regarding James. I've a need for your tolerance and your tongue; more of this bickering I cannot and will not endure."

He turned, startled to find his small retinue of guards all staring into the room much as he had done. At his questioning gaze the fellows cleared their throats and stepped back. Charles paused then, a wicked grin curling his lip, for he knew the palace. Within a short time all would hear that the Lord and Lady of Chatham so craved one another that they had no patience to achieve a bed once their passions had flared.

Charles paused, unable to restrain his natural humor. He turned about quickly, catching the Duke of Rochester's daughter in a deep flush, pulling the white sheath of gown closer to her breasts.

"Lady Chatham, is there something not quite right with the bedding? I'd not be lax in hospitality!"

"Nay, sire!" she gasped out, coloring in a most bewitching way all over again. She realized herself caught in his humor then, and quickly lowered her eyes. Warwick's arms tightened around her.

Charles did not continue out; he did not, at first, know why he lingered. Then he realized that he was quite taken with the pair of them, and that the future boded nothing but ill for both. He wanted to see them laugh and smile, to enjoy what time they might allow themselves.

"Have you been to the races, Ondine?" he asked.

"Newmarket? Never."

Charles nodded, satisfied. "I believe I shall make a move for the court. When the tedium of my mewling nobles ends today, we shall set our sights for Newmarket! That is, Warwick Chatham"— Charles's voice took on that tenor that warned the wise his England was his first concern, no matter what frivolity was displayed— "if you think you can manage to hurry along your appearance."

With that subtle warning, he closed the door at last.

When he was gone, Warwick, still crouched behind Ondine, sighed and rose, reaching for his hose and boots, stumbling into them.

"This again!" he muttered, casting her a dry gaze. "And it never will end, for Catherine bears no child, and James remains warned away from court by the king, but he's still the Catholic heir! Half the nobles still clamor to have Charles legitimize his bastard son, the Duke of Monmouth, and, by God, Jemmy would make a fine king. Many swear they'll never accept a Catholic king; others swear that civil war will rage if James is swept from the secession."

He swept his shirt from the floor, buttoning it as he continued to speak. "Then, across the sea, we have William and Mary— the Orangeman panting for his uncle Charles's death, then that of his father-in-law; he sees the crown of England in his future, and he might well one day achieve that goal."

Ondine frowned and shivered, bereft of his warmth, yet fascinated that he spoke to her so.

Like a wife.

"Charles is in prime health—" she began.

Buttoning his coat, he leaned and kissed her lips lightly. "That he is; as long as I live, I will be among those who guard that health and life! But I tell you, he is right—these rumors and pressures regarding the secession grow tedious, and James does little to help, offending even those who fought for him well and once thought him a noble commander.''

Ondine stood, carefully wrapping her gown about her, as Warwick at last reached for his weapons and hat. He paused, sliding his sword to its hilt, watching her.

''Would that I could stay!'' he murmured suddenly, fiercely. He gripped her bare arms, dragged her to him. Passionately he kissed her lips. When that was done, he pressed his lips to the hollow of her shoulder, the rise of her breast, holding her tightly. Then with a sigh he released her, moving to the door, lest he forget he owed a king allegiance.

Ondine still trembled from his touch, glorying in the glow that surrounded them. Though it was magic, make-believe, it was still sweet glory.

''Will you enjoy the races?'' he asked her lightly, his eyes upon her tender, whimsical.

''Aye, that I will.''

''We move again. Will you pack for me?''

She nodded, still clinging to the sheath of her gown.

He smiled, dipped low in stately courtesy, but paused before he left her, his smile fading.

''Don't leave. Jake will remain here.''

''Along with the king's guard,'' she reminded him softly.

''Wait for me; don't leave.''

''I won't,'' she whispered, and he kissed her hurriedly and left.

It was late when they came to Newmarket, for the king's retinue was large, and he was a man of such vast energy that not all who chose to serve him could keep his pace. There was often little warning that he would appear, and on such occasions the innkeepers, merchants, and servants ran in circles, for supplying those involved with the king demanded great resources.

Ondine was fascinated by all the activity. She rode with Warwick and Justin, and it seemed their moods were all the best, laughter flowing well and easily. Justin demanded to know the whole story of how Warwick had come upon her, and between them, Warwick and Ondine managed to make light comedy of the story.

''Damn!'' Justin exclaimed suddenly, pulling the drapes from the carriage window. "Hardgrave follows us still. And that vixen Anne! She waves most gaily!"

Warwick shrugged. "Let her wave. 'Tis not against the law."

Justin waved back, green eyes narrowing. "She strikes unease in me each time she doth appear cheerful!"

Again Warwick merely shrugged. Feeling his movement, Ondine turned to stare at him. She discovered that his eyes, amber and musing, were on her. She flushed and spoke to Justin.

And that night, that night! Later, when she was alone and frightened and tempest tossed, she would remember that night. A glowing candle to stave off the dark reminder of time, a streak of beautiful, blinding peace against a sea of storms. Remember, ah, yes, ever would that night live in crystal memory, a fragment of eternal beauty.

They were given a small cottage all their own, with simple things. They had a single room, with unadorned table and chairs, a massive hearth, and a massive bed.

Upon their arrival, Ondine found gifts from the king on the bed. There were belted robes in white, with their initials embroidered in gold upon the great lapels. Warwick commented that he was gratified to be held in such esteem, for it was obvious that a dozen seamstresses had sewn all morning to create the robes.

And that seemed to be most of their conversation that night. He ordered simple wine and cheese and bread; he left her that she might don the robe and returned to wear his own.

They ate upon the bed with the tray between them. They finished as if of one mind, and their eyes locked upon one another's. Warwick removed the tray, and they still sat, cross-legged, not an arm's length away. He moved to slip her sash, to part her robe, and for the longest time he simply stroked her flesh, drawing tender lines between the valley of her breasts. In time she uttered a sound and rose to her knees, still fascinated by the depths of his eyes, longing to touch him. She slipped the robe from his shoulders and cast her fingers upon him in leisurely discovery. She felt the line of muscle and sinew, played within the vast mass of hair upon his chest. For long moments the silence between them continued, broken only by the eloquence of their eyes. The warmth of the fire crackled. She threaded her fingers into his hair, rested her chin atop his head, and felt his face cradled against her breast. Then he, too, was on his knees, and slow simmering ardor blazed to vast and seeking hunger. He sank to his haunches, wrapping the slender length of her legs around him. Whisper followed whisper, tenderness tempered urgency. All the things he said, the things he did, movement and measure, she would remember.

Ecstasy upon ecstasy . . .

So would he recall, with vivid imagery, the sweet magic beauty of that night. So would he recall . . .

They came, at last, the next afternoon to the races. Warwick showed great enthusiasm for the horses, finding Justin and swearing that it was a shame they'd none of their own breed that day. Justin said that his colt could beat any mount upon the field; Warwick retorted that whether the colt could would matter little—Dragon could take any horse he'd seen to date.

There was gaming and gambling, betting and good cheer. The king was attended by his queen, the skies were clear, and the day was astoundingly sunny and clear. Staring at all the elegantly dressed lords and ladies, at the hawkers and merchants, Ondine smiled easily, in love with life itself. There was but one flaw this morning; one sour note that could make her smile falter.

Anne and Hardgrave stood not far behind them, Anne as glorious as ever, Hardgrave stocky but attractive in lace sleeves and velvet maroon breeches and coat.

He saw Ondine's eyes upon him and smiled in a manner that made her heart leap with curious fear. It was not that he gazed at her with such an evident leer—men, she knew with a sigh of resignation, often wore such ridiculous expressions. Nay, it was something more. She frowned, then realized her concern.

He did not look like one merely lecherous, but one who thought—no, expected!—to fulfill his every fantasy.

Ondine held Warwick's arm tightly. He patted her hand absently and pointed out a dappled gray steed to Justin, swearing it would win by a full length.

Moments later the horses were running. Warwick and Justin

stepped forward with enthusiasm. Ondine turned slightly and saw that Anne and Hardgrave were not far behind.

There was a wild array of shouting as the horses raced over the finish line. People grouped more tightly about the track.

"You're sure? You're absolutely positive that you procured the right vial from the king's laboratory?"

Ondine frowned, certain that Anne was speaking in a hushed whisper behind her. She heard gruff laughter and strained to hear Hardgrave's reply, but she could not. Too many lucky gamblers were laughing and congratulating one another about them.

To her surprise Anne and Hardgrave approached them. "Did you choose a winner, Warwick?" Hardgrave inquired politely.

"I usually do," Warwick replied.

"Did you gamble, then?" Anne asked pleasantly.

"Alas, no, we came too late." Ondine noted that Warwick answered pleasantly, but that his lazy gaze upon the two was nevertheless intent and wary.

"Oh!" Anne said suddenly. "Perhaps we could move to the oak—there—and have a better view."

Justin gazed at his brother. Warwick arched a brow, but it was true that they might better inspect the horses from that vantage point. They moved to the oak.

"They start!" Anne announced. "Who shall win?"

"I say the bay!" Hardgrave boomed.

"The bay!" Justin protested. "Nay—that chestnut, yon. See his great breadth of shoulder."

Warwick laughed. "You're both wrong! 'Tis that great black stallion will take the race. I'll stake a hundred pounds upon it!"

"I'll see that bet!" Hardgrave challenged.

They are children—the lot of them! Ondine decided with disgust. Give them a bit of entertainment, and bygones were bygones so that the game might be enjoyed.

"And what do you say, Ondine?" Anne queried her.

"Why, the ebony stallion, of course," Ondine replied more tartly than she wished. "I would support my husband."

Anne grinned and idly looked around as the men crowded the fence. "They do sell the most wonderful things about here. Pastries that are delicious, ribbons and bows, buckles and lace. We must walk about later. It's wonderful fun, don't you think?"

"Aye, that it is."

A shot was fired; the crowd roared as the next race began. They were pushed and shoved from behind, and Ondine suddenly felt herself roughly jerked toward the oak.

And then she didn't understand in the least what came to pass, for it was so quick. A clothed hand was clamped over her mouth. She tugged upon it madly, determined to shriek and scream, yet she could not. There was some scent about the hand, about the rag shoved over her mouth, that stole all sense and reason. She saw the sky, the people, the horses, and all swirled around her. She felt as if she were being lifted, up, up into the oak, into the sky.

Dear God, what was happening? How had she come to be so very far away? And whose hand was this that constrained her, and what was this sickly sweet odor that robbed her of strength and sense and motion? Her fingers clawed and failed, grew weak and helpless . . .

She heard a scream and thought that it might be her own, but it was not; it was Anne who screamed. She was on the ground, clutching her torn bodice to her breast. Hardgrave was bending to her; Warwick and Justin, confused in the melee, were drawing their swords.

Ondine saw it all as if from a great distance. She wanted to fight; she desperately wanted to scream for Warwick. She could not. Her limbs had gone leaden; her voice had no substance.

Then everything faded around her and all was darkness.

She awoke with a groan, disoriented. Her head was pounding with a miserable velocity, and she felt quite nauseated. It seemed that she was upon a ship that rocked with the waves in an endless and miserable roll.

She opened her eyes; the world seemed to spin and her head to pound more fiercely. She closed them quickly, wincing as memory came to her. She had been standing with the others at the tree. Then suddenly she had been touched, caught by that unknown hand and—drugged! She remembered now, and still it made no sense. She had been attacked, yet Anne had screamed. Anne had lain upon the ground, as if abused.

Who had been there? A set of thugs? They were bold offenders surely to perpetuate a crime with so many in attendance! Why the attack, and where was she?

She had to open her eyes, had to discover her whereabouts.

She willed her eyes open once again. Light seared into her brain, creating new pain, but she held through it, and in moments her vision cleared. She tried to move and discovered that she could not. Her hands were tied to narrow bedposts, and she felt that she pitched and rolled because her prison, it seemed, was a musty ship's cabin, stale and disheveled, small and tight. A single window brought in the light, which displayed nothing to quell her growing panic. In the cabin there was a chart chest, a trunk, and the bunk she lay upon, nothing more. An open bottle of rum sat upon the chart table and a dirty coat was cast over it. There was a pitcher on the trunk and a washbowl that seemed permanently etched with grime. The cabin had an unwholesome odor that threatened to make her ill where she lay.

Nay, nay! She gritted her teeth together, willing herself to think. There was no great mystery here; she had been kidnapped and dragged aboard a ship. But by whom? And for what reason?

Anne! Ondine remembered the words she had overheard, the lady Anne demanding if Hardgrave had taken the right vial from the king's laboratory. Vial! A drug to steal the sense from her . . .

Was this to be murder, then?

Panicking, she strained and thrashed, yet achieved nothing. Her flesh grew raw, for the more she struggled, the tighter the ropes became. She quieted suddenly, her heart a drumbeat in her ears, for she heard footsteps beyond the door, then voices.

"Hey! What do ye do there, matey?"

"I'm in to 'er, that's all!"

"She's to be left; them's orders!"

"Orders be damned! I'm the one who risked life and limb to snatch her, and I'll look if I damn well choose!"

The door slammed opened. Ondine closed her eyes, thinking it best to pretend that the drug still claimed her.

Two pairs of footsteps approached the bunk, and with them a stench of long-unwashed flesh that well suited the cabin. She prayed that she would not cough or sneeze at the offense, that she might lie still and listen and learn some bit of information.

Yet it seemed that she lay there for aeons of agony, with the men saying nothing, and her only sense being that of smell; she smelled the tars so thoroughly that she longed to scream.

At last one spoke in a whisper, the braggart who had "risked life and limb" to snatch her.

"She's fair and fine, Josh, that she is. Young and firm! Would that she'd awake."

Josh snorted. "Fer what, my friend? Ye've heard the order; she's not to be touched."

"And why not, might I ask? She's married, she is—no virgin lass. And think on it, probably wed to an old and graying noble; she'd appreciate sport such as I could give."

"Sport such as you, you weasel?" Josh sneered. "Forget it! She goes to the bloke downriver—for the rest of the gold!"

"We get the gold; she'll be delivered goods. C'mon, Josh," the weasel cajoled. "Wot's he to know the difference? Steal the lord's lady was me order! Well, steal her I did! I deserve some reward!"

"You'll not risk my part of it!"

"Who's to know?"

"Him—the man who's paying us, that's who! 'Less you plan to tear out her vocal chords, and he'd not like that a bit! He said he wanted her unscratched!"

"Bah! I'll not scratch her!"

There was a silence, a silence in which Ondine thought she would surely die, scream, or go wretchedly mad.

And then he touched her. He caught her hair between his fingers, then placed his stinking paw over her bodice.

She did scream. Her eyes came open wide and horrified, gleaming into the weasel's. And, oh, he was vile! More snake than any a man—jailor or inmate!—she had ever crossed in Newgate. His teeth were jagged, filthy, yellow. And his hand, the hand that touched her, seemed all but gray . . .

"Don't! Don't! Don't dare! I swear I'll kill you—"

He interrupted her with a pleased wheeze of laughter. "Spitfire, vixen! All the better. Kill me, will you, bitch? And how?" He reached to the post, tugging at the rope to wrench her wrists in a painful grasp. He started laughing again.

Josh stepped forward; he was not so bad as the weasel, Ondine thought quickly. He was cleaner by far. His clothing, though, was near as threadbare, and he was an older man, lean and pale, apparently agitated by the whole affair.

Ondine held her breath, then let out another long and furious scream, one that pierced the ears and surely threatened doom.

"Leave her, you fool!" Josh commanded.

The weasel chuckled, leaning over her. She inhaled the foul, rummy stench of his breath and thought she would be sick. Dizziness almost overwhelmed her as she realized that he intended to press his stinking mouth to hers.

Her hands were tied, she realized then, but her legs were not. She brought up a knee with all her fury and strength and slammed it fiercely against the weasel's britches.

He screamed and doubled over, glaring at her hatefully. "Hoity-toity bitch! Nobility! Thinks she's too damn good for the common man! Maybe not, milady, maybe not! Maybe I'll decide that the devil can take the gold, and I'll teach you how to really scream. I'll—"

She thrashed, aiming for him again. He seemed about to attack her when Josh caught his arms, dragging him away. "Leave her, damn you! Leave her now. That gold is part mine, and part the captain's, and you'll not steal it from us!"

He gave the weasel a fierce shrug. The man shook himself, then stamped from the cabin.

"Where am I?" Ondine demanded of Josh. "What gold do you speak of? Free me—and I'll promise far greater riches!"

Josh didn't reply. He walked to the table, his back to her.

"Please! I am the Countess of North Lambria! I can—"

"You'll be nothing but a rich man's doxy and whim soon, lovely," Josh said with a weary sigh, turning about. Ondine's eyes widened as she saw he carried a soaked cloth.

"No!" she screamed.

"Y'er trouble!" he told her flatly. "Too much trouble!"

She squirmed and kicked and twisted, but there was no help for it. Josh sidestepped her legs, swearing that they needed to be tied.

Then the cloth descended over her face. She gasped desperately for breath and found nothing but a void of darkness once again.

Chapter 19

Just as Anne screamed, Warwick realized that Ondine no longer held him, yet that scream took his attention and instinctively he sought the injured party, his sword drawn and at the ready as naturally as he breathed, mind and body ever attuned to danger and well honed from past services to his king.

And from that point on, it was madness for Warwick, madness and blind panic.

While Anne gasped prettily, Justin noted that Ondine was gone. Warwick took off into the crowd, bellowing her name.

A young girl selling pastries told him she'd seen a groom carrying an exceptionally heavy load of blankets from the great oak tree to the road. Warwick, with Justin at his heels, rushed to the road. Confused at first, Jake then gasped, remembering that a supply wagon had gone by—and that one of the merchants had mentioned it was bound for the shore and a trader called the *Marianne*.

The wagon carried a bulk of blankets that might easily have carried the slim body of a woman.

Warwick, cold and numb with terror, was ready to dash off alone. 'Twas Justin forced him to wait, until the ever adventurous Buckingham and his cronies could be summoned, with ten of the fleetest racehorses to carry them swiftly in pursuit.

* * *

Hardgrave held Anne, soothing her from the assault. Yet, in truth, the two whispered together.

"You must ride with them!" Anne told Hardgrave.

Hardgrave, never so subtle as Anne, answered in a fury she was forced to quickly hush. "Me! See here, lady, what if the filthy swine we paid coin to knows my face—"

"Hush! Only one has ever seen you—the captain of the vessel. That is why you must ride! If Warwick discovers the wagon has gone to the river dock, he'll not stop until someone confesses to complicity! Implicating us! The captain knows you. He *must* die in battle! Would you have us both in the Tower, or exiled? Or worse still, would you meet Warwick in battle again, without the king to demand that the blades be shielded?"

"I'll meet him again anytime," Hardgrave said bitterly.

"Well, I am not prepared to reside in the Tower while you die a glorious death! You have failed, yet all can still be redeemed. Go!"

Warwick and his party of men raced with the wind.

The town slipped behind them as they swept along the road, past shady trees and valleys, rich and verdant rolling hills, flocks of sheep, and fields of grain.

Warwick shuddered as he rode, feeling blinded and maimed by the fear. He was grateful still that he saved her from the hangman, but what a fool he'd been to think he might use her as a pawn. A less arrogant man would have seen her endless beauty and courage, known that she would be an enchantress to humble the strongest man, to seize his heart . . . God in heaven, he loved her.

This love—it weakened, it crazed a man. Without Justin and Buckingham, he would have just set off and slain any in his way with madness, till he was brought down himself. By the devil, he was no fool! Battle had always shown him cool, a warrior who fought with wits as well as brawn. But this, ah, this love, it robbed him of sense and strategy! It ripped his body again and again with fear. Before God, it was dangerous, and though he would gladly lay down his life for her, that life might not prove to be enough.

If—Oh, Holy God! It could not be "if"! When he found her, he would make her safe! He would wait for nothing before sending her away. Her life was ever in danger for being a Chatham; if that precious life ever became forfeit, he would no longer own a soul.

"There, Warwick! I see her! The *Marianne!*" Justin called from his side. "Third upon the river; cast betwixt the fishing craft. Her sailors are casting the ropes away!"

It was true, he saw quickly. Sailors moved about the vessel, breaking her from the dock.

"Hard forward!" Buckingham called, and horses that had galloped hard were urged to greater speed. They tore into the dockside town, clattering against cobblestones, causing all who ambled in their way to shriek and scamper for cover. Carts of fruit and vegetables broke and fell, dogs barked madly, and men about their daily business paused under cover, gaping at this break of a work-weary day.

Warwick's heart thundered along with that of his poorly used steed; he cried no orders, gave no heed to the others, and thought only to reach the *Marianne* before all the ropes could be broken, the walk hauled in.

He jerked in upon the reins, dismounting from the horse even as it came to a halt. He dimly realized that Hardgrave was at his side, eager to confront battle.

It was Justin, though, with the sense to attempt a cry.

"Hold, sailors of the *Marianne!* Hold, by order of the king! Captain of this ship, I charge you, hold!"

"Hold! Never!"

The captain, a lean fellow with a patch over his left eye, a filthy beard and evil leer, held tight to the rigging and bared his sword. "Hey, mates? there's not a dozen of them noble dandies; we're two score! The king's order! Bah! Take us if you can, gents! Mates, cast her away, these fellows might want a swim!"

The command brought great activity. Men rushed swiftly to clear the remaining moorings, but too late, for Warwick leapt across the plank, his party a swarm behind him. They were met with pistols and cutlasses, yet from the first onslaught, fewer in number but greater in skill, they attacked like righteous angels of God. Warwick had barely laid down his first swarthy contestant before he noted that the captain of the vessel had already been engaged in battle by Hardgrave. It appeared that he would speak even as he fought, yet if he'd decided to surrender, that thought came far too late. Hardgrave smiled, expertly flicked the man's sword aside, and skewered him with a deft blow.

A snarling fellow, short and muscular, toothless and minus his lower left earlobe, came at Warwick in a rush. Warwick stepped aside, spun, and pinned him to the deck, quickly looking about for the next assault. Bodies were down about the ship, sailors, or pirates, rather, it so seemed. Blood spurted from Buckingham's shoulder; he was fighting on with his pistol as a club. Justin was engaged in combat with two blackguards and Warwick rushed to his side.

"Brother!" Justin laughed, avid with the challenge of it all. "You insult me! They're but a pair of swine!"

"Rather insult you than bury you!" Warwick parried back, clipping the wrist of one of the fellows and sending him reeling to the deck, begging for mercy. Warwick stepped past him. He had no heart for slaughter—he sought only his wife.

"Go on!" Justin urged him. Buckingham, holding his injured arm, but smiling, came to them, and gazing at his friend, Justin continued with a broad grin, "This is but a sop-up now of a pig sty!"

"Find your lady," Buckingham said, "and we'll see whom we might discover to give light to this adventure!"

Warwick needed no further urging.

He found a ladder to a hallway leading aft. A foul odor warned him he neared the galley; instinct caused him to pause, an instinct well heeded, for two burly mates, apparently unaware that the battle was lost topside, came to block his way from the galley hole.

Warwick arched a brow at the pair, his sense of humor somewhat restored at their appearance. Their bulk was caused by roundness at the middle, and he thought that they looked like a pair of eggs.

"Give way, me gents; your mates are dying, and I've blood enough on my hands today."

The one laughed and nudged the other. "Is he blind—or has he but one eye? There's two of us, milord!"

"And if I kill one, what is another?" Warwick queried pleasantly in turn.

The one who had challenged him with laughter lost his surly smile; with a shriek of rage he came at Warwick. Warwick barely stirred, but narrowed an eye at the man's angle of speed, and when he was almost atop him, he at last lifted his blade.

The sailor fell upon it himself, sinking slowly to the floor and staring upward, amazed to discover himself dying.

The second man stared at Warwick, then fled down the hall, entering the last cabin, slamming the door in his wake.

Warwick stepped over the fallen man and hurried toward the cabin, certain that it was the deceased captain's, and equally certain that it would be where Ondine was being held. Horrible images came to him, racking his heart and mind, as he quickened his speed. Ondine . . . a captive of this loathsome crew! With all her beauty, her fairness, her fire, her golden hair . . . If they had touched her—

If they had touched her, he thought grimly, he'd slit their throats to the very last man, mercy be damned!

There'd been so little time, he tried to assure himself.

But rape took little time, and murder even less.

That thought so enraged him, bringing his blood to such a chill of fear that he gave no thought to trying the door. Instead he slammed against it with his shoulder in cold, deadly determination. The door shuddered; he pitted his weight against it again, and the sea-rotten wood gave to his touch. He held still, wary before entering, not wanting to discover a knife in his back from behind.

She was there; that he knew instantly. Her hands were strapped to the posts of the portside bunk—even her ankles were tied. Fury rose in him at the sight of her chafed and reddened flesh where those tight knots bound her, yet that fury was tempered by fear and confusion.

She slept, her hair a halo about her, her face ethereally beautiful and peaceful in that mist of flame and sunlight. For a moment he feared that she was dead, then her brows tensed in a frown; she shook her head as if fighting some inner fog, and her eyes opened.

He exhaled in a vast surge of relief. She lived!

"Get him!"

The whisper sounded from the far corner of the room. Warwick stiffened and, with narrowed eyes, observed that corner.

There were three men: the fat brute he'd come upon in the

hallway; a skinny fellow, with teeth so yellow they might have been a jackal's; and a third, no cleaner, yet not so much like a treacherous varmint in appearance.

"Gents," he said quietly, "give way. And I tell you, if she is in any way touched—"

"Damn you, Josh, for a coward!" the one with the yellow teeth cried out. "Slay him, man, he's alone!"

Yellow teeth drew his knife with a growl; Warwick gazed with narrowed eyes from him to Ondine. She stared at him, as if confused, barely recognizing him, but she seemed aware. He thought that he must free her first, lest they think to unman him with a threat to her person. He could not afford to have the threat of harm to her held against him as a lethal weapon. He stepped into the room, his sword held high, and quickly slashed the bonds that held her.

"Go!" he charged her. "Topside, to Justin!"

She tried to move; she was so dazed and sore that it was a difficult measure at best. The weasel was coming at Warwick then, crouched low, his knife in his hands. A heavy fellow she hadn't seen before was taking courage from that action, advancing from the side, near her. Josh was taking the other side.

"Get out of here, Ondine!"

She couldn't; she was dazed, but she couldn't leave him to such odds. Glancing around, she saw the filthy water pitcher on the table, and as the men paid her no heed, she reached for it, swerving terribly in her attempt.

The weasel lunged first—apparently he had no notion of Warwick's talents with his weapon. The sword whistled through the air; the weasel gasped and sank into a pool of his own blood.

The other two were stunned, then panicked. Together they rushed for Warwick, as if innately aware that neither could be hero or coward; survival meant combined strength and action.

Ondine raised her pitcher in a heavy lunge, then gasped in horror, for she struck neither the weasel nor the burly man, but caught her husband square against his temple.

"Oh, God!" she gasped.

He caught his reeling head and barely twisted in time to slice the burly fellow's arm from wrist to shoulder, reducing him to a heap of groaning helplessness.

Josh backed away to the corner of the room, dropping his weapon.

Warwick, stunned, turned to stare at Ondine.

"Madam, just whose side are you on?"

"I'm sorry! So sorry!"

"I told you to get out of here!"

"I—I couldn't leave you!"

"Go—now!"

She tried to step; she swayed. He caught her, keeping a wary eye upon the last man as he did so.

"What have you done to her?"

He fell to the floor, hands clenched in prayer. "Spare me, Your Grace, spare me! 'Tis a drug, nothing more! Will wear away in minutes now, I swear it upon my soul!"

Ondine stared into Warwick's eyes. He returned her glare, but with no tenderness. He touched her face, and the feel of his hand was not cruel, yet he seemed so—harsh.

"I'll know what happened here!" he told the man.

Josh shook his head in desperation. "We were paid! Paid with coin and well! She was to be taken to a gentleman downriver."

"Who?"

"I don't know, by God, I don't know! I'd tell you if I did! Only the captain knew the man—he didn't want himself known to any."

And the captain was dead, Warwick thought bitterly.

There was movement behind him. Warwick, with Ondine cradled against him, quickly spun, raising his sword.

"Warwick—'tis me!" Justin warned him quickly. "Just me and Buckingham."

Warwick thrust Ondine into his arms. "Take her," he said hoarsely. "Take her—and start back."

Justin didn't understand his brother's raw emotion and stiffness. He sighed with relief and caught Ondine, baffled, for she seemed unharmed, yet she could not stand on her own.

"Wait!" she called. "Warwick, I—"

"Get her out of here! Bring her back to our rooms and order Jake to guard her, to sit on her if need be!"

Ondine gave in. Her head still swam; she had no strength. Justin lifted her into his arms, and she merely closed her eyes with weary relief, clinging to him.

Buckingham stepped into the cabin as Justin left it with his burden. "Some rubbish remains alive," he told Warwick, staring at their captive.

"Aye," Warwick murmured, "but I learn nothing."

"Only the captain knew—" came the plaintive cry of their prisoner, but Buckingham cut him off with a cold and cruel laugh.

"Only the captain knew! Aye, we've heard that one. But we've ways and means, my fine fellow! Wait till you feel the caress of the Earl of Exeter's daughter!"

The man paled, for the "Earl of Exeter's daughter" meant the rack, and no man remained unscathed from such torment.

"I tell you—"

Buckingham turned calmly to Warwick. "It seems we've saved not only your bride, Warwick, but a score of beauties kept in the hold! This captain and his crew claimed to trade with Spain; kidnapping young lasses was their real business, bound for the harems of Morocco."

Warwick arched a brow. He could feel little guilt or pity for so much blood strewn now that he knew the purpose of these men.

But neither could he feel relief, for he believed the mewling wretch before him—this man did not know who had paid the sum to have Ondine delivered to him.

Hardgrave! he thought in fury. Hardgrave and Anne! Yet Anne had almost fallen prey to these pirate slavers herself, and Hardgrave had fought beside him with a determination to equal his own.

"Leave him to the courts of law, Buckingham," Warwick said, shaking his head. "We'll get nothing from him." He turned, disgusted, and strode his way back to the open deck. The stench of the place was enough to rot a man.

He held tight to the rail at the starboard side, gritting his teeth as a convulsion of anguish swept through him. How he'd quivered to see her alive and well! How he'd loved her when he'd seen her, dazed and dizzy—striking him, but meaning to be there for him, ready to fight at his side. Ah, her face, her beautiful face! The expression upon it had been sweetly comical when she'd realized her mistake.

By God, she was his heart, his soul, his every breath of desire.

He wanted with every fiber of his being to reach her, hold her to his chest and cherish her face, her lips, her hair, her form, her very life—her laughter and her warmth, her temper and her spirit. He winced, for he knew he could not. Today had proved him a wretched protector. And he had underlined the fact to a shattering degree that she seemed to be safe nowhere, not while she was his wife.

He sighed deeply. In time the king's guards would arrive to round up the living remainder of this motley crew. He could ride back to the cottage at Newmarket, where they had found such absolute peace and bliss in each other's arms.

And there, tonight, he must refute her, coldly and cruelly, for he knew her courage and spirit. She would fight him; she believed fiercely that she owed him the debt of her life, and even if she was frightened, she would not willingly leave him until she felt she had paid her debt to him.

She had to leave him! She had to live! Even if he had to play the beast in truth to force her to do so.

Ondine awaited Warwick with the greatest anxiety. She didn't understand him, but she knew him well, and in that she knew he had changed once again. He had ridden like the wind to her rescue, yet it seemed that then he directed his anger against her!

Jake was, as ever, good to her, but remained detached. As Warwick had commanded, he all but sat upon her.

She had felt so touched by filth that she had instantly bathed; but then she had felt so lonely that she'd asked Jake to fetch Justin, and though Jake hesitated, he finally did as bidden.

Ondine was irritated to a flaming wrath with both Warwick and Jake. How could anyone suspect Justin of foul deeds?

But when Justin came, Ondine learned that he knew very well his brother held him in suspicion, and though he did not cry out against Warwick, it was apparent that he was very hurt.

He sipped the port that they morosely shared, staring into her eyes, cleared at last of the drug.

"He believes that Genevieve was murdered, I see that now. But that he could think that I—"

He stopped, choking on bile.

Ondine, convinced of his innocence, tried to soothe him. "I think, Justin, that he loved her so very much that he is still crazed by it. He—he did adore her?"

Justin rose and shrugged. "He was always gentle and tender and very good to her. Yet who knows what my brother thinks in truth, for he is capable of great reserve and silence. And today . . . I can't believe he means you any cruelty, Ondine. He is merely furious because he was so frightened for you, and because he cannot discover who was behind it all." He hesitated a minute, not wishing to distress her further. "You do know that someone— some man—had paid those knaves a vast sum for your delivery?"

Ondine rose suddenly. "Anne!"

"Anne?" Justin frowned. "Ondine, I saw her myself, wretched and shaken by the snake that almost took her!"

She shook her head furiously. "Justin, I heard her! I heard her telling Hardgrave something about a vial from the king's laboratory. They stole the drug used upon me! She feigned the attack so that none would notice my disappearance; Hardgrave was then the man who would have had me downriver!"

Justin stared at her strangely, then shook his head and touched her cheek with tender affection. "I don't doubt that Lyle Hardgrave would pay a pretty sum just to touch you with one finger, my sweet beauty! But Hardgrave rode with us and fought bravely."

"A sham!"

"Perhaps," Justin murmured, "but think on this. His lust for you has naught to do with murder. Ondine, Hardgrave wants you alive and healthy and—well—you know, lovable!"

Ondine sank back into her chair, for Justin was right. A kidnapping on behalf of sexual appetites did not lend itself to an association with a ghost that haunted from the tomb!

Just then the door slammed. She stared, feeling as if a cold wind had swept in to haunt her.

It was Warwick. Cloaked and plumed, he seemed immense in the doorway, implacable, unapproachable.

There was silence in the room as he pulled off his gloves, staring coldly at the two of them. At last he said harshly, "Justin, leave us. I want a word with my wife."

Justin looked as if he might argue, but not even he had ever

een Warwick so rigidly cold, tense, and without the least sense
f emotion or mercy.

Justin turned and took her hand, kissed it, and offered her a
roubled smile. "I'm near if you need me."

"Brother, I have yet to beat a wife," Warwick said narrowly.

"Yes . . ." Justin murmured. He stared at Warwick. "Perhaps
you will 'yet' do many things. I swear, I understand you not—"

"Justin!"

"Stop!" Ondine cried, on her feet. "Justin"—she lifted her
chin defiantly, staring at Warwick—"it eases me not to have the
wo of you at odds. I have no fear of this particular beast, although
I do think him near mad to change his moods like the wind. Please,
go, and bear no rancor for one another."

Justin glared at his brother; Warwick ignored him, waiting for
him to leave.

He left the room, and Ondine continued to stare at Warwick,
her head high, but her heart riddled with confusion and despair.
What had she done? She was the injured party!

He walked into the room, tossing his gloves upon a chair,
warming his hands before the fire.

"We leave here tomorrow."

"That makes wonderful sense; we have just come."

He turned, hands clasped behind his back as he surveyed her.

"You, madam, are trouble. I—"

"I am trouble?" She repeated the words, astounded that he
could use them. "You brought me into this insanity—and I am
trouble?"

"Aye, madam, you are trouble—and useless. I attempt to delve
into an intrigue that I must, for all honor and duty to those beyond
the grave, solve. Yet with your face and form, you attract all
manner of being! We are returning to North Lambria—"

She broke in with laughter that neared hysteria. "From where
we have just departed!"

"You will not be staying. I have booked passage for you on
the *Lady Crystabel* out of Liverpool. You will go to Virginia as
Mrs. Diana Brown. I've arranged for a house in Williamsburg,
the hiring of servants, and a solicitor to see to your financial needs.
You will remain there—a widow in mourning—for the period of
a year, in which time I will arrange for a divorce. At that point

you will be free to live where and how you choose, with an income for life.''

Charles had warned her; she could not believe this—not this icy cruelty, this total lack of concern other than for financial insurance. How had she ever fallen in love with such a man? The stone of Westminster provided greater warmth!

For several seconds she could not speak, so stunned and chilled had she become. What manner of man was he, fire and ice, to love her so passionately, disdain her so heedlessly? She dared not speak, or move; she would shatter, she would break. What had come of all the love they had shared?

At last she turned her back to him and managed to speak.

''You are mad, Warwick Chatham! Completely. You hire a bride to catch a murderer; the murderer comes close and you cast her away. I know what happened this day, and it was no fault of mine. And as to passage to the Colonies, I thank you very much. I'm sure that Williamsburg is most intriguing, but I'll not go. Nor do I need your income. We part ways here, milord.''

He exploded with a furious, impatient sound. ''You will do as I say! And what is this of which you speak? What happened today?''

She spun back around, chin lifted regally, her eyes as frigid as his. ''Your mistress, Lord of Chatham. I heard her speak of a vial stolen from the king's laboratory. That loathsome vapor that so stole my consciousness! 'Tis obvious, sir. She and Lord Hardgrave plotted and planned this mischief.''

He shrugged at her words, as if they had little meaning, and she could not begin to fathom his lack of interest. ''The lady Anne was assaulted. She is still most distressed. Hardgrave rode with us at the front of the fray.''

''I tell you—''

''And I tell you, madam, what you might have heard means nothing. Nothing at all, for there is no way to prove it. The only man who had connection with the scoundrel who paid for your flesh was killed in the fighting. I cannot go before the king with accusations and no substance. And if what you say is true, I counter again with the fact that you are trouble, and the sooner you are out of my life, the greater pleasure I shall have with it!''

''Well, then, sir, you may consider me out of your life this

ight!'' she gasped. She had to leave him; she had to go! She
would double over with awful, wrenching pain. Even now tears
shimmered in her eyes, and she thought that she would wail and
scream.

She had known ... she had always known he intended this!
But time and the recent magic of their night here had come to
delude her into a fantasy in which life and heart and soul and
mind were bliss.

Life! Her own life! What was she thinking? Dreams of love
were illusory; she must be as hard as he, as sharp, as cunning, as
negligently determined. She could not leave England—she had to
escape him now, for the situation had become desperate. How
could she ever hope to clear her father's name and reclaim her
estates from those who had caused his murder if she was far across
the ocean?

Her mind would not clear; all she knew was pain, the death of
magic and belief and glorious illusion.

''You are not going anywhere this night,'' he snapped harshly.
''And you will do as I say.''

''Why should I?'' she demanded heatedly.

''Why?'' He arched a dark brow with absolute arrogance.
''Because you are my wife.''

''A state you intend to rectify.''

''I never intended to be chained to a common thief for life!''

She felt as if his words were physical blows, lashes that dug
into her, knives that twisted and turned. Dear Lord! She would
have sworn that though he might not love her, he had cared with
a certain tenderness! Ah, if he would just leave her! She could
fight the tears and the injury and find strength to plan her future!

''Trust me, milord,'' she said lightly, sweetly. ''I am eager to
be rid of a beast! Yet I will not leave England, sir. Nor do I walk
from a bargain duly made, my honor bound payment for my life.
I do not fear your ghosts, nor your mistress, nor even Hardgrave.''

''Fool, woman!'' he exploded, leaving the fire to stride to her,
doing what she had prayed he would not do—touch her. His hands
gripped her shoulders with a bite. He shook her with impatience
until her head seemed to snap from her shoulders.

''Fear them you should! Do you know what near happened
today?''

"But it did not."

Warwick felt the tension in his fingers, in his body; he knew the cruelty of his grip, and astounded, he stared at her in ripe anger. Her words . . . she despised him, so it seemed, yet she clung so stubbornly to this foolery he'd invented himself! Duty, honor, debt! Courage shimmered from her eyes; she would defy him, she'd defy the whole of England if she chose! How could she not despise him, feel that his cause was a madness? She did not comprehend the danger!

"Listen to me, Ondine, and listen well. We go to Chatham to settle your belongings. We spend one night, and you will not leave my side in that time! Then I will place you upon a ship bound across the ocean, and, by God, you will call yourself as I have warned you!"

"Nay, I will not—"

"You will listen! You are my wife; my property, if you will! My possession. Mine to dispose of as I see fit!"

Growing frantic, she tried to wrench from his grasp. He laughed with no humor at her efforts, and his laughter spurred her to greater tempest. She broke free and brought her hand across his face, raking it so as to draw a thin line of blood against his cheek. Startled, he held his face, and she broke from him at last, backing away. "Go somewhere! Leave me! You are rid of me now, well and good! Go to your injured Anne; go to the devil! Just leave me—"

Two steps brought him to her, and he might well have been the devil incarnate at that time. His lip curled in a brutal sneer, unlike any expression she had ever seen on him, and she had known many. Never before had she seen him so cruel.

And never before, even when they had first met, had she feared him so. Aye, he might well have been the devil, with the burning fires of hell alive within his eyes.

His touch when he caught her again crushed her to his chest despite her hysterical cries and desperate struggles.

"I'm going nowhere, madam."

"Then I shall leave—"

"Nor are you."

She ceased struggling for a moment, stunned, her breath held.

her eyes round pools as she realized the insinuation of his tone and touch.

"Nay, fool! You're so eager to be rid of a common bride, yet you think I'll fall into your arms! And what would you want? A lowborn thief? How have you managed thus far? Oh, shame! Great Lord of Chatham! Don't dishonor the purity of your breed so!"

His fingers moved into her nape, tearing at her hair so that her neck arched, and her face was forced to behold the laughing countenance of his own. "Milady! Even the king seeks carnal pleasure among the common folk. In fact, I think, for such base enjoyment, none gives more pleasure. There is something ... primal there, you see. 'Tis your status only as my wife that offends me; I find your talents between the sheets most uncommonly wanton, and that beauty betwixt your thighs doth exceed that of your fair face."

"Vile bastard! You'll not—"

"Alas, I am still your husband. But then, cry as you will. I will touch you, and you will respond. Base instinct, my love."

She went wild; she kicked him and twisted and clawed, amazed and enraged, and wondering from some daze of horror how she had so misjudged this man, this cruel and brutal stranger, hell's own devil, ever more powerful than she.

She screamed and shrieked and pounded against him, and his only response was torturous laughter. He lifted her like baggage and tossed her upon the bed, impassive to all her blows, amused only by her desperate, frantic fight.

She landed hard and gasped for breath, thinking that she still had to escape, for he would leave her to shed his clothing, and she would race like the wind for the door, and, wife or no, surely the king would not leave her with this lunatic beast!

A breath, a pause; she thought to roll, but he was beside her, heedless of his garments. Stunned, she realized there was little he must remove, and she cried again to escape his strength. But she might as well pit herself against a sheer stone mountain, for she was quickly exhausted and gasping, half sobbing as she was finally subdued.

"By God in heaven, do I hate you!" she swore.

He grew still then, and if they had not fought so viciously. If his words had not carried such scorn and debasement, she might have believed that it was with a breath of anguish that he whispered, "I know."

He held her for a moment, tightly to him, cradling her head. Then he began to make love to her.

And for the life of her, she hated him more. He had not lied. She wanted to respond, to a heated kiss she knew so well, and had come to crave, to the warmth of his flesh, the pressure of his form.

She bit into her own lip and willed herself to rigid stillness. For her life, for heaven's salvation, she would not fall to his seduction that night. She would prove him wrong.

She stared at the ceiling with sightless eyes until he shuddered and groaned over her, then lay spent at her side.

There were no more words between them.

Hours passed, night threatened to turn to dawn. Warwick tensed as he felt her rise. He heard a shaky sob escape her as she gathered the remnants of her nightgown and faltered in her steps to reach the low burning fire, sinking there to huddle before it on her knees. She was silent; he could see her back quivering with the force of tears she still managed to keep from sound.

He knotted his fists into the sheets; ground his teeth into his lip until blood filled his mouth. God! How he wanted to go to her, take her into his arms and tell her she was the greatest woman he had ever met; that her beauty was a part of her person, the shining glory of her face, the compassion and pride and honor that gleamed in the miraculous wonder of her exquisite eyes. He wanted to tell her that he loved her above all else in life. But that could cost her her life!

She never returned to the bed; he never slept.

It was a miserable party that set forth for Chatham when dawn came, Justin at odds with Warwick, Ondine completely withdrawn, and Jake morose with the pathetic tragedy of it all.

Chapter 20

Perhaps it was only natural that the fine weather failed as they neared North Lambria. As they came upon Chatham Manor the sky grew dark, though it was early afternoon. The wind picked up, cool with a feel of rain. Trees and brush swayed by the roadside. A slash of lightning lit the sky, and thunder cracked as if to render the very heavens in two. Ondine thought it fitting.

All that had sustained her throughout the miserable journey had been the self-sworn promise that she would escape Warwick in Liverpool and follow her own quest. She would return to her lands in Rochester, find and steal that evidence against her, and—dear God!—somehow discover a way to clear her father's name.

"We're home," Warwick, sitting across from her, murmured suddenly. He leaned forward, lifting her chin with his thumb, eyes shielded in shadow, brooding, dark. "What plots pass through that swiftly moving mind of yours, my love?" he queried her.

She twisted from his touch and sighed. "None that concern you, Chatham. May we alight?" she asked coolly.

He opened the door and stepped out. They were upon the drive before the house. Jake and Justin were down already; Mathilda was rushing from the house, and Clinton followed behind her.

"Welcome! Welcome! Has been strangely lonely here, with all

the household gone!'' Clinton greeted Warwick. Mathilda had little interest in either Warwick or Justin; as ever she was differential and polite, but Ondine was her main concern.

''Ah, lady, you do look well and fine!'' Mathilda said, beaming. ''And now that you're here, I'll give you the greatest care. 'Twill be a boy, I'm ever so sure. Male children do dominate this family line. Whatever, though, 'twill be a child, a babe, to bring youth and laughter back to this house!''

It seemed that the wind died suddenly, leaving everything still and silent with the portent of explosion.

Warwick stepped between them.

''There will be no child born here, Mathilda. I'm gravely sorry for the injury you will feel, but I will not claim the child as mine.''

''What—?'' Justin began incredulously, but Warwick's voice rose in harsh tones above his.

''For reasons known to my wife, I am dissolving the marriage. Her child is no Chatham; as of now, I no longer call her wife. As of tomorrow morning, she will be gone. Any and all who dispute my decision are welcome to leave this place and never return.''

Shocked silence followed this announcement. Warwick stared at them all, ending with Ondine. Then, in great mockery, he tilted his hat in her direction, then strode from them all in the direction of the stables.

''Why, you unholy bastard!'' Justin spat out in fury. ''Warwick!''

Warwick turned, but Ondine raced to Justin even as the color fled from her face, leaving it pinched and white.

''Leave it!'' she implored him.

Warwick stared at Justin, waiting, then shrugged and started on his way once again.

Mathilda burst into tears. Jake shifted uneasily from one foot to the other.

Only Clinton stared after Warwick curiously. '' 'Tis not like him. 'Tis not like him at all,'' he murmured thoughtfully. Ondine gazed at him, swallowing, remembering that logically she had presumed the haunt of Chatham to be this very man.

Yet now he offered her a reassuring smile and came to where she stood with Justin, taking her hands. ''Take heart, lady, this is not the man, the cousin, that I know. We are of an age. As babes

ve played upon mats together, as toddlers we waddled and tousled
nd spat, as youths we learned our lessons well. I know him as I
now myself, my blood, my soul—this cruelty is not of his nature,
nd it will pass.''

He bowed to her most courteously and started after Warwick.

Justin, holding Ondine, was as tense and rigid as bone. ''Clinton
as not seen Warwick's strange behavior; he does not know the
angers of his mind. I'm near to believing madness rages here,
nd near to thinking my brother—he that I once knew and loved!—
wells no more within that shell!''

''None of it matters, Justin,'' Ondine said softly. She escaped
is hold and raced up the steps, eager to reach the sanctity of her
hamber.

Once inside, she started up to the second floor, fleeing past the
ortrait gallery, hurrying to her own chamber.

Once there she pitched onto the bed and indulged in desperate
weeping. On and on she wept, the brewing storm outside a tempest
hat raged and swept through her soul.

Somewhere through her fog and misery and desperation she
ealized that someone was pounding fiercely upon the outer door.
t was not Warwick, she knew, for he would never ask entry, but
always take it as his right.

She forced herself to stiffen—to remember that she must pursue
er own honor!—and answer that knock. It was Mathilda who
ought entry. Mathilda with a silver tray and her wretched goat's
milk, but a Mathilda who quickly melted that newly acquired
hardness in Ondine's heart, for she shook with sobs and tears that
streamed wet and heavy down her cheeks.

Ondine stepped aside, letting her in, and smiled despite it all.
She took the tray from Mathilda, set it on Warwick's desk, and
gently urged the housekeeper into a chair.

''Please, please don't be so upset—''

''Clinton's right! This isn't like Warwick at all. Some madness
has seized him!''

She shook her head painfully, then knotted her fingers in her
lap and looked at Ondine. ''He'll come to his senses tomorrow!
I refuse to believe this! And who does he think he is! Not even
our splendid sovereign Charles seeks a divorce from his wife, and
that poor lady is barren! He'll not get it! This is—lunacy!''

"Mathilda, please, do not be so distressed. I'll find some brandy, that should help."

Ondine brought the bottle from Warwick's desk, mistress becoming server as she pressed a small glass in Mathilda's hand. "Drink it, Mathilda, please. You'll feel better."

She wished that there were something she could say, some assurance that she might give, but there was none. She'd never seen anyone quite like Warwick when he was set on something, nor did that matter. She was through with Chatham Manor, through with its lord. By tomorrow, one way or the other, she would be gone.

Mathilda absently drank the brandy offered her; Ondine then pried the tiny glass from her fingers.

"It will not happen!" Mathilda said suddenly. "It simply will not happen! I will not let it!"

Perhaps Ondine should have argued with her; she didn't have the strength. She smiled at Mathilda, and was then amazed to find herself stifling back a yawn.

"Oh, poor dear!" Mathilda exclaimed. "The milk, you must drink the milk! He's run you so ragged! You must drink the milk."

Ondine went to the tray and consumed all of the goat's milk. It was a small price to pay for the happiness it gave Mathilda.

Ondine set the glass back upon the tray. Mathilda came to her like one in a daze and took the tray without looking at her again. She went, like a sleepwalker, to the door and only there paused. "It will not happen. It will not happen."

She left. Ondine closed the door behind her, then walked back to her own chamber.

With determination she went to the window first. Her heart sank, for there was surely no escape that way. A fall would kill her.

She stared out at the weather. The sky was almost black. The wind continued its haunting cry.

Would the storm hinder her escape? Or would it shelter and hide her? That didn't matter either. The rain had still not started, but everything seemed alive and vibrant with its threat.

Ondine pulled back into the chamber, frowning, remembering the first whisper she had heard. There had been nothing here, but it had come from here.

An excitement began to grow within her. Step by step she tread the floor, staring down at it. She saw nothing but ordinary floorboards, scrubbed clean and fresh, covered here and there with elegant rugs.

She refused to give up her quest. She was not mad, and she had heard a whisper that night. Someone had been here and had escaped.

Ondine next began to comb the walls, looking for fissures in the stone, for any little thing out of the ordinary. Nothing appeared, and she began to grow despondent and weary.

Then it occurred to her that she had not pushed aside the curtain to the latrine, that private place where the chamber pot was kept.

With vast excitement she swept it aside, bypassing the seat with the pot. Her fingers worked hurriedly over the wall, and anxiety rose in her along with the excitement.

Then she found it, a stone, an ordinary stone. But when she pressed against it, it moved in, and an entire section of the wall gave way just as if it were a door.

She stared at it in amazement, then in high elation. This was it; her escape. It worked upon a lever and hinges, set into motion by pressure on that one stone. It was ingenious, it was wonderful. But where did it lead?

She stepped back quickly into the room and grabbed a candle, then came back to the dark opening. Holding the candle high, she began to follow the corridor.

Oddly, she heard no squeak of rats, nor did spiderwebs tangle about her. Someone used this passageway and had used it recently.

She moved quickly ahead, more desperate than frightened, more determined than careful. After a walk of about forty paces, the corridor suddenly turned and gave way to a narrow spiral stairway.

She followed that stairway.

And, to her delight and amazement, it brought her to a small wooden door, one that gave easily to her touch. The door opened outside the manor house, several feet from its western edge. She wondered that she had never seen the door before, but then realized that it was below the earth, that she had to climb uphill several paces to reach the ground, and that it was blocked by a high set of spreading hickory trees.

Shivering with relief, she leaned back against the stone of the manor. She closed her eyes, fighting a sudden attack of dizziness, brought on by the thrill of discovery, she assumed.

Ondine gazed calculatingly at the manor, then narrowed her eyes against the darkness to see to the stables, far beyond.

Oh, if she could flee right now! But she dared not; she needed a heavy coat for her journey, the simplest that she had, for she must pretend to be a pilgrim. And she would need whatever coin she could receive, for she would have to purchase something new in London and return to her estates in a hired carriage.

But the stables . . . she should go there now and plan which mount to steal, see from where she might quickly snatch a saddle and bridle. Night was upon them already, and the storm was almost there; no one should be about; the horses would already be stabled for the night.

She set her candle upon the ground, near the door lest the wind should take it; then she started off, sprinting across the lawn. She shook her head, a little dazed, for the distance seemed suddenly much greater than it should have been, and the ground wavered beneath her feet. Her stomach lurched as she ran, and she swore silently against the awful goat's milk that never had agreed with her.

When she reached the stable, she discovered that she had to cling to the wall for several moments, barely able to stand. The stalls were not straight, but curved before her eyes.

God! she prayed suddenly, fervently. What new cruelty of fate was this? She stood ready, thrilled by her recent discovery— escape was a wondrous open doorway for her! And here she was, discovering herself the victim of some strange illness.

Nay, nay! Like Mathilda, she denied the truth strenuously. This could not be! She simply would not be ill; not until she was far from Chatham Manor! She forced herself to stare at the stalls. The bay she had ridden once before whinnied, and Ondine decided that this mare would be the best mount. The tack room was at her side, and all the bridles, saddles, and trappings were within easy reach, neatly arranged. It would be easy to slip out the secret corridor after midnight, run to the stables, and leave with the mare. Blessed hope! This was not some daydream, but reality!

"Ondine! What are you doing here? It's going to storm!"

She screamed out, startled and then terrified as the voice came to her and a hand set down upon her shoulder.

Clinton.

And he carried a hoof pick in his hand, small, but, oh, so lethal looking as he stood in a shaft of moonlight, tall and muscular, staring at her curiously.

Clinton . . . no matter how kind in manner to her, perhaps he was capable of murder . . .

"Ondine!" He seemed to whisper her name, and she thought of another whisper she'd heard in the night, haunting, frightening, meant to drive one mad.

"Damn him!" Clinton said suddenly, fiercely. "Has he so upset you that you've no reason left? Does Warwick know you're out?"

"I—"

"Does anyone?"

She couldn't speak; some cruel lethargy was hard upon her; her limbs were as heavy as lead, her mouth as dry as dust. And here he stood, Clinton, discovering that no one knew where she was . . .

"Come on!" he said suddenly, harshly.

"No—"

And then his hand raised, the hand with the pick. She saw the muscle of his arm, hard and bulging and strong. He slammed it toward her, suddenly, lethally . . .

She opened her mouth, longing to scream, it was all so quick; it seemed like an absurd motion.

His hand, the pick, slammed harmlessly against the wall beside her head. He shuddered, controlling anger, then looked at her more closely. "You're ill. I'll see you back to the house."

She placed a hand on his sleeve. "Nay, I . . ."

"Don't fear; I know that he does not allow you out, and would not be pleased to see you with me. I'll lead you as far as the door, and then I'll call for Mother."

She couldn't protest; she couldn't even answer him. She was terribly afraid that she wouldn't even be able to walk.

But she could stumble, held by his arm. But though he talked to her, she could barely hear him. She could see Chatham before them, but the manor wavered before her eyes just as the stalls had done. Dear God, what was this? This awful, awful sickness?

"We're at the steps; hold, and I'll call Mother."

Her mind . . . where was her mind? Where was thought, and knowledge and strength and logic? She gripped her temples between her hands and tried to press the dizzying numbness from her head, but her hands were as numb to touch as her mind was to thought.

It was almost as if she were drugged, almost like the horrible stuff the pirates had used. It wasn't the same at all in one way; it was exactly alike in another . . .

"Mother's here. She'll bring you to bed."

Ondine heard the words. She looked up at Clinton, who smiled and started off into the darkness. She lifted a hand, thinking that she could call him back, that something was wrong. Danger lurked.

Except that she couldn't identify the danger.

Arms came around her. "Milady! Are you ill?"

"Yes . . ." she whispered. "I'll . . ."

"I'll take you to bed; come, let me help you."

She managed to stand, leaning heavily against Mathilda. "Ah, lady, what are you doing wandering about? You shouldn't be. You'll not leave here; I said that you would not leave here. I've the answers that you need; I know what happened to poor Genevieve. I know it all; I found the secret in the chapel. Warwick will know all. You'll never, never have to leave."

The words filtered slowly into Ondine's mind; they made no sense, they made every sense. She clung only to a few.

"The answer?"

"I have all the answers. In the chapel."

"The chapel?" Ondine wet her mouth with her tongue and formed the words. The answer . . . Warwick's answer! Tonight. She could have done with it all—pay that debt for her life this very night, before pursuing her own.

But it was wrong; all wrong . . . why couldn't she see it, understand it?

"We'll go there now," Mathilda told her conspiratorially in a soft, hushed whisper.

Ondine never said aye or nay; Mathilda took her up the entry steps and through the foyer, but did not lead her up the stairs. Instead, they passed through the ballroom, empty now, echoing the wind and shadow and darkness.

They came to the chapel entrance. Mathilda pushed open the door and led Ondine in. She walked her straight to Genevieve's beautiful altar, and only then did Ondine see that the stone was opened again, that the recess to the tombs below gaped like a black pit before her bleary eyes.

Two ropes with sturdy nooses dangled from the altar to the pit, like ropes of a hangman. They were hung so that the lovely marble angels with their heavenly faces could stare down upon the dead.

Ondine opened her mouth; she tried to scream. No sound came from her and—oh, God!—it was most chilling, for now she knew, she understood fully that Mathilda meant to kill her, yet her body was so numb that she could barely move, barely speak.

"Drugged . . ." she managed to whisper as Mathilda seated her calmly in a pew to continue her preparations. And then, "Why?"

"Oh, you pretty, pretty thing!" Mathilda crooned, and too late Ondine saw the total madness in her eyes. She had known there was madness seeping into Chatham, but never had she suspected Mathilda to be the well from which it sprang. Mathilda! Who had claimed to love Genevieve so dearly. Mathilda, who had cried such terrible tears when she and the supposed baby might be sent away.

"Why?" Mathilda murmured absently, checking the loops on the two ropes that held them to the marble altar.

"You—loved—her. I thought . . . you cared . . . for me."

"I loved Genevieve dearly! And, sweet girl, you are lovely, too. See, I have here two nooses, so as not to send you off alone! Ah, yes, that was the mistake, you see, that I made with Genevieve."

"No . . ."

"They cry out!" Mathilda said suddenly, fiercely. "Oh, lady, have you not heard them? They, the lady dead and my dear mother! That was the crime, you see? I was there that day; I saw it all! My mother, pushing Lady Chatham to her death! Then that horror, that absolute horror when she fell through herself! Ondine, ever since that day they have cried out to me! Genevieve . . . I thought that she would satisfy them. That a Chatham bride, dead in beautiful youth, would fulfill their needs and let them rest. There was the mistake—Genevieve was not enough! Don't you see? It must be two. A Chatham countess for the countess; the mistress's bastard daughter to take her eternally damned place in the hollowed halls of this place!''

"No . . . drugged.''

"Ah, poor lady! Of course the milk was drugged, to ease thee from this life! You mustn't fear, I'll take your hand. I'll hold you as we depart this life for our role in the next!''

She tried to open her mouth and scream. She tried to fight Mathilda as the small woman slipped the noose around her throat and dragged her toward the pit. She tried. She had no strength, no will at all, it seemed. She could only stare at the horror—now too late—finding the logic of insanity a motive for murder.

Warwick barely nodded at Jake, leaving him free to go about his business, when he slammed into his own chambers. His temper by now was truly foul—Clinton hadn't said a word to him when he'd made arrangement to have the carriage ready again by dawn. He'd felt his cousin's reproach, and that was far worse than any argument.

From the stables he'd gone to his office and procured a large supply of gold coins. She would refuse them, but she'd take them, and she'd be on that ship to sail far away from England if he had to have her bound and gagged until the ship was too far out for the little fool to dream of returning.

Warwick paused in his study, frowing to find the brandy bottle on his desk. No matter, he took a long burning swig of the stuff, knowing he would need it. He would face his final confrontation with her tonight, and it would take everything that lurked within him to keep himself from touching her, from breaking, from telling her not that he despised her as a peasant, but that he adored her as a woman.

She had to leave. He was not a superstitious man, but he felt as if the very walls of Chatham were closing in around them, as if the storm and darkness and howling wind were a warning that death was closing in once again . . .

He straightened his shoulders, then strode through his chamber and the bath, ready to confront her. He swung open the door to her chamber, then stopped, frozen with amazement and fear.

She was not there.

"Ondine!" he called. The wind moaned the only reply. In seconds he tore about the place, searching every nook and cranny, beneath her bed, beneath his bed, in the bath, the closet, everywhere.

She was not there.

He stormed out to the hall, shrieking for Jake. The little man ran anxiously up the stairs.

"She's gone!"

"She can't be! I swear by my life, she passed me not!"

Justin emerged into the portrait hallway from the dining room, staring warily at his brother's torn features, then at Jake.

"What—"

"She's gone! By God, I have to find her. Justin—"

"I've never touched one of your wives!" Justin railed furiously, and then he, too, seemed to sense some import in the night, and his face paled. "Why do we stand here? We must confront the danger."

The front door opened and closed. Clinton entered, carrying the household ledgers. He stared up at those tense men in surprise.

"What is it?"

"Ondine! Have you see her?"

Clinton stiffened and hesitated. "If you intend to offer the lass more ill use, Warwick, I'll not tell you a thing! And if you so desire, I'll be glad to depart this place in the morning! You behave as no decent man, but as the beast the title claims you to be!"

Warwick came tearing down the stairs and clutched his cousin's shoulders frantically. "Clinton, for God's mercy! I intend no harm to her! I am frightened to the bone!"

Clinton tensed, aware now that something was wrong, and that Warwick was frantic. He hesitated just a second longer, then spoke gently.

"She is in her room. She seemed ill; Mother took her."

"What? Nay, Clinton, nay—she is not in her room. I came from there—she is gone."

"Then . . ."

"Where is Mathilda?" Justin asked suddenly.

Silence followed his inquiry. Then Jake spoke, his voice quavering uncertainly.

"The . . . the chapel? There 'twas where she disappeared before . . ."

His sentence fell. Warwick, with the others at his heels, raced like the raging wind to the chapel door. It was barred. He slammed his shoulder against the wood, but it was sturdy stuff. He slammed against it again and found his brother and cousin at his side. With the next heave the latch broke, and the door went tumbling in.

For one moment they all paused, icy horror enwrapping them. Mathilda sat on the stone by Genevieve's altar, her legs dangling over it, as she dragged Ondine ever closer to the orifice.

Ondine . . . She seemed to sleep, her sweet peaceful beautiful lips curving upward in innocence. Could she be dead? Nay! For a noose was about her throat; a noose well tied and tightened! It was strung to the altar so that once she fell, the short length of rope would hang her quick and well.

"Warwick! And Justin, too, I see. Dear, dear Clinton! 'Tis almost done now. I take my lady with me—and future Chathams may now reside in peace!"

"No!" Warwick shrieked the word; the sound rose like thunder and cascaded about them, anguish deeper than life or death.

Mathilda smiled sweetly, then edged herself into the gap.

"No!" Even as he raged, Warwick moved, leaping across the chapel with a great cat's power and rage.

He was too late; Mathilda was gone, and Ondine's lovely form began to follow hers.

It was not too late, it couldn't be, dear God, it couldn't be!

He threw himself toward the cavity and, catching his wife's skirt, tugged and pulled and lifted—and dragged her back to his side, panting. Justin was there, quickly easing the noose from about her throat. She was so white, so pale, so cold!

Warwick pressed his head to her chest, listened and prayed.

"She lives!" Justin shrieked. "She lives! I hear her breathe."

And then her eyes opened. Lost, she saw Warwick above her, saw his haggard features, his golden eyes.

She smiled, and her eyes fell shut once again.

Warwick cast the rope far away. He rose to his knees, swept her into his arms, and stood, resting his cheek against her hair, tears stinging his eyes at the precious, precious beauty of her warmth.

He turned to take her away from this loathsome place of death, but paused then, for his eyes fell upon Clinton. Clinton, who had tenderly lifted the small weight of his mother's body from the hole of darkness. Clinton, ravaged now and stunned by the events.

"She was mad," he whispered raggedly, still trying to understand it all. Then his gaze rested on Warwick, fell upon Ondine with a flicker of happiness.

"By God, Warwick, I am so sorry." He shook his head painfully. "I didn't know; I had no idea . . ."

"I know that," Warwick said softly. "And I, too, am sorry, Clinton. It was the generations past that so destroyed her."

Clinton, dazed, cradling his mother's cheek, nodded. "Before God, Warwick," he said hoarsely, "I love your wife, as a cousin should. Never would I have seen harm come her way if I'd had any idea at all . . . Oh, God! Blessed saints, I know sorrow, yet I feel the keenest joy that Ondine lives and breathes! If it will ease you, Cousin, I'll bury my mother, then leave—"

"Nay, Clinton," Warwick said gently, raw with Clinton's pain. "Nay! We are Chathams, all. We three have paid this night for the sins of our fathers, but that horrible debt is paid. From it all we have one another. Chatham is yours, as well as mine. She was your mother—my father's half sister. We will bury her; and we will go on, together, to see that the past remains truly buried."

Then Justin spoke. "Take her, Warwick; take Ondine from here. I will see to Mathilda with Clinton."

Warwick nodded. He stepped outside into the wind, for he felt he needed that cleansing touch.

Far out in the northern hills the wolves began to howl.

And he was glad, for he knew that it was a natural sound, and no specter to haunt the night, ever again.

The rain began, cleansing, refreshing.

He started for the house, anxious to bring Ondine back to consciousness, anxious to love her with all his heart.

Chapter 21

A log snapped and crackled on the fire, bringing Ondine back from the depths of the fog that had claimed her.

She opened her eyes slowly and saw the golden blaze of the fire before her. It was the only light in the room; no candles burned. Only that soft glow came to her.

It wasn't her room she lay in, but Warwick's. She knew that, even as her eyes adjusted to the shimmering blaze. She was upon Warwick's massive bed. The sheets felt clean and fresh, as she felt herself. She lifted her hands and saw a white ruff upon her sleeves and knew that someone had bathed and dressed her.

A chill swept through her, despite the warmth of the blaze, despite the serenity and security of the room. Memories of the recent past swept over her with a rush of terror—her feeling of utter helplessness, of watching her own doom, of having no part in it. She shuddered as she thought of the rope about her neck—a sensation with which she was growing dreadfully familiar!—and the sheer madness of Mathilda's eyes.

But Warwick . . . Warwick had been there, to catch her when she would fall once again.

And yet, despite it all, she was glad. She had fulfilled her promise, and not so much for the debt of her life, but because she loved him. He would no longer live in pained frustration, wondering what brutal power had chosen to haunt his life and kill his beautiful bride. She would be free—and so would he.

Ah, still the things he'd said rankled deep in her heart; her pride decreed it so! Still someday she might dream to come before him, her lands and title restored, and smile sweetly while she chose any man but him! Such a thing was pride. Yet such a thing was love that she already felt the horrible aching void of leaving him while she lay here, in his bed.

A despair fell over her, threatening to overwhelm all good intentions. She had to leave. Tonight. She could not trust him; the danger was over, but so was her role. He might well want her in the Colonies anyway—shoved away and out of sight while he pursued his fight for a divorce with Charles and the Church of England. She dared not linger, but she didn't know his mind.

She sighed, then feared that the sigh would turn to a sob; she opened her eyes wide, stretching. She noticed then a movement beside her and turned quickly to discover Warwick, his features shadowed, haunted, his eyes pure gold and glittering like the sun upon her.

"Ondine . . ."

She smiled, tremulously, determined now to reassure him, for all that she might despise his temper and his arrogance, he was a man of his word. Never had he faltered in her defense, never had he forgotten his vow to preserve her life—always had he been there, somehow, when she needed him.

"Can you speak, can you move?"

His hand touched hers; she wound her fingers around it and smiled. "I'm well, I feel no effects."

His eyes and touch moved to her throat, where he gently probed that flesh. "A chafe, I believe, no more. 'Twas poppy seed that drugged you. I had Lottie comb the kitchen and cellar, for I feared the drug upon you as much as the deed that—near came to fruition."

"Mathilda is . . ."

"Dead, aye, gone to peace, poor woman."

"And Clinton?"

"He aches, as is natural." He fell silent for a moment, then closed his eyes tightly and opened them again. "She was my aunt, you know. Here, as long as I remember. Always a part of my life. And none of us knew, we never imagined . . ."

"I'm sorry, Warwick."

He sighed and said nothing, then looked at her once again. "It was easier, this, than had it been Justin, or Clinton. Easier to find madness the culprit than avarice. And, then again, 'tis easier to have it known and ended."

"Have you—made your peace with Justin?"

He nodded, idly taking her fingers, playing gently and absently with his own. "Aye, that I have. 'Twas not so hard, for he understood that I lived with a madness of my own, that madness being fear. He did not know till we spoke tonight that you had once been attacked in the chapel before, cast into the crypt. And Clinton . . . Clinton knew nothing. You see, when I first claimed that Genevieve had been murdered, no one believed me. They thought I had gone into a deep pit of grief and was lashing out blindly. Clinton felt guilty that he had not recognized this madness in his mother; he felt he should have known. Justin and I have tried hard to reassure him that none of us knew what nightmares haunted her and twisted her mind."

Ondine lowered her lashes, watching the long brown fingers move on hers. She felt like crying; she must not. He spoke with such weariness, he appeared so very exhausted and haggard, such a toll taken from him. When had he slept last? Certainly not long or well on their journey home. He had been stiff and distant, but always near her, always on guard. He certainly had not slept on their last night in the cottage. That night! That night she must remember now! His cold brutality; his words, daggers in themselves! His arrogance, his determination to dominate all with absolute and ruthless control. Warwick Chatham, master of his realm, of his life, of all that came beneath him.

This she must remember, for she had to leave.

"Warwick, what now? What of Mathilda and Clinton? Suicide, the Church claims, is the greatest sin, yet I cannot believe that God will not take pity on her wretched soul—"

"Nor can I," Warwick assured her flatly. "My grandfather gave her life; she will lie in Chatham ground. And suicide . . . I say that it cannot be called so, for it was an illness as sure as the plague that killed Mathilda, and Masses will be said for her soul. Have no fear on that account."

She plucked at the sheet, nodding, glad. Had Warwick discovered that murder had been cold-blooded for gain, she felt sure the killer would have received no mercy. Yet in this she was not surprised, for she thought him honorable in such things, and was both glad and proud that all the Chatham men knew when and how to bind together in support of one another, the legitimate heirs and bastard all the same.

"Clinton was most distressed. He felt he handed you over, straight into the arms of death. He did not know."

"He mustn't feel that. He had really meant to—to shield me from you."

"Aye!" Warwick said, his tone lowering to that dangerous one she knew so well. "And what were you doing, wandering about? How did you get past Jake? He swears you did not go by the door."

She hesitated, then decided there would be no harm in answering him. It was best that he know about the corridor, the spiral stairs and the door. She would need that escape route no longer; once he slept tonight—which he must, for he was so very weary—she would leave with all silence through the door.

"There is a panel in my chamber."

He scowled. "I've searched that place—"

" 'Tis behind the latrine," she told him softly.

He swore beneath his breath, thoroughly self-disgusted. "Tomorrow it will be opened! Ah, this place! We hid so many Royalists and priests! But the time is over now for the refuge of fugitives; I'll have no more secrets in it."

She smiled absently, for that would be none of her concern. She started to rise, saying, "I must see Clinton. I want to tell him that I am sorry, that—"

"Nay, not now. You'll have the morning."

The morning ... so he did, indeed, intend to see her gone by afternoon. What had she imagined? Ah, but he was tender tonight, and so very warm, when she had known such coldness from him! She wanted his touch so desperately; some fresh memory of all that had been beautiful between them to take with her into the horrible emptiness of the future! She wanted no more words between them; no more thoughts of the mourning that must engulf Chatham.

She wanted one last glimpse of magic, be it illusion, be it a dream. She hoped to forget the world for just a few hours . . .

He touched her forehead, smoothing back a lock of her hair. He pressed his lips against her forehead, and they were hot and fervent and tender. Then he backed away from her, smiling ruefully.

"There's much to be said; much to be planned. But no more tonight. I shudder each time I think of how close it came . . ."

"You were there," she whispered.

"Just barely," he told her. "Jake thought of the chapel; some blessed sense of suspicion and recall came to him. Without Clinton and Justin, I'd never have broken the door. It was a close rescue, madam, frighteningly so. So now you will try your strength no more, but sleep, and I will pray that the nightmare leaves your mind and that you are truly well."

"I am well!" she protested with a frown. He was standing, preparing to leave her to sleep—this last night.

She caught his hand, a fire of panic sparkling in her eyes, making them shimmer like a liquid sea in the soft glow of the blaze that made an intimate haven of the room. She came to her knees, holding his hand, halting his departure.

"Warwick, I—"

"No words tonight!" he commanded her. "You must lie back, sleep, recover!"

"There is naught to recover from!" she said swiftly, faltering, uncertain—frightened that he would reject even this overture from her. "Please," she whispered, then hesitated, lashes sweeping over her cheeks once more. "I—" She paused, finding the courage to stare up at him. Then she thought of her own person, and an entry to the conversation she sought to find.

"How . . . did I come to be here—so?" She indicated her long white gown and the cleanliness of it all. And—God help her!—as intimate as they'd been, a blush suffused her cheeks and her voice was a bare, husky whisper. "Did you bathe and gown me so?"

"Aye, that I did, with Lottie's help," he told her.

He touched her cheek and spoke earnestly with a rueful smile,

"Ah, lady! Brute that I have been, fear nothing from me this night! Even beasts have their limits! Ondine, this—"

She brought a finger quickly to his lips, casting him into a questing confusion. He grew silent, but hiked a brow to her, barely breathing.

"Milord, I want no words. Just as you say, morning comes, and matters might be settled then. But tonight . . ."

"Tonight?"

"Tonight I pray that you do not leave me."

"I'll not, lady, if that is what you require. I'll sit by your side all night—"

"Oh!" she cried in frustration, staring at him with flaming eyes. "Surely, Lord of Chatham, you are the daftest among all beasts!"

A slow smile curled into his lips, and he watched her with vividly sparkling eyes.

"Lady, watch your words, that they say what you mean. It costs me harsh and rigid control when I must be near and keep from touch! My heart has been heavy and near shattered; such bliss as that of your arms is pure temptation. Yet, you have been sorely abused by relation to my name this night, and I would have you know only peace."

She crawled from the bed and stood before him, desperate to make her wishes known, for never again would she place a palm against his most beloved cheek, or know the exquisite ecstasy of his love. Tender, savage, tempest, sweet; his passion was wondrous, and she yearned to know it, hungered deeply, this last night. Ah, she was aching, empty, quivering, touched by wildfire by having him this near, pondering what might come.

"Milord! The last that I seek at this moment is peace!"

Still he stared at her. She emitted a soft cry of aggravation and hated him briefly for forcing her to such a wanton perusal! But if needs must this night, she would pursue! For surely, surely, pray God, he could not refuse her!

She touched the gown where it lay on her shoulders, shook her body lightly, and it shimmied down from her. The gown wafted luxuriously along the length of her body and came to her feet like a mist of soft fog, leaving her naked before him, her body touched to richest flame by the fire's glow, sleek and rich by that enhancing light; angelic and pure—and totally carnal.

Warwick inhaled sharply, stunned and rigid, instantly tense, and instantly aroused beyond all measure. He swallowed quickly, felt the speed of blood that raced and bubbled, of the pulse that beat from his groin and echoed throughout his body. And, oh, this! This most wondrous, most incredible love. For all that he had done to her, she could still come to him . . .

His magic sea-nymph, she was truly given life by her marriage to a mortal, standing before him like some Aphrodite, eternally glorious. Ah, she was the fire, she was the light, she was everything that guided him now! This love was pain, it was fear, it was all encompassing . . .

Who was she, this water nymph of his? Something ever so fine, commoner or countess, it was true, she was the greatest lady he had ever met; she was his beloved.

"Warwick!" she breathed at last, a cry, a desperate plea.

He reached for her hand. She gave it to him, and he rose, still then in the blue depths of her eyes, adrift—and completely aware of her and himself and the explosive power between them.

He came to her, touching her hair, then clutching her shoulders and pressing his lips ardently upon that bare flesh, where he held for the long heartbeat of an eternal moment. Then his lips grazed her ear, and his whisper came hoarse and ragged.

"Be sure, madam, that this is what you wish this hour, for if I stay longer here, I will not be able to leave."

She slipped her arms around him and pressed close to his body. She stood on her toes and touched his lips with her own lightly, again and again, parting them, nipping at them, coming to them again, and finding a fiery mating with his tongue.

His arms embraced her in a crush. A glad and muffled cry tore from him, and he was indeed lost. Ah, all that she was! A cascade of sunlight and fire, wind and tide, sweeping through him, over him, within him. He started to speak; she stopped him with another kiss. "No words this night," she whispered.

"No words . . ."

No truths would come between them; no harsh realities would dispel illusion. There would be moments when the wind beyond the walls rushed with the soaring flight of their longing, when the rain beat no harder than the pulse of their blood. The storm outside was a storm inside, beautiful and wild, impetuous and free. He

held her breasts and gloried in their weight, kissing the fair peaks
and savoring the taste. He carried her to the bed and laid her upon
it, shedding his clothing; then he came to her again.

Every touch was a reverence, each stroke an adoration; each
kiss a cherishing anew.

Ah, sea nymph, witch, most magical creature! She touched
him, again and again. She loved him sweet, loved him with most
exquisite abandon. She moved, her body liquid over his. She gave
to him as never before.

And he gave to her, all of him. He filled her, again and again,
held her, shivering, trembling, quaking, shuddering . . . again and
again, until she sighed against him and buried her head into the
dampness of his chest, exhausted and spent.

"Ondine . . ." They were there; words he didn't know how to
say; eloquence had deserted him. They were simple words: I love
you. They hovered on his lips, and they must be spoken.

But once more she touched her finger to his lips, shaking her
head strenuously. "No words!" she pleaded, almost sobbing. "No
words tonight, I beg you!"

He cradled her against his chest. They were both aglow with
satiation. His arm was strong around her, and exhaustion claimed
him at last.

There was always tomorrow. Tonight . . . tonight excelled
dreams and fantasies.

Tomorrow there would be time for words. And perhaps none
would be more eloquent than their love this night.

He nodded and dared close his eyes, secure at long last that he
could sleep without fear—for her.

She knew that he slept quickly; he had been so very drawn, so
dearly in need of repose.

His breath became even; strain eased from his features, and
for this rare moment he appeared very young, handsome and
wonderfully tousled.

She remained beside him for at least an hour, watching him,
taking all of him into her mind and heart and memory. The texture
of his face, its strong and rugged lines, the full and sensual curve
of his lip, the arch of his brow, the length of his nose. She dared

even to run her fingers over his chest, to feel the muscle there, the dark tufts of hair.

She stayed and watched and felt her tears rise.

Then, at last, she rose, silent, broken.

She paused at his dresser, smiling slowly, bitterly. It was laden with gold coins, coins she knew he meant her to take to the Colonies.

And, after all, she forced herself to accept the bitter truth.

He was a master lover; a man of lusty appetite, and he'd never denied attraction to her. But attraction was easily discovered, easily had and lost—easily a delusion of love.

All bargains were fulfilled—and now she should be grateful for the proof that he intended still to ship her away; she needed the coin.

She treaded softly into her own chamber, most grateful for his absolute exhaustion, since she'd learned early how lightly he normally slept.

She dressed in her simplest gown, a plain velvet in soft dove gray, in warm hose, and her best boots.

All had been bought by his coin, yet the Duchess of Rochester could pay him back easily and well. She found her warmest cloak, dull brown wool with a heavy cowl that gave the appearance of a pilgrim's garb. She dared not take more clothing, for she needed to travel light; speed would be of the essence.

At some time he would wake. Possibly he would give chase, for the simple reason of his arrogance—the lord of Chatham did not tolerate disobedience to his high command.

The lord of Chatham . . .

Time spun too quickly for her then, but after she had carefully dropped the coins into her pockets, she still could not leave, but watched him again, completely in love.

In love! Oh, it was weak, it was shattering! Honor and a daughter's duty called. Her pride and the morals bred into her since birth forced her hand. But love, this treacherous, fickle thing, kept her here, craving the sight of him, her beast, her beautiful, beautiful, manly beast.

The sweet sound of a bird's cry at long last startled her from tender hypnotism. Now it was all still beautiful, before morning's

ight, and the truth of his feelings could tarnish memory or send
er captive far away.

One last touch . . .

She kissed his forehead, willing back her tears. Then she fled,
and to her mouth to hold back a moan of anguish.

There was no Jake in the hallway—no loyal friend to guard
he night—there was no more danger. She found her way along
he hall and down the stairs, and out of the manor.

She did not dare look back, but raced to the stables. Quietly
he whispered to the bay mare. With as little fuss and noise as
ossible she set bridle and saddle to the mare, praying that no
oung stable boy would awaken in confusion to accost her.

She mounted the mare and took her from the stable. And then,
nly then, did she turn back.

The rain had ceased; the wind had died. Chatham stood upon
ts mound in all pride and strength, for always it would brave the
wind and the storms of the rugged north. Chatham, harsh and hard,
t bred men as graceful as its lines, as strong as its stone, tender,
rutal, fit as the manor to face the wind and storms.

Warwick! her heart cried.

She was no longer Countess of North Lambria, Lady Chatham,
o longer Warwick's gallows' bride. From this moment she would
gain be the Duchess of Rochester, a power in her own right.

"Away now to home!" she told the horse. "My home," she
dded softly. "My rights, my heritage." She swirled the mare
round and sent her galloping into the night.

It was strange then that she heard the wolves howl. There were
laintive cries, sharp cries. They were mates calling out to one
nother—males, she thought, with bittersweet amusement, crea-
ures bound to claim and hunt their females, taken for life.

It did not occur to her then that a Chatham might be like
he beast, the wolf, that prowled his forest, that he, too, would
elentlessly pursue his mate, no matter how far she might wander.
he was far too wretched to think much at all.

"Rochester!" she cried to the breeze.

Taunting her, it seemed to echo the name.

PART III

The Duchess of Rochester Full Circle

Chapter 22

Ondine managed to travel as far south as London with a group
f holy sisters on pilgrimage. There she spent Warwick's coin in
ood measure on a proper wardrobe in which to return home in
plendor.

It was the twenty-first of October when Ondine at last came in
er hired carriage down the cobblestoned drive that led to her
ome, Deauveau Place, as it was called, for the family name. It
tood like a crystal palace, blanketed in new snow, the first snow
f the season.

She pulled apart the drapery of her hired carriage's window,
lutching the new silver fox cloak she had purchased in London
) her throat. Home . . .

Ah, it was so beautiful! she thought with a gripping pain of
)ve and nostalgia. It was so gracious, so fine. Unlike Chatham,
 was not an ancient structure, having been built at the beginning
f the century during the reign of James the First. Her great-great
randfather had been a Frenchman, assigned to service in the
ousehold of young Mary, Queen of Scots, when she had spent
er brief time as the French queen, until her husband's death. On
Iary's return to Scotland, Deauveau had come to Edinburgh Castle
) serve; in time, he had become invaluable to the young James,

Mary's son, and again, in time, had come with him to London on his first ascension to the throne after the death of Elizabeth the First.

It was then that he had been granted his lands, and was proclaimed Duke of Rochester. That founder of the English line had built not for defense, but for beauty.

Deauveau Place stood tall with turrets, but they had been fashioned for view onto the gardens and entry. Her windows were arched and mullioned, her lines entirely graceful, and her stones were whitewashed. The great entry always stood open, as it did now, so that guests would first come into a courtyard, where they could be met at the main door by the master.

Master! That Raoul could ever think to claim such a title!

She stiffened then, biting her lips for redness, pinching her cheeks for color. She passed then through that elegant entry in the courtyard, and within the house, she knew, servants would be running to inform either her uncle or Raoul that a carriage was arriving. They would, perhaps, await her entry. Or perhaps curiosity would bring them to the entry steps, frowning to see who might have come and for what reason.

The carriage came to a halt. She didn't wait for her driver, but pushed open the door and alit, pulling the silver fox more tightly about herself as she stared up at her home. It was so beautiful, shivering and shimmering beneath the frost, so very much like an ice palace.

The great arched and carved entry doors opened, and Jem, her father's aging valet, stood there, gaunt and wrinkled, showing his years as he had never before. He stared at Ondine for long moments, seemed to waver and go pale, and then he came down the steps shaking and still white.

"Ondine?" He whispered her name incredulously, with the greatest reverence.

She smiled, ready to cry at this tender welcome. The old man came to her, and she put her arms around him, hugging him vigorously, then easily, for it seemed that his bones had gone very brittle and that scant flesh remained to cover them.

"Jem!"

He pulled away from her, and she smiled radiantly with tears stinging her eyes. She'd come with no real plan—except to face those who had wronged her. In these few seconds she felt that whatever she suffered, whatever road she might have taken, this was the right thing to do, for in that brief reunion with Jem she knew that neither she nor her father had been forgotten.

"Lady, lady, lady!" he gasped, still grasping her hands, still staring as if she were an apparition. "We've searched half the country for you! Prayed and begged before God! At times all sense decreed we give you up for dead, but I never could do so in my heart! When I heard of your father, I was ill, for never was there a better master. To this day I puzzle over it! I cannot believe him a traitor! He would not vote to kill the old king, why the new? And you, lady, part of it all! Never!" Panic lit his crinkled old face suddenly. "We should hide you—"

"Jem!"

The irate order came from the doorway.

Ondine stiffened at the sound of her uncle's voice. She realized that the hood of her fur covered her hair and that he could see none of her yet.

"If we've guests," her uncle continued, "bring them in, man! Don't stand there like a dolt!"

Ondine turned slowly, casting back her hood to face her uncle.

William was no Deauveau, except by some distant relation. Ondine's grandfather had married William's mother after his first wife's death, and William had taken on the name Deauveau. He had been raised with Ondine's father, treated as a full brother. He had, in turn, served his stepbrother. As a child, Ondine had never realized that William raised his own son in the presumption that the two children would be wed, and that Deauveau Place would fall to him in that manner. She ground her teeth together even as she smiled at him, for she wondered sickly whether her father might still be alive if she had only agreed to marry Raoul. Anything might be worth the price to bring him back to life.

But she hadn't known, she hadn't even imagined that such a sinister and devious plot had brewed behind William's smiling swarthy features.

He was a man of near fifty years; yet with rich dark hair still, and slim features that held his age well. His nose was very long and slim; his lip, too, was narrow and could curl with cruelty, for his humor was quite dry. He was very tall and slender and, in his way, a man to be reckoned with.

"Hello, Uncle," she said simply.

"Ondine . . ." He said her name as if he, too, gazed upon a vision. And perhaps she was, having dressed most carefully for this day. Beneath the frothy silver of her fur cloak she had chosen to wear all white—a full white velvet skirt over a bodice of white linen and lace. The only color about her was from her eyes, her cheeks, and the sunburst spray of her hair against the fur when she cast the hood back.

After all that time in which he had surely become convinced she had been eaten by some wilderness beast, she was back, decked in splendor, all elegance and all beauty.

William's eyes narrowed sharply; his hand came to his heart, and though Ondine continued to smile sweetly, she hoped inside that he was about to suffer apoplexy. For long moments silence surrounded them, silence, and the gentle fall of snowflakes, crystalline and beautiful.

"You live," he said at last.

She laughed softly. "Aye, Uncle."

"And you dare to come here, traitor!"

Again she laughed, but this time with an edge. "Come, Uncle, 'tis me to whom you speak! Not some misguided fool!"

He looked quickly from her to Jem, then thundered out with obvious annoyance, "Get in the house! What we have to discuss will be done in private. Jem—see to your lady's things. Ondine—come."

She smiled, lowered her head, collected her skirts, and started up the steps. At the top he grabbed her arm in a thoughtless gesture, his long fingers biting into her so that she almost cried out her loathing. She reminded herself that she must play her game most carefully, buying time.

"Into my study!" William rasped harshly into her ear.

"Yes, Uncle," she said demurely.

They came down the entry hall, bypassing the great room to their right. Ondine gazed inside and briefly saw that nothing had changed since that long-ago day when she had left. A fire burned from the wall-length grate. The long Tudor table still occupied the middle of the room. The sideboard was still neatly decked in her mother's finest Irish lace, and the silver services still gleamed from atop it.

"Come!" William said sharply, urging her along so quickly that her feet could barely tread the floor. With her head still lowered, she smiled grimly, glad that he was anxious to remove her to privacy before more of the household met her.

He threw open the door to his study—his! 'Twas her father's study, in fact, she thought painfully. A long window looked out upon a row of secluded hedges; the rest of the room was lined with cases and books, French mostly, for William always believed that things French gave him an air of sophistication.

Ondine heard the door snap shut behind her. She continued on to the windows and stared out at the beautiful falling snow, aware that he watched her.

"Where the hell have you been?" he snapped out.

She turned, negligently slipping from her fur and allowing it to fall upon the window seat.

"Many places, Uncle, among them hell itself, I do believe," she replied casually.

Eyeing her warily, he strode across the room to where a score of bottles, various wines and various ports, were kept within a recess of the wall. He stared at her while he poured himself a shot, drank it, then poured another.

He seemed to find a grip on himself. He shoved back the chair to his desk and sat in it, waving an arm for her to sit.

"Don't be uppity with me, Niece," he warned her narrowly. "I have it in my power to snap my fingers, call my men, and have you hauled off to the Tower. I have, at my disposal, proof positive that you conspired with your father to assassinate the king."

Ondine started to laugh. "Oh, come, Uncle! We're alone! Who is this act for? We both know that neither my father nor I conspired to kill the king! You, Uncle, rather, conspired to steal my father's place and property."

He rose, smiling then with the cruel curve to his narrow lips. He poured her a small glass of his port and brought it to her, not batting an eye as he stared into hers.

"Ondine, I have felt the majority of my life that a good switching would have done you incalculable good. You are a fool. If you lived, you should have preserved your life. You were a fool to

come back here. You may talk yourself blue, you little bitch, but
you'll not change what appearances are. Your father died in his
pathetic attempt to kill the king. We, your family, live out of favor
because of it. The king is aware that I have documentation that
proves your complicity. He knows, too, that doting uncle as I am,
I am loathe to bring this forward. Charles has a softness for women,
Ondine. Especially young, beautiful ones—led to wayward actions
by their misguided elders.''

He paused for a moment, calm now, pouring more port and
lifting his glass to clink against hers.

''You had your chance, Ondine. Marriage to Raoul. This house
united. But you spurned my son. It will cost you your life. You
know that I cannot let you live.''

Her heart was thudding madly. She smiled and drained her port,
hoping the fiery liquid would give her courage.

''Will you slay me, here, then, in your study? I think that the
servants would definitely talk!''

She smiled vaguely and walked past him, idly thumbing the
accounts that lay on the desk. Then she swirled around to him
again. ''I remind you, Uncle, that while I do live, I am the Duchess
of Rochester.''

''But I am your legal guardian, until your twenty-first birthday.
Two more years, Ondine. Are you so anxious, then, for the Tower
and the headsman's ax?''

She came around, seating herself at the desk, changing their
position, and smiling most sweetly.

''Nay, Uncle, I am not eager for death. And that is why I have
returned.''

He went still for a moment, then came to the desk, planting his
hands upon it while he leaned close to her, watching her for some
trickery.

''You mean to marry Raoul?'' he demanded thickly.

''That was the arrangement you proposed all along, was it not?
If I marry Raoul, this 'proof' you propose to present to the king
will disappear. That is correct, is it not?''

There was a sharp rap at the door before he could answer her.

''Who is it!'' William thundered out impatiently.

''Raoul.''

William emitted some sound and came to the door, ushering

his son inside, then quickly closing the door behind him. Raoul did not even glance at his father, but strode to the desk, staring at Ondine.

He was very much like his father: tall and slim, dark haired and complected, mahogany eyed. He might have been a very handsome man, were it not for the sly cast to his features, a look of cruelty not unlike William's, and understandably so, for it was the father who had bred avarice into the son. He had been using the family fortune well, Ondine observed, for his pants were of the softest fawn, his shirt was thickly laced at collar and sleeves, and his surcoat was of the richest brocade.

He stared at her as the others had done; disbelieving her presence, amazed to see her so. He reached out to touch her hair, a free cascade that fell down the velvet softness of her gown in a crescendo of sun and fire, and the expression in his eyes changed completely, frighteningly so, for she saw in it a lust that made her blood run cold. She almost cried out at his lightest touch, one that merely assured him she was real and no mirage.

"You are back!" he said.

She was glad that the desk separated them. Once he had been her friend, a surly one at times, but a companion of youth. She had not known until that terrible day at court that he had meant to possess her and all that was hers at any cost.

"Aye, she's back," William said crossly from behind him. "And showing no signs of wear!" William had lost his sense of amazement at her appearance and felt no qualms about accosting her. He strode around the desk, catching her chin in his hand, twisting her face to his none too gently, and staring deeply into her eyes.

"You come in even richer apparel, my dear, than that in which you left us. I repeat, where have you been?"

"Uncle," she said softly, with all the regal dignity she could muster when she chose, "do not touch me. I have come to deal, and that you should keep your bloodstained hands from me is my first demand."

He laughed, shortly, with little humor, but he released her, seeming oddly disconcerted despite his bluster. "Girl, to live you will marry Raoul, and I assure you, as his wife, you'll give yourself no airs!"

She lowered her eyes, wishing she might tell him she would be instantly and violently ill if it ever came to the point that she should share a bed with Raoul. Always, always, she would see her father's blood upon both their hands!

But that was not something she could say now. She kept her eyes lowered then, afraid that she would give herself away.

"Uncle, I am not yet his wife. And when I am—" She shuddered inwardly. Oh, she despised them both! But she must carefully play this game. "It will be his touch, and his alone, that I endure. Until that moment, I demand that I be left in peace!"

"You demand—!" Raoul snapped in a whirl of fury, but his father pushed past him, planting his hands upon the desk once again.

"You demand, Ondine?" he asked softly. "You have no demands! You have come here—given yourself into my hands! It is at my whim whether you live or die, and you still think to speak to me as some crystal-pure princess! I will make the demands, Ondine, and you will jump to the tune of my voice."

She leaned back sedately in the chair, eyeing them both most serenely, though her heart continued to plague her with its erratic beat. "Raoul!" she said softly. "We are not, as yet, wed. And until we are, I do have demands!"

He did not touch her, but he came so close that he well might have done so, and it was all that she could do not to shrink away in fear, for he bore no resemblance than whatsoever to the childhood companion she had once known. She wondered at the things she saw in his dark eyes, rage, frustration, greed—and even a certain pain, something that might have been coupled with loss. She wondered, too, if at some time he might have really cared for her, and if that caring had twisted to something more deadly.

"Cousin, I see your feelings for me, yet I care not what they are. Scream if you will when I touch you, still I will do so. Most pleasantly, my dear love, God has made it that you maintain your beauty, despite your mouth. It will give me the greatest pleasure in the world to mold you into a good wife—to break you, Ondine. And don't delude yourself, sweet innocent. 'Tis more than possible that I can also turn you into the most ardent of lovers. I want you, Ondine. Let it suffice at that. I want you, and I want the land.

That last I shall have one way or another. The other, well, it is by your choice. My kiss, or that of the ax.''

She pushed the chair away, rising as calmly as she could to escape them both. She tried to keep her fingers from shaking as she poured herself another badly needed drink.

''It is not completely my choice,'' she said, her back to them both. ''We must see if an agreement can be reached.''

''Agreement!'' William thundered, coming to a red-faced rage again. ''I remind you: I hold the cards—''

''Let's hear her out, Father,'' Raoul said smoothly with a tinge of humor to his voice. ''Don't you wish your victory complete? None could wrest the title or the land from us—ever!—if she were to be my wife!''

So! Ondine thought, quickly lowering her eyes. They were afraid! There were cracks in this ploy of theirs, and it seemed that even her uncle would rather have her alive than dead. It was true, a marriage would secure the claim.

''Duchess!'' Raoul sneered nastily, bowing to her. ''Let us hear your demands.''

She spun around, uplifted by the port—and the added faith that she could play for time.

''One month.''

''One month?'' William queried warily.

''One month. I will marry Raoul one month from today. In that time he will not touch me; nor shall you. I will live here again as is my right and—accustom myself to the future.''

''And why,'' William asked, ''should I give you any time at all?''

''Because, if you do not, I will scream 'traitor' all the way down the aisle. I will tell the servants, I will shout to anyone that I see, that you were the ones to attempt to kill the king. I might well reach the Tower, but it will not be silently, I do assure you! The servants here, they loved my father well. Give them but a chance, and they will all be surly and suspicious. Give me the time I ask, and I will keep silent, and perhaps''—she sighed, then cast Raoul a hesitant smile—''perhaps we might consider it a normal betrothal time, in which two people come to know one another before their nuptials.''

Ah, how quickly Raoul took the bait! She might almost have

pitied him for the hope that leapt into his eyes, except that it was true, she would never forget the blood that stained his hands.

"A month, then," he said huskily, stepping forward.

But his father waylaid him, pointing a finger upon Ondine's breast, despite her demand that she not be touched.

"Not so fast, Raoul! You all but drool, yet you do not know the facts. I want to know, Ondine, where you have been all this time!"

She sighed once again, very wearily. "I told you, Uncle, many places. I hid with thieves in the forest for a while. I—I found work in one of the north country manors—"

"You did not purchase this clothing through honest labor, Ondine. I'll know where it came from and now."

"I did purchase it, in London."

"Where did the coin come from, girl?"

He kept pointing at her, and she found that she backed away from him, despite all resolve, until she sat upon the window seat with him staring down at her.

"Gambling! And that, Uncle, is partially what sent me home! I hated filth and poverty! I took my earnings from the North and came back to London, and there fell into a game of dice. Luck was with me, and I had coin once again to buy these things! Oh, I was heartily sick of having naught. I realized then that Raoul's offer could give me that life to which I was accustomed, and that to keep running, I must do so in poverty and filth!" She lowered her eyes, praying that they could not see the lies within them. "I thought . . . I thought that if I could have the time . . . if I could just come to know him again, I could accept it all to regain my position. I—I just need time."

"The time is yours! We will come to know one another again!"

Raoul was on a knee at her feet, holding her hands in passionate promise. She stared at his long, slender fingers, untouched, uncallused by work, and thought of Warwick's. Lean and hard they were, roughened by his labor, browned by the sun . . .

She wanted to cry. She could not endure this smooth touch and all it stood for, and not when she compared it to one she had come to love so dearly. Her head spun dizzily as she thought of the times she had twisted and writhed in bed in sweet passion with Warwick. Even that night when he had been all but brutal, his touch had not failed to reach into her heart. And Raoul . . . Raoul thought to share such intimacies with her! The very thought of it was so totally repugnant that it threatened to overwhelm her and send her, fainting, to the floor. She wanted to snatch her hands away, as if he scalded them with something impure.

She could not; this was not the time to spurn him. That blessed time was to come, yet never would it come if she did not play this game, this new role, and play it brilliantly.

"No deal is yet struck!" William said, returning to his desk and sitting behind it to view the two of them.

Raoul stood, facing his father.

"I want her! She is ever more beautiful—"

"And still, I wonder, where has that beauty been?" William said laconically. "I'm truly interested to discover if our duchess has not become a whore."

"Father!"

William shrugged aside his son's reproach. "It's no matter of great mystery. We need but call in a physician to attest to your betrothed's chastity before the nuptials. You will be interested, I do assume. You are so eager for her, yet there are things you must remember. If she carries another man's brat, that child will stand to inherit. And I shall be damned if, at this point, I have come so far as to leave this estate to a wench's bastard and not my own blood!"

Ondine could feel the blood draining from her face, yet she knew she dared not display distress. One month . . . she had so little time! And if they were to call in a physician, it would be before the wedding Mass was celebrated. She never intended to go through any ceremony, but now she would have to move all the more quickly.

"Whatever you wish will be done when the time is right!" Raoul announced coldly. "Now, Father, shall we consider this done, then? I'll ride to the bishop for the banns to be cried, for arrangements to be made. Ondine receives her time for her silence. I will unquestionably take on the title. And you, Father, will unquestionably retain the rights to the money! It seems to me that we have accrued all that we originally intended."

William stared hard at Ondine.

"I don't trust her," he told his son, not shifting his gaze.

"What is there not to trust? She will be my wife. I will keep
her sharply in line, Father. That you needn't fear."

"Whatever it takes?" William inquired, a sneer for Ondine
curling pleasantly into his lip.

"Whatever it takes; that you know."

William shifted. "The deal is made." He stood and walked
over to Ondine, careful not to brush her in any way. "Aye, the
deal is made," he repeated softly, challenging her eyes. "Duchess,
your things will be brought to your old suite. Don't forget, though,
dearest Niece, that I will be watching you. And I am not in—lust
with you, as is Raoul. One month from this date, you will say
your vows with Raoul. You will not think to usurp my position
here. And you will tread a tender line, my dear. Oh, and one more
thing! I think that you are a liar; I am hoping dearly that you are
not a whore. You may say what you will; I have ways and means.
And I do intend to discover, Ondine, just where you have been
since you ran. And with whom."

He straightened, eyeing his son. "Raoul—go. See that the banns
are cried immediately. This will be a most public wedding."

Raoul nodded and departed the room swiftly.

William turned to smile once more at Ondine, sweeping her a
sardonic bow.

"Welcome home, Duchess."

Chapter 23

If ever the halls of Chatham Manor did tremble and quake with the thunderous howl of a beast, it was that morning Warwick woke to find Ondine gone.

Yet she was, in truth, gone. And in this frantic dilemma, he turned to his brother and cousin, the three having grown closer in tragedy, and told them both the truth of the matter, from beginning to end. He swore to them his behavior toward Ondine had been cruel only because he'd hoped to save her, and then he swore again, assuring them that he and his wife had been most—amiable before he had fallen asleep the night before.

Between them they commented at last that they'd all been fools; they should have noted that the lady of Chatham certainly carried her own air of mystery. Warwick quite suddenly swung a fist against the table, declaring that the king knew something and he was going off to seek Charles. Justin determined to accompany him; Clinton and Jake would join him in London once Mathilda had been lain to rest, and with Jake, too, they would scour the countryside to find her.

* * *

Warwick and Justin reached London in record time, yet it did them little good, for the king had conversely traveled north. They spent the time waiting at St. James's Place, for Buckingham had assured them that was where the king intended to come.

At last Charles returned. Warwick gave him no time to settle in, being so impatient and anxious by that point that he felt like a pistol, cocked and ready to explode. The king had barely left his carriage, barely entered his chambers, when Warwick burst in upon him with no protocol whatsoever, startling the king's servants, bringing his personal guards to arms.

He did not bow to the king, but burst out with a harsh, "I need to speak with you now. Sire." The last was a hasty amendment, since he was stared upon so sourly by servants and guards alike that he might well have been slain at that point.

Charles arched a dark brow. "So I see," he said dryly. "Leave us," he told guards and servers alike. "Lord Chatham seems sorely lacking in etiquette this day, yet still I think he means me no harm."

Warwick flushed darkly, but was too agitated to notice much around him. He barely waited until the door closed behind the last man before he spoke again.

"Where is she?"

"Where is who, my dear man?"

"My wife. She's gone—and I know that you know where she is!"

"My good fellow!" Charles said indignantly. "I've yet to abduct the wife of a friend—"

"Nay, nay! I accuse you of no such thing, Your Grace—"

"'Your Grace'! He does remember who I am!"

"Charles, she has disappeared! Now, you tell me, sire, that you know nothing about her! When I first brought her here, she quaked like a leaf and tried to escape me at that time. Once she had seen you, she seemed loathe to depart! Now, sire, I have been preoccupied with affairs of my own—"

"Yes, I've heard that your difficulties were solved."

"Aye, Charles; 'twas not really such cruel murder as it was madness. Mathilda sent Genevieve to her grave; she thought to take Ondine, but her life was spared, and Mathilda is gone."

"I am sorry, Warwick, yet relieved. I thought you crazed with guilt when Genevieve died; you were completely sane. I lend my sorrow to your family, yet am glad that ghosts should haunt your manor no more,'' Charles told him.

Warwick nodded, grateful for the king's empathy, yet still impatient. ''Sire,'' he said as quietly as he could manage, ''you've yet to answer me on a matter grave to my heart and health—and sanity!''

Charles sighed, casting his boots away, and staring into empty space as though he looked beyond it. Then he shrugged. ''So,'' he murmured, ''your mystery was solved, and upon that fruition your lady disappeared.''

''Aye,'' Warwick said over tightly gritted teeth.

The king gazed at him, apparently amused with the great effort it cost him to remain in control.

''You asked me to inform the Church that I approved a divorce for you from this lady you now plague me about.''

''God's blood!'' Warwick swore, losing his thin hold upon his anxiety and his temper. ''I did not want her murdered for association with me!''

''Ah, my friend, then you love her?''

''She's my wife, Charles!''

''I did not ask you that. I believe the marriage legal and binding. What I inquired about was your concern.''

''Aye, damn you, I love her, Charles! Somewhere, somehow, she became my life's blood, a part of me, and, by God, Your Grace! I have served you wisely and well since you came to the throne of England, with life and limb and wit, and so help me, now I beg—nay, I demand!—some assistance from you!''

Charles raised both brows, reminding Warwick for one moment that this was yet a Stuart king; a man staunchly believing in the divine right of kings—and a man not adverse to a certain ruthlessness when he considered it necessary, despite his affability.

''You demand?''

Warwick locked his fisted hands behind his back and stood his ground, saying nothing.

''For the life of me, Chatham, but you are a rude beast! However, in lieu of service justly tendered, as you have said, I will forget and forgive your use of the language. But—I hesitate in what I say to you because of that very temper that so brings you here.''

"What?" Warwick murmured.

The king waved toward the door. "Call for some ale, good and stout. Seemed a long journey I just took myself, and I would quench my thirst before this explanation I must give you."

"But time—"

"Time is of no essence, Warwick. There is nowhere that you might rush, like a dragon-slayer, to snatch her from harm's way into your arms. Call for the ale."

Warwick knew the king's stubbornness; he opened the door and found a servant waiting—along with two guards who continued to regard him suspiciously. He impatiently awaited the ale, then discovered that he was well glad the king had sent for it, for he had acquired an aching thirst himself. Closeted in privacy once again, Warwick found himself seated upon the king's bed while the king thoughtfully paced the floor before the fire, sipping at his ale.

"This, Chatham, is a story that begins long ago. There once was a duke in royal service, yet he was no Cavalier, for he was strongly opposed to my father, determined that he must rule with his parliaments, and could not disband such a body of lawmakers right and left. He was no Roundhead either, yet he wound up with such men who served Cromwell, certain that my father's policies must be stopped." Charles stopped pacing, and once again he looked to some distant past, then shrugged. "My father truly was among the best of men—yet he was, for his time, the worst of kings! Ah, but I think few really thought that he should come to lose his head for treason!" The King sighed. "I'm sorry, I speak of the past, and this is the present. Well, this duke did not vote for my father's head; yet such was his involvement that I near to requested his when I first came to the throne. Time can bring reason to a man; this duke was also among those who had claimed that I should be brought back upon Cromwell's death."

He stopped again and stared at Warwick directly.

"Do you remember the day of your joust with Hardgrave?"

"Aye, Charles," Warwick said, frowning, and very glad of the ale then as the story grew along, " 'twould be hard for me to forget such an occasion."

"Ah, yes!" Charles murmured. "My apologies again; I had forgotten that, too, was the occasion of Genevieve's death." He cleared his throat. "Well, it was upon that day that I came to a decision to bring the old man back into royal favor."

Warwick recalled the day, running over each detail carefully in his mind. Suddenly he choked on his ale, coughed, and queried on a wheezing whisper, "The attempt on your life! The man slain."

"Aye. Well, the old Duke of Rochester had a daughter—"

This time Warwick choked so violently that the ale spewed from him, and Charles felt obliged, with a weary shake of his head, to pound Warwick strenuously upon the back. Warwick waved a hand and rose, confronting Charles with a strangled cry.

"Ondine?"

"Aye," the king said agreeably, rescuing from Warwick's hand the mug of ale that threatened to slosh and spill all about his apartments.

"Then how in God's name did I find her upon the gallows out of Newgate?" Warwick exploded.

"You've listened to half a tale, Chatham, now hear the end!" Charles said impatiently. "Sit! Warwick, I tell you, sit! Stay calm, man, or I'll tell you no more!"

With a furious oath barely contained, Warwick perched at the end of the bed once again. Charles eyed him for several seconds, then warily passed him his ale.

"I'm telling you now, Warwick Chatham, you must take heed if I go further! Her position is precarious, and only she can solve it, and only if she takes great care."

"Charles, for God's sake—"

"Patience, Warwick, and discretion, please! You know that the duke was accused of an attempt on my life; he was supposedly slain in the act."

"What do you mean 'supposedly'? Weren't you there?"

"Of course, Warwick! But my back was to the action; I've not eyes in my spine! All I knew then was that someone screamed, that the duke was suddenly down and dying, and that his beautiful daughter was running for her life while those who slew the duke were whispering in horror that she had conspired with them! No one was there but a servant, I believe, and perhaps two of my guards. By all apparent fact, it seemed that the duke had chosen just that moment to end my life."

Warwick said nothing; he just stared ahead, then whispered, "The girl at the stream!"

"What?"

He stared at Charles, startled. "I—I saw her, too, that day. I rode out after the joust. I wanted some peace so I took Dragon into the forest. I was disrupted by an argument, and a girl suddenly burst from the trees, and when I would help her, she disappeared into the water. I could not find her and began to think I might well have imagined the whole thing. I told Jake that I thought I had seen a mermaid, and in truth, it seems, I had."

He stood anxiously. "From whom did she run that day?"

"Warwick," the king said somberly, "this is where I beg you to keep discretion. I cannot identify for sure with whom she argued, for I was not there. I can only assume it was either her uncle, William Deauveau, or her cousin, Raoul. They're step relations, and the remainder of her family. I'd heard rumor of a marriage between Ondine and Raoul, but Rochester denied them to me. His daughter, it seemed, had other plans for her life, and if she tells me true, her judgment was good, for she swears it was her cousin and uncle who made use of her father as a pawn, claiming he was the one to draw sword on me, so they could legitimately slay him, blackmail Ondine, and claim the lands."

"But if you know this—"

"I know nothing for fact, Warwick. I can only go by feeling in this matter, and I believe the girl. But those who witnessed this event were apparently tricked into believing that Rochester performed the deed—and a king must uphold the law. Had she been apprehended then, she would have been detained in the Tower for questioning, and no doubt, it's true that those two greedy relations have some forgery or substance to connive a court into a conviction of high treason."

Warwick felt as if he'd come afire, as if his blood rumbled and boiled all within his being. The world before his eyes spun, and all seemed covered by a blood-red haze.

"And so you've sent her back to these two?" he demanded.

"Listen to me, man!" the king thundered. "She must discover what they plan; what it is they intend to use against her!"

"You are the king; you could pardon her life!"

"It would not be enough for her! Surely you know her, Warwick! She will never rest with her father condemned of treason."

Warwick slammed his mug against the mantel and stared bleakly at the king. "You suggest that I wait? That I do nothing while my wife lives in the midst of men who seek to kill her? Charles! She is my wife by law! I have every right to ride in there and demand that she come back to me!"

"You have the right—but if you do that, Warwick, you will never have the woman. Wife or no, she could well reach the Tower. And even with my pardon, she would have no innocence for her father, and before many eyes, she would live a life in which she breathed, but was condemned for that treason."

Warwick lifted his hands.

"You tell me that she has gone home—to these two viperous beings—and that I can do nothing?"

"I don't know that she has gone home, I can only assume it. I did, in fact, suggest it."

"You what?"

"Warwick—may I remind you that you married her, merely to set her up to catch a killer in your own domain?"

Warwick groaned, then his voice rasped out like a razor's edge. "She might already lie dead by their foul hands!"

The king shook his head. "Nay, I do not think so. William wants her for Raoul, for uncontestable right to the title and lands. The cousin, Raoul, merely—wants her. If she is careful and clever—which she is—she will survive well enough."

"There is no way, sire, that I can know this and not become involved!" Warwick stated flatly.

"I know, I know." The king sighed, but a grin played about the corners of his lips, and in truth, he was well pleased. "You should be near, to slay a dragon should the absolute need arise. Yet I beg you, do not rush in. Find some other way, if you really love her, to help her prove her innocence. And for God's sake, Warwick, do control that temper of yours!"

"I'll do my very best," Warwick replied stiffly.

"Both your lives may well depend upon it."

Warwick inhaled and exhaled deeply. "Where do I find this place, these lands of Rochester?"

The king smiled again, quirking a brow. "Why, the duchess

resides not two hours from this very place. Southwestward, Chatham. The manor 'tis called Deauveau Place. It's a most splendid palace, quite comfortable, really. In fact, far more so than that barbarian manor you keep up in the North.''

Warwick cast the king a most damning gaze; the king saw fit to laugh, though he knew the situation to be grave.

''I shall plan a visit myself, I think,'' he murmured, ''in the next week or two. It will be most interesting to see what has transpired in that time. I wonder if I shall find you near?''

Warwick smiled at the taunt. He set his mug of ale upon the mantel, and unlike his rude entrance, he bowed most politely to the king as he left.

''Sire, I do most earnestly promise that you shall, indeed, find me near.''

Chapter 24

Released at last from her uncle's study, Ondine fled up the fine oak stairway to her set of rooms, closing the doors behind her and sliding the bolt. For long moments she stood there, her back supported by wood, while she gasped for breath. It was done! She was here; she had passed through that first confrontation with life and limb still intact.

Gasping once again and aching from weakness, she fled across the wide sitting room to the next set of doors. She came to her bedchamber and lay down upon her mattress, tears stinging her eyes.

Here, too, nothing had changed. Her rooms remained as she had left them. The cover on the bed was still the lovely damask spread her father had bought from the Spanish traders. The light silk gauze that framed the Flemish posts came from the distant Japans, and the water ewer and bowl upon her white-and-gold dresser had been bought by her father years ago from the Venetians.

She bit down hard on her lip to keep from sobbing. She'd learned what seemed a lifetime ago not to feel, not to mourn. But coming home impressed upon her heart her father's absence. This house was his, and those who had deceived and killed him ruled it, tarnishing all that they touched.

"Oh, Father!" she whispered aloud.

Then she forced herself to breathe deeply, for she did not wish to cry out; her uncle might well have enlisted spies among the household to listen at her door!

She caught her breath, trying to dispel the panic that settled over her along with an overwhelming sense of doom. Here she sought a needle in a haystack—and had given herself scant time for the search. Only thirty days . . .

Blood suffused her face and she rolled onto her stomach, burying her burning cheeks into her pillows. A physician! To see that she remained pure and chaste for marriage—with the vilest of snakes!

"Oh, dear Lord, help me!" she whispered aloud, for she had much to fear.

Nay, there was nothing to fear. Long before the wedding drew near, she would have discovered what "documentation" they had forged of her treason, or else she would have run once again. She must smile and give demure assent to any such requirement that they voiced.

There was a far greater terror to be faced! William did not trust her; he had sworn he would find out where she had been . . .

She rose and paced the room nervously. Coming to the great floor-length windows that opened onto her balcony, she threw them open and stepped out to the small oval protrusion. She looked out upon the lawn, covered now in its crystal blanket of snow. Even the great oaks that dipped on either side of the balcony were touched with ice and looked as if they carried stars of heaven on their branches. So beautiful . . .

Chatham. What would Chatham look like now? An ice palace, too, encompassed in winter? Hung with crepe in mourning, perhaps? By now poor Mathilda would have joined those haunts she heard in her mind; her body would lie in the crypt; masons would be working upon her memorial. Clinton's heart would be heavy still; but he was a man to look sorrow in the face and move on. Justin would be practical, smooth, and gentle, easing things toward normality once again. And Warwick . . .

Where would Warwick be? Surely he had ranted and raved when he discovered her gone! He brooked no disobedience to his orders. Ah, how tender he had been that night, how caring . . .

Autocrat! He'd sought their divorce already. There was naught

to cling to in his tenderness, for, with blunt and brutal words, he'd
assured her once that the lust of the flesh had nothing to do with
emotion. Perhaps—having found that he could not cast her across
the distance of an ocean, since she was not available to be cast!—
he had already traveled back to London, ready to hound the king
for his freedom. His blood was no longer tainted by ghosts; he
might choose an heiress from anywhere he wished.

She closed her eyes tightly, annoyingly near tears again. She
must have a firm grip upon herself! She must hate him, despise
him, and then forget him, casting her mind entirely to her own
cause. Ah, but he was part of all that frightened her now, for she
knew not what avenue William might pursue in his quest for her
past.

Great tremors began to rack her, and she gripped the balcony
rail despite the ice upon it. If William were to discover her already
wed, he would surely find the means to kill her himself.

She turned from the balcony and came back to lie upon her
bed, unaccountably weary. But rest gave her no solace, for she
did not sleep. She ran her hand over the spread and felt the softness
of the mattress. When she dared to close her eyes, she saw not
darkness, but Warwick. Her husband was lean and corded, his
shoulders naked in the moonlight, his eyes a glitter of gold, intent
with purpose, as he stalked her, a man in quest of his wife . . .

"Oh!" she groaned softly and twisted in shame, for she could
not forget him. She could not forget how he held her when he
had come to her, could not but yearn and imagine that he would
find her here, sleep beside her on this bed, hold her naked and
quivering and yet secure to his heart . . .

With an exclamation of fury she was on her feet. She would
think of him no more! Rather she should plan now, for her search
in this haystack for the precious golden needle! Tonight when
everyone slept, she would search her uncle's office. Dismally she
thought that nothing would be there; William was too sly to be
so obvious.

There was a tap upon her door; she hurried to her sitting room
to answer it.

Jem stood there, with two lads behind him, bringing her her
trunks of newly purchased finery. She smiled and bid him enter,
glad once again for the pleasure she had given him.

"Into the bedroom with them, lads," Jem instructed, and the boys obeyed. Ondine did not know the two, which gave her a moment's unease, for she was forced to realize that her uncle had changed most of the household staff. Indeed, it seemed somewhat strange, in view of all, that Jem remained in his position.

They deposited the trunks, and Jem instructed them to return to work in the kitchen.

When they were gone, he took Ondine's hands. "Dear, dear girl! If you need me, I am here! Think, milady! You mustn't marry Raoul! Not while there is life and breath—"

Ondine shushed him quickly, looking about to warn him that the very walls might have ears. "I'll not marry him, Jem, have no fear. Yet I implore you to take care in your distance from me, for if ought should go wrong, I would not have you pay."

His aged and crinkled face carried the deepest dignity. "I'd pay with my life, lady."

"Nay, nay! Make no sacrifices, for your life cannot aid me! Trust in me, Jem, that I shall take care."

He nodded slowly and miserably.

"Shall I send your maid to help with your trunks?"

Her eyes widened with a sudden pleasure as she thought of Liza, the sweet young girl, her lady's maid, she had left behind.

"Liza!" she cried. "Oh, aye, for dearly I'd love to see her!"

Jem shook his head dolefully.

"Liza is to remain in the kitchen. William has ordered another for your personal care. Berta."

"Berta?" Ondine frowned. She knew no Berta.

"She is new, lady." Jem hesitated. "Your uncle's lackey, that she is, spying on the rest of us!"

Ondine exhaled a long breath, then nodded in resignation. She had known that William would watch her like a hawk. She lifted her shoulders listlessly. "Send her, then, Jem. I might as well spend this time in setting my private space to order!"

Berta arrived with uncanny speed once Jem had closed the door behind himself. She was a tall woman, Ondine's own height, but much heavier, though not prone to fat. Rather, Ondine thought with a certain dry amusement, she was built like a knight! She had broad shoulders, muscular arms, and a blunt square face with wee piggish eyes that were neither dark nor light, but some vague shade of taupe. She entered the room with her arms crossed over her ample breasts and stared at Ondine with all but a sneer and snicker.

"Milady, I've been asigned to serve you," she said pleasantly.

And Ondine came near to laughter. You've come for anything but to serve! she thought. Yet she smiled sweetly and said, "Thank you, Berta. I'm sure we shall get along famously. Would you see to my trunks, please, then?"

Berta nodded and lumbered past her. Ondine decided that though Berta might be a rugged foe in a test of arms, she would never be fleet of foot!

She wandered back to the balcony, glad of the fresh cold air as she listened to the sounds of Berta unpacking. Cumbersome she might be, but efficient, for the woman finished quickly and returned to Ondine.

"His Lordship has said that dinner will be at eight, and that you are to join them at precisely that time. It grows late. Shall I order your bath?"

"I don't believe that I shall bathe before dinner."

Still Berta remained.

"His Lordsh—your uncle has suggested that you shall bathe each night at dark."

"Suggested?" Ondine queried heatedly, trying to control her temper.

Berta had either the good sense or the grace to lower her eyes and speak with a modicum of care and kindness. "Raoul wishes, er, that you should be fresh at all times, milady."

"Raoul! Raoul!" she snapped without thought. "My cousin feels that contact with water more than once a month will render him dying of a lung malady, yet he orders me—never mind!" She spun around, shaking with fury, trying to remind herself that she loved to bathe, so little hardship would come to her.

Berta cleared her throat. "It has also been . . . suggested, milady, that if you refuse, you be given assistance."

Ondine swung back around. "Meaning, Berta, that you are ordered to drag me into a tub should I refuse."

Berta said nothing, but shuffled her feet.

Ondine sighed. "Order the bath, then!"

She fumed all the while that preparations were made, aware

that she was made a prisoner in her own home, taught that her place was little better than the servants', nay, even less so! For the servants were not the subject of her uncle's strict scrutiny, nor of Raoul's demented cravings.

When Berta went to touch her with the soap, Ondine came near to slapping her. She managed to contain herself, crisply enunciating that she would be left alone at this point.

Berta did leave her then, and she sank into the hot water, relieved by the steam. But her peace was scant; Berta returned quickly to be there when she rose, ready with a towel. Nor did she escape further administrations, for Berta remained to comb and brush her hair, and in this the unlikely lady's maid was surprisingly talented, smoothing tangles from the long skeins of hair while affording a minimum of pain. Disagreement arose again then, for Ondine wished to have her hair coiled atop her head; Berta informed her that Raoul wished to see it free and untethered down her back.

Ondine held her temper just barely, then shrugged.

She asked for one of her new high-necked gowns. Berta brought one from her closet that had been there before her return, an organdy with a deep neckline. Ondine thought that her temper would surely erupt, yet she contented herself with throwing her brush across the room and thinking nasty thoughts of Raoul. Look, Cousin, all you will! Stare, then! For I swear you'll burn in hell before you ever touch me!

Dressed at last—exactly as had been ordered!—Ondine came back down the stairs and through the hallway to the great room, where her uncle and cousin awaited her at the table. They rose for her to sit, and though she kept her eyes downcast, she was vividly aware of their stares. William's was suspicious; Raoul's both appreciative and smugly satisfied.

"Good evening, Niece," William said pleasantly enough, seating himself again once she was down. "Welcome . . . to your table."

"Is it my table?" she asked sweetly.

He set his lip grimly and moved to pour her wine.

"You look . . . lovely," Raoul commented.

"Just as you wished?"

"Aye, just as I wished."

Ondine managed to retain her smile. Raoul was the weaker of

the two, and she might well need this advantage. She turned about as a platter of lamb was offered to her, then frowned, for she didn't know the man carrying the silver tray; Jem should have been serving.

She waited until they had been left alone in the room and then asked, "Where is Jem?"

Her uncle broke off a piece of bread and chewed it thoroughly, watching her before he spoke.

"Jem will work in the kitchen now."

Ondine gasped with outrage. "He is too old for such heavy work! You will kill him—"

"I think he will manage," William interrupted dryly.

Raoul reached his hand across the table, winding his fingers around hers. She thought to pull them away; he held them fast, and her eyes, too liquid with tears, came to his.

"It is best this way," he told her.

"It is the best, Niece, that you and Jem will get!" William said flatly. "I find myself suspicious of him. And you, my dear, are aware that I trust you not in the least. Stay apart from each other, Ondine, unless you would cause this dear friend greater discomfort!"

She tried to sip her wine, but choked upon it, snapping out, "Oh, I despise you both!"

Raoul stiffened; William smiled. "Watch this beautiful kitten you so desire, Raoul. She is far from declawed!"

Raoul's fingers tightened punishingly around Ondine's. "What matters, Father, her heart—she is beaten. And she will yet learn to wear her collar with grace. One month, Ondine," he added softly, "and I will see you completely humbled."

She managed to wrench her fingers from his and folded her hands in her lap.

"You're not eating, my dear," William remarked pleasantly. She said nothing in response, and he apparently lost interest, indulging his hearty appetite. He turned to his son. "The lead carriage horse has lost another shoe. We must find a new blacksmith by tomorrow."

Ondine shrieked out an oath that astounded them both and was quickly on her feet, challenging them furiously. That they should send Jem to the kitchen was sorry enough a complication, but Nat, the blacksmith, had served Deauveaus for generations, and she would not see him cast out on her account.

"Jem is not good enough for you, Uncle?" she demanded, her hands set rebelliously on her hips, her chin upthrust. "You must vent your cruelty upon Nat, too? I'll not see him or speak to him, I swear it! But don't cast him away, I"—she hesitated, swallowing back bile—"I beg you, I implore you," she said more softly, lowering her eyes in surrender. "Please, I'll make whatever concessions you demand, but do not leave Nat without a living as winter approaches!"

She dared to look at William again, only to discover him smiling with the greatest amusement and cynical pleasure. "Very, very pretty, my dear! But alas! I've nothing to bargain with! I did not cast Nat out of the property on your account; he died last week, of the most natural causes, a happy old man."

Chagrined, Ondine hesitated, then faltered. She stared across the table to Raoul. His dark eyes were curiously intent upon her, and she realized with a little rush of fear that her passionate defense of Nat had only served to excite his interest.

Raoul might prefer her soft and acquiescent, but he was not adverse to the excitement of a challenge. He would, indeed, enjoy breaking her to his will.

But she dared not think of such things, else she would find herself running now, no closer to justice than she had ever been. She raised her chin once again and asked quietly, "Is this true?"

"Aye, Ondine. His goodwife said that he came to his cottage one night, hale and hearty as ever despite his age, yet fell asleep and simply did not waken."

She swallowed once again, lowered her eyes, then sat. But though the lamb was delicious, herb laden and minted, she could not eat. One swallow made her queasy, and she thought it a result of her wretched discomfort with her return home.

She kept her head lowered and meekly requested their leave to return to her room.

And again she knew that William watched her bowed head, trying to fathom her pretense. "You'll have to learn, and quickly, Duchess, to appreciate the company of your family."

"I am weary only, Uncle," she said in a soft tone. "The travel today, the excitement of coming home . . ."

Her voice trailed away. He watched her a moment longer. "You may go to your room," he said at last.

She rose and swiftly moved to leave the room.

"Ondine!"

She paused in the hallway, drawing a deep breath, for Raoul was following her. His hands fell on her shoulders, and he turned her to face him.

For long moments he stared at her, and she thought again that he might well be handsome to another woman, so defined of feature, so dark and suave. Yet all that she could see in his face was cruelty and the weakness that came of treachery. He was but his father's puppet; yet he was not adverse to spilling blood slyly to attain his goals.

She forced herself not to wrench from his hold, but lowered her head in feigned subjugation.

"What is it, Raoul?"

He hesitated; she felt his nearness, and the bile that lay in her stomach seemed to churn fearsomely.

He touched her cheek, and she clenched hard on her teeth. He raised her chin and she looked into his dark eyes.

"You are incredibly beautiful. I have longed for you all my life. I've no real desire to hurt you. Go gently here, and you will fare far better, my cousin."

She shrugged. "I am here, Raoul. Your father has well established his rule of the house. What can I do but succumb to all that you desire?"

"Grow to love me!" he told her heatedly. "By God, I never wished to harm you!"

"That is why you slew my father, Raoul?" she could not help but query disdainfully.

"By God, Ondine, it is you who slew him!" Raoul replied in a hushed fury. "Had you but shown a preference for me—"

"The saints be thanked!" Ondine interrupted him sarcastically. "You do admit your guilt!"

"I admit nothing! I came to talk some sense into you; to save you from yourself! But you go on, wretched, arrogant bitch! You will, my lady, receive your just dues! Once those vows are taken, madam, you will pay!"

She was not prepared for him and was stunned when he lowered

his mouth to hers, grinding his lips there cruelly, seeking entry
for a deeper kiss. Caught against him, she could only twist from
his assault with her heart painfully beating, choking in her throat
and struggling desperately for freedom.

"No!"

She pulled from him with a sudden burst of strength, bringing
her hand to her bruised lips and staring at him with horror. The
taste about her mouth, the scent; oh, she felt ill . . .

"You promised! You swore you would give me time!"

He seemed about to strike her at first, but when she shrank
back, he stiffened, held his temper in check, then said in a curious
tone, "Is that it, Ondine, time?"

She thought quickly, desperate to stave him off with no further
contact.

"I need that time!" she whispered in a plea. "Time to forget
my father's blood on your hands! Time to become accustomed to
you! Please, I will tread gently! I will be with you, walk with you,
talk with you—but give me time!"

He hesitated, then pulled her against him. She was ready to
fight once more, but held herself back in time.

He merely kissed the top of her head and set her from him.

"Good night, then. Tomorrow we will ride together and talk."

She nodded, yearning to escape to her chambers.

"You will let Berta tend to you to my pleasure?" he asked.

She nodded. Oh, hurry, say what you will! she thought frantically, for to her amazement she realized that his kiss had actually
made her nauseated; she was truly about to be sick.

"Go on, then; I'll send her to you now," he said almost gently.

"No!" she gasped out, then pleaded of necessity, "Raoul, I
wish to be alone now, please!"

He caught her to him, kissed her on the forehead again. "Ondine,
Ondine . . . I only wish to cherish you, to worship the font of your
body! It will be wretched only if you make it so! Go, then, sleep,
and dream of me and our future."

Dream! Oh, most unholy nightmare!

But she curved her lips with effort into a shy smile. He released
her, and she fled hastily up the stairs to her own suite.

She knew he followed her departure with his eyes, but she could
give no thought to him. Within her room she quickly bolted the

door, glad of Berta because her room was warm and the fire blazed and offered her light.

As the bolt clicked she knew she had no more time. She brought her hand to her mouth and raced from the sitting room to the bedroom, and to her dresser. She barely managed to free the pitcher from the bowl before she was violently ill.

Spasms shook her again and again. She thought that she would die with the vileness of it, yet eternity though it seemed, the sickness at last came to an end, leaving her weak and gasping. Fumbling, she found the water pitcher and splashed water over her face and throat and hands, using it all before she could feel clean. She staggered then, out to the balcony, out to the bitter cold of night, for only there would she feel refreshed and breathe easily.

Bleakly she railed in silence against herself. How would she ever manage this, if she were to be so pathetically weak?

You have endured so much! she shrieked inwardly. Near starvation in the forest; rotting in Newgate! The feel of the hangman's noose about her throat! The drugs and evil designs of foul-smelling slavers, and the more pathetic danger of Mathilda's twisted designs. All this she had endured. She could not fail now!

Ah, but through the last travail, she had been Warwick's countess; ever he had been there for her! There had been those magic moments when he had held her, when the sweeping force of his possession had taken her mind from all fear, from all thought, from all else but the ecstasy . . .

Ah, milady, he is gone now! she reminded herself. He cannot be a part of this!

But such reminders could not ease the tumult of her thoughts. She stiffened her shoulders and realized she grew frigidly cold, yet that cold felt good. She forced herself to think with sense and logic.

Her only chance lay in meekness, in convincing Raoul that she meant all that she said, in learning to speak gently to him. And William, too, needed to feel a confidence; if he did not, she would never have the opportunity to put him off guard.

"I will do it!" she whispered aloud to the moon, cast high over the snow. First she must harden her heart—and her stomach. She dared not let Raoul know yet that his touch made her violently ill.

And as to Warwick . . .

"Oh, damn him, too!" she muttered fiercely. But with that, she felt strong again. She returned inside and held her breath and cleaned up all the messes she had made, using snow from the balcony to freshen her bowl. Then she drew a chair to the fire and waited.

Hours slipped by. She donned her heaviest nightdress, one of thick material, and quietly let herself out her bedroom door.

All was silent.

She tread softly down the stairs, and silently into her uncle's office. A moon gleamed richly beyond the walls of Deauveau Place, but she could have wept, for it did not give her enough light.

She hesitated, then brought a long tinder match to the small lamp on the desk. The glow filled the room, and she hurriedly began her quest through the drawers. She had to find his forgeries and destroy them. That wouldn't clear her father, but it would end his threats to have her sent to the Tower!

Time swept by as she desperately and methodically stuck to her task, drawer after drawer. But she could find nothing amiss. There were quills and ink and blotters, accounts and ledgers, wages paid and monies earned from the tenants.

She thought most acidly that William Deauveau was a splendid foreman—he collected every last shilling due!

As she opened the last drawer she felt depression overwhelm her. There was nothing here! Ah, she had known it, hadn't she? That this was far too obvious a place—

She froze then, aware that a footstep had landed on the stair. There was a pause and then another fell, and she realized that someone was trying to stalk her.

Thinking quickly, she grabbed a book from the shelves, collected the lamp, and hurried to the window seat, curling into it with the book in her hand, the lamp at her side.

The doors swung suddenly and violently open. She uttered a little scream, grabbing the book to her chest.

William Deauveau stood there in nightdress and cap, staring at her with the greatest suspicion.

"Oh, Uncle!" she gasped. "You frightened me sorely!"

He stepped into the room, grimly silent, looking about. She was eternally grateful that she had replaced things as neatly as she had found them.

"What are you doing here?" he demanded harshly.

She tried to gaze into his eyes with a look of pure innocence. "I could not sleep; I thought that I might read."

He strode over to her, staring at her more closely. He snatched the book from her hold, sneering at her.

"Do you often read with your story upside down, Ondine?"

"What? Oh, I dropped the book when you slammed the door so!" she accused him in hurt return.

He kept smiling, slipping the book behind his back. "And what were you reading, my dear?"

She might have screamed inside; she could not. She dredged from her subconscious mind all that her conscious thoughts had hidden. It had been a dusty green bound book, one with beautifully gilded pages.

"Shakespeare!" she gasped out.

She had guessed right; his eyes registered his surprise.

"And what collection?"

She searched her memory, yet already breathed more easily. *King Lear* is the first play in that particular work, Uncle," she told him serenely.

He opened the book, gazed at the first page, then snapped it shut and handed it back to her. "It's very late; you might tire of a sudden and sleep with the lamp askew, thus starting a blaze that might well kill us all. Go to bed."

Ondine had no thought whatsoever to argue. She clutched the book to her breast and ran quickly up the stairs. Safe in her room with the door bolted once again, she sank to the floor, trembling.

She must learn to be cautious—so, so cautious!

In time her heart slowed its frantic pace. She rose and went on into her bedroom, then into her bed, praying that she could find some release in sleep. But sleep, when it came, gave her nothing. The images that plagued her were not nightmares of Raoul, but haunting memories of Warwick.

Ah, memories that made her wake wretchedly exhausted!

"Autocratic bastard! Must you linger with me, command even my sleep now! Ah, that I could only flaunt the true fact of birth to your noble face!"

She whispered out the words, then turned into her pillow, groaning. She clutched her temples, made painfully aware that last night's illness had followed her to morning.

She felt horrible, even lying down. Queasy, dizzy . . .

"Oh, God!"

All color fled from her face; she was eternally grateful that she was alone, that Berta had not come to serve her yet.

Her mind went horribly blank, then filled with dates and times and figures; detail upon detail of intimate times together went flashing through her thoughts.

"Oh, God!" she repeated.

And she knew that Raoul—totally loathsome creature that he was!—had not caused her illness, nor had exhaustion, excitement, nervousness, nor any other easily dismissed disorder.

She was carrying Warwick Chatham's child—not in pretense, but in devastating fact.

Chapter 25

Clinton and Jake had reached London by then, and it was Jake who discovered where they might glean the most information on the lands held beneath the thumb of William Deauveau.

Not far from the outskirts of London, yet a scant forty-five minutes from Deauveau Place, was a tavern called the White Feather. It was a bawdy place, most frequently filled with the rougher working class, some honest, some not. A man, it was said, could buy most anything there, for the right amount of coin—women and ale, chemists' potions and poisons, and information.

Clinton was the one to recommend caution in their apparel, and so he and Jake, along with Warwick and Justin, first purchased simple woolen garments, unadorned and cheap. They rode to that tavern as northern laborers, not at odds with those they had served, but desiring to come nearer the great city of London, farther from the foulness of the weather.

They ordered ale by the keg, beef and mutton, and spent much of their first night observing everyone about them. A buxom blond barmaid had a dither of a time deciding if she best liked Warwick or Justin, so they teased her together, set coins into her bodice, and when, for a few more coins, the innkeeper was persuaded to let her join their table, they plied her with great tankards of ale.

Her name was Molly, and she was a coarse, yet good-natured sort, affording just the type of assistance Warwick felt they needed.

She stayed, quite complacently, between the two brothers, giggling into her foamy ale. Justin talked foolishly to her; Warwick asked the more important questions.

"Tell me, lass, where could a man, good with his hands, find labor about these parts?"

"Ah, matey, but I'll bet ye're good with yer hands!" she replied, bursting into gales of laughter. Over her fluffy blond head Justin grimaced at his brother. Clinton cleared his throat.

Jake thought they might have ordered too much ale.

"Most seriously, lass. What of the grand manor I heard talk about? This Deauveau Place?"

"Deauveau Place! Ah, now, 'tis a hard taskmaster rules her now!"

"Tell me of him."

The girl chuckled. "Ah, now, that's a story, man, so 'tis!" she said, slurring. "Once he were a kind man, quiet and reserved. But the waters ran deep, so they say, for it seemed he attempted to kill our good king Charles, along with his whelp. None would have thought it surely, for she were a most beautiful thing, ye kin"—she jabbed Warwick in the ribs and winked—"the like of which our good king, fer all his experience now, might seldom ever see! The rumor is high that the lass was in with her da, yet she disappeared. And now the brother—not even a true Deauveau, but some stepson!—owns it all." Molly lifted her ale to her lips with a full-lipped grimace. "Seems a sad story to me, for I hear tell she's returned and that she's to wed her cousin." Molly shivered. " 'E's a handsome devil, that one, but makes the blood run cold. The lass, those who served her there say, was always patient and kind, and I pity her, that I do. Not that it's too uncommon, mind you, gents, but he looks the type to beat a bride, even a noble one at that!"

Looks passed quickly around the table; Molly was too far into her ale to note them.

She stared up at Warwick, smiling.

"If you've the stomach for such a man as Deauveau, though, they do say that the wages are good."

"Are they, then? What say you the chances that the man might hire me on?"

Molly stared at him blearily for a moment, then gasped with sudden pleasure. "Why, the old smithy just died, he did! They be needing a man, since the apprentice were just a boy! If ye've a mind for solid labor, you might want to try your luck tomorrow."

"Tomorrow? When? Where?"

"Why, in the town center, of course."

"Thank you kindly, Molly," Warwick said, rising.

"Well, where ye be off ta now, so quickly?" Molly demanded indignantly.

"A night's sleep, if I'm to be a working man on the morrow, dear mistress!" he informed her, then lifted a brow in mock apology to his brother.

"But fear not, lass; me brother here be a lazy lout, yet one for fun, if you know what I mean. He'll take care of you, girl!"

Take care of her! Justin looked stunned, but Molly had already transferred her attentions to him, and he couldn't do or say a thing to Warwick, since he was well occupied guarding his privates.

Clinton laughed and rose, Jake followed suit, and Justin grew desperate.

"Molly! I'm promised for the priesthood, I am."

"A finely built gent like you? Noo!"

"Ah, but I am, alas! I'd thought I'd have me a few last flings, but already I feel my soul flying to torment. Oh! The pain!" With great drama Justin managed to rise, flash Molly one last smile and one last coin, and race after the others, leaving the tavern, though they'd a room there, since taverns were well known for carrying tales.

"The priesthood, eh?" Clinton doubled over with laughter at the sight of Justin, running quickly behind them.

"The pain! The pain!" teased Jake.

Justin grimaced, casting Warwick a baleful glare. "She wasn't exactly my type!" he accused his brother. "If you must pick up women, you must dispose of them, too, Brother. I damn well was in pain! She's fingers like a spider!"

None could take him too seriously, and Warwick burst into hearty laughter. But by then they were far along the road from the tavern, and no one was about to hear them. Gasping for breath after laughing in the harsh cold, Clinton leaned against a fence and stared more somberly at Warwick.

"I should go for the blacksmith's position. I've spent half my life around horses."

"And I haven't, Cousin?" Warwick arched a warning brow.

Clinton waved a hand impatiently. "You've spent your life managing the estate, and on the king's business. I am the one who knows horses."

Warwick shook his head. "I know enough. And I have to be there."

"Perhaps, Lord Chatham," Jake remarked, "ye're precisely the one o' us who should not be about her."

"I'll do nothing rash, damn you all!" Warwick swore. "I've common sense aplenty, but I must see her. She is my wife."

Justin ribbed Clinton with his elbow. "Actually, I'd rather enjoy seeing the lord of the manor as a blacksmith. He's pathetically low on humility, if facts must be faced."

"Oh, aye, pathetically," Clinton agreed. Jake sniggered.

"Justin—"

"Just a comment, Brother, nothing more!" Justin said cheerfully. "But now"—he rubbed his chin—"he's a bit too clean for a man of his means, wouldn't you say, Clinton?"

"Oh, aye, pathetically clean."

"He needs a good romp in the mud."

"Well, there is no mud about, good fellows, so you'd best forget that!" Warwick stated.

Clinton grew sober. "Warwick, 'twould be best if you did not appear so refined. You might easily make this William Deauveau wary. There's mud near the tavern entry. Ye need some dirt under your fingernails, at least."

"Callused and filthy! I will enjoy this," Justin announced.

Warwick stared at his hands. "There are calluses aplenty on them as it is," he said.

"Aye," Clinton agreed, "be grateful for them; were they not there, you'd never pass as a smith."

Warwick shrugged. "All right; lead me to the mud. Justin, you'll not be around to see anything. You and Clinton are heading back to court."

"We are?" Justin asked.

Clinton nodded, watching Warwick, aware already of the workings of his mind. He gazed at Justin then. "We're to see what there is to discover. Surely someone, somewhere, saw something amiss that day."

"Don't go to court, but take rooms in London," Warwick advised. "I think we need to look among the common folk. Perhaps listen to the gossip in the taverns. Someone might be afraid to step forward."

"And what of Jake?" Justin asked.

"Jake will stay here, should I need him. He can glean the most from the people."

"And besides," Jake added, his wizened gnome's face crinkling into a smile, "I rather like Molly, meself!"

Laughing, they all linked arms and headed for the mud. Justin seemed most talented at applying it to his brother. No man should go slovenly for such an appointment; he simply should not appear as if he enjoyed bathing and indulged in that habit regularly.

After a time, though, the laughter died again, and Justin tensely queried his brother. "How do you know you'll earn this fine position? Maybe a number of hearty and better known townsfolk will also be applying."

"I don't intend to wait for the interviews; I'll present myself at Deauveau Place in the morning." He hesitated. "I can't wait; I can't hold my distance any longer. I must be able at least to see her, and see that she moves healthy and well!"

At dinner the following night, Ondine was in a much stronger frame of mind. She had spent the afternoon riding over the snow-covered estate with Raoul. She had been pleasant, and he had not come too near. When they spoke, they talked about things distant: the theater in London, opera, and art. Raoul was an avid admirer of the great painters; he was well read and had a keen eye for talented men and masterpieces.

She had been painstakingly charming and sweet that day, well aware that charming Raoul might be her only hope of salvation if things went too far beyond her control.

Such as being with child!

She lured herself from the thought continually, for there were no answers to the dilemma, but simply more problems. She could not think that she would adore the child, that she would be pathetically eager to lavish upon it all the love she had never been able to give the father. She could not wonder if it would be a husky boy, born with rare golden eyes like his sire, or a wee girl, perhaps, golden blond, lovely, and sweet . . .

She dared not wonder, even in the depths of her heart, what Warwick would feel. Would he wish her back—should she live to discredit this pair here!—for the sake of a legally born heir? He was ever so possessive a man; lord of his domain! And worse still, perhaps more frightening than even her uncle's treachery, was a haunting fear that he would be furious that she should have left him so, carrying what was rightfully his. Having stolen gold coins would mean nothing to him; those she had earned. But leaving with flesh and blood, his flesh and blood, an heir . . .

"Are you ill, Ondine?"

"What? No!" she gasped out, looking from her cousin to her uncle.

"You give no attention to your food," William commented.

"My sleeplessness last night, I suppose," she murmured, biting into her fowl. She smiled. "It is delicious, Uncle."

William wrapped a hand over hers briefly, curiously. "How charming you can be when you so choose, my dear."

"And I have so chosen, Uncle," she said softly.

"Umm." His syllable carried a tone of doubt, but she gazed at Raoul with a smile, and Raoul, it seemed, wanted no doubts.

"What do you think of the new smith?" William asked Raoul.

Raoul thought a moment, his fork delicately poised in midair. "He suffices. Big brute, though, isn't he?"

"One couldn't have a weakling for a smith," William commented, turning to his food. He shrugged. "He's a surly fellow, it seems. The north country breeds arrogance. He's powerful, though, with shoulders that do well in a forge. We shall see how he works out." He gazed at Ondine then, but she did not notice, for this night the fowl was truly tender and delicious, and she was famished. Her sickness had miraculously left her; it was almost like a trick of fate, coming to point out to her what recent circumstances had caused her to ignore.

"Will you play the spinet tonight, as you used to?" Raoul asked her.

"I—" She had thought to escape him early, but she needed to woo Raoul to her confidence, and playing the spinet did not call for much hardship. "If that is what you wish, Raoul," she finished.

Dinner completed, they entered the ballroom at the left wing of the house, a wonderful vast room with good acoustics. It was chilly here, though, even with a fire raging, for the ceilings were high and the place difficult to heat. Ondine played tune after tune, humming at times, singing at others, finding a certain peace in the activity. William sat in a great chair, sipping brandy, quite at home with this pastime that marked him a true gentleman.

Raoul held a glass of port, but did not drink. He stood, leaning slightly against the spinet, and watched her.

This is my home! My heritage! she longed to rage.

But it could only be hers if she could oust them from it, and that would take time and patience.

At last her uncle stopped her, saying that it had grown too cold for them to remain in the ballroom. He took her arm to lead her from the place. At the foot of the stairs he relinquished her to Raoul.

Raoul made a great display of kissing her hand.

She could not wait to wash it, but smiled and told him sweetly that she would see him on the morrow.

Ah, what glory it was to shut her door upon them! She leaned against it in relief, then started, for she could hear them speaking in low tones just outside in the hallway. She pressed her ear to the door, barely breathing so that she might hear them.

"I tell you, it must be done now!"

"Father! She just comes to trust me, to see my company! If you do such a thing now—"

"Do you want a whore for a wife?"

Raoul laughed bitterly. "If she's a whore, Father, she might well please me at that. Lady or whore, she is the duchess! Sexual appetite does not change that fact."

"Well, I would like to know!" William said stubbornly. "If he's been off with other men—of what caliber we've no idea!— I'll be damned if she'll stride about this place with her cloak of virtue! I tell you, I intend to send for a physician now, to solve this thing one way or the other.''

"Father! I am the one to wed her!"

"Then discover something of her, or I shall see to it myself. I give you a few days time and that is all."

Raoul replied, but Ondine could not hear him, for the two men walked away. Worried, she walked into her room, tapping her finger against her chin in vexation. What was she to do now?

Raoul . . . he was her only hope. Should she throw herself at his feet in some wild scheme, praying that he could stave off his father?

She started, certain that she had heard some sound from the balcony. She moved there, brows knit, and saw that the doors were not fully shut. She stared outside, then shivered, certain that she saw a tall and muscular man below, leaning against an oak. She came nearer, but the figure turned and disappeared.

Wary, she closed the balcony doors against the cold of the night. Aye, would that be fate, ironic fate, if some petty thief should come and slay her in her sleep!

She turned about, ready to prepare for bed, aware that she badly needed rest. Tomorrow morning she planned to sneak into her uncle's chambers while he attended to plaintiffs in his office. It would be dangerous, and she would need to take grave care. She must not be skittish and tired.

Yet even as she lay down in her bed with a heavy covering about her, she shivered.

She thought that she would rather some brute strangle her for her jewels, or William discover her searching his chambers, than that Warwick should find she had left him carrying his child!

Nay, he would not even want the baby.

He had announced that he would send her to the Colonies.

"Oh, dear Lord!" she whispered in a weak little prayer, then grew impatient with herself and tossed about. She must worry about this dilemma later; she could not think on it now. She had to get into her uncle's chambers, she had to think of some story to tell Raoul, and, oh, dearest God, what on earth was that going to be? Think, think, don't worry. Warwick was miles and miles away, not here to chastise her, not here to hold her . . .

He was part of another life.

* * *

As several more days went by, Ondine decided that Berta was
the least of her difficulties. She would come in with tea in the
morning, having learned that Ondine loved to read while she sipped
it. She would help her dress, Berta choosing the gown. She would
arrange her hair, which was not so terrible a displeasure, but rather
an easy thing, then depart. Ondine would wander down the stairs,
breakfast with her uncle and Raoul, then wander off so that they
might discuss business.

She had to pretend a great disinterest in the estate, lest they
worry she should expect to manage her own domain!

But she was glad of that, for one morning when they retreated
to the office, she pretended to return to her rooms after agreeing
to bundle warmly and meet Raoul at the stables in an hour.

There was no one to disturb her when she sauntered past her
own door and through her uncle's. Once there, she had to pause;
these had been her father's rooms, and once, long ago, her mother's.
The desk was her father's, the Van Dycks were her father's, the
great claw-footed Italian bed was her father's. Everything was her
father's, taken over by this horrid—pretender!

She couldn't let the misery dwell in her. With a single deep
breath she moved into the room, reminding herself that she must
listen carefully.

She did, pausing every few minutes as she searched the desk,
the shelving, the fireplace, the drawers, the trunks, the wardrobes.
Nothing, nothing came to light, and once again she felt like
weeping.

A clock chimed from below, and she realized that her time was
up. Wearily she decided that she must go through everything again;
she had been too hasty with the desk.

She opened the door a crack, checked the hallway for servants,
and slipped out. She was one step away from the door when Berta,
puffing, made an appearance at the top of the stairs.

"Where have you been, Duchess? I pounded upon your door
for the last hour!"

Ondine made a great pretense of yawning. "Did you? Perhaps
I slept. I'm surprised you didn't just enter."

Berta lowered her eyes. "I respect your privacy, madam!"

Ah, like hell you do! Ondine thought, yet she was filled with a certain elation, for she was certain Raoul had ordered that she was not to be disturbed at rest.

She smiled radiantly. "Berta, would you run for my cloak, please? The silver fox. I'm to meet Raoul, and that is so very warm against the cold."

Sullenly, perhaps suspiciously, Berta went to obey her. Ondine waited, continued to smile as the woman slipped the cloak about her, then waved a hand in dismissal. "Thank you, Berta! Oh, do please keep my fire burning warmly. I'd not like a chill room for a bath!"

The stables were not far from the house, but still she felt the chill of the cold as she approached them. Snow crunched beneath her feet, and she pulled the silver fur tightly to her throat.

Raoul was outside, awaiting her impatiently. As she reached him he clutched both her hands and kissed them fervently, then frowned.

"You are not dressed to ride."

"I thought it a little cold," she told him. "Raoul, I need to speak with you."

"We'll go back to the house."

"Alone."

" 'Tis chilly here," he said, then mused aloud, "ah, there is a shelter behind the smith's, a buffet from the wind. And the heat from the forge will warm us."

"Lovely," Ondine said.

Together they scampered past the stables to the next long building. Behind it they came to an overhang, and there was even a bench beneath it where the smiths could come—away from the heat—to rest a moment from vigorous toil. A door was open behind them, sending out blessed waves of heat.

Still, Ondine was at a loss. Once she started this speech, she knew she must complete it, and complete it well. She did not dare be squeamish!

"Raoul . . ." she whispered painfully, taking his hand into hers and delicately drawing lines over the slim blue veins on the back of it. "Oh, Raoul . . ."

"What is it?" he cried to her, turning to see the very real distress in her eyes. He took both her hands in his, holding them tightly as he spoke earnestly. "Ondine . . . I've threatened you only because I must! But I have coveted you forever, my beauty, and will be your husband. If you've trouble, you must tell me!"

"Oh!" she cried, and managed to squeeze a tear onto her cheeks. "It's your father, Raoul, if he knows—"

"Forget Father!" Raoul said heatedly. "You will be my wife; the duchess; I will be the duke—not Father! Tell me, tell me anything, and I will protect you!"

"Would that you could!" she whispered. It was not so difficult to speak; she was merely acting again, and a good performance created its own satisfaction and reward.

"Do you doubt me?" he swore hoarsely. "Ondine, if only you cared . . ."

She took it a step further, elegantly sliding to her knees at his feet, allowing the silver hood to fall back as she faced him.

"I do, Raoul, oh, I do! I don't know why I ever ran! I still need to know you . . . but I am so certain that we can be happy together . . . could have been happy together."

"Could have! Come, Ondine, off your knees, into my arms!" He put his arm about her, drawing her to him. He attempted nothing like his brutal, disgusting kiss, and so Ondine rested there, smiling a bit secretively, since he could no longer see her eyes or lips.

"What is this 'could have'! There is nothing, nothing that will keep me from you!"

"But there might well be, Raoul!" she wailed. "I lied to you, Raoul. You see, my fear is not for my life, but for my immortal soul!"

"What is this nonsense?"

"I do not really know, yet I'm afraid! Raoul, when I ran from here, I hid in the forest. There was a man there who helped me, and I married him. At least, I think it was legal. But then, I left him. I ran, for I realized that he was crude, nothing but a lout of a peasant. But if he still lives, Raoul, then I cannot marry again. Not unless he can be found; not unless—he dies, or the marriage is annulled. We must find him to do that, Raoul."

Raoul jumped to his feet in a sudden fury, turning to stare at her. "Then you are no innocent! Yet you refuse me—"

"Nay!" she cried in her most pathetic voice. "It is not you I refuse. Oh, Raoul, you know that isn't so, please, know it! But

my soul, Raoul, he must be found!'' She bit her lip, amazed that
she could make her eyes glitter with tears. "Raoul!'' she whispered
brokenly, and he was back beside her. "Your father intends to
bring a physician. He'll part us then! I'll never be able to love
you!''

"Love me now!''

"Oh, that I could! But my soul, Raoul!''

"Damn your soul!''

"Ah, my life I could damn! But not my chances for eternity!''

"Oh, God!'' Raoul swore, clenching his fists.

Neither of them noticed that a tense and haggard face, kept
barely in restraint, gazed upon them from the open doorway of
the smith. Fists were clenched more tightly than Raoul's, eyes
blazed a fury that well cautioned of eternal damnation.

Barely, barely did Warwick hold his temper. Barely, barely was
he able to keep himself from reaching out and wrenching her to
his side, slaying Raoul with a single blow from his hammer.

Wait, dear God, patience! he warned himself.

But patience came hard as he gazed upon her, a thing of molten
beauty, fire and ice, in her silver fox.

He forced himself to breathe deeply, to loosen his hold upon
the hammer.

Lean back, my friend, he cautioned, enjoy the show. Act Two
would be his, and it would come very soon.

Raoul next fell to his knees at Ondine's feet. "I swear, I'll find
this man! And my father will not touch you, that I swear, too. Just
keep silent for now, and trust in me.''

"As you say, Raoul.'' Smiling, she smoothed back his hair.
Then she shivered, and he suggested they return to the house.
Hand in hand, they walked back through the snow.

Ondine was so elated and confident that the rest of the day went
very well indeed. She called Berta in early so that she could wash
her hair and dry it by the fire. Berta chose the most daring of her
gowns, one with a ludicrously low bodice, yet Ondine demurely
slipped into it without a word.

For the moment it was wise to keep Raoul panting. She could,
in fact, almost feel pity for him. He was so weak against her will.

Yet he was weak in the hands of others, too; that above all had to be remembered.

Still . . .

Ah, it was so much easier to go down to dinner that night. It was easy to smile to welcoming comments, easy to consume her meal with relish, easy, even, to meet Raoul's gaze across the table, to blush and allow her own gaze to fall, then meet his once again.

Even William seemed disarmed that night, glad of the camaraderie between the two. She played the spinet again, shared brandy in the study, and most blushingly accepted Raoul's kiss on her cheek when she mounted the stairway.

It was her uncle who stopped her that night, catching her hand right before she would enter her room.

"Duchess—even I could swear that you have truly had a change of heart."

She widened her eyes in surprise at the doubt in his statement. "Ah, Uncle! I believe that life can only be what we make it! What would I do, here alone? Who would I have, without you to protect and guide me?"

"You are truly resigned?"

"Why, sir, I am even content!"

He nodded, perhaps not really believing her, but content with her behavior for the moment.

Ondine smiled, then withdrew her hand in a leisurely manner and continued on into her room.

She closed and bolted the doors behind her, leaned against them, and even chuckled softly.

Then she swept through the sitting room, her hands already busy on the laces of her gown. All was going well; she would not have to fight her uncle, Raoul would. Tomorrow morning she would return to William's desk and search it thoroughly.

She started to hum a little tune as she breezed into her bedchamber and slipped out of her gown, allowing it to lie at her feet. In her chemise only, she stretched luxuriously, believing for once that there was hope, that will alone could make her the victor.

"Good evening."

The words snapped her instantly from her reverie. She opened her eyes wide, stunned to see a sooted and blackened figure seated easily upon her dresser, idly swinging long, long legs.

She opened her mouth, gasping for breath to scream, yet the sound never came. He was instantly up, clutching her from behind, sliding a hand across her mouth even as he pulled her against the muscled strength of his chest.

"Don't scream, milady; gallows' bride; Countess. But then it is Duchess now, I believe! *Tsk, tsk!* How confusing. But no matter, don't bother to scream. 'Tis only me—that crude lout of a peasant you so woefully married!"

Chapter 26

"Warwick!"

She gasped out his name as his hand eased from her mouth, so stunned that the night seemed to swim all around her.

"The same, lady."

She didn't like the hard tone of his voice, or the tension she felt from his arms, his hold. So many emotions raced through her heart that she could barely fathom them all: elation, that he should be here, holding her again; amazement . . . it was indeed Warwick; terror and trembling, for if he was discovered here, he would be slain in a matter of seconds, and no one would condemn a guardian for killing a man in a "maiden's" bedchamber!

Oh, and love! And then terror all over again, for he was most certainly livid with anger at her, and though he had somehow appeared in this ridiculous attire, she didn't—couldn't—understand the situation at all.

"The new smithy!" she murmured suddenly.

"Ah, yes, once again the same, madam!"

Oh, still the room swam! This . . . this seemed more than she could handle. She thought that she would swoon, and then she thought that she should swoon, as her experience with Raoul was teaching her that men were malleable creatures, tending to be gentler when they feared they caused a lady distress.

She fluttered her eyes closed, emitted a last sighing gasp, and cast her weight against him.

He lowered her carefully to the floor, but she felt no tenderness from him. She didn't even feel his touch.

She raised her lashes just a slit to see him leaning upon one knee, casually resting his elbow upon it.

"All the way, Ondine. 'Tis not Raoul you're with, lady, but me, remember, that peasant lout of a husband."

"Oh, do go to hell!" she snapped, opening her eyes fully. He chuckled softly, yet his expression remained grave, or what she could see of it, for his cheeks were ill kempt, shadowed with beard, and he was dusky colored from constant exposure to the fire and soot of the forge.

"You're filthy," she murmured.

"Alas, yes, we've come full circle, so it seems."

He simply stared down at her, and she realized the disadvantage of her position, prone while he glared upon her from a certain height. She tried to sit, but he pressed her back, and the best she could do was to raise up on her elbows to contest him.

"What are you doing here!"

"Simple, I should think. I've come for you."

"But—" She swallowed, frightened she would cry and terrified that such an action would turn to hysteria.

"Deceitful baggage, my darling duchess, but nevertheless, still my wife."

"This is no concern of yours."

"On the contrary; what concerns you must well concern me. Think, my love, of your immortal soul!" he mocked.

"Oh, do get out of here! How in God's name did you get in?"

"The balcony—and I will not be going for some time yet."

"Don't you understand? They'll kill you!"

He shrugged. "Would that distress you?"

"Certainly! I owe you *my* life; I don't wish yours taken!"

"Ah, the emotion that gushes forth from you, love! Would that I were Raoul, so that you might cast yourself at my knee!"

She gritted her teeth. "Raoul is easy—"

"So are all your men, it seems."

"All my men?"

"Ah, yes, Raoul, Justin—Clinton, for that matter. Jake! Hardgrave—the king! What is it that you do, my darling?"

"Will you please leave! You make a ridiculous blacksmith!"

"And I am not easy, is that it?"

"Warwick!" She lowered her voice and whispered more urgently, "Honestly, you do not realize—they would kill you!"

"Lady, I should like to see your uncle or that sniveling Raoul make such an attempt. I'd most gladly skewer either, or break their bloody necks!" He placed his hands idly before him. "And I do take offense; these are, most conveniently, wonderful hands for a blacksmith. They've well the strength to tackle the tools—or a neck, for that matter. Or even an errant wife."

"I'm finished with you, Warwick Chatham!" she hissed to him, praying he'd not truly lost his senses, for it seemed he didn't even bother to keep his voice low. "You married me to discover what had become of—of Genevieve. Now you know. You promised me my freedom—"

"But you did not remain long enough for me to have that chance, did you, milady?"

"I—could not!" she murmured, lowering her eyes from his. "As you seem to know, I could not be sent from the country!"

He blinked, holding tight his expression, wishing most fervently that he had forced her to listen that night she had come so very close to losing her life . . . forced her to stay, to love him in return.

"This is a fool's quest!" he told her harshly.

"A fool's!" she cried softly, indignantly. "Chatham, are you blind! This house, these lands, are rightfully mine! Yet that is not what matters! Damn you, how—"

"I went to the king."

"Then you know," she whispered, "that I am still suspect of treason and could easily lose my head!"

"Nay, I know that when you ran, you ran in terror, too young and innocent to realize that running but made you more a victim of their game. Charles would never blindly kill—"

She interrupted him with a soft groan. "Warwick, there were witnesses; hoodwinked, but nevertheless honestly believing what they saw."

"Charles can pardon you."

She shook her head. "Perhaps he could, but how would that look if the law condemned me? I would never be free of the taint; nor would history ever forgive my father for a deed that was not his!"

He exhaled long and low, and she could not tell what he was thinking. "Ondine," he said at last, "when we met, you were about to lose your life on the gallows. Pride is not so great a thing to die for! You could have claimed your rank—"

"And died by the headsman's ax instead!"

"That time is past; you have seen Charles. You know that he believes you innocent."

She closed her eyes tightly, inwardly pleading that he understand. "Charles cannot prove me innocent either. Only I can find the answer to that dilemma."

He rose and slowly paced the floor. Gripping the bodice of her chemise tightly to her chest, she sat, watching him. At last he returned to her, hunching down before her, eyes a golden fire of intensity as he spoke.

"You know, too, don't you, that I could leave here and return with the law—half the king's army—and demand your return. You are my wife, duchess or no. I can claim my rights and settle it all myself from there."

Tears stung her eyes, and she lowered her head. "I've time!" she pleaded softly, not knowing if he cared, or if his temperament was simply such that he did not let possessions go except by his own decree, in his own manner.

"Please, Warwick! I've less than a month now before being forced to a—a—"

"Bigamy is the term, my love."

She moistened her lips nervously and shook her head. "I never intended to go through any ceremony—"

"Ah, dear Duchess! But what a convincing and fetching pretense you gave today! You were lucky, madam, that I did not end it then and there."

"Warwick! I must find this forgery! In my possession, it could perhaps be evidence *against* them!"

"I cannot bear nearly a month, Lady."

Her heart seemed to skip a beat. She swallowed. "Then you will leave? You'll not interfere."

"Oh, I'll interfere, all right, if you press me too far. And I do not like this one bit; it's foolhardy and dangerous. Nor will I leave this place; I'll be here, love, day and night. You do not have a month; you've two weeks, if I can manage it."

"Two weeks!"

"The closer you come to this 'wedding,' the more dangerous things will become. And when I warn you, lady, to cease some action that distresses me, you will do so. Immediately."

She tossed her head back in a sudden fury, making her hair cascade down her back in a sun and fire trail, her eyes ablaze like precious sapphires.

"Sir, I thought perhaps you'd noted that I was no simple common lass. By blood, Warwick, not by marriage, I am the Duchess of Rochester. You'll not treat me like—"

"My lady, I do not give a damn if you carry the blood of a thousand kings! You will listen to me because you are my wife, because I wish to keep you from danger, and because—I do promise you most assuredly!—I will not have what is mine mauled and petted and coveted by another. Now, have we come to an understanding, do you think?"

She lowered her head, clenching hard and miserably upon her jaw, but nodded. "Oh, Warwick, don't you see! You are the one in danger here!"

"Hush!" he said suddenly.

He stared past her, through the bedroom to the outer door. She, too, heard footsteps in the hall. They held silent for a moment, then Warwick relaxed once again. The footsteps had passed by.

"Please!" she whispered. "You must leave here."

He shook his head, and she noted the gleam about his eyes that sent her heart racing in shivers of excitement—dread, and yet the sweet anticipation of her dreams.

"Warwick—"

"I'm not going anywhere tonight."

Oh, dear God, the danger! He was near mad!

She started shaking her head, so terribly nervous of his intent.

"Nay, Warwick—"

"You're still my wife."

"Not here, I can't—"

"Anywhere, my love."

"You're, er, filthy!"

"Do excuse me!"

"Warwick . . . "

Her protest trailed to nothing, for it seemed the time for talk had left them. He reached for her, cupping his hand at her neck, drawing her face to his, her lips touching his own. It was a sweet and burning sensation, and she did indeed feel that she would faint then, pitch headfirst into a drowning pool of joy in his very being, joy in the warmth and splendor that riddled her body.

It was a gentle kiss, moist and longing, vastly tender, lingering, inquisitive. He moved from her and watched her eyes, smiling wistfully. His voice was husky.

"You are not, then, so terribly displeased to see me?"

She shook her head, lowering her lashes in sudden confusion.

"Then come to me."

She raised her eyes, and they were wide. "Warwick," she whispered most sincerely, "I cannot! You're so very grimed—"

"Ignore the dirt; come love the heart."

She shook her head again in vast embarrassment. "You don't understand! They've a giant to watch me! Berta cares for my things, and she would—ah—"

"What?"

"Notice such filth upon the bedclothing!"

He sat back, grinning, then chuckled aloud. "No problem, my love." Standing, he retrieved from a chair his cloak, a vast garment in dull wool, but set with a lining of soft linen. And it was clean, since he did not wear it in the smithy. He cast it over her bed, and its great size amply covered the finer fabric there.

"Come to me," he whispered, reaching for her hands.

She took his, watching his eyes, disbelief and wonder still expressed in her own. But when he would pull her against himself, she protested softly with a little cry.

"Wait!"

"What now!" he demanded sharply, dragging in a ragged breath, his patience near at an end.

"My chemise . . . your clothing will soil it!"

He swore out some soft oath, then instantly set about tugging upon his boots and shedding his worker's heavy trousers and shirt and thick wool hose. Ondine found herself standing very still to watch him, entranced, and somehow very sedate, smug, and pleased. He cast his clothing aside with such ease, such natural grace, such disregard, as if he need bear no consciousness in the act, for she was so much a part of him. It was either that, or, she reminded herself, he had such confidence and pride in his simple, basic being that hesitancy could have no place in him. Ah, and why should he falter, for was that not part of her own pride? Blackened or fastidious, he entranced her, the hard line of his body beguiled her, fascinated her, making her hands yearn to touch him without command from her mind. She loved the breadth of his shoulders, gleaming beneath dust and grime in the firelight. She adored the oaken sturdiness of thigh and calf, the leanness of hip, flatness of belly, rounded wonder of muscle and sinew, the beat of the pulse at his throat . . .

She smiled, secretively, thinking that, aye, she loved all of him, and most certainly, that wonderful evidence of "endowments," hers now, potent and rigid, alive and impatient with desire. And ever more her smile increased, for there was the sweetest pleasure of all in knowing that she was what he yearned for—she the creator of all this male beauty, she the total heartthrob of his being. He made her feel a bliss, a liquid trembling, warm and shaky. And now she was ablaze, savoring just that ecstasy of anticipation, knowing that soon they would touch . . .

"What? You smile, or laugh, milady?" he accused her, coming toward her.

She shrieked softly, eluding his hold.

"My chemise . . . "

"Best remove it, then. Quickly," he warned her in a tone so much like a growl that she chuckled softly. Yet quickly, indeed, she made haste to obey, most aware then by his expression that his ardor left no more room for care or reason.

She shed the chemise, letting it fall to the ground, and found herself most instantly crushed against his chest, a prisoner of his arms. So delicious the sensation! Her flesh was so bare against his naked own; she felt him with all of her, softness of breasts against hardness of muscle. She was so vulnerable, so trusting, so smiling in wonder, her head cast back, the sea-magic and liquid beauty of her eyes gazing into the amber glow of his.

"Duchess, lady, wench—wife! You dare to laugh at me still!" he chastised her with ferocious challenge.

She shook her head, smiling still, near to feeling that the liquid of her must soon seep through him, embrace and blanket him.

"I smile, milord, with delight only," she answered honestly, so dazed with this night, she could not pretend.

He gave some distant glad cry of triumph, and that hoarse, guttural sound made her smile curve deeper, for with him she had learned that triumph was an equal thing, given, taken, shared. As was surrender, for even as she succumbed to him, a part of him became indubitably hers, captured for all time, an eternity.

In his arms she came upon their bed of rough linen; in his arms she tasted rhapsody, heard its joyful ringing. That rough touch of his stubbled beard was coarse against the tenderness of her flesh, yet she cared not; sensation came all the greater. She could give no heed to the dangers that lurked beyond the door, for heaven help her, once his touch stirred her blood, her mind knew no other reality. She wrapped him in the silken ribbons of her limbs; he buried himself in the erotic entanglement of her hair. Thrusting rhythms lifted them on the wings of heartbeats where that very pulse became a song of union, of glistening flesh, naked bodies, straining limbs . . . yet with all the ethereal purity of endless clouds, silver magic. And only when their song, their beat, reached its crescendo did she feel the earth again, for his hand covered her mouth, muffling that ardent, mindless cry which would have escaped her.

Staring into his, eyes she flushed, and he chuckled softly, a sound breathless and deep, for still he remained with her, loathe to leave the sheath of her body. She buried her head well against his chest, sighing, and then as the heat of passion cooled in drifting satiation, she tensed, for fear had returned.

"You've got to go!" she urged him.

Reluctantly he rolled from her at last, staring sightlessly up at the ceiling. "I tell you, I do not like this."

"Please, Warwick, we—"

He rolled back to her, clutching her hands beneath his fingers, fervently pressing his lips against her breast. He stared deeply into her eyes and said, "If at any point I feel no hope remains, you will come—leave this quest—when I say."

She lowered her lashes humbly, grateful that as yet he knew nothing of their child, for surely then he would drag her away, kicking and screaming if need be.

"Aye, Warwick."

Still she felt his eyes upon her, and slowly she opened her own, meeting his curious gaze.

"I love you, milady."

"Oh, Warwick!" She freed her hands from his grasp, threw her arms about his neck, and pressed herself to him in a new ecstasy of joy. Dark clouds seemed to shatter and break; all seemed sunshine and the sweetest whisper of a clean breeze.

"Wench or lady, horse thief, Duchess, I love you," he added tenderly, arms tightening in return. And she whispered that she loved him, too, had loved him for an eternity . . .

On it went—muffled, inaudible words, clearly understood. Yet Warwick, so determined that his avowel must come now, and so desperate to hear hers in return, pulled away with explanations still unsaid, for the hour grew late no more, but early. Outside dawn came too near.

"My love—"

"Love . . . " she repeated, near delirious in her happiness.

He cleared his throat, catching her hands and eyeing her once again with a satanic gleam of wanting.

"My lady wife, my love! Though I find this the greatest ecstasy ever offered by life, I beg that you not bring your hips so hard against me, nor torture so my flesh with the stirring beauty of rosebuds and cream mounds, else I shall not leave, but drown again my lover's sword in the velvet cloak of your body. Alas, 'twould be the most beguiling action of the moment, but perhaps not the most wise."

"Oh!" she murmured, suddenly wide-eyed and sober and well warned, for only then did she know that his ardor was once again growing strong against her thighs.

"Go!" she pleaded, pushing him from her.

He chuckled softly, kissed her one last fleeting time, and, with the greatest reluctance, rolled from her and rose.

She closed her eyes, twisting away, not daring to watch him dress, heartsick to see him go.

Warwick, clad once again, pulled on his boots and stared at

her, a smile of great tenderness curving his lip. How glorious she appeared there, so wondrously sleek and rounded, pure and fair upon the poor material of the cloak. What a golden sunburst the rich strands of her hair seemed against the dull brown covering.

"Ondine!" he whispered softly.

She turned to him, and he smiled. "I need my cloak, lest you would keep it. Ah, if you wish, gladly will I freeze—"

She was instantly up, naked and beautiful, snatching the garment from the bed to toss upon him. Yet even as he wrapped it about himself, she cast herself into his arms, and once again they held tight, lovers blissful in the discovery of love, ecstatic—yet torn and anguished.

At last he set her away from him, glad that she could be so easily natural in her state of nudity with him, wishing that she were clad so that his leave-taking might be less difficult!

But then worry for the future seized him, and at the last it was with a hint of roughness that he touched her.

"Watch your step with Raoul, milady! Take the gravest care; all will most certainly be lost should you come too close to each other in my presence, and my temper should shatter."

"I never—"

"You did! Today, my lady, it almost ended—your would-be husband might well have died a quick death from a hammer wound!"

She flushed. "I will take care."

"And I, my love, will return to you here."

Smiling at last, he kissed her forehead. She backed into the room, shivering as he opened the balcony doors.

Then he was gone.

For a moment she stared after him, touching her lips with her fingers, still amazed at his kiss . . . amazed at his love, at the very fact that he had been there, that he had come to her . . .

That he loved her, oh, really loved her! There was a future beyond this horror that loomed over her, a future together, a life of love and laughter, good and rich. All things lay ahead with promise and splendor.

But there was still this matter of danger first, treachery to be revealed.

She went to her closet for a gown, nervously scrutinized the

oom, became content that nothing was amiss, and returned to her
ed.

There she could not dwell on the present. She could only sigh
with contentment, run her hand over the place where he had been,
and dream of the day when she could tell him that their love had
bore fruit, that they would soon be parents; dream of the life that
grew within her, of that day when she and Warwick would welcome
that beloved being into their world . . .

All things seemed possible now. She would know no weakness.
Warwick was with her again. And he loved her.

Loved her . . .

She was radiant when she awoke, humming when Berta
appeared with her tea, oblivious of the woman who had been such
a horrid thorn in her side. She drank her tea in a leisurely manner,
smiled at Berta's choice of a gown, and inquired with cordial
concern as to the woman's state of health.

Berta, naturally, eyed her with suspicion, yet Ondine could
continue to smile with great smugness, for there was nothing
suspect, nothing that Berta might find.

Downstairs, Ondine greeted her uncle and Raoul with unfeigned
enthusiasm; it was easy to do so now. With Warwick about, she
was certain that she could soon bring about the downfall of these
two, and that belief brought her confidence.

"You slept well, did you, my dear?" William asked, and she
knew that he was baffled, ever suspicious, but as with Berta, what
could he discover? Ondine's smile was radiant, her eyes were
bright. She was able to look upon Raoul as if she were indeed
anxious to claim him as a lover.

"I slept wonderfully, Uncle. I have never found such comfort
in my bed!" she said demurely, eagerly helping herself to fresh
baked bread.

Raoul laughed, excited by her appearance, believing that the
brightness in her eyes shone for him, that all she offered would
soon be his.

"There will be greater comfort when you come to mine," he
said.

She might have laughed in his face; she carefully lowered her eyes instead, glad that a flush suffused her cheeks, for it seemed to please her uncle mightily.

And so breakfast passed. Ondine idled about, sipping more tea, when her uncle reported that he had work to do in the study and asked Raoul to accompany him. When they were gone, Ondine once again took care that no one noticed her and slipped upstair to her uncle's chambers.

She tore into his desk, determined, excited, and then slowly disappointed, for even with her most tedious perusal of all paper and documents, she could find nothing.

She sat back then, despondent, yet even as defeat settled over her, excitement began to grow again.

She leaned forward, for she noticed something ingrained on her uncle's blotter. She moved forward, staring more closely, and shivers filled her as she realized that though the documents he had threatened her with were not here, they had been written here She could see that someone had practiced her handwriting here Practiced it, until her signature was almost perfect. What perfec proof against them!

Oh, how she longed to snatch the blotter from the desk! She bit her lip and removed her hands from it. She could not go running from the house with it! And yet it might well be exactly what she needed. Any man of decent eye could see what had been practiced against her. However, she needed to have strength behind her strength to invade the place, to seize the evidence. If she gave herself away now, the blotter would be destroyed before she could use it.

Ondine departed the chamber carefully, slipping back into her own room, where she might have privacy to control her excitement But she'd barely closed her door before Berta knocked and entered without leave to do so.

"I've come back to clean," she told Ondine sourly. "Seems there's mud all about your bed!"

"Oh?" Ondine murmured. "Perhaps my boots carried it in."

Berta just stared at her, then said, "Raoul waits for you down stairs."

"Does he? Thank you."

She quickly escaped Berta's glare, rushing down the stairs t meet Raoul. He caught her hands and snapped his fingers at Berta, who had followed her to the landing.

"Bring the duchess her cloak, Berta. We're going for a walk."

Berta complied, and Ondine swept the silver fox about herself, waiting patiently with downcast eyes while Raoul adjusted the hood about her head.

She took his hand meekly, yet when she saw that they were returning to the bench at the lean-to by the forge, she was ready to pull back.

"Raoul, 'tis so cold today—"

"My dear, 'tis the only place we can talk without being overheard!"

Oh, if you only knew who was listening! Warwick's temper was such a slender thread, and knowing now that he listened made her performance ridiculously difficult.

Once seated, Raoul ardently took her hands. "You must tell me everything about this man—his looks, his name, exactly where you came across him. I must find him quickly!"

"Uh—he's blond!" she replied quickly. "Very blond. His hair is almost as pale as moondust. And his eyes are very blue. Nordic descent, I would think," she mused.

"And his name?"

"Tom."

"Tom—what?"

"Miller. Aye, that's it. Tom, the miller's son. 'Cept he turned to thievery rather than grain. And if he has not been hanged yet, he hides out in the forest near Westminster."

"I'll find him!" Raoul swore. "I'll find him! And then, my love, nothing will stand between us. Ondine, kiss me! Give me just one kiss. Feel the ardor in my lips, the passion in my heart! Let me touch you—"

The door to the smithy suddenly swung full wide. Warwick came upon them, a red glowing shoe held out before him in a set of prongs. He stared at the two with a feint of surprise, but without apology.

Raoul stared at him heatedly, swore something beneath his breath about uncouth peasants, and then yelled, "What are you doing here!"

"I am the blacksmith," Warwick said, watching the shoe cool.

Ondine drew her hands hastily from Raoul's, aware by the glitter of Warwick's eyes that his temper was as hot as the shoe he had formed.

"Raoul, I'm freezing!" she muttered. But it seemed that Raoul was distracted then, too. From the steps of the house his father waved to him in impatience.

"My love, I'll be right back."

Frowning, he ignored Warwick, touched her cheek, and went off at his father's beckoning.

Warwick did not come near her, but his whisper sent a chill sweeping down her spine.

"I warned you, my love, to watch your step!"

"It's near over!" Ondine said excitedly, careful to keep her eyes forward. "I've found something—"

Raoul was turning back to them.

"Tell me in your room tonight."

"Nay! You cannot come there!" She discovered herself blushing furiously. "Berta found all your dirt!"

"Then, my love, see that you track in mud of your own, for I shall be there!"

"Warwick!" she gasped, yet to little avail. He had already turned back to the forge. Ondine jumped to her feet, eager to elude Raoul before he could persist. She thought that she could handle her cousin; she did not think that she could manage Warwick.

She passed Raoul by on the snow. "I am so cold! My dear cousin, we'll meet again at dinner!"

She sped back to the house, highly agitated, yet still elated. She found solace in her room, alone with the beating of her heart, with her excitement—and with her dread.

Too soon, though, Berta made an appearance with a meal tray, and it seemed as soon as that tray was gone, her bath came. It didn't matter. She was still in such a high state of nervousness that she barely noticed Berta.

But Berta noticed her. She eyed the girl's young body when she stepped from the bath, moving slowly with her towel.

And though Ondine gave Berta no thought whatsoever, Berta was thinking only of her.

She judged, and came to a satisfied conclusion.

She finished with Ondine's hair, then quickly took her leave

Ondine was very, very glad to be left alone. She sighed as Berta left.

"Thank God that witch is no more upon me!" she railed in a whisper of disdain.

Yet she would not have been so elated if she had known that Berta had gone straight to William.

But at that moment she had no premonition of doom. She was dreaming of Warwick again, daydreaming of the night they had shared together, dazed with the beauty of love so sweetly requited.

She went to dinner, still in that dreamy state. Raoul was unerringly polite, and with Warwick's iron-hand presence nearby, she was even better able to play the sweet betrothed to the hilt. And she was so glad of her discovery that morning, so confident, that she noted nothing strange in her uncle's behavior. William was most decidedly in a rare courteous mood!

"Your glass, my dear, is empty, shall I fill it for you?"

"Aye, Uncle."

"More beef? More fowl?"

"Ah, nay, I think. Thank you."

"Ah, you appear a little worn! You mustn't play tonight, or tarry here, but go to your room and rest."

"I am a bit weary."

Weary! She was overjoyed. Everything was going her way . . .

After the briefest kiss upon the forehead from Raoul, she was able to escape to her room. She dressed herself in a simple gown and waited. Then, waiting, grew restless and anxious. She stripped away the gown she had donned and wrapped herself instead in the silver fox fur cloak. With that cover and nothing beneath it, she hovered near the balcony, waiting again, anxious again.

Midnight came, and with it appeared Warwick.

She greeted him with a glad cry, throwing her arms about him.

"Oh, my love! I'm so glad to see you, but so frightened. It's dangerous . . . "

"I had to come, you know that. I tried to be cleaner, but I dared not shave."

"I care not how you come to me."

"Love me . . . "

"I do."

He wrapped her tightly into his arms, rubbed his chin against her hair, breathing in her scent. His arms were about the soft fur of the cloak, and he thought that he'd never seen her more beautiful, felt a touch softer than the silver fur, unless that touch be the silk of her flesh.

"Love me now . . . "

"Gladly, oh, Warwick . . . "

"The cloak—there's nothing beneath it."

"Nothing—but all of me. All that loves you, so desperately, milord!" she replied, and his hands cast the cloak from her, and he thought that, aye, here was softness, sleekness, beauty, greater than silver or gold.

Ah, yes, glory came with darkness, with midnight, with words whispered in firelight and shadow! He threatened her again about Raoul, but not until they'd satisfied those first intensive needs, not until they lay together, damp with contentment, arms entwined. Then she teased him with questions about his past—about the lady Anne and the nights he had ridden away from Chatham.

"I had to ride out or else go mad!" he swore to her. "For you see, I did not dare to love you."

"It wasn't another woman?"

"Never," he swore. "Never, from the very first time I laid my eyes upon you."

"Oh, Warwick!" She kissed him hard and with loving enthusiasm, leaning against him, adoring just that very natural and intimate contact of their bodies, the amber glow in his eyes, the rugged wonder of his face.

"But what of Anne?"

He shrugged. "Anne was just—there. Ondine, I did not deceive Genevieve—ever. And though she was tender and sweet, I did not love her, not as I love you."

"Oh, Warwick!" she repeated, and she kissed him again.

"As to Raoul . . . " He growled low in his throat.

And only then did she remember that they were very near out of the dilemma.

"Warwick!"

"What!"

"I've found it, well, not 'it,' but something that might well clear me! There's a blotter, on my uncle's desk, and it's quite easy to see that someone practiced my handwriting there!"

He scowled where there should have been pleasure. "You were prowling around his chambers."

"I had to—"

"Nay! What if he had caught you!"

"But I must—"

"Nay! I will get this blotter. Tomorrow. You will not go near those rooms again. I'm at the end of my patience. I will get that evidence you have discovered, and we will have done with this. I'll find it tomorrow, and we leave tomorrow night."

She paused, burying her face in his neck. "Warwick, it will not be enough."

"What?"

She swallowed back a little sob.

"Please . . . give me just a few more days! The blotter might prove something, but it will not clear my father's name!"

He sighed. He didn't believe she could find proof to clear her father's name. "Three days, Ondine, no more. I cannot tolerate Raoul even touching you! On the third night, we leave!"

"You'll come for me here?" she inquired softly.

"Nay—you'll come to me at the blacksmith's cottage, as soon as you can escape after dinner." He hesitated. "I like not the idea of your slipping from the balcony." Again he paused, turning to take her passionately into his arms.

"I love you, Ondine," he said, holding her tight, all the rugged planes of his face tense, strong, and endearingly handsome. "But alas, it seems that very balcony beckons me again."

She clung to him, despising the moment that he left her.

"Will you come tomorrow night?"

"Aye."

" 'Tis so dangerous!"

"Madam, I cannot stay away!" he told her. Then he held her once again, loathe to go, knowing he must.

Daylight was returning.

London

Chapter 27

Clinton and Justin had taken a small house right on the river. It was not a difficult task for them to question and query, mainly because Justin had always been friends with young Buckingham, and Buckingham was known for his vast social endeavors. They spent their time in a whirlwind of activities, from theatrical entertainment at court to carousing the streets in near drunken stupors. They invited guests for dinner, they played in ribald fashion with any number of young swains and certain ladies known for being far less than discreet.

To most eyes it would appear that they were no more or no less than the noble rich, sewing wild oats with a certain decadence.

But it was from one of the young ladies—an earl's sixth daughter with little chance of a dowry and an even poorer chance of securing a sound husband—that Clinton received his first decent clue.

One extremely pleasant evening as they lay together in his bed, he learned from her that one of the king's guards had retired from the court after that long-ago day of the joust, giving the king no valid reason for his request, yet begging that he be released from duty. When Clinton demanded to know what his companion could really know of such things, she admitted that she had been clandestinely involved with the man, and therefore had a good understand ing of his feelings. Her father had ended the affair, determined that she marry within her station, even if her husband should prove to be an aged ogre.

The lady's name was Sarah, and Clinton grew quite fond of her, not only for her youth and beauty, but her frankness, honesty, tenderness, and passion. He did not go so far as to make any admissions to her, but he told her that it was most urgent he meet with the man. She agreed to help him. By the following afternoon she returned to the house on the river, telling Clinton that he and Justin might meet with the man at an alehouse near Charing Cross.

Night came. Though Clinton was too enamored of Sarah to trust his judgment regarding her, Justin was not, and he decided to trust her. He looked Sarah up and down when they were due to depart, noting the excitement in her lustrous brown eyes and her obvious adoration when she gazed upon his cousin. He knew of her from Buckingham. Her father offered her nothing and kept her in tight rein. She had in turn offered her own form of obedience, chancing no elopement, but lifting her small chin and living her life as she would, a guest at the king's court, a companion to his queen, free to enjoy some of her youth before that "ogre" of a husband, eager for young flesh with dowry or no, might be found.

"She'll have to come with us," Justin told Clinton. "How else will we know that we've discovered the right man? It would be even more dangerous should we make a mistake in identity."

Sarah placed a small hand into his. "John Robbins is wary of this meeting, Clinton. I understand none of this, but he is deeply afraid of something. He said that he will see you only where there are a multitude of people. I believe he fears that someone seeks his life."

Justin gazed at Clinton over Sarah's burnished brown curls and raised an eye. They had to trust someone, and in time, others might talk and realize that they had been quizzing everyone about a long-ago day when the Duke of Rochester had lifted his sword against the king and had been slain in turn.

"We all go, I say," Justin stated softly.

Shrugging, Clinton helped Sarah into her cloak, and they went out into the streets to hire a carriage.

The alehouse was crowded when they entered, filled with the riffraff of London, riotous and smoky. Men were puffing on pipes, and with the soot from the cooking and heating fires, the place seemed cast into deep mist and shadow.

"Charming," Justin commented. People were everywhere; it seemed doubtful that they should find a place on a bench to sit, much less discover a certain man amongst so many.

"We'll go toward the far corner," Sarah suggested, "for the greatest shadow is there, and then John Robbins will look for us."

A bawdy drunk tried to waylay Sarah on their journey through the room. Clinton whacked him once upon the arm, and the man groaned with shock. "Eh, guv'ner! Meanin' no disrespect! Just tryin' fer a little fun, sir!"

"Try elsewhere!" Justin snapped. "Can you not tell a lady of breeding, man?"

The husky drunk began to laugh. "Ah, sires, you know not the place, eh?"

"What?" Justin pressed him.

The drunk reddened and stared into the foam of his ale. Then he gave off a wheezing laugh.

"Breeding!" He looked back up to Justin a little apologetically. "Ye're some noble line yerself, my young lord, so I can see. Yet not so young, methinks, to have ascertained that noble blood can little rule noble flesh!" He fell silent, gripping his mug, then motioned for Justin to come closer. "'Tis a room in back, sire. Commoner and lord, wench or lady, may go there and find whatever they wish in"—he grimaced—"deviations in *amore!* Ye kin what I'm sayin'?"

Justin lowered his lashes in a secret smile; aye, he knew what was being said. Buckingham should have known this place well! A lord might come here for a casual and easily paid affair; equally, a lady of the finest pedigree might don a cloak and mask and find entertainment secret from family or friends. The drunk had merely assumed Sarah to be a young lady on the hunt for an adventure that "society" would not allow her.

He dropped a coin on the man's table, glad to know more of this place they had come to haunt. "Have an ale on me, friend, but warn your companions—this young lady is not for the taking."

"Thank ye, sire! Thank ye!" the drunk mumbled, and Justin hurried along to join Clinton and Sarah.

They found a bench in the far corner. Justin ordered ale, and they sat, eyeing everyone that came and went within the alehouse. In time a figure approached them, a tall, lean man, heavily cloaked in gray wool, appearing much like a holy father or a pilgrim.

He knew them, or he knew Sarah, for he slid into the bench beside Justin, reaching for his ale, as if it had been ordered for him. He kept his head lowered, and it was difficult to see his features, yet Justin did glean that he was a man of about thirty years, aged and beaten for that time, nervous and sad of eye.

"I have come for Sarah's sake only," he told them. "Talk quickly to me, and I will answer what I may."

Once, just once, he stared quickly up at Sarah. Something wistful touched his eyes and passed, and again he stared into the mug of ale.

"I need to know something of a day when the king's life was threatened and a man lay dead in the wake," Justin told him.

John Robbins stiffened. " 'Tis long past," he said, "and nothing to be gained of it. The duke is dead; his daughter also, I must think."

Justin gripped his arm. "Nay, she lives! And so does she need help."

John Robbins stared quickly about the room; even here he was afraid.

"Man, we do not threaten your life!" Justin assured him. "Does someone do so, then?"

"Aye, and not my own! Were I to be discovered in this speech—" He sighed, swallowed a long draft of ale, then said, "I've an old mother, living out her final days. Four sisters, young, lovely, and innocent. Perhaps 'tis not me that would be struck, yet these I love."

"By who?" Justin demanded.

At last the cowled man looked him full in the face. "You tell me—that she lives? The daughter? What proof have I? She ran that day, and all that I could do for her was to refrain from catching her! Even then I dared not speak, for *all* were so enraged on behalf of the king. *I did not know what I had seen myself,* and before the time came that I pondered the incident clearly, a man had come to me."

"What man? Deauveau—William Deauveau?"

He shook his head. "Nay, the son. Raoul. He carried on his

hands the old man's blood. And he told me he knew well the place where my mother lived, and that were he to die himself, the order was already set and paid that my sister should be taken—her throat cut.''

He paused, lifting the ale to his lips once again, as if he could not wet them enough. He stared about the table bleakly. ''Even were it not for the threat, there seemed little I could do. You understand, it was like a magician's trick—done so fast. The sword was not there—then it was. And then the old duke died, and all were outraged, seeking his daughter, ready to slay her upon the spot.''

''There is nothing to fear!'' Clinton told him heatedly. ''The king himself is eager that the girl be cleared; that she seize Deauveau Place from those who hold it!''

John Robbins stared at them distrustfully. ''What is this thing to you, then? How do I know there is reason to risk those I love? What tells you that the daughter lives, and what assurance have I that the king is on your side?''

''Chatham,'' Justin said softly. ''My brother is the Earl of North Lambria—''

''Charles's great champion . . .'' Robbins murmured.

''Aye, the same. Even now he lurks as a servant on the Deauveau estate, keeping watch upon the duke's daughter, because she is his wife. We are Chathams, and I swear to you that we carry great weight—''

''Chathams!''

It was a female voice that interrupted him from behind. In great dismay Justin turned, already wary of the voice. He stiffened, like one preparing for battle.

''Lady Anne,'' he muttered.

''Aye, and so wondrously surprised to see you!''

Crooning, she moved around to join them; her appearance was too much for John Robbins. He bolted, knocking everyone from his path.

''Oh, be damned!'' Justin roared, jumping to his feet to give chase. He was but vaguely aware that Anne was unconcerned at all the activity, and she sat in the very spot from which he had departed.

Justin stumbled his way through the drunks and tables after

John Robbins. He lost no time, yet when he reached the street, there was no sign of Robbins. Though he looked in all directions, he could not find a clue to follow, for the snow was trampled to a black mush that allowed for no prints.

Heaving a great sigh, he at last gave up and returned to the tavern.

Anne! Oh, bloody damn her! If she wasn't always turning up when she was least wanted! Turning up—and twisting knives, so it seemed. She was leaning over the table, talking, as Justin approached their group. He shook his head briefly to Clinton in silent admission that their quarry had been lost.

Anne! He should have known, he realized ruefully, that she might be part of the clientele of such a place! Having failed in pursuit of Warwick, she was too lusty a wench to spend time seeking out another of his ilk. What drew men to her also caused them to tire of her. Her very mien spoke of forbidden and carnal pleasure, and promised at the same time that she should never be trusted.

Warwick! He swore to himself as he thought of his brother. Little might Warwick have known that simple pleasure would have these consequences. It had been a heated affair, a negligent indulgence upon the part of the Earl of North Lambria, but it would haunt them all, so it seemed, for an eternity. Warwick's marriage still meant nothing to Anne. Fair or foul, Justin knew, Anne meant to have him back. She could not comprehend that Ondine was no light infatuation for Warwick. Much more than his wife, she was the one woman he could adore, in passion and tenderness, forever.

He sighed wearily. Anne was just a damnable thorn in his side for the moment, accosting them at precisely the wrong moment. Yet she was far more than a mere irritation, for now they would have to hunt and pray and spend long, long hours searching for John Robbins and swearing to him that they could protect him and his family if he came forward with the truth.

"Justin! How very rude for you to depart just as I arrive!" Anne said sweetly, moving so that he could sit.

Justin noticed that Clinton appeared so tense, he might be ready to kill; Sarah was flushed, yet her eyes were bright, like one ready to do battle.

"You disrupted us, Anne," he said lightly, retrieving his ale then, for he felt he needed it badly.

"Oh, I saw! I do apologize, yet who should suspect that you were involved in a mysterious assignation!" Anne laughed. "Do tell me all about it, Justin! Who was that man?"

"I told her that we'd a horse stolen," Clinton said quickly, impatiently. "That we found this character to give clue to the thief—but have now lost him."

Justin shrugged and stared at Anne. "So you have heard." He smiled pleasantly, determined to become the aggressor before she could plague them further with questions.

"Anne . . . Lady Anne! Now, what on earth would you be about in a lowly—brothel such as this?"

Anne shrugged, tossing back her dark hair, smiling at Justin, eyes sparkling with vivid energy. "Oh, I do grow bored of some of the endless protocol at court! 'Tis fun to view the lowlife now and then; 'tis exciting, don't you think?"

Justin stared at her a long moment and thought that she was, indeed, a striking woman. Beautiful . . . and so completely sensual in every word and movement that any man felt his blood stir at the sight of her, at the sound of her husky words. There was that undeniable sultriness about her. Yet he thought that she did not compare with his sister-in-law. Ondine's golden beauty was an even greater thing. The carriage of her head was so alluring, the sound of her voice so lovely, even beguiling. She had courage in abundance, which Anne did not lack, but she had more. Ondine carried a passion within her that Anne lacked: where she loved, she would love deeply; whom she honored, she would honor forever. Despite that sensual stirring that Anne could cause, Justin felt that all masks had been lifted; he knew Anne for all that she was—and wasn't—and decided that he was enough the rogue himself to enjoy a game of wits with her.

He smiled in turn at brilliant eyes.

"Tell me, do you come here only to 'view' others?"

She laughed softly, untouched by the taunt. "Justin Chatham, you, sir, are a blackguard. Tell me why the question, and perhaps I will give an answer."

"An idle one, merely."

"Umm," Anne murmured, then her eyes flashed across the table. "How strange that Sarah comes here, too!"

"On my cousin's arm," Justin commented.

Anne's eyes widened with mischievous humor. "Ah, yes, and what a fine arm! Clinton, at times I do believe you the finest specimen of a well-structured breed! Why, 'tis your work, I would think. Shoulders broad, arms that bulge. Ah, yes, fair Sarah! What an arm you've chosen! Yet don't deceive yourself, dear. Your father'll not approve Clinton. He's no real Chatham, you know, but takes his name from the house and grounds! He's the bastard branch, poor Sarah! No marriage there, alas! But I must agree . . . for the sake of lust alone, surely you could have chosen no one better, for I do understand that abilities run in families, just as eye color, or height! You choose your lovers well."

Justin held his breath; he wanted to throttle Anne then and there—Clinton's temper was notoriously near to Warwick's. Only Anne would dare to say such things, and perhaps even she had pushed too far this time. He turned to answer Anne in scathing fashion before Clinton could reply, yet it seemed unnecessary, for Sarah was no little mouse herself.

"Ah, Anne, you do speak truly! I'm ever so glad of that strong arm to lean upon! I choose my lovers with the very greatest care, and then, though marriage eludes me, I give my heart to one at a time. Chatham? Aye, I find that the name fits him well, for 'tis a noble family, and I find him most noble."

"Bravo!" Anne cried, clapping delightedly. She turned once again to Justin, carelessly dropping the matter. "I'd heard that you and Clinton were drinking and rousting and probably deflowering a score of unwary young virgins. Where is that brother of yours, the great lord of Chatham himself? And his fair and delightful bride, of course?"

Justin sipped his ale and grinned conspiratorially. "Ah, I would think that you could well imagine the scenario, Anne! They're young, they're lovers, so passionate, so in love! They've told none of their actual whereabouts; they've gone off, entirely alone, to enjoy none but one another!"

Anne kept smiling, yet she spoke through her teeth, affording Justin endless satisfaction.

"How—lovely. And how romantic. Yes, I'd say I can well

imagine the scenario. He takes a common gallows' bride. The two of them—off to live as peasants!''

"Needing nothing but love!" Clinton added charmingly.

Whatever wounds she had inflicted upon them were avenged in that one smiling moment. Anne stood, having tired of the conversation, so tense that her smile was strained indeed.

"Well, I must be off. I shall leave you to your hunt. But, oh, I have heard you're arranging the most wonderful dinner parties! You must invite me soon."

"With the greatest pleasure, Anne!" Clinton stated, winding his arms around Sarah and pulling her to him. "That is, of course, if you can bear the company of a bastard branch."

"Don't be silly, Clinton! I find bastards—like this rubble—most amusing!"

She was gone, but Clinton took no offense. He laughed, then shook his head, staring at Justin. "How could anyone so very beautiful be so evil?"

"I don't think she's evil, darling," Sarah murmured, stroking his cheek. "She's like a spoiled child; if she does not get what she wants, she thinks until she discovers a way to procure it—no matter who she hurts in the way. And," Sarah mused, "she wanted Warwick Chatham very badly. I think she actually loves him."

"I don't think she knows the meaning of the word," Justin said impatiently. "And she did some serious damage here tonight."

Sarah slipped a hand across the table to cover his. "I can find John Robbins again. I know that I can."

Justin nodded worriedly. Time was playing against them. He didn't like the fact that Warwick was at Deauveau Place. Warwick was usually as careful in planning as he was powerful in a fray, but this, this was different. Justin could not forget how his brother had looked when they had given chase the day that Ondine had disappeared from the races. Nor could he forget the utter horror on his face when they had discovered Ondine so very near to death in the chapel.

He sighed. "Time . . . time plays against us. We must hurry. We need John Robbins to come to the king; we need to sweep into Deauveau Place before . . ."

"Before what?" Sarah queried softly.

"Before my brother sees his wife too close to this vicious cousin of hers and loses his mind, and thus his temper!"

"How did you two allow him to go there!" Sarah exclaimed.

"No one tells Warwick what he will and will not do." Justin sighed, then he rose, discouraged, yet determined afresh. "Come, let's get out of this wretched place."

Clinton and Sarah followed his lead. Justin noted Sarah's soft hand on his cousin's arm and felt a little pang. Though she was whispering, Justin could hear Sarah's words.

"She is right, though, you know. My father would never let us wed. Yet I care not, for I do love you—and I will be with you!"

Damn Anne! Justin thought for the thousandth time—so casually did she wound others!

But then he dismissed her from his thoughts, for he was worried once again about how they should find John Robbins a second time. Robbins would now be forewarned, and if he was the least hesitant, he could surely make a true disappearance into any number of hellholes within London.

Justin had no idea of it at that time, but he should have been much more concerned with Anne.

She had not left the alehouse, but retreated to that room beyond where drink was imbibed with a heartier measure; where deals were made, fantasies brought to light, if only for an evening.

Hardgrave was sitting there, bleary-eyed, laughing as he diced with the owner of the establishment. Two very young girls sat swaddled at a bench beyond the gaming table. Anne absently ascertained that Lyle had planned those two for his night's amusement, yet he felt the night so young he had ample time to gamble before wenching.

She had no patience with any of it.

Ignoring the game at hand, she rushed up to him, hands on her hips.

"We've got to go!"

"Go!" Hardgrave growled with annoyance, casting her an impatient glance. "Why, I've just begun—"

Anne leaned down and whispered to him. He looked up at her

with a gaze of bleary confusion, then slowly seemed to comprehend her words.

"Where?" he asked her hoarsely, pushing back his chair to rise.

She smiled, very aware that she had his full interest. She placed a hand upon his arm, treating him as she might a small child.

"Now, Lyle!" she cajoled. "We mustn't race off madly—and chance this thing! We must think and plan carefully, and then set to work. There is a way—"

"So you told me before!" he snapped harshly.

"Lyle! Come, now, we must be alone to talk. Perhaps this will be our very last chance, so we must take care. I do have an idea."

Hardgrave groaned. "Your last idea came near to setting me in the Tower!"

"But we've better forces working with us now; I think we'll find ready accomplices."

"How do you know all this?"

She brought her lips to his ear, whispering heatedly.

"I overheard a telling conversation! Justin Chatham was here— I tell you *I know what I heard!* And they are both very vulnerable. Warwick and his golden girl! Lyle, she is no commoner—yet better, still, for our designs. Oh, Lyle! Think on it! Feel it! Feel how dearly you want revenge on him, and think how dearly you crave her. Lyle, this strange partnership of ours may yet bear fruit. The girl for you, and Warwick, wholly mine, at last!"

Hardgrave tensed and reddened, fighting emotion. He dropped his dice on the table and grinned at the owner of the place. "Ye've made money on me tonight, Taddy, and I can't even sample the goods. Good night to you, lasses." He swept his hat to the girls on the corner bench. " 'Twasn't for lack of temptation, ladies!"

Anne caught him by the lace lapels on his frothed shirt, determined to get him out then; they needed some secretive and careful planning. Ah, she could almost feel Warwick in her arms again, desperately in search of solitude after the loss of another bride.

Hardgrave stumbled, then caught her arm, and together they left the alehouse. Outside, the clear cold air sobered him quickly, and he gazed down at Anne pensively.

Ah, yes, this strange partnership of theirs! It had nothing of love—yet it went deeper than that emotion. It was based on more than sex, more than an equal delight in sampling all that the world offered with no pretense.

It all centered upon Chatham—upon fostering lust and vengeance.

"Lyle! Think on it! That little witch of his made her appearance into our lives on the very day of your joust with Warwick! The joust you lost! She was there—running! Things do come full circle, do they not? Your greatest vengeance will be to take her from him!"

Lyle gazed into her scheming eyes, aglow with excitement for the future.

"Mmmm," he murmured. "As we planned it before, I shall have her—while a death certificate is forged. And you, at last, will have Chatham."

"Aye!" Anne breathed joyfully. "He'll forget her in time. Oh, I know that I can make him forget her! I shall make him happy, I can please him; I can please any man."

"I don't doubt it, my dear," Lyle Hardgrave muttered. "I don't doubt it at all." Dear Anne, he thought in silence, that is just where we part ways . . . You see, I do not want him happy again. I want him dead. Stone dead, like the walls of Chatham itself . . .

"I am still at a loss," he told his most perfect conspirator as he raised a hand for his driver to bring his carriage forward. "Our peasant girl is a lady, returned to her home. How shall we bring her forward—what accomplices?"

Anne moaned impatiently. "Do you remember nothing of that day?"

"Only that I was beaten," he retorted bitterly.

"The Duke of Rochester was slain that day for treason against the king's very person! Aye—you probably were too busy sulking to have known most of it! 'Twas the same day that Genevieve died, so I remember it all very well. Ondine, the silly nit of a girl, ran, and her family estate fell into hands that coveted it well! A relative took it over, an uncle or somesuch person. I believe from what I heard that she's returned home, and Warwick has gone there—as a servant, no less! There must be some grave dissension—I heard tell of a cousin she was to marry, but refused.

"Now surely, my darling lord, the densest man must see between these trees! The man who has taken over the property will not want it returned to the rightful heiress! And it's suspect that he would want the son to marry her now, lacking any knowledge of where she has been. I should think that she might easily, easily be purchased!''

''I would think that he would prefer her dead.''

''Nay, not dead! Just gone. We must think of something to promise him, that she will be taken from the country, never to appear again. And when you tire of her, such a thing can easily be managed!''

''As in the last time, Anne?'' Hardgrave taunted.

She lifted her chin in the air. ''Are you a coward in truth? Still afraid of Warwick Chatham?''

Hardgrave went rigid and a pulse ticked against his throat; she knew she'd hit the right chord.

''Let's get near this place, then, shall we?'' he demanded thickly. ''And get a message to this man that we might have, er, mutual interests.''

''Aye, let's. And let's do it in a hurry!'' Anne purred.

Chapter 28

There was something taking place in the morning; Ondine knew not what, but she awakened to the sounds of argument below.

She was still very tired—dazed as she came slowly to awareness. Such was the toll of her clandestine evenings. She recognized that someone argued, then she recognized the voices as her uncle's and Raoul's, but by that point a warning had come to them from somewhere that their shouts could well raise the roof and all and sundry would soon know their private business.

Ondine wondered if Berta hadn't been the one to warn them that they should be overheard, for soon after the voices lowered, Berta came into the room.

Ondine rolled over, groaning and pressing her face to the pillow. She didn't feel like dealing with Berta or facing another day! Yet what choice had she?

"Duchess, come, you must awake. Your uncle requests your appearance below with all haste."

"Does he?" Ondine murmured dryly.

"Duchess—"

"I am awake, Berta. I am awake."

She sipped her tea quickly and had little patience for assistance while she dressed. She was as anxious to see William as he was, apparently, to see her. It must be a busy and productive day; Warwick did not want her prowling about—she had to prowl about! Time was her enemy.

She sat on the edge of the chair before her dressing table as Berta worked on her hair, muttering nastily about the tangles. Ondine felt a brief humor then, for she longed to tell Berta that it was simply impossible to keep her hair totally unmatted when her husband chose to play with it all night.

Seconds later she descended the stairs. She found neither William nor Raoul seated at the table. Instead, both of them stood stiffly, at odds across the room, ignoring the steaming platters that awaited them on the sideboards. The stranger—the tall muscled sallow-looking man who had taken dear Jem's place as steward and valet—waited just inside the doorway for the meal to begin, his hands behind his back, a facial expression nonexistent.

"Ah, at last, dear Niece!" William exclaimed, staring upon her with jaundiced eyes. "You've decided to join us."

There wasn't even a pretense of courtesy to his words; they were barked out in severe warning that more would come.

"Am I late?" she asked sweetly, sliding into her chair.

"Late, aye, Niece."

In question and reproach, one delicate brow slightly arched, she stared at Raoul, sullen and terse across the room.

Raoul blushed and looked away from her. Ondine shrugged, then turned to the apelike servant in the hallway, a man surely chosen for his blind obedience to her uncle alone.

"The tea, please. Now. I do not know your name."

The man started and looked to William. William appeared as if he were about to explode, but then he smiled with a casual and evil leer and said, "By all means, do serve the duchess her tea! His name, Ondine, is Berault, should you need anything further."

"Thank you, Uncle. Thank you—Berault."

"Berault, you may leave us," William snapped.

Ondine, quaking somewhat inside, for she knew not where this was leading, or what William might have discovered, added cream to her tea with what she hoped was nonchalance and stared across the room at Raoul again. This time he met her eyes with pleading in his own. He was keyed and angry.

She finished fussing with her tea and gazed toward her uncle, expectantly. "You complain of my tardiness to a meal, yet once I appear, you spend the time staring at me. Have I grown horns, Uncle?"

"Horns, Ondine? Nay, 'tis not likely. You yet appear as sweet as honey—and pure as driven snow."

He walked to her at last, standing over her. Then placing his hands upon the table, he stared into her eyes.

"By the saints, girl, you do look weary! Shadows beneath the eyes—pale, drawn. Are you quite sure you've come home with no illness?"

"I feel absolutely fine. And yet, sir," she added, narrowing her eyes in prayer that she might cordially force him to his point, "I am ever so amazed that my health should concern you so! Truly, Uncle, there is little pretense between us! I imagine that you would be sublimely pleased to hear that I was ailing desperately—upon my death bed, at that."

He touched her chin, lifting it, and his touch did not disturb her, for she felt such hatred then that it was easy to return his stare with loathing in her own.

"You're very young, my dear, with too much vitality, to so conveniently leave this life!"

"That is correct, Uncle," she retorted softly. "I'd never do anything—anything at all—to make things easy for you! And since *God* knows my right, I believe that I shall maintain splendid health!"

Grimly he released her. "Splendid health! We're back to the matter at hand! You see it is precisely since you are young—betrothed to Raoul—that I needs must look to your every concern. If you will not die, you will become a part of our inner family."

She sipped her tea, feigning a disinterest, yet growing ever more nervous.

"That has all been decided and arranged, has it not?"

"Oh, yes; it is in the offing. For Raoul's pleasure—certainly not my own!"

"Then . . . ?" she inquired pleasantly.

He smiled at her, with such pleasure and malice, that she was certain he had made a damning discovery. Warwick! Had he been caught coming from her room? Was he injured, slain? Oh, God!

Her stomach seemed to catapult within her; the room took on a hazy hue as that terror settled over her.

"Ondine, my dear—" William began.

But he was not able to continue. The door suddenly burst open; Berault had returned, and no longer did his sallow countenance bear no expression. He was highly agitated.

"I did not call for you!" William shrilled.

"But—"

"Must I repeat myself endlessly? I do not wish to be disturbed!"

"But it's the king!" Berault managed to say hastily.

"The king?" William repeated, amazed.

"Aye, the king! Even now, his carriage comes up the drive! He has an escort of at least a dozen. We're ill-prepared; we know not what to do!"

Ondine slid uneasily from her chair, so very grateful that Charles was near, still so terrified that it might be too late for Warwick. Oh, dear God! What had happened? Then she remembered that she should be frightened of the king before her uncle and Raoul.

"Oh!" she gasped in distress.

William cast her an absent gaze. "Don't be a fool! Act naturally! I've made no complaints against you—you'll be fine. Berault, go to the stables, quickly, so that all might be advised that his carriage need be taken, water offered the horses. Then go to the kitchen and advise Jem. He will see that our best ale is tapped, and that there is food prepared to offer His Majesty."

Berault instantly moved to follow William's orders.

Ondine watched him leave the room, then gasped, tears filling her eyes with sudden pain as her uncle grasped her hair at the nape, jerking it cruelly. His hold pulled her against him so that he might threaten in a hissing whisper at her ear.

"But, fair Niece, take care with your every word and motion. That you have returned, I can cover; if you should attempt to betray me with the slightest word or deed, I will instantly produce proof that you were in league with your father, plotting the king's murder. If I fall, girl, I swear you'll tumble with me! Death can be quick, as well you should know. You watched your father die. Oh, so fine a line exists between daylight and the grave! Force my hand and I will see that there is no choice by law but to sever your lovely neck; think to trap me, and you will die instantly, a knife within your heart.''

He did not release her, but dragged her down the hall with him. ''Leave go of me!'' she commanded her uncle heatedly. ''We've made our bargains; you do not need fear me!''

He did not release her, not until they all stood outside, awaiting the king.

It was true that the king had come with a retinue. Five guards rode ahead, five behind. The lead man announced the king's arrival, yet already all was in motion for his royal reception. Men raced from the stables to take the horses as the king's guard dismounted from them. The footman moved with a flourish to pull the step down for the king, and then Charles alighted, looking curiously about himself, a mischievous smile upon his handsome lips.

''Your Majesty!''

Ondine came quickly to him, dipping a low and graceful curtsy, kissing his ring. Her uncle was quickly behind her, ever as gracious. Raoul, too, was quite capable of a very elegant courtesy, making the entire greeting a pretty picture of perfect etiquette.

If only her heart were not so heavy with fear for Warwick. What else could have upset her uncle so?

Then she saw him. Even as she lowered her lashes before Charles, her eyes widened again, for Warwick was there. He had come with the men from the stables and was holding one of the guard's mounts, watching the display with the others.

''Duchess, 'tis glad I am to see your fair face!'' Charles said pleasantly, greeting her first in turn and kissing both her cheeks. ''Ah, child, I was so distressed that day you ran! You'd not have suffered without some proof of complicity, my dear. I heard rumor of such a thing, but no proof came to light, and so glad I am to hear that you've returned to your home!''

''Thank you, sire,'' she murmured, trying very hard not to burst into laughter, for Charles was a fine performer, and knowing that Warwick was very much alive and free had sent her into delirious relief.

''William, Raoul, 'tis good to see you, also.''

''Your Grace,'' William responded with a bow of the head. ''We are most grateful that you visit us here, at this our humble home.''

''Humble!'' Charles burst into laughter, then clapped William on the back. ''Why, sir, these are some of the finest lands in the country! Humble! Why, in purse, I'd dare to say that Rochester far exceeds my personal wealth.''

''Will you come into the house, Your Majesty?'' Ondine inquired. ''We are most eager to serve you.''

''Aye, of course. I've come for just a brief spell, but I did yearn to satisfy my own curiosity. Ah, pardon! It seems the snow has dirtied my boots—''

He paused, looking about, and Ondine frowned, not knowing his intention. She hadn't realized that Charles had noticed Warwick, roughly clad, unshaven, and sooted from the forge.

But he had. Oh, he had, and why not? For he had known Warwick many years, and they were as close as friends could be, given that one was the king. Charles appeared near devilish, and Ondine soon discovered why, for he lifted a hand to Warwick. ''You, young man! Aye, you, the tall fellow with the fine shoulders. Come here!''

Warwick started for but a moment, then turned over the mount he held to a young apprentice and approached the king, kneeling before him awkwardly.

''Good man for a smithy, Deauveau! Seems the job would become him, and him the job. How do you like service here, young sir?''

''Ah, it is good,'' Warwick murmured, still upon his knees. It appeared that the king was in no mood to release him quickly.

''My boots, young man, have become encrusted. Do clean them for me while you're down there, good fellow, will you?''

''Aye, Your Grace.''

The answer came a bit slow, but well and strong. Ondine barely kept from bursting into merry laughter as she met Charles's eyes over her husband's head. It seemed that only they had heard the grating of Warwick's teeth, that only they, together, could truly enjoy this moment of seeing the great Warwick Chatham, champion at arms, so sorely humbled!

''Ah, very good, my thanks there, boy! The best of luck to you, then!''

And with that, Charles stepped past him, slipping an arm about Ondine to lead her into the house.

He kept them a distance before William and Raoul and whispered into her ear, "I could not resist! A smith, eh?"

"A smith, sire, and I must say I enjoyed your entrance tremendously!"

"Knowing the circumstances of your relationship, my dear, I was quite sure you'd felt the blade of his domination now and then, and that our dear lord Chatham deserved a taste of his own medicine."

"Aye!" Ondine laughed softly, her heart light, her eyes sparkling brilliantly. "You knew, then, that he was coming here? That he intended such a thing?"

"I told him everything, my dear. He knows me well; he knew I hid the truth from him. You are not angry that I betrayed you?"

"I could bless you for it, yet I am afraid for him, for he does not wear humility with ease."

But the king grew sober then, his voice becoming softer. "Play 'tis one thing, and it seems we must all enjoy it when we may. Yet I—who did perhaps encourage this situation—do not like it much now. Have you discovered anything?"

She wanted to tell him about the blotter, that it gave clue at least to evil purposes. But she had no chance to speak—William was upon them.

"You have heard, Your Majesty, that my son and the duchess will wed, and the house will be one?"

"Ah, yes, indeed, I have heard rumor of the impending nuptials!"

They came into the hall. Charles shed his cloak, and Ondine saw that he was in full Stuart dress uniform, his sword at his side. Two of his guards followed him closely. When the king sat at the head of the table within the hall, they flanked him on either side.

He cast his gloves upon the table, a congenial guest, and accepted the ale that Jem quickly brought him from the kitchen. He gazed about and murmured pleasantly, "I have interrupted your morning meal! Come, and I will sit with you."

They took their places. The king refused to dine, but continued to smile as Berault served them food now grown quite cold.

No one remarked upon it.

"Alas—as long as all is well," Charles said, "I am pleased. My dear, in truth, I bear you no grudge for your father's act—

certainly, it was but a moment's madness on his part. I could not bear to think that you, such a fair young lass, might have conspired against me. But here I see it all! The peace and harmony amongst you! What more assurance could I have when these two men—your doting family—have given you their faith!''

"It did grieve me most terribly, sire," William vowed, "when my brother came to that fit of madness! That he should raise his arm against you . . . Sire, it was the most woeful day, yet now we seek to live past it."

"And live past it well," he murmured dryly, pulling his small blade from his hip and idly paring his nails with it. He emitted a sudden impatient oath. "Damn, but this blade needs a honing. Raoul Deauveau! Call that smith of yours here! I've a mind that man could make a finer thing of my blade!"

Raoul was instantly up, bowing and out. The king commented on the hall; William said again that they were grateful to him, glad that he had lifted his disfavor, though it was true that the family had been deserving of his anger.

Then Warwick entered the hall on Raoul's heel, his golden gaze already wary of what was to come.

"There you are! It seems I've a dull knife here, yet I'm convinced that you can set it to rights."

"Your Majesty, I shall do my best."

Warwick once again knelt at the king's side, next to Ondine, as he extended his hands to accept the knife. Charles dropped it to the floor.

"Ah, it seems the cold has numbed my fingers!"

"No difficulty there, sire," Warwick said smoothly, ducking to retrieve the knife. "I do live to serve you."

"Do you? How charming!" The king applauded. Ondine quickly looked down at her plate, lest she be tempted to laughter once again. Yet she had the feeling that the king meant more here than idle play, though she did not understand quite what he was doing. She longed to talk to Warwick herself, away from all prying ears, and discover whether he had managed to retrieve the blotter from her uncle's desk.

Perhaps Warwick had been called in so that he and Ondine could have a moment together, because Charles suddenly stood, moving far across the room to point out the window and ask a question about the usage of the land. William and Raoul came quickly to his side, leaving Warwick kneeling down beside Ondine.

She pretended to sip her tea, but whispered instead to him, her long hair a shield that hid their hurried conversation.

"Have you the blotter? We could get it to Charles now—"

"Nay! We cannot!" he responded with a hoarse breath of air. His golden gaze touched hers with firelit sparks. "It was gone; the desk was clean when I went there."

She stared at him with horror. He uttered some terse warning sound that reminded her they were not alone, and she swallowed back the despair and frustration that had seized her, turning to smile for the king.

"Ah, off your knees, man!" he told Warwick. "Go—see what you can do with my knife!"

Warwick rose, bowed briefly, and hurried from the hall. The king lingered long enough to finish his ale and comment once again that he bore the family Deauveau no grudge. Then he said that he must be gone, but would return.

"We'll send for your knife—" William offered.

"No need; I'd enjoy a view of the forge!" the king said, and sweeping his cloak about his shoulders, he started out himself with his customary long strides.

Raoul and William gazed at each other, then leapt to their feet to follow him.

Ondine remained where she was, pensive and worried once again. The blotter was gone. Yet how could they have known that she had seen it? Maybe they did not know. Maybe, once again, time had worked against her, and William had merely decided to clear his desk.

Oh, God . . . but then why her uncle's sharply sarcastic anger that morning? Something was afoot. But surely, now that the king had been here and seen her here, they would not dare to harm her.

Nay, she decided bleakly, that was a slender thread to cling to indeed! They had managed to murder her father before witnesses and come from it the heroes. Perhaps Warwick was right, and it was exceedingly dangerous to linger here at all. And now her scant hope had disappeared.

She sighed softly, squaring her shoulders. Dangerous or no, she would have to start over again. She had loved her father so dearly, and she loved the life she was carrying with all her heart. How could she not pit all her heart and strength into justice for that generation gone, and that to come?

Charles knew that William and Raoul Deauveau had followed him; he knew, too, that they would not dare to intrude upon him once he had closed a door.

And that was what he did, as soon as he entered the forge.

Warwick gazed up from his stone seat by the fire. He was not about to kneel again—he'd been on his knees enough to last a good ten years, much as he did honor his king.

He smiled ruefully, instead, offering Charles his sharpened blade, then sweeping a bow with the same mockery he'd received. "Your Majesty! I most humbly pray 'tis sharp as you desire!"

" 'Tis sharp as your tongue!" Charles retorted quickly, grinning, but he sobered quickly. "Tell me, in all haste, what goes on here."

Warwick sighed despairingly. "Nothing! Ondine thought she was on to something, but when I scaled the walls to retrieve this evidence she had discovered, it was gone. Charles—there is no hope here! She must understand that. She is blinded by that love she bore her father, too proud to retreat. If she finds these documents—these forgeries—they hold over her head, to what avail is that? It does not prove that her father did not raise his sword against you. I've told her I'll give her three days—including this one—and that is all. I'll take her from this country if need be; but I will take her from here, as is my right, so help me God! Those two are evil in the extreme, and we have come too far; she has endured enough. How many times may one woman cheat death?"

Charles stared at his passionate servant and sighed. "Ah, Warwick, that is why I determined to come now. I assumed that once they had seen me—and I had seen Ondine here, beneath their care—they would think twice before seeking to harm her." He hesitated a moment. "I am in accord with you, though. Linger here no longer than three days more. 'Tis better to forfeit the lands than her life."

Warwick nodded tensely.

"I must leave; I stay with a smith too long. 'Tis well I'm known for a liking of the common man!"

"Charles!" Warwick called when the king would leave. Charles turned back curiously. Warwick knelt to him once again, and this time in all sincerity and truth.

"Thank you. For your belief, for your care."

The king grinned slowly. "You saved my life once upon a time. Remember? And Chathams have remained loyal; I'll not forget the blood spilled on my father's behalf. You see, Warwick," he added, grinning crookedly with pain, "I understand Ondine's feelings well. My father, too, was killed by treachery, though it was of a different nature. Get off your knees now, for in all honesty, you are not a man to do well upon them!"

Warwick stood, and the king embraced him, then hurriedly took his leave. Following him and standing at the doorway, Warwick was able to hear the king cheerfully comment that he was well pleased with his knife. He watched the royal party depart, then turned back to the fire, glad that there was work to do, work to keep his hands busy while his mind remained in eternal worry and chaos.

Yet he paused when he would have set to melting steel, for with the king's departure, William and Raoul Deauveau had not returned to the house. They came back toward the forge, engaged in a fierce argument.

Warwick came to the open doorway and hovered just behind it in shadow, straining to make out their words while remaining beyond their vision. It was not difficult to do, for the tenor of their voices kept rising.

"I tell you it's true!" William rasped in fury.

"And I tell you it is no more than supposition!" Raoul retorted.

"Supposition! So tell me, Son, does that supposition not dismay you?"

"You're taking the word of a thick-bodied and thick-minded stinking peasant!"

There was a long silence; then came a long, long expulsion of air from William Deauveau.

"Berta is large, yes—I needed a large woman, in case your lovely and devious betrothed decided to be troublesome. But she is bright and knows women well. She would not make a mistake. Your sweet little virgin is definitely with child.''

Warwick was so startled that it seemed his heart ceased to beat; coldness . . . a blanket of coldness, like a river of snow, seemed to engulf him. His mind raced blankly for a moment, then pitched into a fever of emotion.

By God, he felt like thrashing her with a thousand lashes! How could she have done it! Left him, left Chatham, when she was carrying his heir? How could she play this dangerous game, when even more than their own lives was at stake?

Oh, fool that he was! A chambermaid had noted it, and he had not! He, her husband, who held her and cradled her and loved her through the night . . .

''I knew that she was no virgin, Father. She came to me with the truth—a truth she dared not tell you. And what matter does it make to you? I am the one taking the bride! One tryst, and virginity is lost; the difference is but a night—''

''You're not listening! The girl is not only deflowered, but carrying some lout's child!''

''That, too, Father, is easily handled! We need only keep her hidden once her condition is discovered; the child can be disposed of with little effort.''

''She'll surely love you and serve you well once you've slain her child!'' William scoffed.

Raoul began to laugh. ''What matter that, sir? We've already slain her sire!''

''We need to get rid of her now—''

''What? The king would surely be suspect! Damn you, Father, I will have her!''

''You are a fool! All sense and mind tucked into your pants!''

''Father—''

''Nay, I'll argue no more! Marry the bitch if you are so keen upon her! Take her—you but take yourself straight to hell!''

Warwick wound his fingers into fists of tension at his sides.

Nay, Raoul Deauveau and sire William, he thought, so enraged that before his eyes the world had turned red. Blood red. It is I who shall take you straight to the gates of hell!

''I wash my hands of it!'' William exclaimed, then said on a curious tone that was by far lighter, ''Do what you will, Raoul.

Ah, see to things here, Raoul. I'll not be about for our evening meal.''

"Where are you going?''

"Nowhere special. I've received a message from an old friend; I shall spend some time with her this evening.''

"A woman?'' Raoul chuckled. "Ah, Father. The fires of lust still burn brightly, eh?''

"Umm. Perhaps. We shall see. I shall go now, so you may have your precious beauty all to yourself for the evening. Your black widow, that is!''

"Father, I tell you, she has been broken to my will!''

William answered something, but they were walking away, and Warwick could hear them no more.

Perhaps it was good that they walked away. The awful anger, the anger that washed the world in a mist of red, was still within him. Had they lingered longer, he might have emitted a primal, tearing scream and rushed out to slay them both with his bare hands, or die in the attempt.

Ah, foolish action! For if he were to die, he would but leave Ondine at their mercy. Ondine . . . and their unborn child.

Yet one thing was certain: It was no longer Ondine's battle alone. In his heart, to the depths of his soul, he knew that the two usurpers must die—in fair fight—by his hand.

Ondine . . .

He set his mouth grimly, for at the moment he also had a most serious argument with his wife!

Chapter 29

At a bench in the rear of the White Feather, Jake sat lazily sipping a tankard of ale, legs pulled up, his back comfortably resting against the wall. He grinned, watching the activity in the room; a dice game in one corner, cards in the next. Men drank and laughed, and the tavern maids, their wondrous bosoms well exposed, laughed in turn and served more ale. A haunch of venison roasted on the open flame, creating a tempting aroma. It was cozy and warm, a fine shelter from the blustery cold that encompassed everything beyond the doors.

All in all, Jake thought, smiling as he saw that Molly was fixing him a plate of the venison, spooning rich gravy over the meat, he'd made out rather well on this particular adventure. The lord of Chatham was busy at an anvil, while Justin and Clinton were on the prowl in London. All he'd had to do was to endure the days with his eyes open and his ears tuned—a most convivial assignment! As it happened, Molly seemed to enjoy the warmth of his heart and minded not his gnome's face, so leisure had become a handsome sport, and he would most certainly be sorry to leave this place behind.

Molly placed his food before him, blushing like a bride, smoothing her hands over her skirt. "Ah, what a lass ye are, Molly!" he told her, placing the coin for the meal between the lovely plump pillows of her breasts. She flushed again, lightly slapping his hand.

"Now, ye eat that, sir, while it's still hot and good! And watch yer hands amongst the management!"

Jake broke into easy laughter, for the management was willing to sell most anything. But he cast a wink Milly's way and dipped a hunk of bread into the gravy, savoring the taste. For whatever else might take place here, none could deny that the White Feather boasted a fine cook and warm filling food.

"A taste to savor, Molly, lass!" he said approvingly, and added, "Only ye, yerself, lass, have the power to please the palate greater!"

"Ah, get away with ye, ye silver-tongued flatterer!" She stooped to give him a quick kiss, but Jake tensed suddenly, his eyes upon the tavern door.

It had swung open suddenly, taken from the hands of the latest customer by the force of the winter wind. Gusts swept into the place, carrying a sprinkling of snow.

Yet it was neither gusts nor the snow that Jake noticed, but the latest patron of the tavern.

It was the lady Anne.

Clad from head to toe in an encompassing cloak, all that one could see were her beautiful dark eyes, but Jake knew those dark eyes, aye, he knew them well!

Some young hearty called out against the cold, yelling that the door be closed. And then Jake saw that Anne was not alone; a great hulk of a man entered behind her, silencing the shouts by his mere appearance. His size and height signified a dangerous fellow, strong, and accustomed to using the sword and pistol in his belt.

"Hardgrave," Jake muttered in shock against Molly's lips.

Molly mumbled something, freeing herself from him in a fervor. "Now, Jake, a pinch on the rump be one thing, but—"

"Molly! Molly!" he brought his voice to a urgent whisper, needing to hold her near until he could shift around, placing his back toward the two who had just entered. "Molly, girl, do ye love me?"

"What is this, Jake?" she demanded suspiciously.

"Molly, do ye love me—just one little bit? 'Cause if ye do, then I need yer help now."

Molly frowned, but seemed to sense his tension. "All right, then, Jake, me love, what is it?" she asked in return, whispering as he did.

"Those two—the lady and gent what just came in—ye must wait on them, Molly, and ye must listen sharp to what they say."

Molly looked around to regard Hardgrave and Anne curiously. They were seating themselves at the long bench across the fire from Jake. Hardgrave cast his gloves upon the table, looking around the room with distaste. "Eh, innkeeper! Service here!"

"Why, he's not even sitting yet!" Molly said indignantly. "Must be some great lord or t'other."

"Molly, go ta him, please! Like a good lass. Hurry, now! And keep silent 'bout me, now!"

Molly hesitated just a second, then went scampering over to the table with her head humbly low.

Jake shrank as close as he could to the wall, straining to listen, then realizing that he didn't really have to. The tavern din, silenced when the door had burst inward, slowly rose again. Lord Lyle Hardgrave seemed to have no thought of being overheard.

"What have you got for wine here, girl?"

"None, this night, sir. We've ale—"

"Bring your best, and mind you, it must be your best. Give me no pig swill, or you'll wear it over your head, mind you!"

"Aye, the best!" Molly said, bobbing a curtsy. He went on to command a plate of venison and warned her that it must be fine, else she would wear gravy. Molly bobbed again. Lady Anne shook her head impatiently at the prospect of food, but would certainly take ale instead of wine. Molly hurried away from them to fulfil the order, and the lady Anne chuckled at Hardgrave's displeasure.

"Lyle—what would you here? The place is a country sewer no more! Were you expecting a list of specialties from the vineyards of France?"

She laughed with delight at her own joke, and Jake saw that she seemed exceptionally excited this night, diamond-eyed with pleasure.

"We should have dined in London," Hardgrave complained with a grunt.

"How can you think of food at such a moment!" Anne snapped impatiently, but her humor seemed quickly restored, for she smiled like an angel when Molly returned with bread and ale; she told Hardgrave she found the service ample.

Molly curtsied and scurried away once again. Jake watched her at the fire, fixing Hardgrave's plate. He frowned, unable to hear the words at the next table as Hardgrave suddenly lowered his voice.

Anne laughed again, a tinkling, melodious sound that worried Jake gravely—more gravely than the fact that the two of them were here! It could be no accident. This was none of those places of ill-repute that the nobility were known to haunt!

Molly set the plate before Hardgrave, hovering there as long as she could, but then Hardgrave seemed to lose patience with her.

"What are you, girl, a moth? I've the food before me—now get your rump gone!"

Molly left him, disappearing into the kitchen, returning with another foaming tankard for Jake, though he had ordered none. She was a bright girl, that Molly, for she had used it only as an excuse to whisper into his ear.

"I cannot linger, Jake, perhaps if I stand by the fire—"

"Nay, Molly, I can hear them fine, mostly, meself! Go about yer work, love!"

She nodded, astutely leaving him so he would miss nothing more.

"Will you hurry with that!" Anne urged Hardgrave. "I don't want you about when Deauveau arrives!"

"And why not?" Lord Hardgrave asked Anne, smacking his lips over his venison, washing it down with a swig of ale and a sigh. He wagged a greasy finger at Anne. "Why do you wish to meet him alone to begin with—"

"Oh, we have been through this!" Anne said impatiently. "You will grow impatient; you will be—uncouth! This is a business deal we make here. I wrote the message, did I not? And we received an immediate response! Lyle, he is a man—and I best deal with men! Now, shall we have this go smoothly, or no?"

Hardgrave muttered something that Jake could not hear, no matter how he tensed and strained. Yet already it seemed that the

blood had gone cold in his body and raced like icy streams throughout him. Deauveau! Some kin of Ondine's—the uncle or the
cousin—was coming here to meet with this most untrustworthy
pair, spelling trouble if not complete disaster.

Hardgrave stood suddenly in anger, wiping his mouth against
his shoulder sleeve, yelling once again for service. Molly came
to him quickly.

"Clean this mess away, and be quick with it. Bring a fresh
tankard of this donkey piss you call ale!"

"Aye, milord, right away!" Molly promised.

Lyle Hardgrave stared down at Anne. "I'll be outside; the fresh
air will be welcome."

"Don't be—obvious, Lyle! I don't want him seeing you tonight!
Not until we've fathomed his thoughts!"

Hardgrave strode out of the place, his grip on the door so severe
that it seemed not even the wind dared best him.

Anne remained at the table, her lovely face shadowed by the
hood of her cloak, her head lowered, yet her smile still visible.
She studied her small, delicate hands with idle pleasure while she
waited, sipped more ale, tapping a foot against the floor.

Jake waited more impatiently than she. He felt himself like a
wire, drawn too taut, near to breaking.

Men continued to laugh, wenches to flirt, dice to fall. The fire
snapped and crackled, smoke and warmth filled the room. The
passing minutes did not seem to disturb Anne; she waited serenely.

Jake jumped and cringed inside with each sizzle of the blaze,
keenly aware of everything and suddenly too hot.

The lady Anne looked up. He pressed himself more closely
against the wall, so closely he might have become a part of it.
But she did not see him; she seemed only mildly interested in
what went on around her.

Finally, when Jake thought he might well go mad, the door
opened again. A man entered. He was no young man, but one of
middle age, yet still straight as a poker and handsome of face and
form.

The uncle, Jake decided. There was no question that this was
the one who was to meet Anne. He was finely dressed, wearing
dull soft gray, but his breeches were of velvet and his overcoat
was fur lined at collar and cuffs.

It did not take him long to discern Anne from the rabble within. He came straight to the table and stood before her, eyeing her carefully. Anne returned his scrutiny with amusement.

"You are the lady who sent the message?" Deauveau asked at last.

"I am."

"How can I trust you?"

"Sit down, my fine sir, and I shall tell you!"

Deauveau sat. He didn't indulge in the ale, but pushed the tankard away with disgust.

"Who are you?" Deauveau demanded.

"Oh, I don't care to have my name known," Anne said charmingly. "Call me Jake, if you wish."

"How—"

"I'll tell you what I know, sir, then perhaps you will understand! You are the adoptive brother of the late Duke of Rochester. The lands by right belong to his daughter, your niece, yet I think you've no real mind ever to turn them over to her! You've a son—"

"Raoul," Deauveau breathed.

"Oh, precisely!" Anne chuckled. "And, yes, I can imagine it well! The fool boy has been tricked—"

"What do you know of this?" Deauveau demanded hoarsely.

Anne leaned closer to him over the table, eyes aglitter like a cat's.

"I know the, uh, duchess is a little slut! 'Tis no true bride your son would be taking!"

Anne must have been stunned that her beauty failed her, for Deauveau suddenly caught her wrist in a punishing grip. "Is this blackmail?" he rasped out harshly.

Anne appeared stunned, then she chuckled with pure tinkling delight. "Blackmail, nay, sir! I intend to offer you a heavy sum of money!"

"For what?" Deauveau queried suspiciously.

"As I mentioned in my letter, I believe we have common interests. Sir, I think that you would love nothing so much as your niece's total disappearance—with a death certificate involved—so that you may, by way of being legally next of kin, take all that is hers with none to bar you. And you would no longer have her there—your son's bride—a nasty thorn slicing into your ribs!"

Deauveau stared at her long; he inhaled and exhaled slowly.

"Why should this be done? What do you gain? From where would I receive the money?"

"You are interested!" Anne exclaimed coquettishly. "I'm ever so glad . . ."

"Details!" Deauveau snapped.

"There is a gentleman, a friend, greatly enamored of the girl. He will pay a fair price—"

"Nay! For she could escape him and reappear."

Anne shook her head. "This friend will not let that happen; he will take her to France until he tires of her, then—umm, shall we say—he may regain his financial loss through another business deal, this with certain sailors who have discovered a pretty face can be their most lucrative cargo."

"She'll live—"

"Aye, but justly so—can't you imagine? No longer duchess or lady, but concubine to some stern sultan!"

Deauveau hesitated, then leaned back, eyeing Anne now with uncertainty. She smiled and placed a small leather purse upon the table. "Gold," she whispered to him softly. "Go on, touch it! Feel it. Taste it . . ."

Deauveau's gleaming eyes grew round. He hesitated only a second longer, then reached for the purse, weighing the contents first, then sliding it across the table to himself to peek within. He looked around, then drew out a coin and bit into it, quickly slipping it back into the purse and secreting the purse within his coat.

"What is your interest in this?" he asked Anne.

"Oh," she purred, "rest assured, sir, I will gain from it!"

"When? How?"

"Tomorrow evening my friend and I will come with a closed carriage. When you dine"—she paused, indicating the purse he had taken and hidden at his breast—"you must see that the vial of powder you find at the bottom of that bag goes into her drink. Then see that she retires quickly, for in less than half the hour she will sleep like one dead."

"That is it?" Deauveau queried crossly. "Then how will I explain her death, her disappearance, to the king?"

"Ah, easily! Easily!" Anne claimed. "You have some servant, surely, who could don something of hers that will hide him? You pretend the next morning that you are going for a drive. Thieves, sir, bandits, will attack you. You will have only to become disheveled then, and make a hue and cry. My friend and I will see that a body is found in London, and that it will be identified as that of Lady Deauveau, Duchess of Rochester. Clean and neat, milord!''

"Nay—not so clean or neat! What of my son?''

"Send him away on business; he need never know.''

Deauveau digested that information for a moment. "It could be done," he said slowly.

"It can, sir, and will." Anne smiled beguilingly, then added, "Ah, see, too, sir, that something is done with that blacksmith of yours for the eve.''

"Why?'' Deauveau narrowed his eyes warily. "What do you know of him?''

She laughed—nervously, Jake thought, and rightly so!

"I know nothing of him, except that he is a big brute and could be dangerous.''

Deauveau did not seem happy with that; Anne offered him no more information. Deauveau reached for the ale he had previously rejected and drained it quickly, grimacing as the liquid went down.

"Come, sir!'' Anne urged with annoyance. "Do you want her gone or not? If you do what I say, none can point to you!''

"Aye, I want her gone!'' Deauveau said with vehemence.

Anne smiled and raised her hand, looking about for their tavern maid. Jake frowned then, for he couldn't see Molly about anywhere. What had happened to the girl?

"Ale here!'' she commanded.

"Nay—I need no more.'' Deauveau stood, staring down at Anne very carefully once again. "Madam, know this: Beauty moves me not at all. If this plan fails and leaves me beholden, I will find you—and kill you in her stead.''

Anne was not frightened. "Deauveau, I cannot tell you how devoted I am to this bargain of ours! It will not fail; I seek that death certificate with greater vengeance than you can imagine!''

Her passion must have convinced him, for he nodded and strode from the tavern.

Jake barely kept from moving, yet he didn't dare. The lady Anne would certainly recognize him if she saw him. He would have to wait for Hardgrave to return, for the two of them to leave this place, before he could seek the means to get a message to Warwick.

Once again time dragged. What was Hardgrave, truly the devil's own, doing to endure the cold so long?

Once again the minutes dragged endlessly. Even Lady Anne grew impatient, frowning, drumming her fingers against the table, staring at the door again and again.

At least ten minutes passed before Hardgrave arrived, coming ridiculously close to Jake when he went first to the fire to warm his hands and backside.

"What in God's name took you so long?" she snapped when he joined her.

He shrugged. "I wandered, I lost track of the time. Is the deal made?"

"It is!" Anne exclaimed, too wickedly ecstatic to care any longer that he had taken such time.

Hardgrave nodded. "Good. Then let us quit this place!"

He tossed a coin on the table, and Anne rose. Hardgrave set an arm about her shoulders, and together they left.

Jake had just started to rise, to move limbs cramped from frozen inertia, when Molly burst back into the tavern from the front, shivering with cold, rubbing her red and chafed hands together. But she was so full of excitement that she rushed straight to Jake, heedless of her chills.

"Molly," he began, "I need help—"

"More than ye know!" she exclaimed in a terse whisper. "The gent—that nasty, arrogant fellow—I saw him from the kitchen, I did. Waitin' outside, yet waitin' as if he had something on his mind! I knew ye wanted to know everything, Jake, so I snuck out after him—"

"Without a coat? Bless ye, girl!"

"Hush, hush, listen! When Deauveau—"

"How'd ye know it was Deauveau?"

"I told ye about the Deauveaus, remember!" Molly said indignantly. "Now, listen! When Deauveau came out, calling fer his horse, the other man hailed him before he could leave. Deauveau was impatient; the lord was insistent. He started talking about that friend of yers—"

"Warwick?" Jake demanded.

Molly rolled her eyes at him with reproach. " 'E's no black-smith, that one, he ain't!"

"Ah, Molly, I know, it's just—"

"Ye couldn't trust a tavern wench, I know!" she chastised him. "Well, it seems ye must now, Jake!"

"Molly, I trust ye! Fer God's sake, tell me what happened next!"

"Lord What's-his-face told Deauveau that he was the 'gent' in question—that all that the lady had said stood, but that there was more. He told Deauveau that the blacksmith was the duchess's lover. Deauveau said that he'd kill the cur; the lord said no, that he wanted to kill the man himself, but that the lady inside was to know nothing of it! The lord was very insistent, even when Deauveau started raging. He said that Warwick was his, and his alone to slay, and that he'd been waiting for that vengeance for a long, long time. Deauveau finally calmed down, and the lord gave him some package, saying that it was more of a 'powder'— all Deauveau had to do was put it in something that the blacksmith drank, and he'd be out like a downed bull in a matter of minutes. He said to make it all happen tomorrow night, at the dinner hour."

Jake grabbed her cheeks between his hands and kissed her soundly.

"Ah, Molly, yer one in a million fer sure, girl!"

"I like ye, too, Jake. Ye know that!"

"I've got to reach Warwick immediately," he murmured worriedly, but Molly chuckled and swung herself happily onto his lap.

"One in a million, that I be, Jake! My sister's married to the son of one of the old servants at Deauveau Place; she can have her boy bring his grandpa a new knit shawl. And old Jem can get a message to the blacksmith, all right, you mark my words! Jem's been staying on there just on the chance the girl might come back—he'll be yer most willing friend!"

"Then get me a quill, Molly, girl! And know this, ye've just made a friend yerself, and that friend be one of the king's favorites. Rewards, Molly, will be yers!"

" 'Tis not fer reward, Jake!" Molly admonished him with a cuff upon the ear. " 'Tis for love!"

* * *

At his cottage, far from the main house, as such workers' lodgings were, Warwick lay upon his thin pallet staring at the ceiling, waiting for time to pass, for the night to grow deep and dark. Firelight danced upon the ceiling, and he watched its pattern, yet his mind raced as he did so, his body tensed and eased, tensed and eased.

Ah, these feelings! They tortured him, they ripped him in two. He saw again a blood-red fury as he thought of the Deauveaus, William and Raoul, and his fists would clench, his muscles constrict. How he longed to face them in a battle to the death! Come hell itself, he would do so! Cold-blooded murderers and worse! Traitors, debauchers, blackmailers; conniving, sniveling snakes!

Raoul—ready and eager to slay a babe! His babe!

Agh!

He rolled and twisted, bracing against the bed to still his rage. And yet it was something he could contain, in his fashion, for he determined with lethal intent that he would, in time, find a way to force the men into open battle. Cowards—they were no true foes! They had used trickery to perform their murder, slaying the duke before he ever understood their treachery!

But Ondine . . .

He rolled again, staring at the dancing patterns on the ceiling. He was almost afraid to see her this night, yet he was compelled to do so. He longed to drag her over his knee and redden some fair part of her anatomy! God! How could she have done this! Left Chatham, come here, left him, entered into this liars' maze when she carried his child! Dear God, he couldn't yell in her room—he was overflowing with oaths. Time had not eased his bitter anger against her; it had increased it. He shouldn't go there; he had to. He had to tell her that she was to meet him tomorrow at this cottage, and that they would leave then—be damned to all else! He was her husband; he was her law. He was the father of the life within her that she so carelessly endangered; he was the man who loved her beyond all else!

He swung his legs over the cot, ready to don his cloak and scale the walls to her chamber. Tomorrow, he thought grimly, he would get her away from here, then come back for justice and vengeance himself. Charles could banish him from the kingdom for fighting if he chose, yet Warwick did not give a damn.

He started suddenly, holding still and listening. Something furtive moved by his door. He was about to yank it open so that the intruder might pitch in when he heard a soft rapping. Curious and wary, he opened it.

An old man stood there, shivering in the night. One of the servants from the house, Warwick realized, recognizing him. He was certainly no threat, being well, well on in years, small and gaunt—and trembling like a windblown leaf.

"Come in, old man," Warwick said, reaching for the fellow's arm and dragging him near to the fire. The man nodded gratefully, taking the one plain but sturdy chair there and rubbing his hands before the blaze as Warwick crossed his arms over his chest and stared down at him, waiting patiently.

Slowly the man's teeth ceased their chatter, and before Warwick could speak again, he began an outpouring of words. "I've a note for you, smith. A message from the White Feather, from a man called Jake."

"A message? Hand it over, man!"

Frowning with surprise and deep concern, Warwick took a sealed envelope from the man's trembling fingers. "There's tea in the pot over the fire; warm yourself," he told the man absently as he ripped into the envelope.

Jake's words were brief.

"A plot afoot," the message read. "Come to the tavern now. Urgent. Do not go near Ondine this night!"

Scowling, Warwick looked back to the old servant, now attempting to pour himself a tin mug of tea, still shaking so badly that the pot banged against the tin.

Warwick took the pot from his hands, poured the tea, then haunched down by the old man's feet, waiting impatiently for him to warm his blue lips with the steaming liquid.

"How did you come by this message?" he demanded.

Proud eyes gazed into his. " 'Tis no trickery, sir, not by me! I've a son wed to a lass who's sister of a wench at the White Feather. My grandson came to the back door tonight, with a package for me. He told me I must get this envelope to you, and then he said that I was to stress that you must not come to the house."

"Can you get a message to your lady?" he asked tensely.

Eyes burning brightly, the old man nodded.

"I don't wish to place you in jeopardy—" Warwick began.

"Sir, you are no smith; that I can see, and so would those two who label themselves 'lords' if they had any interest outside themselves! If you're here to help the duchess, then readily will I place myself in jeopardy, for I have loved her many years, and would die a thousand deaths not to see her wed to that treacherous scum!"

"Good man!" Warwick said softly, smiling. "Then tell her this, and it is urgent! Tell her she must slip away in the morning; tell her she must come here before noon! She must act their perfect lackey in the morning, yet not fail to arrive here! Can you do this for me?"

"Aye. They have tried to keep her from me, and me from her, but, sir, I will reach her! I swear it!"

"Thank you—"

"Jem, sir, my name is Jem."

"Thank you, Jem. Bless you. If all goes well tomorrow, you'll see your lady again, anytime that you wish! All that you must do is await my word."

Jem handed Warwick the tin cup and stood, no longer shivering. His slender shoulders were straight.

"You'll take her away from here—tomorrow?"

"Aye."

"Then bless you, sir! God bless you, and God go with you! And God damn the two of them for all eternity!"

"Amen!" Warwick agreed.

He let Jem out, then reached for his cloak. He had a long ride ahead of him, a long ride out to his curious assignation at the White Feather.

Chapter 30

Ondine never did discover what caused her uncle's foul temper of the morning. After the king's departure, William had come into the house only briefly, then departed again with only a few words mentioning that he would not return until late, and another of his condemning glares.

Raoul did not return to the house at all during the afternoon. Berault informed her that he was about business. Ondine thought that this "business" was most provident, for if she could but elude Berta's ever prying eyes, she could search Raoul's rooms.

She was thus involved—searching his wardrobe—when she was discovered by Raoul.

"What are you doing in here, Ondine? I cannot believe that a great concern for my hose brought you into my private quarters."

She flushed quickly, then somehow managed to laugh. "Nay, Raoul! 'Twas not your hose that brought me here. I came to—"

"To what?" he snapped.

She panicked, then spoke. "I—well, I wanted to see your rooms."

"Duchess," he said tensely, dark eyes as menacing as the nervous constriction that tightened his body, "tell me what it is you've come to see!"

"Oh, Raoul! I was simply attempting to draw a comparison! We're to be married in less than a month now and I was assuming, well, that we should choose a set of rooms, and I've always been exceptionally fond of mine. Yet I thought it not entirely fair to think that mine was best. I meant to judge on size, and position, and comfort—for two. And while I was here . . . well, I must admit to a woman's curiosity. I peeked into your things and found this horrid squalor!"

It seemed an agonizing eternity before he slowly eased, before he accepted her sweetly spontaneous lie as truth.

He touched her hair at her forehead. "I've never had a wife to care for me before," he told her.

He was too close! "Oh, 'tis dark already! I must hurry to bathe for dinner," she cried. "Raoul! With your father out this evening, we'll be alone." And so saying, she fled his chamber.

She didn't know that she still shook until she reached her own door, opened it, and once inside leaned heavily against it. She gasped for air, sighed deeply, and closed her eyes, pleading that her blood should warm again, her limbs cease to quiver. She realized then that she hadn't said a word to Raoul about his father's behavior of the morning, or asked about his disappearance. Escape had seemed of the greatest importance then; at dinner she would need conversation so they could readily discuss William.

"Duchess, you do look pale!"

She opened her eyes, irrationally annoyed to find that Berta was already there, standing before her with her chubby hands on her squat hips and staring at Ondine in that smug way that was little more than a sneer.

"I thought you did not enter my room if I did not bid you to do so, Berta," Ondine said dryly.

Berta lifted her hands innocently. "Milady! 'Tis late indeed! I brought your bath. You must hurry, for the water grows cold."

Ondine smiled and contented herself with sweet vengeance toward Berta, stepping into her tub, but dropping the soap again and again and politely using the woman as a hunter might a golden retriever. She was doing it on purpose, of course, and Berta knew that, but what could she do?

Once dressed, she began to shiver again. Raoul had frightened her this afternoon when he had come upon her, and she wondered at the true workings of his mind—just as she wondered about his father's.

She raised her chin for bravado and started down the stairs. Before entering the hall, she brought a soft smile to her lips, then swept in.

Raoul awaited her, standing before the fire, hands laced behind his back. She floated nearer to him, drawing his attention. Then she curtsied and swirled in a perfect pirouette so that he might admire the deepest mauve and lightest organdy gown that he had selected for her this evening, having certainly given Berta the order that brought the sour-faced battle-ax to produce it from Ondine's wardrobe.

"Lovely," Raoul approved, then Ondine decided not to be quite so charming, because she despised that look that came into his eyes.

It was not the same look that Warwick sometimes gave her, one that gleamed golden and insinuative but also appreciative, so heated that it brought fire to her blood and a sweet quivering inside her. This, this was different. Perhaps the intent of it was the same, but the manner was different. Raoul meant no harmony, no give-and-take, no sweet sharing. His was a leer that hinted of something evil, and she felt tainted each time he looked at her so.

She hurried to her chair at the table, not even noting that the despised Berault was behind her, ready to adjust her seat. Stiffening, she felt him there and allowed him his task. Raoul came after her, choosing his father's position at the head of the table, since William was not there.

She leaned toward him whispering softly, as Berault moved toward the sideboard to fetch the serving platters.

"Might we dismiss him as soon as the food is before us? I've questions of grave importance and privacy for you."

Raoul looked at her curiously with his dark eyes, then nodded his assent.

Berault was back, at her side. Ondine helped herself to veal and stewed vegetables and watched Raoul do the same.

"That will be all," Raoul told the man.

Berault hesitated, as if, Ondine thought dryly, he had been ordered to spy upon the two of them during the meal.

"I said, that will be all!" Raoul snapped.

Berault really had no choice. He left the hall, closing the double doors behind himself, reluctantly.

Neither Raoul nor Ondine cared about his reluctance. Raoul sipped his wine and watched Ondine. "What is it?" he asked her.

She pushed food around on her plate, then looked up at him. "Why was your father in such form this morning? Quizzing me with such a vengeance, so determined! Then when the king came, he all but tore the hair from my head, threatening me! Raoul, the title still is mine—or mine to share! What is this thing with your father? Will you be the duke, the master here, or shall he?"

He answered her slowly, carefully, still watching her as a vulture might watch a thrashing prey.

"You have said you are the duchess; I shall be the duke."

She sniffed irreverently and gave her attention to her plate once again. "I must wonder, Raoul," she said softly, "for he did seek to tear me to ribbons today, and you came not to my defense, though you've sworn to protect me!"

"It's difficult, my fair betrothed, to come to your defense when you give me lies and half-truths!"

She stared at him reproachfully. "What lie? I came to you with the truth! I told you I had married! Is this foolish mistake on my part the cause of your father's fury?"

"Nay," Raoul said, eyeing her still. He gave no attention to his meal, but leaned back crudely in the chair, planting his boots upon the table. "My father discovered nothing of any legal wedding, of a husband, living or dead."

Raoul's eyes seemed to burn very brightly; she knew before he spoke that he watched her for a reaction, and even before his words came, she tensed, taking care.

"It is the child you carry that has father so enraged."

"Oh!"

No amount of preparedness had her ready for that blow. Her heart sank, that William might have guessed. How? She had gained no weight, given no sign as yet!

"Then it is true," Raoul said with a heavy sigh. A sense of hopeless terror struck her; she thought if he desired he would think little of spilling her blood then and there—he had gotten away with murder once already.

"Aye," she whispered numbly; denial would make no sense. She had, in stunned surprise, betrayed herself.

He moved his feet suddenly. His fingers curled around hers and he leaned close, his long sharp nose near touching hers.

"I believe that Father wishes to kill you," he informed her tonelessly, drawing a chill to her very bones. "Yet, you see, I am loyal indeed. I can forgive the child. It shall be no matter to me to claim it. I have told him so, and so it shall be. I will be the duke, and your master, and as you see, you will have strong occasion to be grateful for it!"

She couldn't help but look into his eyes, to feel the fury and coldness that came from him. His father wanted to slay her, but despite his words, she knew that he was no better. He had spoken of claiming her child, but it was the child that he would slay!

Berta! she thought suddenly. It was that great hulking cow who had betrayed her, sniveling about, marking tender changes in her body she had barely begun to discover herself. Berta, that damnable, wretched woman!

Ondine pulled her fingers from Raoul's, knotting her fingers in her lap. She lowered her head in a humble fashion, yet it was not humility she felt; now she needed the sweeping mass of her hair, a shield to hide the true loathing in her eyes.

"So you would marry anyway," she said softly. "And claim my child, seed of a peasant, as your own! Truly, Cousin, I am stunned and amazed. And most gratified, too, of course."

Her manner seemed to both please and amuse him. He sat back once again, stretching out his legs, able this night truly to imagine himself the lord of the manor.

"You will have to bear Father's insults."

"Aye, I can see that."

"He will be brutal."

"Aye, I can imagine."

"But I will be there. I would do anything to possess you."

She raised her head at last, meeting his eyes, hers touched by the fire's sizzle, a smile playing about her lips.

"Me . . . the title, and the lands."

He shrugged. "They come as the same, do they not?"

"They do, I suppose, as long as I live."

His feet fell to the floor again. He was annoyed when he

addressed her next. "I will have what I want! Father must bend to me in this matter. As long as you come to me meek, bear his fury as well you deserve, step with care and obedience, all will be well."

She pushed back her chair, her food barely tasted. He rose as if to stop her, yet she placed a pleading hand upon his arm.

"Raoul, I am, most naturally, distressed. I—"

"We've the night alone!" he said with dismay.

She shook her head. "I feel ill. Please, forgive me, Raoul. Forgive me in the knowledge that soon, ah, soon we will always be together. Please!" The last came a bit desperately, for it was true—before God!—she had to escape him.

"Raoul! I am grateful, I am amazed; I am in awe of the days that will come before us! But this night, this night I cannot help the fear, and I feel weak with it, exhausted!"

That was not so much a pretense; she felt dizzy, miserable, and very, very frightened.

Slowly he nodded.

She waited for no more from him, but turned, swirling her skirts behind herself. She hurried up the stairs and did not feel at all safe until she was within her chamber with the door bolted.

Not even that safe haven, though, gave ease to her agitation. So her uncle knew . . . Oh, God, what did that foretell? And Raoul, Raoul was a liar of extreme vileness, for bitterly she knew that he would never tolerate another man's child, and certainly not that of a man he believed to be an illiterate peasant!

She had claimed exhaustion; she was far from it. Time and time again she walked the length of her chambers, from sitting room to bedroom, then back again. Raoul still believed that he was marrying her—she was certain that William had determined that he would not. William, then, must be planning some other fate for her, but what would that fate be?

She paused at last, lying on her bed, placing her cheek against the coolness of her pillow. Perhaps Warwick was absolutely right; perhaps this had been a fool's quest from the very beginning. It might well be the time to flee, without waiting for another day . . .

Warwick! Ah, if Berta had seen her condition, it was only a matter of time before her husband, her lover, discovered it likewise.

She wondered with a soft groan if he would ever believe she had come here ignorant of the babe she carried and that she loved the babe, his babe.

Warwick . . .

He would come. He would come to her tonight, slipping into the room like a powerful shadow. He would be there to hold her, to cherish her against the fear and terror that seemed a new and devious noose, tightening for the impending kill.

When he came, when he held her, when he leant his strength to her, she would agree that they must run now, that they mustn't wait another minute, that there was nothing to be gained in staying. Oh, but she was a fool! She was risking so much here! Her life, the babe's—and even Warwick's. For he would never leave her, and it was true, should he see her in difficulty, he would cast himself upon her assailant, heedless of weapons, heedless of number . . .

Her face burned, even against the coolness of the sheet. She closed her eyes tightly, then resolved to fight her fear and think productively on what was to come. She had only to wait, to embrace her lover when he came as surely as the night wind, to place in his hands her heart and her life.

Determined, she stood and rinsed her face. Still anxious, she sat before her dresser and began to comb out her hair. She felt the warmth of the fire, the darkness of the night beyond. Ah, it was a cold night, the earth blanketed in snow, the wind beginning to whisper and moan, swirl and threaten.

She cast the brush away and stood, and thought again with quivering awareness that he would soon be with her, strong and powerful. No words would be needed at first. He would come to her an inferno, eager for her arms, eager to appease the fires that burned so high when they lived like this, apart and thinking always of the other, apart and wary of danger. They would long to crush and hold and assure one another that they were alive still, together still . . .

Smiling wistfully, Ondine stood and slowly, carefully, began to shed her clothing—her shoes, stockings, garters, overskirt, and underskirt. Then, shivering, she crawled quickly into her bed, beneath the covers, hugging them to her.

He would come. He would come. He would warm her . . .

Firelight played across the room. She watched its movement

across the ceiling. She thought of his touch, his love. She imagined his face in her mind, his eyes, cheeks, and chin, so stubborn, so gallant. She saw his hands, bronze against her flesh . . .

Her sweet dream was suddenly and violently interrupted by a fierce pounding at her door.

She bolted up, hugging the covers to her chest, her heart slamming against her chest in a frenzy.

"Ondine! Let me in!"

"Ah, one moment, Uncle!" She spoke the words, but they barely came out. She had to moisten her lips and repeat them.

Yet that utterance broke the spell of terror upon her; she flew to her chest, anxiously ripping through her things. She found her heaviest nightdress and quickly clawed it over her head, struggling with the buttons even as she hurried to the door. Dear God! Whatever his quarrel, she had to get rid of him quickly, before Warwick could appear . . .

Breathless, her hair a tangled stream about her, she cast the door open.

He pushed her aside and marched in, striding through the sitting room, then into the bedchamber. He came back to her. For an instant in the flicker of the fire she saw his eyes and nearly quailed; there was such hatred for her there—a fanatical hatred, as if she had been the cause of every nuisance and injustice in his life!

Then, amazingly, he blinked, and that strange stare was gone as if it had never been, to be replaced by a cunning one, lacking all gentleness in its look of mockery.

"Ondine . . . ah, dear child, I was greatly worried!"

"Worried?" she repeated, pointedly dubious.

"Aye," he murmured, moving to her fire, warming his hands there. She followed him, yet kept her distance, wondering what new treachery this act could be.

"I've been to town," he told her, glancing at her over his shoulder. "Seems there's a madman haunting our area, Niece. A killer, given motive and motion by the full moon, seeking out young maids through windows and balconies, butchering them where they lie."

"A crazed killer, Uncle?" Ondine repeated, frowning but wide-eyed in her pretense of innocence, desperate lest Warwick arrive!

"As I heard of it, I immediately turned toward home, thinking how the oak stands next to your room, and how such a man—crazed!—might easily scale it.''

Ondine lowered her lashes, determined to test him, for above all, she had to be rid of him.

''Uncle, were there a crazed killer about, I believe you would gladly point him to the tree and boost him to the window. William, I am aware of all that you know about me; I know you would dearly love to see me dead. Perhaps you hesitate from murder only because of the king. So tell me, Uncle, what is this tale of yours?''

''Ondine!'' he protested, leaving the fire to take a firm seat in the chair that angled from it. ''Ondine . . . aye, 'tis true, I know all about you. And I despise you for the conniving harlot that you are!'' He smiled at her in an amazingly pleasant fashion for the bitter brutality of his words. ''But, alas! That fool child of mine has set his heart upon you; therefore, I, the doting father, must do all in my power to keep you safe! And, my dearest child . . .'' He rose, coming to her with such a silent tread that she did not think to elude him, and brushed her cheek with his knuckles. ''Ah, yes! Dear child, were I to wish you slain, I would prefer the pleasure come from my own hands, and those of no other! Nay, rest assured, girl! Tonight I have come to protect you from whatever demons might attempt to scale those walls!''

White and trembling, she stepped away from him. He smiled once again and went back to the chair with a sigh of satisfaction.

She stared at him in ashen horror for long moments. He maintained his victor's grin. She tried to think; her mind had gone numb with the rest of her. Then an agonizing realization rushed in about her. He did not intend to leave! He meant to stay in that chair, all the night long!

Nay, he could not! He could not! Warwick would come; he would leap within, unarmed. William would attack him with pistol and sword, and Warwick, unarmed, would be at his mercy.

''Girl, you look like a ghost, staring at me so!'' William snapped furiously. ''Go to bed!''

She couldn't move. Surely he couldn't suspect Warwick! He might have discovered that she was with child, but he must believe his son's tale, since the tale had already been told. He must believe that she had married a thief in the forest, that from him came the child.

"Go to bed!"

I cannot, I cannot, I must stay near the balcony, and warn him if he should come near.

"A killer, Uncle?" she repeated, finding life at last. "A slayer of innocents, coming in the night?"

She hurried to the balcony doors and cast them open, praying that Warwick would be down in the snow, that she could warn him.

But there was no sign of her lover yet; no sign at all.

"Ondine! Get back in here!"

William was on his feet again, rushing to her, slamming the doors against the cold, and pulling her back inside. "Go to bed, girl! Now! I will sleep in the chair!"

Sleep. He had to fall asleep. That seemed her only salvation.

She lowered her head, nodded, and fled past him, jumping into her bed, pulling the sheets to her chin once again in misery.

Don't come now, my love. Don't come now! she prayed.

Ah, how heavy time could hang when one lay in terror and misery! Every crackle of the fire, every gust of the wind, played upon her tortured nerves. She twisted, she bolted, she shivered horribly. The wind would not cease, nor the rustle of the old oak.

She sighed softly, then took up a position on the floor near the balcony. If he appeared, William would know. He might well seek to tear her hair out, beat her or even strangle her upon the spot. But Warwick, at least, would escape, for she would scream and scream until he was justly warned.

Time . . .

It ticked by. She tried to remain straight. She dozed, then awoke with a start, panicked at the scratch of a leaf against stone. Stiff she would remain, cold, aching, until she would doze again, awake again . . .

At last she awakened, startled by the cry of a bird, to discover that the dawn was breaking.

Dawn; he would not come now.

Tears filled her eyes; she did not know if Warwick had been

forewarned, or if he had deserted her. Of if—oh, heaven forbid!—he had somehow been discovered and lay bleeding somewhere . . .

Where was Warwick! Oh, God, oh, God! What had become of him?

Chapter 31

Ondine lay upon her bed until the sun began to rise, dispelling the shadows of night. Desperately she tried to fathom what events might have brought William Deauveau to watch over her the whole night through, and desperately she wondered what had kept Warwick from her. She tried to assure herself that nothing could have happened to Warwick. William was obviously suspicious of her nightly activities, lest why invent such a lie—a lie that entailed the use of her balcony? But if he knew that Warwick came to her, he would have surely discovered some means of doing away with Warwick, and if that deed had been fact, then why spend a night of misery in a chair?

Nay . . . Warwick had somehow learned of William's suspicions, and had therefore not been caught upon the balcony! William had spent his night in vain, and Warwick was well.

She could lie abed no longer; she had to find a way to see Warwick, to assure herself that he was really alive and well. She couldn't even concern herself with what her uncle knew or suspected. She had to reach Warwick—and agree that they should run now!

She dressed quickly, rushing in the hopes that she could get downstairs and out of the house before Berta could arrive and her uncle awaken. Clad in her warmest gown and fur-hooded cloak, she dared not breathe as she silently scampered past William's sprawled form and to the door. Once there, she inhaled and exhaled, then held her breath again, praying that she might slide the bolt open without making a squeak.

Only when she was outside the room did she dare breathe again, and close the door as softly as she might.

She ran down the stairs and into the hall toward the entry, but paused there, for Raoul blocked the entryway, giving orders in his autocratic way to one of the tenant farmers. There was some disagreement: Winter was exceptionally harsh this year, and the farmers were behind in rent. It seemed that Raoul did not care; he did not intend to let the man in out of the snow, nor did he intend to give any leeway on monies owed.

For a moment Ondine's heart seemed to pitch to her stomach. She felt herself the greatest coward, for these were her people, her father's people, and any lord with a grain of kindness must know that blood could not be squeezed from rocks—that mercy now would but draw interest in the harvest to be reaped at a later date.

She bit her lip, wishing she might intervene. But she could not; she had no power here now, and no way to regain it when it seemed she was in some grave danger herself.

She could only be glad that the argument was taking Raoul's attention, giving her a chance so that she might retreat through the hall and find an exit through the kitchen.

She raced through the still curtained and darkened hall to the pantry, and through it to the kitchens, aware that the servants would be up now, busy with their daily tasks, yet praying that neither Berault nor Berta would be among those in the kitchen. Pausing as she entered the sunny place, she held still, breathing deeply again, adjusting her eyes. There were but two servants here as yet; a young girl who turned a capon over the fire, and Jem.

"Jem!" she whispered happily, certain he would never give her away and grateful that he was here. He turned from the block where he sliced bread, and seeing her, his face seemed to light like the day, as if a grave concern had just been answered for him.

"Milady!" he gasped, then glanced quickly at the girl by the fire, saw that she gave them no heed, and shuffled quickly over to where Ondine stood, still against the doorway.

"Milady!" he repeated, his voice dropping to a soft and anxious whisper. "I've a message to you from the smithy. He's taking you out of here, today. You're to reach his cottage—the blacksmith's cottage—before noon. Do you ken, lass?"

She nodded fervently. Oh, God be thanked! Warwick *was* unharmed, he had somehow been forewarned, and all would be well as soon as she could reach him.

"I barely slept," Jem muttered, "knowing the urgency; not knowing how to reach you! Ah, milady—"

"Duchess, there you are!"

Berta! Behind her! Oh, God, of all the things she did not need, it was this wretched bovine spy upon her!

"And all dressed up in your lovely cloak, milady! Like as if you were to be going out!"

She straightened regally from the wall. "I am going out, Berta. The heat of the house has oppressed me; I feel quite desperately the need for some fresh air!"

She started across the kitchen and was amazed when Berta actually grasped her arm, stopping her. She stared at Berta's hand upon her as if it were no better than dirt, but her utter disdain did not affect Berta in the least. The woman smiled. "Not now, you'll not, Duchess. Your uncle is awaiting you. That dear man was distressed to find you gone when he awoke! After guarding you the night long, milady!"

"I shall walk before breakfast—" Ondine began, but Berta kept smiling as she raised her voice and called sharply, "Berault! Berault!"

That awkward hulk of a man instantly made his appearance behind Berta.

Ondine realized that they meant to take her back to the hall, whether she walked, or whether they dragged her. She lifted her chin and shook Berta's hand from her arm, dusting the fur carefully as if Berta had sullied it. Best to come willingly now; after breakfast she would escape. She gazed up at Jem and saw that he was watching her helplessly, so she smiled an assurance to him, then turned to Berta with a great display of impatience.

"Oh, for heaven's sake! If I walk later, I shall walk later!"

Berault looked upon her suspiciously, as if she still might need his urging to return to the hall.

"Berault?" She lifted an eyebrow delicately. "You will excuse me, please?"

He moved aside. Ondine swept on through the pantry into the hall; Raoul stood by the fire, surprised to see her enter by way of the kitchen.

"I'd thought to take a walk in the snow this morning," she said coolly, in response to his unuttered question. "It seems that others have different ideas for my actions."

"What—?" he began, frowning at Berault and Berta, who hovered behind her.

Neither needed to give a response; William Deauveau made his appearance then, still rumpled from his night in the chair. "Ah, there you are, ingrate of a chit!" he exclaimed to Ondine.

"What is going on here!" Raoul demanded in frustration.

William sauntered casually into the room. "I learned in town of a madman," he told his son briefly, "and saw fit to stand guard myself all through the night for your betrothed. And after my sacrifice, the girl disappears on her own! Berta, take the duchess's cloak; she'll not need it now."

Berta complied, taking Ondine's cloak and leaving to return it to her room. Raoul protested.

"A madman—" he started to query, but his father silenced him with a wave of his hand. "Aye, some fellow out after women, poor wretches. Nothing to worry on; we shall protect our own. I'm impatient only with Ondine, since she thought not to thank me, but to worry me further!"

"I wished to take a walk!" Ondine exclaimed. Oh, Uncle, you are a devious liar! And, Raoul, you are a devious idiot!

Yet she was still as confused as he; she had no knowledge of what her uncle knew to make him act so strangely. She could only be grateful that Warwick had been forewarned, and that she would fly to him as soon as she could.

"I shall take you for a walk as soon as we've dined," Raoul assured her.

Nay! she thought, yet that worry was oddly taken from her by William himself.

"I'm afraid, Son, that you'll be too busy to take your betrothed walking. You must set out today for Framingham—"

"Framingham!" Raoul protested. "That is a day's journey, a night's stopover! Why should I go to Framingham?"

"To meet with a Spanish merchant carrying the finest silks from the Orient—"

"Silks! Rubbish! What need—"

"A gown for your bride, Son, and wedding clothes for yourself! Have you no interest—"

"A new gown!" Ondine declared, clapping her hands with joy, and thinking that, yes, Raoul must depart for the day! She must be able to escape to the smith's cottage alone.

Berta reappeared in the room, slinking in silently to stand behind Berault once again. Raoul ignored them both, still looking disgruntled. "Father, a merchant should come to us—"

William shook his head, inclining it toward the servants and warning his son that disagreements should not be voiced in front of them. "Berault! See to our meal!"

Berault disappeared, with Berta thudding along at his heels. William smiled, pulling Ondine's chair from the table for her. "Sit, my dear," he said, smiling, yet staring at her with such a secretive pleasure, she shivered, wondering at the workings of his mind.

"Ondine . . . ?"

She came and sat. Raoul took his place, still scowling at his father. William, too, sat, folding his hands above the table. "Raoul, last night I learned of this man in Framingham. If you would be a duke, you will have the adornment and bearing of one! He has no plan to come this far north—you must go to him. Remember, this man has the finest materials—you must settle for nothing less."

"I'm no tailor—"

"Raoul! You will see to this yourself!"

Berault came back into the room, followed by both Jem and Berta, and the table was quickly set, the food served. Raoul did not care who heard his complaints.

"Overnight? And how am I to deal with this merchandise?"

William waved an arm in the air, adding sugar to his tea. "Take one of the land laborers with you! I care not how you manage it,

Son, but this wedding will be the event of the countryside, and you will—at least!—see to it yourself that you and your bride are suitably attired.''

"Women's work!" Raoul uttered disdainfully. Then his eyes brightened. "Ondine can accompany me."

She nearly cried out and just barely restrained herself. Jem, removing an empty tureen from the table, did not do so well. He dropped the silver server, drawing a cuff on the shoulder and a chastisement from William.

"Get back to the kitchen, you bumbling old man!" His anger stayed with him as he turned on Raoul. "She'll not go with you! She'll stay right here."

"Father—"

"You trust her; I do not. She has set the month deadline. When she is your bride, she will be your domain, yours to control, if you're capable of doing so! Until then, she is my concern, and I do not trust her. She will stay here."

"It doesn't matter, Raoul," Ondine said quickly, feigning a humble sigh.

He grunted something, then bit into his food. The meal progressed in silence. Ondine ate without noting what was in her dish; she burned with the fever to escape and could barely stay in her place.

At last William mumbled impatiently, then turned on his son again. "Are you not finished! Go, get your things together! You must hurry upon the road, or the merchant will be gone before you ever bring your lazy carcass to the town!"

Raoul let out an oath, tossing his fork to the table, but rising at his father's command. Ondine kept her head lowered, thinking it somewhat intriguing that William and Raoul would betray each other if they could.

Raoul came around to the back of her chair. He placed his hand upon her hair, then bent to her.

"Just a night, my love. And I shall buy you the finest material you have ever seen. Your gown for our wedding will be splendid."

"Thank you," she murmured. She was even able to keep from flinching as he kissed her cheek; she would never have to bear his touch again!

He left the room, and she heard his footsteps as he ran up the stairway.

She waited just a moment, then yawned and pushed her chair back. "Ah, I do feel so lethargic! Now that the meal is over, I believe I shall take that walk."

William's hand clamped down around her wrist in a cruel vise. He stared at her, smiling with naked malice.

"Nay, my dear niece! You'll go nowhere!"

Ice seemed to blanket her; she felt like a cornered animal, trapped by a rabid bear. She had to shake herself to clear her mind from the awful hypnotism of his eyes.

"Really, Uncle!" she drawled petulantly, casually trying to free her hand. "I just wish to take a walk—"

"You wish to run to your lover, my dear. I'm afraid I've other plans for you both. Go to your room."

"No!" she gasped, stunned by the assurance of his words, wrenching now with fevered resistance against his hold. His eyes raised; she barely noted it in her efforts to free herself, but quickly discovered the reason.

Berault was behind her, lacing his field worker's arms around her to halt her fury. She would not go down without a fight, she wailed desperately inside.

But it seemed that she was, indeed, going down. She screamed; she clawed at her uncle and managed to draw blood down his cheek. Then Berault's heavy hand closed over her mouth, and she found herself desperate to breathe. She was carried in his arms, staring into stupid eyes, still feeling his hand crushing not only her words, but what breath she had in her lungs.

"Don't hurt her! Don't mar her!" William snarled out softly. "I've promised her in good shape!"

Berault nodded, but it did Ondine no good. His hand remained too tightly over her face, no matter how she squirmed and twisted. She tried to inhale for desperately needed air, she could not get enough. No matter what her will, her strength began to ebb from her. She couldn't see clearly, everything was spinning. Berault's scent was sickening, his touch a horror that cast her into a swimming chasm. She was smothering, she realized bleakly, she was going to die . . .

She did not die, but the world slipped from her. Arms that had flailed in fury fell slack. Berault carried nothing but an empty shell, for consciousness had totally deserted her.

Jem had been sent from the hall, but he had lingered, unobserved, in the pantry. Ashen, he had knit his old hands into tense knots at his sides when the lackey, Berault, had taken hold of Ondine.

Then he stood miserably in agony and indecision. What should he do? Try to reach her, stay to see that she was all right? Yet what could he do? Gladly he would rush into any fray, but his bones and body could do her little good!

He paused just a moment, then looked about himself. Berault was gone up the stairs; Berta was still listening to instructions from William. Ondine's door was not to be opened for any reason until night fell, then he would supervise the preparation of the meal to be sent to her.

Only the one poor kitchen wench—a sweet girl, but simple since birth—remained about her tasks. Jem mumbled something to her about finding a chicken for a stew to be made, then slipped out the back door and started running across the snow.

He should have waited long enough to cloak himself, he realized; the sun had done little yet to dispel the bitter cold. He slid against icy patches, felt a keen pain about his heart. He must go on, he told himself; he must go on.

He reached the smith, but the man was not there. Jem paused, regaining his breath, convincing his legs that they move again. Then he started off again, running, panting, hearing his breath come like a storm against his ears.

He reached the blacksmith's cottage, the first of those in a row where the grounds servants lived. He burst through the door, near frozen and wheezing, so that he was glad to the smithy's quick reactions and strong arms. For Warwick grabbed him, supported his weight, and brought him quickly to the fire, kneeling down before him as he had done the night before.

"What is it, old man? What's happened?" he demanded tersely.

Jem had to gasp for breath for several more seconds. "She tried to sneak out this morning; they caught her. William is sending Raoul away; he has Ondine locked in her room. I believe she fainted in that buffoon's grasp, for she screamed once, but did not do so again.''

Warwick issued a furious stream of oaths, standing and pacing hard behind Jem. ''I knew we waited too long; William knows who I am! Though tonight was to have been his sale of human flesh, he is taking no chances!''

He continued to pace. Jem stared into the fire, all life near drained from him, for it seemed his task was complete.

But the raging knight behind him suddenly stopped and came back to his side, grasping his blue-veined hands.

''Jem, you've got to go back. You must behave as if you are no part of this. Have no fear; I am going for her.''

Jem's eyes widened; his heart skipped a beat. ''How?''

''Through the balcony; she'll have to come out that way, too. Jem, you've been a dear and loyal friend to her—wait patiently, and you will be out, too.''

Jem looked down at his hands, not meaning to speak aloud, but so bleak and anxious in his heart that he murmured another dubious, ''How?''

Warwick, at his side, offered him a taut, dry smile. ''I've no time for lengthy tales now, Jem, but you should know this: She is my wife, legally wed, cherished and loved. I knew nothing of this snake-infested place, though, till she came here. I am the lord of a distant northern realm. The man who sent the message last night is a dear servant of mine; even now he rides to London for kin of mine to come here, should I need their aid. When they come, if all is well and the duchess and I have already departed, you will tell them that the Earl of North Lambria has bid you serve them.''

Jem stared into Warwick's eyes, which burned with such strength and conviction. He nodded, somewhat awed, yet certain that if someone could save his duchess, it was this man, whether his story was true or no!

''Come,'' Warwick said softly. ''You must get back to the house.''

Jem nodded again, not speaking, saving his strength and his breath for the cold outside.

''I will follow shortly,'' Warwick said, opening his door.

Jem decided then that he must speak. "Take care, milord, take care—"

"That I will. Go, Jem."

Ondine awoke upon her bed. For a few seconds she sucked in air, grateful merely to fill her lungs, but then she quickly swung her legs over the bed and raced to the sitting room door. She knew, though, before she tested it, that it would be securely locked.

Nay! her heart screamed out, and she would have pit herself against it, would have banged and kicked and shrieked, except that some small sense lured her from panic and warned that she must not fall prey to hysteria.

She sank to the floor, suddenly shivering. She would never break their bolt upon her door, and the door was solid oak. There would be no escape that way, and even if some miracle did occur, causing the door to dissolve for her convenience, she was certain that Berta sat outside, smugly guarding her beaten charge.

She had to reach Warwick! He would be waiting, he would be expecting her . . .

She stood again, because thoughts of her husband had given birth to an idea.

The balcony. He had come to her by that path; she must go to him the same way.

For a moment she paused, so close to her door that she could hear sounds from below. Raoul had come down again; he argued with his father once again. She could not clearly make out his words, but she knew that she was part of the argument—and the fact that Raoul thought this task too menial for him, and that he wasn't about to carry materials home like a packhorse. His father advised him again to bring one of the hefty land laborers.

Ondine listened no more, but decided with a quick breath that she must now make her escape, while William was busy arguing with his son.

She just barely remembered the cold and hurried to her wardrobe, glad then that Berta had replaced the encompassing fox fur, since she would need it now. She cast it about her shoulders, then quickly burst out the balcony doors, willing herself not to look down, finding that she did so anyway. Ah, the ground seemed so far away; the limbs of the old oak that she might cling to seemed to be all too spindly and weak.

There is no choice! she warned herself and came to the rail. She looked down again. Ah, the snow below was so white! It appeared as if a blanket of clouds lay beneath her, clouds that could comfort and shield her if she should fall.

The snow would not be thick upon the ground; the earth below it would be hard and brutal. If she fell, she would break her bones and possibly her neck, but she couldn't think on that. Nor could she think that she would kill not only herself, but her child. She had to cherish the illusion that the snow was a field of clouds, that she would not fall . . .

She took a deep breath and grabbed onto the nearest sturdy branch, reminding herself that her husband was far heavier than she, and that he had trusted the branches of the tree. She closed her eyes for a moment, dizzy; then she prayed and swung from the rail, grasping the branch.

Hand over hand, she moved quickly to the great trunk of the oak, then grasped and fumbled for a lower branch, and then another. Ah, still, the ground seemed far when she reached the lowest branch! She clung to it, tears stinging her eyes, her breath coming forth from her in gusts that misted the air. She squeezed her eyes tightly shut once again, then loosened her hold, allowing herself to fall.

The snow clogged her nose and mouth; for a moment she lay there panting, trying her limbs, amazed to discover that she was whole. Then she realized the folly of tarrying and came quickly to her feet, hoping that the silver fox fur would help her blend into the snow while she raced along the expanse of grounds to the cottages.

Yet even as she ran, exhilaration came to her. Oh, it was done! The worst of it was over! They had thought to imprison her; she had escaped them. All she had to do was reach Warwick, to come to her beloved, and away they would go.

It was a song, a sweet, sweet melody of triumph that sang in her heart as she raced along, anxious then just to see his face, to feel his touch, to know the promise of life stretching before them!

She was panting, half laughing, half sobbing, when she came to the cottage. She burst into it, his name a whisper on her lips.

Yet she stood still at the entrance, puzzled, for he was not there. A fire burned at the hearth, his very warmth and presence seemed to linger, but he was not there.

She sighed impatiently and thought that he must be fulfilling some last task to cover their escape. Longing for him, she sat upon his lumpy bunk and ran her fingers over the place where surely he had slept, smiling most wistfully. Something must be done about her uncle and Raoul, but that would have to wait. For now, she could be gratefully content that her husband loved her, that she loved him with all her heart, and that in time, she would tell him that they were destined to be a family. Not a bad conclusion for a gallows' bride and a haunted, mysterious groom! Oh, if only he were here! If only they were away! If only this small fear did not live in her breast, a fear that would plague her until they had left Deauveau Place far behind . . .

Someone was arguing at the main house; voices rose so high and viciously that Warwick, slipping past the main entry, could detect undercurrents of violence, if not actual words.

Well and good, he decided grimly; for he was an open target here, slipping through the snow.

He came around the stone corner to the side of the house and the oak that had given him such glad cover on previous nights. Accustomed to the ritual, he quickly shimmied up the trunk and onto a branch, eager to reach the balcony. Yet when his boots found a stance and he quietly stepped through the doors to her chambers, he was astounded and worried to death, for she was not there.

Anxiously he searched the place, and tested the door, frowning as he noted it still bolted from beyond. A deeper worry touched him still, for he realized she must have gone as he had come, and he could only pray that she had not injured life or limb in the unaided attempt.

Quietly he opened and closed the balcony doors again, staring upon the snow there, smiling with both bitterness and love. Ah, yes, her footprints were here, feet far tinier than his, clearly etched upon the fine whiteness. He knew her well, his wife, his love; she could not be imprisoned or beaten. If life lingered in her at all, she would fight, and he loved her for that spirit.

Even so, he longed to thrash her for her carelessness!

Sighing softly, he hopped lithely to the branch, retraced his crawling path, and leapt back down to the snow.

The argument had ceased when he reached the front of the house again, but Warwick gave it little thought. He had only to reach her now, to hold her briefly, and then take her away.

Though Warwick gave no heed to the end of that dire argument inside, Jem was near brought to heart failure by the conclusion of it. Raoul had whined, decrying his absurd assignment. William had insisted and reminded him again that he needn't be a packhorse, he need only take a servant with him.

Raoul had banged his way into the kitchen then, demanding a decent meal and a flagon of wine to take on his way. And it was there, while he had impatiently awaited his package, that he had murmured, "The smith! I'll take the new smith, for that brute has the back and shoulders of an Atlas, and can carry all!"

He snatched his satchel from Jem then, eyes furrowing with wrath. "Wake up, man! Has age made you dense! You're blessed, old timer, that we see fit to keep you in the kitchen!"

He trudged out then, heedless of a reply. Jem remained motionless, heavy laden with dread.

He waited until Raoul had gone, then sighed, for he must go into the snow again. He thought to grab a shawl—oh, such a small thing, a needed comfort! Yet later it would prove that the time had been poorly taken, and that rather should his flesh have congealed than what came to pass!

When the door burst open, Ondine gave a glad cry and came to her feet, hurtling herself against her husband with such velocity that they both came out to stand in the snow. Warwick, startled by her impetus, wrapped his arms about hers instinctively, protectively. She was so beautiful in that fur, in his arms, against the snow. For a moment he forgot his anger and held her there. Then he realized their danger, how easily they could be seen there, and he caught her arm roughly, dragging her back into the comparative safety inside.

Ondine did not feel how stiff he was then, for she was too elated at the sight of him, too eager to hold him, too desperate to speak.

"Warwick! Oh, my love, we must flee! Now! I near to died a thousand deaths last night, I was so afraid! William hovered there the night long. He knows something, I know not what! Warwick—"

His face was stern when he set her from him, jaw set in a twist, eyes blazing. She felt then the tension in his hands and hushed, wary of his look, knowing too well his temper.

"Warwick?" She backed away from him, noting that he followed her with determined, menacing strides.

"Warwick, you don't understand! We must get away—"

"Oh, I understand that perfectly, my love! In fact"—he paused, dropping a few twigs on the fire, eyeing her in the beauty of her silver fox, her hair a trail like the sun, streaming atop it—"we are leaving now. I've sent the lad—the apprentice—around to the stables for the nag I hired. I dared not come here with Dragon, you see, for he is too fine a piece of horseflesh for a blacksmith." He smiled at her, but it was a dangerous smile. "In fact, my love," he told her, "I have never been so anxious to take you from here, for I do intend to thrash you soundly!"

Surely he did not mean it! She stared at him in stunned surprise, then thought his threat was purely masculine bluff, but why? And graver things were upon them now . . .

"Warwick—"

He stood, chuckling softly. "Poor sweet, you do not know the half of it! Let's see, where do I begin? Tonight, Ondine, you were to be drugged once again—and sold to my old nemesis, the lord Lyle Hardgrave!"

"Hardgrave!" she gasped, amazed that he could be a part of this. "I don't understand. How—"

"Jake, milady, has been staying at a certain establishment of ill repute called the White Feather. You know of it?"

She nodded blankly.

"How Hardgrave became involved or discovered our whereabouts, I do not know, only that he has."

''Hardgrave . . . and Anne?''

''Aye,'' Warwick said, stooping to poke the fire, then standing again to approach her, hands on his hips. '' 'Tis a confused group we have here, eh? Seems Anne was the one to find us; she wished to sell only you—so that I would perhaps raise havoc, but eventually come around to a need for her luscious arms once again. Hardgrave, however, means to kill me. You were to have been quietly drugged and taken care of this eve. I should have been left to flounder in bafflement. Anne made the first deal, but Hardgrave accosted your uncle to make the second. Hardgrave, if Jake's fair friend had her information right—''

''Jake's friend?''

''A lovely buxom tavern wench, name of Molly. If Molly heard correct, Hardgrave made arrangements to come earlier—this noon—to see to my death and disposal. Anne would not have known, until I, like you, came to be discovered as vanished—then deceased.''

Ondine shook her head, incredulous at all these curious twists. Warwick smiled grimly and continued.

''Now, added to this confusion, my love, your cousin knows nothing of the matter. He is so enamored of you that your uncle apparently feels it must all be done with him away!''

''Oh!'' Ondine gasped, still incredulous—and still wary, for his anger extended to her!

He came to her then, smiling, his hands flat against the wall on either side of her head as he stared at her with the greatest reproach.

''Ah, yes, ways and means! I know everything, my love. I even know that your uncle wishes you might be slain instead of sold into the slave markets—because you're with child!''

The last came out with all his thunderous fury, and she understood in an instant the explosion of the simmering anger he bore her.

Nor could the charge be denied; she placed her hands against the sinewed breadth of his chest, thinking to plea, for he could not be really angry. They were near to safety, and he must, in truth, be glad of it!

''Warwick, I—''

''Nay, give me not that sweet and innocent face, for I am not some besotted fool, prey to your guileless smile. Madam, I swear, you should go over my knee! You are forever in danger, and you left me! Left me and my home, knowing full well you carried my heir!''

''Nay, Warwick, I did not know!''

''Aye!'' he cried, ever bringing his face and flashing eyes closer to hers. ''Still you protest innocence, to me, your lord and master!''

''Hmmph!'' she responded, with like fire that time, for she would not succumb to his fury. ''Lord, perhaps. Master! None is my master, only if I should choose it so!''

''I make the choices!'' he countered, but she saw there was also laughter in his eyes. She raised her arms, throwing them around his neck. ''Warwick! I swear, I did not know it when I left! Nor *should* I have cared, for you did plan to be rid of me!''

''Never—an act, and you knew it!''

''I did not! You never professed love at the time—''

He stopped her words with a gentle kiss, caressing her cheeks between his palms. Then he looked at her, smiling ruefully.

''My sweet, I do profess love now, and once we're away from here, well will I indulge in it! But I'm still tempted to see you soundly thrashed as such a wandering wife deserves . . .''

''Oh, Warwick!'' She giggled, leaping slightly to fit herself more closely to him, closing her eyes in sweet elation as she held him close. ''I do love you, I do love you . . .''

She was so absorbed in him, nay, they were so absorbed in each other, that neither heard the sounds of stealth outside; neither knew anything at all until they were interrupted by the slamming burst of the door and heard a shout, crazed and demented with fury.

''*Whore!*''

Ondine had time to open her eyes; Warwick never had a chance to move, except to tighten his arms protectively around her.

Then a pistol blast exploded.

Ondine screamed hysterically, barely aware that the ball had sped past her cheek and was imbedded in the wall behind her.

She was aware of nothing except her husband, for the ball had done its damage well before passing on. Warwick's temple was saturated with red. Blood red.

In horror she stared into his golden eyes; in disbelief and agony

she watched them glaze . . . and close. And she felt his arms slip
from her as he crashed, dead weight, down to the floor.

She didn't even see Raoul then; she screamed and fell down
beside her husband, praying deliriously that it could not be true,
he could not be dead. "Warwick! My God, Warwick!"

She reached to roll him over, to rip cloth from her skirt to
staunch that awful flow of blood, his life's blood, her life's blood.

"Whore!"

The charge was leveled against her, and she was forced to notice
Raoul, for his fingers bit into her arm cruelly, and he dragged her
screaming and fighting from Warwick's side. Maddened, danger-
ously hysterical, she bit furiously into the hand that held her so
cruelly.

Raoul swore and released her, but only to send a stinging blow
against her face that sent her reeling, dazed near unconsciousness,
onto the thinly mattressed bunk. She could barely see Raoul's
face, gaunt and narrow with evil emotion, ugly in its twisted
passion, staring down at her.

"He's done, madam. Your filthy lover is dead. You refused
me, while you ran to him! No more, my lady slut! He has received
his just reward; you shall now receive yours. Slowly."

Chapter 32

Ondine could not care; nothing seemed to matter. She was dimly aware of the pain that stung her cheek; well might she have entered a netherworld of desolation and despair.

She might have told Raoul that he could do as he pleased; it did not matter, for she could never be touched again. She was already a doomed creature; life had no meaning to her. She felt cold, as if the snow had already blanketed and claimed her, cold and numb and knowing but one thing: Warwick lay bloodied and dead. There was nothing else left to fight for. They could do what they would to her, for she, too, was like death along with him.

"Harlot! Bitch of satan, look at me!"

He slapped her face again, jarring her from her blank and sightless stare into some world beyond. She focused upon Raoul's face, yet gave no indication that she knew him or cared, for the shock and anguish were so deep.

"By God, I'll make you see me!" he swore with a vengeance. She felt him tearing upon her cloak, knew that he twisted and manipulated her, and still she couldn't care. Nothing on earth could truly touch her again . . .

And yet it did, quite suddenly. She felt his hand upon her bodice, set to rend the material in his frenzy, and it seemed then the greatest sacrilege that he should touch what Warwick had so tenderly possessed, with hands twice bloodied. A shriek came from her, maddened, demented, and she pitted herself against him with new fury, kicking, clawing, raking with superhuman strength. He swore; he fought her in return, yet she had no sense of fear, no thought of weakening, no logic that he, the stronger, would win in the end.

Like a wounded she-cat she flailed against him, shrieking all the while, keening to wake the very dead. He secured her wrists at last, yet still she fought, kicking, biting, more from madness than courage.

His weight fell over her at last, and in some recess of her mind she knew that she was lost. Yet even as he started to laugh, a sound as demented as her screams, the door to the cottage burst open once again.

"Raoul!"

William Deauveau shouted out his son's name; Raoul did not appear to hear him as he caught Ondine's chin roughly between his palms.

"Raoul!"

A hand fell on his shoulder, jerking him away from her. Dazed, Raoul stared up at his father.

"The stinking slut!" he said blankly, blinking his confusion at the interruption. "The stinking slut! She was sleeping with the filthy smith all the while that she turned her wretched nose up to me!"

"I know—"

"You knew!"

"We are rid of her!"

"Rid of her! Nay, I will have her—as everyone else has!"

William's tone became soothing. "Aye, Son, have her, but not like this. She must not be injured."

"Injured! I will tear her limb from limb!"

Stunned and quiet once again, Ondine vaguely noted that Jem— dear Jem!—hovered anxiously in the doorway. Had he gone for William Deauveau? she wondered. Brought him here? Ah, Jem! Truly, it doesn't matter, for I am like one dead—all that truly mattered in life has been taken from me! she thought.

William pushed Raoul aside and touched Ondine's cheek, eyeing

...er as he would a horse up for bid, touching the bruise. "Raoul, listen to me! You've already caused us grave harm; another wished to bring the death blow to that smith! We are paid dearly and well to have her out of our lives—legally dead! But she must be no more bruised or beaten!"

"Nay! Nay!" Raoul protested. "I'll not give her to another—"

"For God's sake, Son! Where is your dignity! This trollop will not be your wife!"

"Not my wife, my whore!" Raoul said sullenly.

"Then it must be quick, for the lord who purchases her will soon arrive; we need pack snow against that cheek so that the bruise will not appear so livid."

"I'll bruise her again—"

"You'll not! Damn you, even if you are my own whelp! You'll destroy all that we've done here! Leave, now! Go to the house! I'll bring her back. Go straight to your chambers, Son, with the right words in her ears to make her miraculously amiable!"

Raoul looked at his father dubiously; William's temper was at the snapping point once again.

"Go now! You waste time, if you would have her!"

Ondine saw through a gray mist that Jem backed away from the door, far from Raoul's observance. Now she was aware only of William Deauveau, for he leaned low against her, placing the flat of his knife against her cheek. Tears filled her eyes, and she began to laugh softly.

"The more quickly you bring that blade against me, Uncle, the greater boon you shall grant me!"

He smiled, bringing the knife down to her throat, then to her breast, and onward, to her belly.

"Have you forgotten something, my dearest niece? You carry that last hope of eternal life for the man you called lover and lord. Would you die so easily yourself? Perhaps you would—but would you condemn an unborn child to death with you?"

She despised herself then, for his deepening grin assured her that she had made some sign or movement betraying the fact that his words had touched her. It was true; Warwick lay dead, but his child, blood of his blood, lived within her. Didn't she—loving him, oh, loving him, but creating the folly that had cost him his life!—owe him the life of their wee babe?

Desolation overwhelmed her again; she was once more their prisoner. She would be turned over to Hardgrave, who would grant her no mercy. She had no chance for herself, or for her child.

But even then it seemed that William knew her thoughts, for he reminded her, "While there's life, my dear, there is hope."

Nay, there is no hope; I care nothing for life . . .

"Get up. Get up now, and accompany me quietly to the house. If you do not, Ondine, I will kill you here and now. But it will not be a swift or simple matter. I will first dig the knife into your belly, cut out your child, and then your entrails. I will do it very slowly, to assure you a sight of your growing fetus before you breathe your last."

She stared at him and knew that he meant it, that he was capable of such a deed, that he would make her see the child. Perhaps she would even know if it would have been a son or a daughter.

No one can touch you now, not really, she reminded herself.

William spoke softly again. "Can you slay your own blood—his blood—so easily? For it will be you who decrees death for the babe!"

She forced herself to stir, to rise. She almost fell, and he supported her. A numbness fell over her again, cold like the grave. She barely felt him as he cast her silver fur about her and led her from the cottage. She did not even look back. The sight of Warwick, dead and bloodied upon the floor, would make her crave death again despite the child.

Jem still hovered outside, falling back from William. Ondine thought to give him a small desolate smile, for poor Jem, he had tried so hard.

They started back to the house. Ondine was vaguely aware of the cold air of the day against her face, of the crunching sound her feet made against the snow, of William's grip, locked tight and grim upon her arm.

Then he began to swear softly, and Ondine saw that a carriage stood in the courtyard before the house. A man alit from it.

Hardgrave was there.

He clumped through the snow toward them. William continued to swear softly, beneath his breath. Hardgrave was bellowing out oaths in a voice that thundered across the snow.

Ondine just stared blankly at them both, even when Hardgrave touched her, jerking her chin about to study the bruise there.

"Damn you, Deauveau! What happened here? I told you that I did not want her touched!"

" 'Tis only a minor bruise—"

"Where is Chatham?"

"Dead already, I fear. I—"

"God damn you, Deauveau!" Hardgrave grated out furiously. "I told you that I—"

"A slight problem here; it was necessary to kill him."

"Can you handle nothing?"

William made an impatient sound. "What is the difference? He is dead, the girl is yours. The bruise is light, some cooling snow upon it, and it will all but disappear."

Hardgrave stared more deeply into Ondine's eyes. "What is the matter with her? She seems as an idiot."

"Shock, perhaps. She has reason left; she needs only to be jolted into it."

Hardgrave started to swear again. "If Chatham is dead, there is no hurt to him in knowing what I will do! Deauveau, I hope you do rot on a trailor's rope! You are a bumbling fool. I've a mind to call this off; to leave you holding your corpse and at whim to dispose of your duchess yourself!"

"I've your gold already," Deauveau reminded him coolly. "And it makes no difference to me if I kill or leave her to your disposal. Do you want her or not?"

Lyle Hardgrave hesitated, his colorless eyes perusing Ondine as he balanced his weight from foot to foot. "Where is Chatham? I would see the body."

"Down at the servants' quarters; the first cottage. He was shot in the head, but remains there, upon the floor. Go, see him for yourself."

Hardgrave glared menacingly at William Deauveau once again, knotting his huge hand into a fist and waving it beneath William's nose. "I shall see to Chatham, then return for her. See that you pack her cheek; dress her in an untorn and unsullied gown, and if you should bumble my orders again, 'tis possible I'll slay the whole stinking lot of you!"

William stiffened, but did not reply. Hardgrave thumped on past them. Ondine felt William's tug upon her arm once again.

"Come, milady. Seems you're to have one last glimpse of Deauveau Place! Ah, yes! And one last lover's tryst with your betrothed, for if we hurry, Raoul might be satisfied, too!"

Jem had not tarried outside the cottage once he had been deserted by the living, but had rushed within, lamenting his foolish decision to cloak his old bones, for if he'd come just a moment sooner, he might have warned the lovers within that Raoul was almost upon him. The lord Chatham might then have turned, might well have ducked or escaped the ball that had cost him his life.

Near tears, Jem hurried to the body, determined to see that the man's eyes were closed, that he might receive that small dignity in death. He rolled the body over, shaking as he saw the blood congealed on the forehead, then starting like a hare as he heard a soft groan shudder from the man's lips.

"You live!" he gasped, and then some form of youth came to him; he was spry as a lad as he hurried to the water ewer, ripped away a piece of his shirt and soaked it, and returned to kneel by the downed man. Carefully, tenderly, Jem cleared the blood away and saw that though there was much of it, the damage was in truth minor; only the flesh had been grazed and ripped; the skull remained untouched.

"Awake, sir, awake!" Jem muttered feverishly, smoothing cool clear water over Warwick's face. "Please, oh, I pray thee God, let him awake! Sir, disaster is upon us!"

Another groan issued from blue lips just now regaining some normal color, and then Warwick's eyes opened, eyes golden and sizzling as they stared into Jem's, keenly battling confusion.

"Jem!"

He moved to sit up, then groaned once again, grasping his head.

"I'd thought you dead!" Jem cried. "They think you dead."

"Ah, it would be kind in comparison to the thunder in my temple!" Warwick claimed, but then he threw his hands upon Jem's shoulders, pain forgotten, memory returned.

"Where is she? Ondine?"

"Taken, sir, in a daze, for she believes you slain! She asked for death herself, but was cruelly reminded of—of your child."

Warwick scrambled to his feet, wavered, and leaned upon Jem for a minute, near to breaking the old man's shoulders. He shook his head, in an effort to clear it, and seemed to cast away all the mists about him. He strode with long firm steps to his bunk and reached beneath it, drawing out a long lethal sword. He stared at Jem once again and asked hoarsely, "They've taken her—to the house?"

Jem caught his lip between his teeth and nodded; already, the blood was flowing thick upon Chatham's temple again.

"So I believe." He ambled over to the door and cracked it, peering out. Then he inhaled sharply.

"Milord! Someone comes this way, firm of stride, noble in dress!"

"Hardgrave!" Warwick swore. His eyes came sharply to Jem's. "Get to the house, Jem, see what happens there. Pass him humbly, as if you have not come from here."

Jem swallowed nervously, thinking this man not well enough to battle the broad-shouldered aristocrat plodding his way so determinedly through the snow.

"Go, Jem!"

He saw that Warwick Chatham was lying down once again, where he had fallen.

"Go!"

Jem left the cottage, torn. What good that Chatham survived death once, if only to fall in truth? Yet perhaps it was true, too, that he needed to make haste, for in some small way he might find a chance to give aid to his mistress.

As he shuffled past the newcomer, he felt despair chill him again, more deeply than the cold. The man with the limpid blue eyes looked like the very angel of death.

Hardgrave slammed into the cottage, furious still, yet suddenly quite gratified, for he felt keen satisfaction to see Warwick Chatham, the great and powerful Earl of North Lambria, nothing but lifeless flesh and crumpled bone upon the floor.

He laughed, sauntering into the room, thinking it a shame he felt no need, for he would like to relieve himself upon the body. He moved closer, thinking to kneel down, grasp a handful of that thick hair, and see how the ball had destroyed that noble head.

He crouched down, then inhaled with a startled gasp, for the corpse moved! Piercing gold eyes seared into his, seared with all the fire and fury of hell, and all the loathing he had ever borne himself.

"Chatham!" He whistled, quick to stand, ready to battle, excited himself that the death might still be upon his hand.

"Aye, Chatham! Alive, my friend!"

Alive, leaping with instant agility to his feet, balancing his weight on slightly bent knees, the sword he had shielded beneath his prone body now lethally raised in his hand.

Hardgrave let out a cry, a battle cry, and drew his own weapon. Steel clashed against steel. Hardgrave ground his teeth together and swung again, sending out a shuddering blow, once again received upon steel rather than flesh.

But then . . . then he knew that he was doomed. Warwick became the aggressor, driving swing after swing against him. Hardgrave was forced back . . . back against the wall. He saw Warwick's face—saw the cold hard resolve in it—and knew that he did indeed battle a demon. Warwick swung again, catching Hardgrave's sword in a mighty blow, sending it flying. Hardgrave slunk to the floor; Warwick's sword tip came to his throat.

"Yield!"

"Kill me! I do not yield."

"Yield!"

"Nay! Never!"

Warwick's lip tightened to a white line. His fiery eyes never left Hardgrave as he walked over to his fallen sword and kicked it back to him.

"Then fight."

Hardgrave smiled, thinking Chatham a fool. He clutched his sword, bounded to his feet, and made a hasty sprint toward Warwick, thinking him ill prepared to parry the straight blow of his weapon.

But Warwick was not unprepared; he stepped aside neatly and leveled his own weapon.

Hardgrave impaled himself upon it.

He stared into Warwick's eyes, even as the realization of death touched his own.

Even then he smiled crookedly, as if having lost some chess match, and lost in good spirit. He clutched the weapon in his back, staggered back, emitted some sound, lifting his hand . . .

And then he died, closing his own eyes almost peacefully.

Warwick stared down at him a moment, bleakly trying to recall the long-forgotten event that had driven them both to become such bitter enemies.

Then he remembered that his wife remained in dire peril, and he drew his sword from Hardgrave's body without a thought and rushed from the cottage.

They were almost upon the house when William Deauveau suddenly paused, muttering that Hardgrave was a fool—more idiotic than even his son. Staring at Ondine he frowned as he eyed the bruise caused by Raoul's attack.

He released her, thinking her little better than a mindless simpleton at that moment anyway, and dipped down to the ground to pack a ball of snow to set against her face.

At first Ondine didn't move. She stared dumbly at his graying head and listened idly as he continued to rant against Hardgrave. Then it suddenly sank into her that William intended to hand her over to Raoul, and then to Hardgrave. This man who had betrayed not only her father, but had brought destruction to her husband, would only further prosper by her degradation and sale. She was not at all sure yet that she really cared to live, for what hope could she give her child?

She knew only then that William Deauveau should prosper for his evil greed no more. A soaring life suddenly came to her; she kicked him hard, with all her strength, and watched as he tumbled facedown into the snow.

She turned and ran, back through the snow, past the stables, smithy, barns, and cottages, through the snow-covered clearing, and toward the trees.

Her heart thundered like a cacophony of drums; she was no longer cold, but burning with heat. Seeing that the thick forest of trees was before her at last, she dared to double over and gasp for breath and stare back toward the main house.

There was a sudden shout. She stood straight again, seeing that Raoul had found his father stumbling to his feet. William pointed toward the trees, and for a brief moment she thought she might have felt the rage of Raoul's stare, meeting hers, crossing all that distance. That he did see her, she knew well, for he started off in a run, directly toward her.

Panting, gasping, near sobbing, she crawled over the root of an ancient oak, naked and barren with winter, and plunged into the trees. She was wild, not knowing where to go, clinging only to the hope that the forest had succored her once before and might well do so again.

Through dull trails cast in somber winter grays, she forged on, her breath escaping her in little cries that seemed like the mournful toll of winter. Dead spidery branches came as obstacles in her way.

Something crashed behind her. She caught her breath, and her heart quickened to a still greater pace.

"Ondine!"

Raoul, Raoul calling out to her . . .

Once, long ago, he had called out thus to her before. She had been running then, too. Running and running. He had caught her, but she had eluded him, found her freedom by pitching into a stream, deep beneath the summer waters.

She had eluded him . . . because Raoul could not swim, and because some glorious knight, cast in chivalrous armor of old, had come to stand between them.

There was a stream, a stream that ran beyond the length of the property, a stream that ran all the way eastward, until it met the icy Thames. If she could but reach the stream . . .

It was winter now; she would surely freeze within those waters.

She had to try for them; they were her only hope.

Coming from the cottage, his sword still dripping Hardgrave's blood, Warwick must have appeared like some avenging angel as he bore down upon William Deauveau, a man still engaged in dusting snow from his body, still engaged in abusive mutterings about Ondine, his son, and Lyle Hardgrave.

Hearing the soft pounding of footsteps against the snow, William expected to see Hardgrave, and he worried only how he would explain this latest turn of events, that the girl had escaped him to seek shelter in the forest, and that his son—as insanely lustful and vengeful as Hardgrave himself—was in pursuit.

But it was not Hardgrave who approached him so fleetly; it was a ghost, a beast. Tall and dark in black wool, wild with a blood-matted tangle of hair loose about his face, and swinging a sword as a heathen invader might have wielded a battle ax, Warwick Chatham swept the distance between them.

William was too stunned to think; instinct warned him to back away, but not in time, and he dimly thought that he was about to die.

He did not die; the breath was knocked from him by a ferocious strength, and he found himself in the snow then, the enraged man upon him, and a bloody sword at his throat.

"Where is she?"

The blade pricked against his flesh; he gasped and gagged, sickeningly aware then that he was a coward, that he wanted no part of pain, that he would say or do anything to get this man and his sword away from him.

But he could not speak; the sword was against his windpipe, and he could barely swallow. He tried to swallow, his own eyes widening to the devil's fire of those that stared into him, threatening to burn him for eternity.

He waved toward the forest and the sword moved away from his throat.

"The forest!" he gasped. "She raced into the forest. Raoul—"

But the last was not needed, nor did it seem to have meaning. The great dark beast was off and racing like some majestic steed down the same path the others had taken.

William brought his hand to his throat and rubbed the pricked flesh. He staggered to his feet and started at a much slower pace in Chatham's wake.

Why, he wondered, did he follow? He should run away now,

before he was forced to face the beast again. But he kept going, for Raoul was in that forest, and he knew not why, but William felt compelled to be there, too. Yet he could not hurry; he could only plod slowly, woodenly, through the snow.

Some voice hailed him; he did not hear it. He just stared straight ahead, thinking that it had all been for naught. He had come so far . . . He had taken the land. He had brought off the most devious and tricky plan! He had done it; he had done it all. And now it was falling down around his ears, all because of a slender golden-haired girl. He had bested noblemen and a king, and he was about to lose it all to a girl who just barely reached his shoulder.

"Hold up there, man!"

He finally did so, shaken not by the voice, but by the arm that fell upon his shoulder.

He turned and almost smiled, for this indeed seemed to be a winter of ghosts. The smith had been the first, arising from the dead.

And now this . . . this strange and miscolored facsimile of the same man. He was slimmer, not quite so tall, but seeming a giant still, staring at him with eyes that blazed a wild emerald instead of a great cat's gold.

William shook his head—there was another ghost behind him, massively shouldered.

"What goes on here?" the green-eyed monster demanded, shaking Deauveau with a fury. William looked past the newcomers and saw another carriage in the courtyard. Ah, a busy day for Deauveau Place! Rarely did more than one carriage come at once! Beside the carriage two men and a woman, all elegantly dressed, lingered and watched.

William raised a hand slowly and waved.

But then the green-eyed stranger was shaking him again. "What's happening? Where is Lord Hardgrave? Where is Ondine? Where is Warwick Chatham?"

William smiled and pointed. "Why, the smith and the duchess are in the forest. Let's all go, shall we?"

"Hardgrave—"

"I believe he must be dead," William said apologetically. He shook his head again. "I knew it. I knew I should have killed her the moment she arrived. Ah, but youth! Raoul just would have

her, have her or die!'' He started to laugh. "And I think now that
he will, indeed, die!''

Justin and Clinton exchanged worried glances, but then as Warwick had, they chose to ignore Deauveau and raced into the wintry
tangle of forest.

It was there before her, filled with tiny crystals of ice, gurgling
and bubbling and beautiful where the sun filtered through the dead
limbs of winter, casting its glow.

She paused just briefly on the snow-covered embankment, thinking that she only needed to cross it to reach the other side. It
would probably not be deep enough now to cover a man's height,
but Raoul might not know that, and he was terrified of water.

"I've got you! And now, madam, you will pay!''

She screamed, for there was a tight grip upon her shoulder; she
had not heard him come those last few steps, for the fresh powdery
snow here had covered the tread of his footsteps. Raoul spun her
about, her head fell back, and her eyes beheld him.

"Damn you!''

He shook her in a fury until her head rolled, until she felt like
laughing. When she laughed, he struck her, and she sank into the
snow, her head lowered, her laughter ceasing.

"Damn you, bitch! I can still save you! My God, do you value
your life so cheaply that for its price you will not turn to me?''

She glared up at him, heedless of her words. "You are insane,
Raoul! Never, never, at the cost of my life or any other, could I
turn to you! You killed my father—'' Sobs caught in her throat.
"You killed my father with his own sword, and you slew Warwick—shooting him from behind his back! Never, never in a
thousand years could I bear you! The thought of death is sweet
in comparison with your treacherous bloodstained hands!''

His face turned crimson with rage; he shook, and a vein seemed
about to burst from his forehead. He raised his hand, and she knew
he meant to strike her again and again, until he had beaten her
unto death.

But instinct caused her to lie prone and roll in an attempt to
escape that first blow. And in motion so, she suddenly discovered
that she was rolling down the slope of the embankment. She came

to rest just at the water's edge. Gasping and looking up, she saw Raoul in grim-faced pursuit, carefully climbing down the slope.

"No!" she screeched, and with that sound came energy and desperate courage. She pitched herself into the water.

The cold was lethal; her coat too heavy. Its weight tugged upon her, and it seemed that her limbs had become like icicles, incapable of movement. The cold called to her and lured her; rest, it seemed to whisper; give up everything for peace . . .

She came to the surface and breathed deeply. Yet it seemed the current meant to carry her under again. She had no choice but to go with it and pray that in its whims it might choose to cast her upon the opposite bank.

"Wait!"

She heard the cry vaguely. It was like the enraged roaring of some wounded creature, yet it carried with it something poignantly familiar. Ah, death! It seemed that surely the shadows were descending, for it was Warwick's voice calling to her. The sound of it was sweet, so sweet and gratifying, for even as icy fingers swept her along, it seemed that he was destined to meet her—upon that opposite bank as it were!

The current tossed her cruelly, for she had no strength. It would not pull her down and have done with her; she found herself above the surface again, hearing that same sweet haunting voice!

"Ondine!" A shrill cry of anguish. "Pray try, wait! I will help you!"

She smiled, for where could be the triumph in death, when he was there to meet her?

But then something swept around her; something strong, something unerringly sure. Something that held her against the current and cold; something that tightened about her like a burning forge of steel, carrying her against the current.

She looked up and saw him. She smiled, for his cheeks were unshaven still; his flesh still stained with smudge from the forge, and his forehead, even, still carried the bloody mark where the ball had taken him.

"My love," she whispered.

And then she closed her eyes.

But they opened again suddenly, for she realized that she was not dead, just shivering furiously, wet against the chill of the breeze, and no longer held, but tossed upon the bank. There was a great thrashing around her, as if all the ground were being torn asunder. Struggling, she raised herself on her elbows and stared about.

"Fight, damn you!"

It was Warwick's voice raging out the demand, Warwick's soaked and powerful back she saw, standing higher on the bank. His hands were upon his hips and he was staring down at some creature he had dragged back from the woods, a creature that now cringed before him.

"Deauveau! I cannot slay a man from the back!" Warwick thundered. "Take your weapon and fight!"

"Spare me!" Raoul whimpered. "You have her; I never touched her! Take her—she's yours!"

"Damn you! Get up like a man!"

The vision suddenly blurred before her, for the quiet, barren forest suddenly seemed to have come alive. There were footfalls everywhere.

Ondine closed her eyes, hoping to clear them. A sweeping warmth suddenly enveloped her, and with her teeth chattering furiously, she opened her eyes wide once again.

A man who had shed his great cloak was standing over her, covering her with its warmth, supporting her with strong sure arms, helping her to her feet; a man with anxious green eyes, and a dearly loved countenance she had thought never to see again.

"Justin!" She touched his cheek with affection. He nodded grimly, holding her to him, since the drama above them was still unfolding.

"Get off your knees, you sniveling coward!" a voice commanded Raoul, yet it was not Warwick who gave the order.

"He'll kill me!" Raoul wept.

Suddenly—without Warwick having moved from his stance before him—Raoul pitched face first into the snow with only a little whimper escaping him. Ondine saw that a knife hilt stuck out from his back and that a blood stain was rapidly seeping around it.

Incredulous, she looked beyond him.

William Deauveau was walking toward his fallen son. Warwick, also incredulous, took a step backward.

William fell to his knees in the snow. He pulled his blade from his son's back, then turned the body face forward and smiled strangely as he closed his son's eyes in death.

He looked up at Warwick then, offering his odd explanation.

"He would not have stood up well in the Tower, you see. He would have suffered agonizingly, awaiting death by the executioner. Alas, he'd have had no honor, no dignity. This was best; quick, merciful."

Silence followed his words, a silence touched only by the winter's breeze.

Then Warwick spun about, dripping still from the stream, yet not shivering, looking only to his wife.

She could not smile; her face seemed frozen. Yet she lifted her arms, lifted them out to him in amazement, for they both lived.

"Warwick!"

The startled cry came from another man, behind them on the bank. Clinton! Aye, they were all here, her Chatham men. Yet she could not muse upon his appearance, for the cry had been a warning, and already Warwick was spinning back, ready to parry the danger.

For William Deauveau had risen and flown after Warwick's back like a crazy, rabid dog. Warwick just barely had time to spin and raise his sword before the man shot on top of him.

But just like Hardgrave, William Deauveau hurtled himself onto his death blade, catapulting at Warwick just as Warwick moved his sword. He felt it searing through him.

Warwick bent slowly with that weight, easing Deauveau back to the ground.

Strangely the man still smiled. He moved his lips, whispering to Warwick. "Thank you," he mouthed painfully. "I could not bear the wait for the headsman either . . . all for a girl . . . Ondine . . ."

Then his lips moved no more. Warwick stared at him a moment later. He left his sword where it was, stood, and turned.

She was waiting for him still, arms outstretched, trembling, her eyes as wide and brilliant as sapphires against the winter's snow.

He came down the embankment, sliding, catching himself, determined only to reach her. From Justin's arms she came to his, those sapphire eyes still upon him with awe.

"You live!" she breathed. "We live."

It must have been too much for her, for her stunning eyes fell shut, and she collapsed against his chest.

Chapter 33

When she opened her eyes again, she truly wondered if she hadn't somehow left the earth, for there was a sea of faces before her, the nearest being that of another man most dear, yet startling to find here. Here . . .

She blinked and realized that she lay in her chamber, in her own bed. She was cold no more, for a fire burned and crackled cheerfully in the hearth and her wet clothing was gone. She was dressed in a muslin nightdress—one with pretty buttons up to the throat—and covered with a sheet and the brocade spread.

The king was on her right, smiling mischievously as he held her hand, but her other hand was warm, too, and turning, she saw her husband at her side, fresh shaven, clean—beautiful. But she frowned at the sight of him, for there was a bandage at his temple, reminding her how close to death he had come; indeed, she had imagined him lost to her, and in that, had cared nothing for herself. She might have most carelessly tossed her own life aside . . . and lost all that was now theirs—a lifetime together.

"Ah, Duchess!" the king declared. "You're with us again!"

Ondine tore her eyes from her husband's anxious amber stare to give her attention to the king. She smiled then, for it was true—they were all there. Dear Justin, Clinton, a pretty woman she dimly remembered meeting at the queen's side, and even a strange man, thin, gaunt, and somehow sad in appearance.

"Your Grace!" she murmured to the king, confused, but then he laughed. "What a crowd to arise to, eh, my dear?"

"Nay, I'm grateful! But how are you here?"

He shrugged, his mustache curling along with the amused quirk of his lip. "I'd thought to return, you see, once I had left. To see all as normal might be easy and well, yet if I returned after having been here already, I thought I might catch someone off guard! As it happened, of course, I arrived when the commotion was actually over, just in time to welcome you back to the free and living!"

She turned her eyes to Warwick again, tightening her fingers that lay in his. Then she released them and, heedless of all others in the room, touched his cheek, amazed still that he lived and that life had come full circle for them both.

He smiled, as heedless of the others as she, caught her fingers, and brought them to his lips.

Justin cleared his throat, grinning as he chose to seat himself upon the foot of the bed.

"Dear Sister, I know you're greatly enamored of this beastly brother of mine, but aren't you even curious as to the situation?"

She grinned in turn at Justin. "Brother, dear, I know the situation! Jake was surely sent to tell you there might be trouble, and you rushed here at that behest! And, Justin—Clinton—doubt not that I am grateful! I thank you for your care, with all my heart!"

"Aye, well"—Justin cleared his throat again, uncomfortably this time—"I'm afraid that you became more endangered due to us! You see, Clinton and I were sent out in search of information. We were accosted by Lady Anne, and though I knew it not at the time, I know now that she must have overheard our words before she presented herself to us and then tied your kin into this deal with Hardgrave and yourself."

Ondine shivered suddenly and looked at Warwick once again.

"Hardgrave?" she murmured.

"Dead," he told her briefly.

"And Raoul and William, dead, too." she whispered softly, then raised her eyes to Warwick once again. "How strange that William should have slain his own son, then attacked you so! He must have known he could not win!"

"Aye, he knew," Warwick said grimly.

"My dear," the king told her, "his game was simply over."

"Ah," she sighed softly. "All is well, and I'm so grateful. Yet now, I fear, I shall never prove my father innocent."

"Oh, but he has been proved innocent!" Justin exclaimed.

"While Justin and I were busy endangering your life," Clinton said apologetically, "we were also busy working on your behalf, and that's God's own truth! Yet it is thanks to Sarah here, and John Robbins, this young gent, that we came to the truth."

Ondine frowned in confusion. Warwick shrugged at her, his love warm in his eyes, but he was determined that his brother be able to explain his own part.

"We met Sarah in London—by asking anyone who might remember a single blessed thing! And she did know something. She had known John on that date; and John was there, one of the king's guards then."

The man, the sad stranger, stepped forward earnestly. "My Lady, my greatest and most humble apologies, but I was a coward! That day, I thought myself mad. In truth, I knew not what I saw. I was confused myself. Then, when I might have voiced that confusion, I was threatened with my sisters' lives. I knew it the truth then: Raoul had drawn the sword, slain your father, and got away with it!"

"Bless you, John Robbins! Bless you, Sarah! Oh, dear God!" she breathed, delirious, heady with the absolute happiness of it all. "I have gone to heaven!" she murmured gratefully.

"No, no!" Justin admonished her. "That's what you're supposed to feel after a tempestuous bout of lovemaking!"

"Justin—" Warwick admonished.

But Ondine giggled and interrupted him. "Oh, Justin, that is true! I do feel that way, most frequently!"

The king laughed, enjoying the joke, then stood with a little "Um-hmm!" sobering them all curiously. "We're still missing one villain to this most unusual puzzle," he reminded them. "Villainess, actually."

"Anne!" Warwick grated out irritably.

"When did you say that she was due here?" the king asked.

"Not until this evening, Charles," Warwick told him. "After eight. Jake is there, keeping an eye upon the—lady."

"Then she should still be at this tavern, this White Feather?"

Warwick murmured, "I think we all deserve the dubious pleasure of going to meet Anne."

Justin chuckled deep in his throat. "One by one, Brother?"

"Exactly."

"A black widow in a spider's web!" the king mused.

Warwick and Justin rose simultaneously. "Sarah!" Warwick addressed the newcomer. "Will you stay with my wife?"

Ondine emitted a strangled gasp. "Nay! That's not fair! Sarah and I surely deserve to come, too!"

"You, my love, will stay in bed!" he admonished her firmly. "You have been through brutal hands and an icy dunking—"

"And you were the one shot! After which you also endured a brutally cold dunking!"

"She is a lively woman," the king said idly to Warwick, as if she weren't even there! "Quite spirited; one can see where a problem might lie with her."

"Alas! Not a humble mouth for a wife!" Justin chuckled.

Ondine threw her pillow at him; Justin caught it easily, so she cast him a nasty glare.

"I can handle my wife," Warwick said confidently, "if you'd all just leave the room for a minute . . ."

"Warwick . . . ?" Ondine moaned warily.

But Charles was leaving; naturally, the others followed suit, and Ondine was left to stare at her husband with a curious mixture of resentment and love.

He sat beside her, taking both her hands, bowing his head, and yet she could see the strange little smile that curled his lip.

"Ondine," he said softly, looking at her at last.

"Warwick!"

"Ondine . . ." He stared at her, his grin tender and open. "Tell me, do you believe that I love you with my whole heart, with all of my life, with all of me?"

"Aye!" she whispered softly.

"Then will you stay here—"

"Because you command me so?"

"Nay, because I ask you so."

"But you were the greater hurt!"

"Ondine . . . !" He swept her into his arms, cradling her head with his hand, holding her against the strength and thunder of his heart. "Never has there been a cat such as you, landing on your feet again and again!"

"Anne, alone, cannot be dangerous!"

"It is not Anne I fear. I wish, my love, that you would stay here, warm and unbuffeted, for the sake of our child!"

"Oh!" she whispered. "Well, I—"

He kissed her tenderly, then was gone.

Jake noted Justin and Clinton the moment they walked into the White Feather, but Justin winked at him quickly, so Jake made no move toward them.

Anne was seated at the bench again, sipping wine, for she'd thought to bring her own. She was quite agitated, for Hardgrave had left hours earlier on some ridiculous errand and now it seemed that he was going to be late for their most urgent appointment.

"Why, Lady Anne!"

Smiling with the greatest pleasure, Justin reached for her delicate fingers and gave them an elegant kiss, then lifted a booted foot over the bench and sat to her right. She had barely registered his appearance with dismay before she felt a presence to her left and discovered that Clinton, smiling also, had taken a seat there.

"Whatever are you doing here?" Justin queried.

"I told you once!" she snapped quickly, wondering what would happen when Hardgrave walked in. Oh, what ill timing! Why hadn't the man been punctual! "I find these places amusing!" She hesitated with the growing sense of unease, for if these two were about, had they come to meet Warwick?"

They had—he walked in right after them, not appearing the smith, but decked in his silken shirt, velvet breeches, plumed hat, and an ink-black cloak.

"Anne!"

He greeted her as pleasantly as his kin had done, sitting opposite her, and smiling, as if they had all met surprisingly upon a Sunday Mass in some obscure chapel.

"Warwick . . ." she murmured. She tried to smile; she tried to appear as pleased, but her effort was lacking. She realized with rising panic that she was trapped; Justin on one side, Clinton on the other—and Warwick Chatham, the arresting, stunning beast, before her.

He indicated the two glasses before her. "Ah, I see you've brought wine for two! May I?—or were you expecting someone?"

She felt a bit strangled, so she waved a hand, indicating that he should help himself.

"Nay, I don't think I will. The tavern ale here wets my whistle well! Molly . . . " He lifted an arm, and Molly sailed over cheerfully, bringing foaming tankards of ale for the three Chatham men. "Molly, me lass," Warwick told her, "I've been thinking that this place may be a bit rough for your tender age. Would you think of entering into private service? I'll be returning north soon. And you might just like that northern clime."

"Well, I just might at that, sir!" She winked across the room, and Anne turned quickly.

Jake tipped his hat to her, grinning affably.

Anne tried to stand; both Warwick and Clinton grasped an arm, holding her to the table.

She tossed her jet hair.

"What's going on here?" she demanded.

"Annie, you don't admit defeat, I'll grant you that!" Warwick sighed to her.

"Defeat—?"

"Lord Lyle Hardgrave is dead, Anne," Justin told her.

She sucked in her breath, staring at them in wide-eyed horror. She recovered, though, quickly.

"You've murdered him! A viscount! A peer! Warwick Chatham, you think that you are the law! You are not! When the king hears of this—"

A tall figure suddenly stood from the center of the tavern and approached their table, raising the brim of his hat.

Charles Stuart bowed most elegantly to Anne and cast her his ever charming smile.

"Lady Anne, do go on. When the king hears of this . . . ?"

"Oh . . ." She was breathless, struck mute. She stared at the king. Charles slid in beside Warwick and looked casually about the place. " 'Tis a bit of a dive, isn't it, me lads?"

Anne found her voice again at last. "Charles! Your Majesty! I had nothing to do with treason, I swear it! 'Twas a joke, a lark, a bit of fun, no more! Hardgrave, dead! I know nothing of it, I—''

"Anne, Anne!" He patted her hand assuringly and spoke in a soothing tone. "Anne, I suspect you of no treason. And thank God! For I would be loathe to think of your beautiful head falling from the block! A lark, a bit of fun, amusement, eh? I'm glad you think it was all so, for the fate you had in mind for Lady Chatham is quite similar to the one I have planned for you."

She went dead white. Her voice was barely a croak. "Sire! You couldn't—you wouldn't—"

He chuckled softly. "Sell you to Moroccan slavers? 'Tis a thought, since it seems I am perpetually lacking funds! Alas, nay, lady, 'tis not quite the same. In fact, I give you a choice. A Tower room, or marriage. There is a certain governor of a certain remote island in the Caribbean who has been a dear and loyal servant, yet he pines for want of a beautiful wife. He's fat as a cat and bald as a buzzard—but sharp as a sword. I think you'll suit one another aptly well!"

"I'll not—" Anne began angrily.

"Ah, but you will!" Charles warned her. He lifted his hand; the groups of rowdies from the table where he had been suddenly rose and cast back their cloaks, displaying themselves as members of the king's personal guard.

Two approached the table.

"Anne? They're waiting for you."

Clinton rose to let her by. He bowed, laughter upon his lips. She stared at the guards; she stared at the king.

Charles's face was set. Anyone who knew him knew that look.

"Oh!" Anne cried in fury and desperation. "Charles!" she tried next with a pitiful plea.

"They are waiting!" he told her softly.

For once, Anne knew that she had been beaten. She swept by Clinton furiously and set herself between the guards. "Get your hands off me!" she snapped when they moved to escort her.

The tavern door closed in her wake. The Chathams looked from one another to the king; then they all burst into laughter.

* * *

Ondine and Sarah were taking tea, both seated cross-legged upon the foot of Ondine's bed, when Warwick strode in, grinning smugly.

Ondine jumped up to greet him, nearly knocking over the China, all but making a disaster of the bed. 'Twas only Sarah's fleeting movement that saved the fragile porcelain cups.

"Warwick . . . ?"

He cast his arms around her, lifting her high, swinging her about. " 'Tis done! All villains apprehended!"

Breathless with laughter, Ondine clung to his arms. "And?" she inquired a bit anxiously.

He kissed the tip of her nose. "She is to have a most fitting end. Charles is having her married off to some fat governor of a most remote Caribbean isle. She'll trouble us no more, my love."

"Oh!" Ondine lay her head against his chest. "I'm glad. It does seem fitting indeed."

"It was that or the Tower," Warwick told her.

Sarah rose, smiling, for the happiness and mutual adoration seemed so wonderfully contagious.

"Well, I'll leave you now," she murmured.

Warwick took himself from his wife's gaze long enough to grin at Sarah. "Clinton is waiting downstairs. And I think he has some rather good news for you."

"What is that?" Sarah frowned curiously.

"He must tell you himself," Warwick told her, and Sarah, smiling nervously, hurried out.

"Warwick—"

He returned his attention to Ondine, and though he knew that he saw her through the misted eyes of a lover, he knew, too, that she was in truth one of the most beautiful women ever to grace the earth, with eyes like a sparkling sapphire sea, hair that caught sunlight or moon light, a fire's glow, and made magic of it.

He pushed her backward slowly, smiling still as he stared down at her. "Have I told you today that I love you?"

"Oh, aye! And I love you, too. But Warwick—"

"Have I told you that your beauty is greater than any sunburst, than any field, than any work of God or man?"

"Oh, Warwick! That's beautiful! But—"

She broke off, startled, for he had backed her to the bed, and she fell upon it, to be quickly followed by him, and held against him as he stroked her cheek, still staring whimsically into her eyes.

"Warwick—"

"Are you well?" he interrupted her anxiously, drawing his hand tenderly over her abdomen. "Do you feel strong? No ill effects of such a day?"

"I am well!" she gasped, for though his fingers moved to seek his child, to her they were beguiling and . . . erotic.

"Warwick!" She caught his hand and held it to her, determined that she must talk. "What is it that Clinton must tell Sarah? Oh, Warwick! She is so terribly in love with him! Glad in it, yet so very sad, for her father is an awful tyrant and—"

"I know," Warwick interrupted her, drawing her fingers to his lips, tenderly kissing them one by one with the greatest interest.

"Warwick—"

"They say, my love, that curiosity killed the cat!" he teased, taking then a studious interest in her earlobe, kissing it, nipping it, whispering against it with moist and heated breath. Then he was staring down at her, eyes glowing like the deepest golden fire, intense, passionate.

"But then you're not a cat at all, darling. You're a mermaid. I thought you so once, that very first time I saw you. I never told you, did I? I saw you—the day of the joust—running from Raoul. Of course I didn't realize then that I was destined to take you in marriage and give you mortal life. I thought you a dream, a fantasy. And still you are so. But in truth, my beloved, it was I who was granted mortal life—and love immortal—through you."

"Oh, Warwick! I love you! You saw me!"

"I did. I saw the vision. A dream. And the dream is now mine."

She wrapped her arms about his neck, meeting his fevered, passionate kiss with an ardor that seemed to encompass all the flaming heat of the sun. She was breathless when he pulled away, breathless when she stared into his eyes and knew that she would love him this way forever, for all their mortal lives . . . and beyond.

He laughed, rising from her to shed one boot, and then another. He tossed his hose carelessly aside. "Vixen, you forgot your question, but I'll answer it anyway. Certain lands and titles had been left vacant. Anne's last husband left no heirs, and Charles decided that those lands should go to Justin. So my brother is now a duke. Then there were Hardgrave's lands, too, you see. Vacant. And the king's prerogative is to bestow titles and land, and so Clinton is a viscount. I believe that should satisfy Sarah's father.''

"Oh! How wonderful!'' She came to her knees, encircling his neck with her arms, hugging him exuberantly.

Warwick chuckled. '' 'Twas not my doing! I hadn't that power. 'Tis Charles you should thank so—nay! I did not say that! You thank the king in this manner, and I shall take stern measure!''

Ondine chuckled delightedly. "Bah! My most beloved beast, you are like most creatures of a forest—all bark and growl, and very little bite at all!''

"No bite at all!'' Warwick protested, rising so that she slipped from him, and gazing down at her with her hands on his hips. She couldn't help but giggle, which drew from him a disgruntled, "Hmmph!''

Then he feverishly tugged his shirt over his head and dropped it to the floor.

"No bite at all!'' he repeated, and tugged next upon his breeches, pulling them from corded muscular legs. Then, once again, he stared down upon her, his beautifully naked flesh shining in the firelight, all sinew and power and completely the man she loved.

She smiled, unalarmed, and then she lay back and stretched out her arms to him.

"A beast, as anyone knows, but bites and growls when treated poorly! And, ah, but I, milord, have learned that lesson well and learned, too, that the most powerful creature, when loved and adored, is ever the most tender!''

He came down beside her, his laughter gone, his handsome face tense with passion, eyes an amber, hungry glow. He cupped her cheek within his hand and whispered with sweet urgency, "Aye, tenderness, aye, love! Well have you tamed your beast, my witch, my mermaid, my love. Come, pour your Nereid's waters over me, for wife, greatly do I thirst!''

Ondine stared deeply into the searing passion of his eyes, and she sighed with delicious surrender and triumph.

EPILOGUE

May 1681
Hampton Court

It was a cool spring, refreshing and pleasant, but upon the court, Warwick felt a trickle of sweat upon his brow.

"Warwick!" the king warned him briefly, for the ball was coming to his corner of the court, and his mind was obviously not on the game.

He made that ball, though, swinging reflexively, groaning inwardly, for the king was so avid upon this game they played against the Duke of York and Buckingham—a strange duo at that!—that Warwick dared not let his mind wander too far. The ball moved too quickly for such leisure.

His shot gave them a lead, though, and as the Duke of York set about to serve, Warwick did glance over to the chaises and managed to feel a modicum of assurance. Ondine still sat there, along with several of the queen's ladies and the queen herself. She saw his glance, smiled radiantly, and gave him a sign for victory.

"Chatham!"

That time, the ball went sailing past him, and Charles was unable to recover for him.

The king came to his side, whispering into his ear as service was set up once again.

"Blessed heaven, Warwick Chatham!" he grumbled. " 'Tis my brother I play! My younger brother! Will you have me lose to him?"

"My apologies, sire, I—"

"You are worried. Well, cease worrying! If the child is destined to come today, it will come today. 'Tis one matter over which I have no royal prerogative! Now, play!"

The play continued, moving so swiftly that for a time Warwick found he could give himself over to it. He mused, though, watching the ball, that it was probably strange that they should be here; most heirs came into this life upon the property that they were to inherit. However, this child was destined to inherit both the properties and titles of North Lambria and Rochester, and neither he nor Ondine could decide which should be the more likely place. Admittedly, both bore specters of the past, remnants of happy days, yet shadows, too. Following that fateful day at Deauveau Place, they had both been quite content to follow the king about in his service. Warwick had been sent to France for several weeks, and after that, he'd served briefly for His Majesty in Holland, at the court of William and Mary. In March, however, he'd begged excuse from further travel. Ondine had been the most perfect expectant mother in the early months, but as her date had grown closer, she had been plagued with anxiety, fearing the drugs used upon her in those early months, and all of her previous activity. Charles, being the parent of no legal heir, but the father of at least a dozen fine bastards, felt a sympathy for the pair, and so had kept Warwick close to home and suggested that since they were both English, though from different parts of the country, the child should be born beneath his royal wing—duke and earl, he would surely grow to serve his king!

And so, quite peacefully, they were able to be at court, with no fears for the running of their vast estates. Jake had married his Molly, and if that industrious pair had difficulty at all with the management of Chatham Manor, they had only to turn to Clinton and Sarah, blissfully wed, and making delightful homestead of Hardgrave's once carelessly run but beautiful old castle.

Jem was in charge of Deauveau Place. While he saw to the house, John Robbins, in love with that countryside, looked to the tenants and the rents, giving the farmers a deep understanding that

had doubled their personal incomes and increased the wealth of the landowners. Warwick grinned even as he managed to slice a ball cleanly past Buckingham. He and Ondine were constantly lending the king monies from their vast supply, though it was they who were in his service.

He frowned then suddenly, thinking of his brother, Justin, for Justin troubled him frequently these days, though he saw him little. Following the events of Deauveau Place, Justin had made a change, growing admirably responsible, yet more grim, and talking constantly of new frontiers. He accepted with quiet dignity the land and title the king had granted him, but just after the Epiphany, he had set sail across the Atlantic, determined to see the Virginia Colony. He'd returned just days ago to be present for the birth of his nephew or niece—Warwick was secretly convinced the child was a boy, for Chathams were known to sire male children—but planned, with great excitement, to return abroad by the end of summer. He had asked Charles for a land grant in the wild interior of the new country, and Charles, bemused at such interest in what he considered a totally uncivilized place, fully intended to make that grant.

Ah, but Warwick worried still, for Justin seemed of such a reckless nature. Warwick thought that he had sewn enough wild oats, and perhaps needed the giving love of a wife. Yet, somewhere in his heart, he thought he understood his brother's hesitancy— and why, too, Justin chose to keep his distance. He loved Ondine, distantly, respectfully—but wistfully—and would surely never settle for a woman with anything less than his sister-in-law's vivacious beauty and unquenchable spirit.

Warwick slammed the ball across the court. The game! It was going on forever—a tight, endless match.

Search far and wide, Justin, he thought, his devotion to his brother as deep as ever. See that you are satisfied; see that you settle for nothing less than this ever-exultant emotion of true and tender love, for it is the sole thing that makes all else in life worthwhile!

He was startled from his thoughts as the king let out something like a conqueror's cry, throwing his racket jubilantly into the air. Somewhat confused, Warwick frowned at him.

"Damn, but 'tis true! You're not with me at all today, Chatham! We won, man! We took the game!"

Buckingham leapt over the net to offer his handshake in congratulations, but the Duke of York followed more sedately. There was a rash of laughter and good camaraderie, drink flowed freely to cool them, then Warwick, nodding absently at the words that issued around him, turned back to the chaises.

Ondine was gone, as were Sarah and the queen.

He felt himself shake and tremble. A guard told him she'd returned to the palace two hours previously. He had been right; oh, he had known this morning by her strange behavior! His child was to be born today.

"I've got to get back!" he muttered.

Charles was there, mopping his face with a tennis sheet. "Chatham, don't panic so! Heirs take time to enter this world!"

The king was wrong. By the time they returned to the palace, Ondine was blissfully lying upon a newly made bed, virginally beautiful in a lace gown with her hair like a sunburst of glory about her, her sweet smile equally as radiant.

Warwick paused at the threshold of the door. The queen and the women who had attended her chuckled softly and bid him enter. Catherine clapped her hands and the maids disappeared; she and the king remained in the door, content despite their own lack of heirs, and stared on as Warwick at last entered the room. On curiously hesitant feet he came to her bedside and stared down at the swaddled bundle by her side.

"Milady . . . ?" he queried.

Still smiling with such contentment and bliss, she unwrapped that perfect bundle. The babe kicked and squalled, quite nonchalantly displaying his sex.

" 'Tis a son!" Warwick cried.

"And wonderfully sound and whole and healthy!" Ondine whispered happily. "Oh, Warwick, count the fingers and toes! He's plump and rosy and—"

"Perfectly wondrous, my dear love, and I thank you for him with all my heart!" Warwick finished for her, leaning past his squalling newborn heir to kiss her lips, the quiver of his own betraying his emotion.

"And such a marvelously easy time he had entering this world!" the queen remarked from the doorway.

" 'Twas my doing!" the king claimed. "I always said that a brisk morning walk was good for all things, and I did keep that fair lady walking each day!"

"I don't think they hear us!" the queen murmured, and the king grinned, for he was certain they did not.

With great affection he slipped an arm about his wife's shoulders and led her from the room, silently closing the door behind him.

Warwick did not know that they had been or gone; he sat there inspecting his son, commenting in wonder.

"My love, see all that hair! A sunburst, like yours!"

"Ah, but it may yet turn dark!"

"His eyes—are blue!"

"I believe all babes are born with blue eyes." She laughed. "His nose is most definitely yours. It tilts quite arrogantly!"

"Nay! It tilts with great dignity!"

The babe, totally disinterested in their parental doting, waved his tiny fists, screwed up his face, and let out a demanding cry.

"Ah, you see! A hungry, howling beast—just like his father!" Ondine declared, but smiling still, she seeped with joy as she adjusted her gown, tenderly urged the child to her breast, and thrilled with liquid delight at his urgent tug upon her.

"Beast, eh?" Warwick grinned, running a knuckle over the wee face, soft as down.

"Certainly—he'll be another Warwick Chatham, Earl of North Lambria!"

"And Duke of Rochester," Warwick reminded her.

She caught his hand and kissed it, and they both stared, dazed still with awe and rapture as all new parents must, at the life they had created.

Ondine's brilliant sapphire eyes met Warwick's golden gaze, and she smiled, feigning a sigh. "I rather thought a sweet and gentle girl would be nice!"

"Sweet and gentle!"

"But I'm ever so content that I've a son—be he a Chatham beast! After all, seems I've tamed one, so I should be quite capable with another!"

Warwick laughed delightedly, the sound husky, from the depths

of his throat. He bent over his suckling babe and with the greatest tenderness found his wife's lips once again.

"If you wish a daughter," he whispered against her mouth, "this 'tamed' beast of yours shall certainly do all in his power to get you with one next! But sweet and gentle?"

She slipped her free arm about his neck, ever so glad with his touch.

"Seems we are both well tamed, my love!" she promised him, and once again they kissed long and tenderly, before the newest Chatham decided it was time they be prodded apart, his tiny fist pounding most ferociously against his father's chest.

They laughed together—and gave him their full attention.

Dear Reader,

Thank you for selecting *Ondine*. For those of you who have been kind enough to follow along with the "No Other" series and are waiting for Sabrina's and Sloan's story, this is not their book. Their story is called *No Other Love*, and will be published by Avon Books in May, available mid-April.

Ondine is, however, one of my favorite books written under the Shannon Drake—or any other—name. It was originally published in 1987, and I'm delighted to see it back on the market. The story originated from a trip to England in which I first went to a place called *The London Dungeon*. *The London Dungeon* specializes in the macabre, but also depicts some of the medieval history of England through its scenes of crime and punishment, and often enough as well, man's inhumanity to man. Among the displays was a scene depicting a hanging, along with it a caption stating that a man or woman could, at times, be saved from the gallows by an offer of marriage. There was the basis for *Ondine*, a story in which the hero and the heroine have separate demons and battles to fight, and find, only through fate, that love does conquer all—and two heads are definitely better than one when trying to solve a mystery. I'm extremely fond of both my heroine, Ondine, and my hero, Warwick, strong-willed people who are determined they will not be bested by life. Charles II, one of all time favorite historical personages, also makes an important appearance.

This reprint is special to me as well because my husband, Dennis, and I posed for the cover art. (And trust me, there is nothing so special in life as being touched up by an incredibly talented artist such as Franco!)

I sincerely hope that you will enjoy *Ondine*, and the tapestry of life in which her story takes place and her characters live, and that they will become as real for you as they did for me.

Thank you so much!

Shannon Drake/Heather Graham Pozzessere